FROM THE REFUGEE CAMP OF GREECE

where a lone young Armenian girl was the prey of terror and where sexual violation and worse awaited her in the human jungle outside the gates . . .

TO A CITY OF GLAMOUR AND CORRUPTION,

Chicago in the era of the gangsters and bootleg gin, where every politician had his price and every chorus girl her "protector," and the brothels and morgue threatened any woman who broke the rules in a man's game of power and perversity . . .

TO A GERMANY SHIMMERING WITH SOPHISTICATION AND SHADOWED WITH THE SWASTIKA,

where the masses were being seduced by the sugared promises of Nazism, as its evil terror prepared to control all Europe . . .

Jo Gregory lived and loved where the action was, willing to go anywhere and risk anything to fulfill her ambitions, yet unable to escape the torment of a heart that was tearing in two. . . .

BYLINES

PART I

1919–1922

"The Starving Armenians! World's Shame!"
Part I of *Children of War*,
by David Driscoll.
June 4, 1919. Exclusive to the *World*.

One

The black stallion reared, his huge hooves flailing in the air, his drooling mouth agape. His Turkish rider brought him down hard, and Jo clearly saw her father being trampled beneath the animal.

Mama had ceased screaming. Her bleeding, broken body had been tossed aside. In death, she grasped her eldest daughter's cold hand.

Hoofbeats and running. Jo fled with Mushgin. They looked over their shoulders and paused to listen, certain they were being pursued.

"Hurry!" Mushgin whispered as he dragged her along. "Hurry!"

"I can't run, I'm caught!" Jo gasped. The sound of horses grew louder.

"Mama!" Jo's eyes blinked open, and she shivered in the darkness, knowing she had screamed, as she so often did when her nightmare came. She struggled to light the lamp next to her narrow bed, her hand trembling. Her feet were tangled in the blanket, and the hoofbeats she had heard were only the steps of a passing teacher outside her door.

3

She forced herself to think of the doctor who had interviewed her over a year ago. "The smarter you are, the greater your imagination, and therefore, the more vivid your dreams," he had told her.

"But my parents *were* murdered," she had replied.

"I know," he said softly. "But your dream is not . . . well, exactly accurate, is it?"

"No, but there were horses."

"You've had a terrible experience," he conceded. "But you must not allow your imagination to relive it over and over. You can control your dreams if you concentrate on pleasant thoughts before sleeping. You're a very intelligent girl. You can overcome your memories."

In the dim lamplight the small familiar cell which was her room took on shape and substance. She pulled herself from the bed, shaking out her long white nightdress. Her eyes moved from wall to wall, finally settling on the comforting picture of the boy Jesus that hung over her bed on the cracked concrete wall.

She bit her lip and shivered, then crawled back into the bed, pulling the coarse covers up to her neck. She sat up, leaning against the iron bedstead, staring at the shadows created by the dancing flame of the flickering lamp.

"Jo Gregorian." She murmured her name as if to summon reality. "Jo" was her own secret name. Her given name was "Josephina," and that was what the other Armenian children and the staff of the Christian Children's Missionary Society orphanage called her. Of course, "Josephina" wasn't a real Armenian name, any more than "Jo" was. "Josephina" was the name her father had given her because he was a man of dreams. She herself had shortened it to "Jo," the name of the heroine in her favorite American book, *Little Women*. But Jo was careful. She used "Jo" only when she wrote

in her diary. She suspected the director of the orphanage, Miss Spring, would not approve of a name which
sounded as if it should belong to a boy.

"Secrets," she whispered. She had her secret name,
her nightmares of which she never spoke, and imaginary lives she lived in her thoughts. In one life she was
a grown woman, a successful American writer who lived
surrounded by admirers. In another life she was back in
Armenia. Nothing had changed, save the fact that she
was older, and had grown as beautiful as her aunt,
Yegsha.

But neither life was real. The reality was that she was
fourteen years old, she had only one living relative,
who could not be located, she was penniless, and she
lived in the Sunshine Home.

The Sunshine Home was housed in a former monastery. It was a rambling stone edifice on the outskirts of
Salonika. The building revealed its own past as surely
as if its crumbling stone walls could speak, Jo thought.
There was a faint odor of dry rot that permeated the
walls, and long fissures which marked hundreds of years
of earth tremors, which were common in Greece.

It was not difficult for Jo to imagine the disciplined
silence of the monks as they went about performing
their penance, moving like brown-clad ghosts through
the maze of passageways, where the only sounds were
the muted jangling of their prayer beads and the steady
trickle of water from an underground spring that bub-
bled down the ancient aqueduct.

The rooms of the former monastery were dark and
austere, its corridors narrow and damp, punctuated by
sudden arches that led into high-ceilinged cavelike halls
lit only by dim lamps. The monks, of course, were long
gone. Salonika had been part of the Eastern Roman
Empire, then part of the Ottoman Empire. It was re-

turned to the Greek kingdom only a few years ago, in 1913. All over Salonika the Turks had left their mark. Like spears raised skyward, an army of tall minarets rose beside transformed churches.

But for all its Byzantine darkness, the converted monastery had advantages. Its courtyards were aflame with the color of flowers grown in the shelter of the crumbling walls. Land was available for extensive gardening, and each of the orphans had his or her own room in a former monk's cell. Each room was furnished with an iron cot, a straight-backed chair made of wood and wicker, and a tiny writing table and lamp. All had identical pictures of the boy Jesus over the bed. However small the rooms, they were an improvement on over-crowded dormitories. In Athens, Jo had lived and slept in a hall with a hundred other children. She was awakened not only by her own nightmares but also by the bad dreams of others. She valued the quiet and privacy of her tiny cell.

Jo reached across the narrow space between the table and the bed and extinguished the lamp, determined to concentrate on pleasant thoughts and to forget the wild horses which were the monsters of her night terrors. Crying, she told herself, was for babies. She wasn't a baby.

She closed her eyes and conjured up the image of her father, Melkon Gregorian. He had been a tall, strong man with a ready smile and a jovial manner. Her mother, Seta, always called him "my gentle bear."

Abstractedly Jo ran her hand over the rough blanket on her cot. It lacked the soft sensual feel of the coverlet she had used on her bed at home. That blanket was carefully hand-woven from the sheared coats of the angora goats her father raised to produce mohair. But owning herds of goats was only one of her father's assets. Behind the village where she and her family had lived half of each year, stretched a sea of poppy fields. They produced opium, a substance widely used in patent medicines in Europe and America, and in its pure form, used as a painkiller to ease the suffering of the ill. Her father was a rich man, cultured and learned. He was primarily a trader, and, Jo believed, a poet in his heart.

"Josephina," her father asked on the morning of her ninth birthday, "do you know why you have been given such a strange name? If I tell you now, are you old enough to understand?" She remembered murmuring, "Yes, Papa," and then her father sat down and lifted her onto his knee.

"Josephina is an Armenian name, and Josephine is its French equivalent. One day soon we will leave Armenia. We will go to either France or America—though I favor America. This has been my dream for many years, and when you were born, I wanted you to have a name that could be French or American. Here, here, I have a gift for you."

With those words her father handed her a package and in it was a copy of a book called *Little Women*. "You will see," he told her enthusiastically, "that the heroine of this book is named Josephine. Now, although you and your brothers and sister have been learning English, I don't think you are yet quite accomplished enough to read this book. But when you are, you will see what a fine American name I have chosen for you."

Jo reached under her pillow and touched the worn book. She still had it. It was her one possession, her one tangible reminder of a life lost. But more, it was also her book of hope.

The Jo of her beloved book was truly American. She

was self-reliant and became a successful writer. "That's what Papa would want me to do," Jo whispered aloud into the darkness, "and I will do it."

Who could have known? Jo asked herself silently. Who could have suspected? Jo had asked herself those questions a hundred times, and she had come to the conclusion that though her father had dreamed of a future in America, he did not foresee the terrible fate of the Armenians. He misjudged the Turks and did not leave soon enough.

Her father had waited patiently for the Turkish government to approve his emigration. He explained that permission was delayed again and again. "Because I will sell everything," her father told her. "And of course, I want to take the money out of the country."

Her father told her stories about America. In Papa's eyes it was a land of opportunity, a land of freedom, a land where no just man feared his neighbor or his government.

"Papa's dreams died," she whispered into the darkness, aware that once again tears were forming in her eyes. It had been five years since the night of the first arrests, five years since her world collapsed, and still the tears were always there, always ready to tumble down her cheeks. She recalled it all, but the most horrible images were the most vivid, and they returned in the darkness of the night, full-blown in horrific dreams. The rest of her memories were hazy: bits of conversation, important events, rituals and traditions. If she concentrated, she could remember the faces of her brothers and sister, she could recall her aunt Yeghsa and Krikor, her aunt's lover. But her memories mixed with what she had been told later, and her years of limbo in refugee camps came between her memories of the past and the hopelessness of her present.

It was when she thought of the day of the arrests and the months spent in the first of three so-called Turkish detention centers that she began to shake. Her fears grew when she remembered the fateful night they all tried to escape. That night had ended in blood. It was the night she began her terrifying flight with Mushgin, her childhood friend. Only she and Mushgin survived, because they were miraculously found by Greek soldiers who spirited them behind Greek lines to relative safety.

She and Mushgin were together in the first refugee camp in Athens; then they were separated. She was transferred to a camp outside Athens, where she spent most of the war, trapped with other Armenian refugees who could not emigrate because of the fighting. Mushgin was sent to relatives in Syria. Then last year she had been moved once again to the Sunshine Home for Armenian orphans. She was sent to the Sunshine Home because her family had been Protestants, a small minority among Armenians, who were primarily members of the Armenian Apostolic Church. She was told, "We'll find homes for the younger children in time, but you are older, so it may take longer."

"Longer, perhaps forever," Jo whispered as she turned on her side and the iron springs of the cot squeaked in minor protest. Emigration to America was still not allowed. It had ceased during the war, and to resume, she was told, Congress had to pass a law. Jo wasn't sure what Congress was, but she envisaged it as a group of elderly men like those who had managed the affairs of the Armenian community, or those who sat on the board of directors of the Christian Children's Missionary Society and who sometimes came to visit and to preach. Such men, she concluded, were prone to forget what they deemed "unimportant" matters, and Jo wondered if the Armenian survivors of the deportations and massacres were unimportant to Congress. Surely they seemed so now. The American papers were filled with stories about soldiers poisoned by gas, with news of the forthcoming peace talks, and with the continuing war between Greece and Turkey. There was no talk of the Armenians, no stories about their forced exile and mass murder.

The door of Jo's tiny room opened and let in a crack of dim light from the corridor. Jo didn't open her eyes. It was probably Miss Spring. She always checked the rooms each night at eight-thirty to see that the lamps were safely extinguished.

The door creaked closed and Jo tossed again on her back. Her dark eyes felt heavy and she knew the fog of sleep was slowly closing in. "No dreams," she whispered, as if to warn her subconscious. "No more dreams tonight."

David Driscoll rolled from his bed in the extravagantly named Alexander the Great Hotel. He stretched, then scratched his unshaven face and rubbed his chin thoughtfully. "Christ," he muttered, looking at his Big Ben alarm clock. It was nearly ten-thirty, and his appointment at the Sunshine Home was set for eleven. With or without breakfast he would be an hour late. And, he decided, breakfast was a necessity, as were a shower, a shave, and a change of clothes.

He had slept in his trousers and shirt. Luckily, he noted, he had slung his jacket over a nearby chair, so it wasn't unduly wrinkled. He felt in his back pocket. "Hell," he swore, realizing that his billfold was gone. He bent over the bed and shook out the sheet and light

blanket. The bed looked as if it had been the scene of a
ferocious battle between man and beast. One pillow-
case was half off, one pillow was on the floor. Even the
bottom sheet was untucked, and beneath that, the mattress pad was bunched up, as if he had crumpled it in
his clenched fist while sleeping. He shook the blanket
again with irritation, and with relief saw his billfold fall
from its hiding place in the folds of the vanquished
bedding.

"David, me boy, you drank too much of that Greek
ouzo stuff last night." He shook his finger at the face of
his image in the sun-stained mirror over the dresser.
And he added ruefully, "You allowed yourself to be
dragged onto the dance floor once too often by that
voluptuous and somewhat impetuous lady of the evening, whatever-her-name-was."

He belched. Clearly the mixture of food he had eaten
didn't mix with ouzo, or agree with his digestive system. His stomach felt like it had its own built-in egg
beater. On reflection, he decided nothing much did
mix with ouzo. "From now on, me boy, whiskey only,"
he vowed, pulling off his wrinkled pants and stained
shirt. After all, whiskey wasn't difficult to obtain in Salonika. From 1915 to 1918, the city had been the base
for Allied operations in the Turkish straits, and it still
bore the remnants of the rude, though temporary, cultural clash.

By any analysis, Salonika was a strange city, different
from most other Greek cities, he had decided. For one
thing, it was full of Jews, though they were a far cry
from the Jews in Chicago, New York, or Boston. They
were largely Sephardic Jews who spoke Ladino, the
descendants of Spanish Jews who had come to Salonika
when driven from Spain over four hundred years ago.
Not that he cared about Jews one way or the other, but

on his arrival a local tour guide had felt moved to explain the various cultural aspects of the city, and he had told the story of the Jews who now made up a large proportion of the population. David also learned that Salonika had been the headquarters for the Young Turk movement that sparked the Turkish revolution of 1908, overthrowing the last absolute sultan, Abdul Hamid II.

Salonika, David observed, had a kind of dark brooding charm, rooted in its history of conquest and war. The scars of its many battles were seen in its architecture and in the faces of its inhabitants. The Macedonians had built it, but the Romans, the Venetians, the Bulgarians, the Normans, the Turks, and the Spanish had all conquered it, leaving the legacy of their cultural markings and implanting their genes among the population. A huge brick-and-marble arch built by the Roman Emperor Galerius survived to commemorate the Roman occupation, Byzantine churches were common, and the domed basilica of Ayia Sophia had been converted into a mosque and then back into a basilica. As for the population, he had seen blue-eyed blonds, ravishing black-eyed brunettes, even raven-haired beauties with golden cat eyes and high Asian cheekbones. David liked women, especially the women of Salonika.

David Driscoll was ensconced in a small hotel—small in spite of its prestigious name. Elite hotels were always full of industrialists, diplomats, soldiers, tourists, and other journalists. But David considered himself on a sort of vacation, and thus a small hotel suited him better. It offered quiet and privacy, and above all was cheaper, leaving him more spending money.

His room was simply furnished but newly whitewashed, clean and free of bugs. What more could he want? After all, the *World* didn't pay him when he was off doing a free-lance feature for possible syndication.

He practically had to beg to get permission to escape from the forthcoming peace talks, which he was certain would be dismal and boring. He'd been condemned to cover enough driveling diplomats since the fighting ended. He'd had enough. Hell, he'd been on the front lines during the war, tramping from one hellhole to another. Then, as if a man could adjust overnight, they'd sent him off to Versailles. Well, he wasn't about to do it, and he'd told Sam Hinch, the head man on the European desk, as much. And Sam had told him there was no money for vacations, so he'd promised to do a story—some human-interest piece that wouldn't take a lot of time.

David finished shaving. He buttoned his fresh shirt and went to the window. Late or not, war or not, what mattered was that he was in Greece. The sky was blue, the sun was warm, and there were plenty of sultry beauties to occupy his leisure hours. As one might have suspected, the Allied forces left a corps of prostitutes in their wake and they were reasonably desperate for customers now that the military had departed.

He reminded himself that he wasn't doing a series on whores of war, but on children. "Children of War," he said out loud. It was a wonderful title for a sob-story series, and certainly Hinch had liked the first installment he had written in Athens two weeks ago. In fact, if all went well, this would be the day his first story appeared in the *World*. "The Starving Armenians" was his heartrending headline.

Shortly after submitting it, he'd been advised by Hinch to pursue the story. Hinch, who always seemed to know everything, told him to go on to Salonika to interview some of the orphans at the Sunshine Home.

"It's run by Americans," Hinch had wired. "Midwesterners, so maybe there are even some local Chi-

cago missionaries involved. That ought to give us some
real local interest."

Salonika! It was where he had wanted to go anyway.
When he finished his story, he planned to pick up a
boat and go island-hopping. As he headed downstairs to
the sidewalk café, he thought how nicely everything
had fallen into place. "Lady luck," he said aloud, "I'd
like to kiss your ass."

When he had left Paris he hadn't the faintest idea what
he was going to write. Then on the train he encountered Maggie Adams, who was on her way to Vienna to
do research for her forthcoming book. "It's called *Children of War*," she confided to him. "I suppose it'll take
at least a year to write. I'll be going to refugee camps all
over Europe to interview children who have been
orphaned."

Maggie Adams, David thought ruefully. She was tall,
dark-haired, and full-lipped. She was always well-
groomed and dressed with a businesslike severity. All
icy self-determination, Maggie was the kind of gal you
wanted to conquer, if only to make sure she was real.
David always found a certain joy in seeing a woman like
that mussed up a little, her grooming gone to pot with
passion. He had spent a weekend in Vienna with her—
the weekend was an indulgence, though he had to
change trains in Vienna anyway. He'd bought Maggie
dinner, wined her, and been charming, urbane, and
romantic. And damn, she had teased him. He thought
they were going to make it, God knows they had come
close. But then, at what might be called the crucial
moment, she pushed him away and recited a lot of bull
about the evils of casual relationships and the need for
self-respect. In the end they'd parted badly. He was
frustrated and angry. Maggie was cold and withdrawn.
"A bitch," David cursed. Well, it might take Maggie a

year to write her dumb book, but it would take him only a few weeks to produce a first-rate series, and the idea had already proved it had merit.

"Make them cry at the breakfast table!" his editor always said. "It's the essence of good journalism. In the absence of hard news or action stuff, there's always the old sob story, or a good solid exposé."

David's mind traveled back to the early days in Chicago. Hinch's advice was similar to the advice given to him by his first editor in 1911. "It's a big press town," Martin Hutchens of the *Journal* had told him. "And you're still wet behind the ears, even if you have been kicking around for ten years. Remember that. This may not be your first job, but it's your first job writing. We'll call you Mr. Driscoll, and a lot of other names too. Now, Mr. Driscoll, as I said, this is a big press town. We're in bitter competition with the other papers; sensationalism sells, but so does raw gut tugging emotion. You tell me you're a reporter. Well, for a reporter, Chicago is like being a kid in a candy factory. Every morning there's a new crop of fresh bodies, kidnappings, rapes, murder—we got it all." Hutchens nodded his agreement with his own statement and continued.

"Action is always the first choice. It scares the readers senseless and they love it. Exposés, on the other hand, titillate. They give our readers vicarious enjoyment. How lucky can a reporter be? Think of it! I doubt there's a single politician in the whole state of Illinois who's not on the take, and even fewer who are sleeping with their wives. Fortunately for us, they sleep with everyone else. Now, your third type of story is the sob story. They're for catharsis. People need to cry. Stick with those kinds of stories, my boy, and you'll give the public all the pleasure they can handle."

David smiled at the memory of his short course in journalism and pulled out the chair in the sidewalk café. The waiter poured him a cup of thick syrupy Greek coffee and on request he added hot milk. After a moment, he brought some hard rolls, jam, and fresh butter. It wasn't bacon and eggs, but this wasn't Chicago. David dug in, wishing all the time for a cup of real American java. Yup, he reflected, he had learned a lot. From 1901, when he was nineteen, until 1909, he had worked at a variety of jobs in factories, on a Great Lakes cargo vessel, and tending bar. Then finally he knew what he wanted to do. He wanted to write. With the help of a press operator he had met in a whorehouse, he landed his first job on the *Journal*, leaving it for the *World* in 1911. He had been with the *World* ever since, and for most of that time he had been in Europe covering the protracted war from the filth and agony of the trenches.

It was eleven when David Driscoll left the café. He ambled off, hands in his pockets. The director of the home was a woman; that would make it easy for him. He stopped to buy some flowers from a street vendor. It always helped to bring flowers if you were late for an appointment with a woman. "Flattery, me boy, will get you everything," he said to himself in his good Irish-American brogue. Probably that's where he'd gone wrong with Maggie Adams. He hadn't flattered her enough. Or perhaps the vicious gossip he'd heard about her was true. She was already a well-known writer, and it was said that she had gotten there less on talent than on her back. He consoled himself that he just wasn't important enough to succeed with her. She doubtless saved herself for her publisher. It was, after all, rumored that they were having an affair.

*　　*　　*

"I can't tell you how sorry I am." David smiled boyishly and bowed as he handed the flowers to Miss Spring. "You're as lovely as your name," he lied with Irish charm. In truth, she was extremely plain and dowdy. Her graying brown hair was a mass of electrified corkscrew curls, her homely face was without makeup, her clothes were two sizes too large, and her glasses constantly slipped over her birdlike nose. Her body was as curveless as a road in Kansas, and her age was indeterminable. Still, for him her thin lips broke into a smile and she giggled unbecomingly.

"It's quite all right, no one is ever on time in Greece. It's the transportation. It's very slow."

He nodded and strained to determine her origins. She was from the Midwest. Kansas or Missouri, he decided. "Do I detect a Missouri accent?" he ventured. "Are you one of the good women from the Midwestern Bible College?"

She smiled and her pale face flushed. "I'm a long way from Poplar Bluff."

David contained himself and didn't comment that damn near anywhere was a long way from Poplar Bluff, a small town in the southern corner of Missouri. "I hail from Hannibal myself." He grinned.

"It's a small world! Fancy two old Missourians finding themselves in Greece!"

"A genuine act of God," David declared, failing to add "Praise the Lord," which he normally did when speaking to missionaries.

Miss Spring cleared her throat and her forehead knit into a frown as she attempted to regain control of the situation. "Tell me, what can I do for you, Mr. Driscoll?"

She didn't mention his name was Irish. If she had, he would have lied and told her his family came from Northern Ireland and were as good Presbyterians as

could be found. In fact his family came from County
Cork and he'd been born in Boston and taken west
when he was eight. His father, an alcoholic and sometime philosopher, told his swelling family of four they
were all going back to the land, where the Irish belonged. "We're headed for greener pastures," he announced grandly. "We'll have our own big farm in
Illinois, the good soil will make us all rich." But the
farming venture failed within months, shortly after his
father discovered that corn didn't grow without hard
work and cows didn't respond to blarney. Greener pastures ended up not to be the promised farm in southern
Illinois, but a tenement in Chicago. His father never
tilled the soil, but rather became a bartender in a pub
on the Near North Side. And there, until his untimely
death at the age of forty, he dreamed his dreams,
recited poetry to his inebriated customers, and philoso-
phized with a certain drunken dignity on the state of
humanity. After his death, when David was ten, his
mother moved her brood to Hannibal, Missouri, where
she supported them working as a dressmaker. David
loved Hannibal. He always told everyone it was his
home. He lied and said he had been born there, that
his father had been a friend of Mark Twain's. In time,
David created an imaginary father who fulfilled his
promises, cherished his wife, and adored his children.
But David knew the truth, and when he thought about
his father's failure he felt bitter. But damn, the old man
could have charmed the pants off a virgin, and David
knew that he could too. He looked at Miss Spring, and
leaned over, smiling. "It is not so much what you can
do for me, dear lady, but what I can do for you. I've
come to offer my services," he told Miss Spring in a
sincere tone.

Miss Spring looked more than a little puzzled. "You

told me you were a journalist. I don't understand. Do you want to become a missionary?"

"No, but I know you have needs. Food to feed the children, clothing."

"You wish to make a donation?"

"If only I had the funds. No, what I propose is to write a story for publication in the *World*, one of Chicago's largest papers. I'm writing a series, you see. It's a series on children, the victims of war. I want to do interviews, so of course I require a translator." He didn't let up, but continued to talk. "Such a story could bring your society hundreds of dollars in donations, perhaps there would even be offers to adopt some of the unfortunate little ones."

Miss Spring stared down at her desk. As if doodling, David noted that she wrote "hundreds in donations" on a scrap of paper. The old girl was hooked, he thought, and silently he thanked his father for his one legacy, the ability to talk a woman into anything. Well, most women. "How can people help you if they don't know about the fine work you're doing?"

Miss Spring pressed her lips together. "We always try to protect the children from any kind of exploitation," she said carefully. "It is our policy not to allow interviews—except, of course, for those with American consulate staff for immigration purposes, but I suppose you know that immigration has been cut off because of the war."

"And it should be restored," David said with conviction. "People forget, they need to be reminded that these children are here. I've only recently finished the first part of the series. I wrote it in Athens. I feel strongly that Americans will respond to these Armenian orphans. They are, after all, Christians. A Christian people set upon in a Moslem land. I might even say a godless land," he added for good measure. It was an overstatement, the Turks were hardly godless, but he was certain Miss Spring didn't accept the Moslem faith as being even remotely valid. She came from the Bible Belt, and her buckle looked darned tight.

Miss Spring tapped her fingers on the desk. "There is one child I could let you talk with. She's fourteen and speaks English. I really shouldn't, but yes, she is older and she's interested in writing, so she might be willing. I feel it's important that she be willing."

"And I agree. How is it that she speaks English?"

Miss Spring sighed. "Her file indicates that her father had his children educated in English and French. He had planned to leave Turkey and go to either the United States or France. I suppose I could show you her history, at least what we have." Miss Spring turned to her file cabinet and pulled open the long drawer. She picked out a folder and handed it to David. "You could help her specifically because she has an uncle in the United States who might take her, but we haven't been able to locate him."

"The power of the press," David said with the appropriate amount of reverence. "It can move mountains."

"Only faith can move mountains," Miss Spring corrected, "but I do believe the newspapers are often quite helpful in these matters."

David nodded and opened the file. A photograph of a young girl greeted him. It was labeled "Josephina Gregorian, age fourteen." The girl had long dark braided hair and an angular face. But it was her eyes that David focused on. They were huge and soulful, great dark pools of sadness. Hell, he thought to himself, those eyes alone could sell ten thousand newspapers. There wouldn't be a dry eye in Chicago, and in all likelihood, other papers would pick up the story. I'm going to get a bonus for this one, he thought, and a great vacation to boot.

"Of course, I'll have to consult her," Miss Spring insisted, breaking into his thoughts.

"Would I be able to talk to her today?" A quick interview, David thought, still time to catch the afternoon sun on the beach, and then tomorrow he could head out for the islands and forget the whole damn world.

"If she agrees," Miss Spring acquiesced. "But I really must caution you. This girl has lost her entire family—she still has nightmares about their murder and about her long ordeal. That's only natural, of course, but the point is, she still keeps her memories to herself. As you can see from the file, there's a great deal we don't know about her. You must promise to be gentle and be patient."

David nodded. Perhaps there was more here than met the eye. He could do two interviews, one this afternoon, one tomorrow. It could be a really good story, and the Greek islands weren't going anywhere. What could a few days matter?

"If you'll excuse me, I'll go and speak with her now," Miss Spring suggested, standing up and moving from behind her cluttered desk.

The golden sun rises over snow-capped mountains, fields of poppies blow gently in dawn's cool breeze.

This is my beloved home, in the valley of the two rivers, in the shadow of Mount Ararat.

Then come the darkening clouds, the thundering heavens open, and we are swept away.

Gone are bright white houses, the barking dogs, the
laughter of my mother's voice.

Gone are my people, drowned in a sea of sorrow and
blood, the survivors cast into the barren desert.

At the sound of Miss Spring's beckoning call, Jo
folded the paper on which she had written her unfinished poem. She carefully tucked it in the pocket of her
crisp white apron. The apron was part of the uniform
worn by the girls at the orphanage. It covered the front
of her plain gray cotton dress.

It was study hour, but she had not been studying.
Instead, she had been writing yet another poem in free
verse. In all, she had twenty poems stored away, though
her latest, she decided, was better than the others.

"I'm sorry to interrupt you, Josephina."

Jo stretched. She had been sitting at the library table
for an hour and her legs felt cramped. "It's all right,"
she replied without looking Miss Spring straight in the
eye. Three years in the camps had taught her always to
look down. The male missionaries thought a girl bold if
she stared, and the lady missionaries invariably asked,
"What *is* the matter? Do you have something to tell
me?" As if to look one in the eye was always the
prelude to a confession.

"You are our best student, so I think an interruption
won't do any harm. Josephina, Miss Lilly, who teaches
you English, says you like to write."

Jo nodded, but silently vowed not to show Miss
Spring her poems. They were, after all, personal, and
even if the language was less than explicit when she
described the deportations, they spoke of things she
could not discuss without crying.

"There's a gentleman here, a writer. Well, he's actually a journalist. That means he writes for newspapers.

He's American. He wants to write a story about our mission and about the children here. He's asked to speak to one of you, and since you speak English and are interested in writing, I thought you might be willing."

Jo frowned. Surely this stranger would ask questions about her family, about the mission, about how she got here. He would probably even want to know the details of the massacres. But he *was* a writer, and writers had to ask questions. And perhaps, she decided, I can ask him some questions about America and about writing. Besides, he wasn't a missionary, so he wouldn't be like Miss Spring or the others. They never wanted to talk about America. They only wanted to talk about the Bible.

"If you object, you certainly don't have to speak with him, dear."

"I don't object," Jo said quickly, realizing that she had hesitated. "I think I'd like to talk to him."

"Then come along. He's waiting in my office."

Jo followed Miss Spring out of the library, which also served as a dining hall. The former monastery was built around several courtyards, and as they walked down the covered walkway, they passed an enclosed garden where some of the younger children were tending the flowers. Beyond the monastery walls, the older children cared for the vegetable patch and gathered fruit from the small orchard. Every hour of the day the orphanage hummed with activity. At seven they all had their porridge together, at seven-thirty they all went to morning devotions, then to Bible class. After that, they were taught reading, writing, and arithmetic, had English lessons, and then they were sent off to do chores. Some children helped the cook prepare meals and tidy the kitchen; others worked in the gardens or cleaned. The boys built furniture under supervision, the girls sewed and made clothing. "Idle hands do the devil's work," Miss Spring proclaimed.

They rounded the corner and Miss Spring opened the door to her office. "This is Mr. David Driscoll. Mr. Driscoll, this young lady is Josephina Gregorian."

Jo broke her own rule and took a long look at Mr. Driscoll before returning her eyes to the design on Miss Spring's carpet. Mr. Driscoll was quite handsome, and he didn't look one bit like any of the missionaries. His clothes were a little rumpled, he was smoking a pipe as her father used to, and his blue eyes looked merry. "How do you do," Jo said politely.

"I do very well." His blue eyes twinkled as if there were already a secret between them. "Will we be able to talk privately?" he asked, turning toward Miss Spring.

"I'm not sure where you could go. The little children are in the garden, the workshops are all being used, and I have a meeting in a few minutes." She wrinkled her forehead and pressed her lips together.

David checked his watch. "Could I take her out for lunch? I promise on my word to have her back by two." He smiled engagingly at Miss Spring, but his thoughts were on the young girl. The poor kid looked as if she could use a good meal. She was tall, and as thin as a reed. One might even say gaunt. Yes, "gaunt" was certainly the word he would use in his story. Her eyes were even more magnificent in reality than they had been in the photo. He wanted to take her into town anyway; he wanted a new picture to accompany his feature story, and there was certainly a photographer in the city. "Josephina Gregorian, her black soulful eyes haunted by loneliness, hunger, and the memory of terror . . ." David mentally wrote his lead line.

"It's against the rules," Miss Spring fussed.

David reached out and took Miss Spring's hand. "Rules

can be broken, especially for a fellow Missourian. I promise I'll take good care of her."

"Well, I don't know if I should."

"You should because you're a fine woman and you know how much good my story can accomplish."

Miss Spring blushed when he squeezed her hand, and Jo suppressed a smile. Mr. David Driscoll might have been an American writer, but he reminded her of her father, even though they looked nothing alike. It was his manner. Whenever her mother hesitated, her father had always complimented her and squeezed her hand. His eyes laughed, and Mama always gave in. Papa charmed all the women. Even her strict grandmother, Christina, could deny him nothing.

Jo's thoughts wandered. That was when it began, she remembered. It would all have happened anyway; it was just that the first horrible event centered around Papa's getting his own way.

Papa was going on a business trip and he wanted to take his elder son, Ibrahim, who was then sixteen, and seven years older than Jo.

"He's too young, Melkon. He's only a boy, and there's plenty of time for him to learn the business," her mother, Seta, had argued.

"And if he stays home and spends the summer with the village boys, he will run around with Krikor and play warrior. No, Seta, he has to go out into the world and learn the truth. He has to learn that not all Turks are our enemies. As long as he stays here, he is filled with Krikor's stories and Krikor's hatreds. I want him to become involved in the business. It will take his mind away from Krikor's stories. Ibrahim is too influenced by the romance of war."

"It is you who want to leave our home and go to America."

"That's because I believe our destiny is in America, not because I believe all Turks are our enemies."

"I still say Ibrahim is too young. He should be home studying."

Papa had taken Mama's hands and squeezed them. "You're a good woman, Seta. And a good mother. But Ibrahim is a man, he must assume a man's responsibilities." Mama, like Miss Spring, had given in, and Papa and Ibrahim had gone on the trip.

On the way home, they were set upon by Kurdish bandits, or at least that's what Papa called them. Ibrahim said they were Young Turks, nationalists who believed the Armenians were supporters of Russia, and wanted the Armenians jailed or deported. "Bandits," Ibrahim confided, "do not scream 'Armenian traitors! Death to Armenian traitors!' "

Ibrahim had been wounded, and both he and her father had been beaten badly. "The Turks want to set the Kurds loose on us!" Mama had cried, but Papa continued to deny it. "Some Turks," he insisted. "But it will be all right. We will be all right, Seta. I've signed a loyalty oath! I am not a traitor. We have friends in Istanbul. It is well known that we're loyal."

Papa, Jo thought, had been wrong. A short month later, the first arrests were ordered, then the deportations had begun. It was the end of their lives. Mama, Papa, Ibrahim, Marianne, her older sister, and Vahack, her younger brother, had all perished. Even Krikor Berberian, whose influence on Ibrahim Papa had so disliked, was dead, as was the beautiful Yeghsa, Papa's sister, who had loved Krikor so very much.

"You absolutely promise to have her back by two?" Miss Spring's voice broke into Jo's memories.

"Absolutely." David kissed Miss Spring's hand and her face again flushed pink.

Jo walked by David Driscoll's side. They left the orphanage and walked across the dusty road to wait for transportation into town. It was an easy walk, but the noon sun was hot, and usually travelers waited to hitch a ride on the back of a farmer's wagon, giving him a few leptas at the end of the short journey. The monastery was two kilometers from the outskirts of the city, half-way up a sloping hill. Below it lay Salonika; behind it rose the Hortiatis mountain range.

A wagon clattered along and David lifted Jo onto the back. It was filled with straw, and Jo leaned back, inhaling the sweet aroma of the dried grass.

"What do you eat at the orphanage?" he asked casually, sucking on the long piece of straw.

"Terrible things," Jo replied, making a face. "Porridge for breakfast, mashed potatoes and sausage for lunch, and bread, chicken, and peas for dinner." She smiled. "They import the peas and potatoes from America in cans. We grow fresh vegetables in the garden, but they're sold in town."

"Why?"

"Because our cook is American and doesn't know how to cook local food. She doesn't even know what some foods are."

David laughed. "And what do Armenians like to eat?"

"Sarma, hommis, pita bread, skewered meat, and rice. Much the same as the food the Greeks eat, but our seasonings are a little different."

"Then we shall have all those dishes for lunch, and some wine too."

"Sarma? Can I really have sarma?"

"Of course, but you have to tell me what it is."

Jo smiled. "Rice, spices, and sometimes meat rolled in grape leaves. It's very good."

"Sounds better than peas. I never liked peas myself."

"I hate them," she confessed. "But there isn't enough food as it is. It sounds like a lot, but the portions are small. No one is starving, and the missionaries do eat what we eat."

David looked at her thin arms and gangly long legs. Her dress hung on her, and he didn't need to question her statement, though he knew full well the mission was better off than the refugee camps in Athens. The Armenian Benevolent Society, which ran many of the other camps, was terribly short of funds, and the Greeks themselves had suffered one economic shock after another.

He had already dubbed the children of his series the "Starving Armenians," and he hoped the tag would stick, bringing a response which would in turn give his series a longer life. "Miss Spring told me you were interested in writing," he prodded, seeking a way to get her talking.

Jo nodded. "I want to be like Jo in *Little Women*. My papa gave me that book. I'm named after the heroine."

"Should I call you Jo, then, rather than Josephina?"

"Would you?"

"Why not?"

"I don't think Miss Spring likes shortened names."

"You mean nicknames."

"Nicknames?"

"That's what they're called in English."

"Do you have one?"

He laughed warmly. "I used to."

"You won't tell me?"

He laughed again. "Not now. When we're friends. Friends don't have secrets."

The wheels of the wagon clattered from the dirt road onto the cobbled path that led onto Salonika's main street. The houses grew closer together, traffic increased.

Bicycles and the occasional car, wagons and horse-drawn streetcars, old men on donkeys, and old-fashioned carriages all vied for space on the narrow cobbled streets.

They passed a restaurant, and David called out. The farmer drew in his horses, and they jumped down from the wagon. David gave the driver some money and they went and sat down in the warm sunshine at a table under a large green umbrella. He let Jo order everything she wanted.

"How long have you been at the mission?"

"A year. Before that I was in a refugee camp in Athens."

"Can you tell me how you got to Greece? Do you remember?"

Jo's eyes settled again on the glaring white tablecloth. She wondered if she could talk about it. She never really had. "I write poetry," she said suddenly. "In English. I truly want to be a writer."

"You'd be a good one—writers should have lots of experiences. Can I read your poetry?"

Jo reached into her pocket and withdrew her poem. "This one isn't finished yet." She offered it to him shyly and watched as he perused the words. She could see the mist in his eyes, and she knew he understood her poem.

When he finished, he looked across at her steadily. "It's good," he said sincerely. She seemed older than her fourteen years, he thought. And there was something really intriguing about her, something that would certainly appeal to his readers, if he could capture it in words. On the spur of the moment he decided to revise his plans. This was going to take time, but an inner voice told him it would be time well spent. In any case, he rationalized, there was nothing really wrong with the beaches in Salonika.

"Victim of an Unknown War—One Child's Story."
Part II of *Children of War*,
by David Driscoll.
June 22, 1919. Exclusive to the *World*.

Two

David had wired in his first story on June 7. He included a note to Mike Hamilton that read:

Dear Mike:
    Is this kid great copy, or is this kid great copy? Look at those eyes! The public will eat this up, there'll be tears all over the Sunday paper. Hell, she's lost her whole family, she speaks English, and her name's easy to spell! You know how Americans hate foreign names! Talk about an ideal subject.

Yours,
Dave

The story was published in the Sunday paper, June 22, and an actual copy had just reached him via train from Hinch in Paris. It was now July 8.

What a layout! David stared at the five-by-eight photo of Jo Gregorian. It was a head-and-shoulders shot only, and those haunting, wonderful dark eyes dominated her face. Next to it, and below, were smaller pictures of the orphanage. Some of the other orphans were depicted and there was a fourth small picture of Jo in her ill-fitting uniform working in the vegetable garden. Below the pictures was Jo's personal story. It was good enough to have been accorded two columns. The remainder of the page was taken up with his own background material. The whole layout ended with a plea to anyone who might know the whereabouts of Jo's uncle.

David laid the paper aside and reread Mike's response:

Dear Dave,

For once your instincts are as good as gold. Here's your story, and I'd like two follow-up segments. Make it three if you can stretch it out without losing momentum. Your series has been picked up by the *Journal American*, the *Globe, and* the *Times* among others. If the kid's uncle is in New York, Boston, or L.A., we'll probably find him. Also, I've got a query from some bigwig book publisher in N.Y. They want to turn your series into a book, which could mean added circulation rights. I'm enclosing the offer with the contract they sent.

Suggest you stay put and bleed this one for all it's worth. Glad to see you come up with a winner, you old typewriter jockey! Good luck and stick with it.

Mike Hamilton

David smiled and tossed back another whiskey and water. He'd go out to the orphanage tonight and show the story to Jo. She'd be thrilled to see her picture and her name in the paper. Slowly he began to reread it. It was almost as if he hadn't written it in the first place. Damn! It was a real tearjerker.

MY LIFE
As Told to David Driscoll

My father came from Constantinople, which everyone in Turkey calls Istanbul. Istanbul simply means

"to the city." My mother came from the east, and when
my parents were married, my father purchased a house
in her village and many acres of land. We used to spend
half the year in Istanbul and the other half at our home
in my mother's village near Lake Van, in sight of Mount
Ararat. My father was called Melkon and my mother's
name was Seta.

Our house in the village was large and built around a
patio. My grandparents lived in our summer house all
year long, and we always felt it to be our real home. I
had a younger brother named Vahack, and an older
brother and sister who were twins. They were called
Ibrahim and Marianne. Like me, Vahack was given an
American name, but it was his middle name rather than
his first. "We'll call him Vahack as long as we're here,"
my papa used to say, "but when we go to America, he
will be called James."

Yeghsa, my father's youngest sister, lived with us
too. I shall always remember her because she was very
beautiful and very much in love with Krikor Berberian,
who was the village hero. He had fought in, and survived, the attacks made upon our people in 1898.

Our life in Istanbul was full of study, but our life in
the village was more relaxed. On Wednesdays our female servants and all the women in my family went to
the bakery owned by Harout Haroutunian. That was
our assigned day to use his ovens, and on that day we
all cooked. Sometimes, because I was the youngest, I
didn't cook. Instead, I used to run away with the baker's son, Mushgin. Mushgin and I were great friends,
and although we now are separated forever, I still think
of him.

When the women went to cook, the men went to the
srjaran, the coffeehouse. Women were not allowed there,
though Mushgin and I once hid under a table and
listened to the men talking politics.

Even in the summer, all the children studied at the
school in the church, but my father hired special tutors

for us because he insisted we must all learn to speak English and French. I used to go to school with the other children in the morning, but in the afternoon I came home and was tutored by Dr. Avorian, a learned professor who traveled with us from Istanbul.

We were in the village when the deportation began, but our personal nightmare began when my father and brother were attacked and beaten. Looking back, I think many of us were afraid. There was much talk. The men talked in the *srjaran* and the women talked in the bakery. It was said that the Turks did not trust the Armenians because they feared we would rise up and become allies of the Russians. It was said that the Turkish army would allow the Kurds to kill us.

My father didn't believe this because he came from Istanbul and had many Turkish friends. He had signed a loyalty oath to the Turkish government and he urged the peasants in the village to do the same.

My father begged the peasants to try to understand and get along with the Turks. Krikor Berberian disagreed. He trained the young men in the village to fight and defend themselves. My brother Ibrahim and my father's sister, Yeghsa, ran away with Krikor. My father was very angry when they left, but after we were taken away to the camps, he said he was glad and he prayed they would escape. I wish Ibrahim could have known that my father forgave him.

When the deportations began, the soldiers came to every house in the Armenian quarter and they told us to bring only what we could carry. They told us we were being arrested for our own protection and that as soon as transportation could be arranged, we would be deported.

I could never forget that night. Up and down the street I could hear women screaming and small children crying. Men shouted in pain as they were beaten. Terrible, terrible things happened that night. Mama wouldn't let me look. She tied a scarf around my face like a chador and she told me to close my eyes and pray. She begged me not to be frightened.

The first camp we were taken to was located just outside the village, by a stream. It was not too bad. We children liked it. We thought we were camping out like travelers without a home to stay in. My mother's Turkish friend sent us food and some warm blankets. She told us to be patient, she said her husband and other politicians were protesting the deportation orders.

But after a week we were marched for three days and three nights. We were put in a camp on the desert. Many older people became ill and some babies died. I can't remember how long we were there. There was little food and water. My grandmother became ill, and she who used to tell us tales of heroes and stories about our past lost her voice and could no longer speak. She would not drink her ration of water, and cried that it was needed for the children. Grandmother died so that we could have her share of the water, and I remember that Grandfather cradled her in his arms all night and cried softly.

Other Armenians were brought to the desert camp. They told horrible stories about Armenians being burned alive in their homes, about rapes and savage beatings. It was said that a whole ship filled with Armenians was taken out to sea and sunk, leaving them all to drown. Vahack cried and cried. I held him, because he was so scared.

My father came to believe that we would all be killed. He and the other men plotted an escape. A riot was begun and many of us escaped into the desert and headed for the mountains. We went in small groups and in different directions. My family went with Mushgin and his father. We walked and walked. At night we froze, and in the daytime it was hot and dry and we boiled.

Then, one night, when we dared to light a campfire, we were set upon by Kurdish tribesmen on horseback.

Mushgin grabbed my hand and we ran away into the darkness together. We hid, but we heard screams. Mushgin wouldn't let me look, and he held his hand over my mouth so I wouldn't scream. In the morning when the Kurds had gone, we found the bodies. My family was dead. Mushgin and I were alone.

We wandered for days in the mountains. Then we were found by retreating Greek soldiers and they took us with them.

The story went on to tell about the orphanage. Jo's story was as she had told it to him, and his surrounding columns provided commentary and background. He described the Kurds as "wild tribesmen on horseback, ignorant and barbaric." In order to write the description of the havoc and horror they created, he conjured up the best description of an Apache attack he had ever read. Not only was the story a tearjerker, it had all the tried-and-true elements of a good cowboys-and-Indians classic. David knew that Custer's defeat at Little Big Horn echoed in his well-chosen adjectives.

David signaled the waiter and ordered another drink. He had been in Salonika for the better part of a month, and now he would have to stay longer. But what the hell! His series was appearing in fifteen newspapers coast to coast and he had signed the book contract. That, as Hamilton had indicated, might mean further syndication rights to another twenty papers, or maybe serial rights to a magazine. "The hell with you, Maggie Adams," David toasted aloud as he downed his third drink. He felt somehow as if he'd gotten even with her for rejecting him. It was a good feeling. He smiled to himself. He sure hoped the kid liked her story. She was smart as a button. A real nice little girl, and he genuinely hoped the paper would find her uncle.

The clock on the kitchen wall had a yellowed face and large Roman numerals. It had a huge key on the bottom that wound it up, and its hands moved in jerky hesitant motions from one five-minute period to the next. Each time its hands marked the hour, it rang a loud clanging bell. Miss Spring told the children she had brought it all the way from Missouri. She said it was a proper school clock.

Jo glanced at the noisy timepiece. It was six P.M. and Mr. Driscoll, whom she called David in her thoughts, would be here at six-thirty. Miss Spring had agreed he could take her out to dinner to celebrate the publication of the story. But regardless of whether or not she would be at the orphanage for dinner, she still had to do her share in the preparation of the evening meal. It was her week in the kitchen, and no one, for any reason save illness, escaped the assigned chores.

Jo put down the potato she was peeling and glanced around. The cook, Agatha Henderson, was in the pantry taking inventory. She was doubtless counting the remaining tins of peas, a huge quantity of which had been purchased from the Allied troops when they departed. The other two kitchen helpers, ten-year-old Daria and twelve-year-old Ellice, were setting the dining tables. Jo quietly opened the cupboard where the pots and pans were stored. She withdrew the cake tin and turned it upside down and studied her distorted image. She smiled, and decided her hair looked greatly improved since she had unbraided it and put a ribbon in it.

Still, she wondered how she really looked. The cake tin was a poor substitute for a real mirror. It was a great pity that there wasn't a single mirror at the orphanage, or at least she assumed there wasn't. She had never

actually been in Miss Spring's private quarters. Miss
Spring might have a mirror, but somehow she doubted
it. "Vanity is evil," the missionaries preached. "Mirrors
make young women vain."

Do I look like Yeghsa? Jo asked herself. She certainly
wanted to look like her aunt. As she stared at herself,
the memory of Yeghsa filled Jo's thoughts, and the
event that came vividly to mind was Easter 1914. Her
family had come to the village early that year. "It's a
healthier climate," her father had announced. "Besides,
I want to see to the fields and supervise the shearing."
Yes, that Easter lingered on the edge of Jo's thoughts.
It was the last holiday her family ever celebrated.

They had consumed a great feast after returning from
church, and Apel, her maternal grandfather, sat in the
chair of honor, the chair reserved for the family patri-
arch. He spun tales of the past with the agility of a
tailor spinning wool for a fine suit. And when he had
finished his history of the Armenian people, he began
with his history of the family so that each child might
know his or her forebears' names, appreciate their ac-
complishments, and feel his or her own place in the
family.

It was late on that same evening when Krikor
Berberian came to call. He had presented bouquets of
flowers to Yeghsa and Mama. He brought a large silver
cross for Grandpapa, and he offered tobacco as a token
of friendship and peace to Papa. Papa fumed while
Krikor waited at the threshold of the door. "How dare
that man come to my house!" He grumbled that although Krikor was a hero, he was still a peasant and a
troublemaker. "He's not good enough for my sister," he
declared.

But on this occasion, Yeghsa and Mama prevailed. "It
is Easter, a caller cannot be turned away," Mama had

pleaded. Yeghsa, feeling no pride, simply begged her brother to be hospitable, and finally Krikor was admitted and his gifts accepted, though, Jo remembered, Papa never smoked the tobacco.

And later, when the musicians played, Yeghsa, who was one of the village's chosen ritual dancers, did a wildly happy folk dance. Her beautiful angular face flushed with happiness when she propelled herself near the place where Krikor sat. His eyes followed her every move as she danced faster and more daringly, her skirts billowing, her long dark hair flowing, and her eyes always returning to Krikor for approval. And then Krikor danced with her, and even though Papa turned away and pretended not to notice, everyone knew that Yeghsa and Krikor were in love.

Jo put down the cake tin. It would be nice to be so beautiful and to have the love of a good man. She shuddered slightly, and she reminded herself that romance was not all there was. Men also did terrible things to women. She knew that, she had seen it. It was the way the beautiful Yeghsa had died. It was the way her mother and sister had died too.

"What are you doing, Josephina?"

Jo started, then turned to look into little Ellice's questioning face. Silently she chastised herself for being vain. It was probably a good thing that there were no mirrors in the orphanage. Mirrors would only increase Ellice's misery, since she could then see her scared, pinched face and the puffy places on the left side of her cheek where tight pink skin tried to stretch across burned tissue.

"Just putting the tin away," Jo answered in Armenian. Ellice spoke little English. She was shy, battered and even more bruised by her experience than Jo. Her village had been burned to the ground, and many of the peasants had been locked in their homes before the fires were set. How Ellice escaped was a mystery, but her face bore the marks of the flames, and her haunted golden eyes spoke volumes.

Ellice shook her head. "You were looking at yourself."

Jo averted her eyes, but nodded. "I'm going out with Mr. Driscoll," she finally explained. "You know, the writer who is telling our story." David was now a familiar sight around the orphanage. He had written about many of the children, and Jo was proud to have been able to translate their stories for him.

"I don't know how you can talk about it. I would cry. I couldn't."

Jo reached out and touched Ellice's arm gently. "In a way, talking makes me feel better. Daria told Mr. Driscoll what she remembered. It made her feel better. Of course, she's younger than you, so she doesn't recall as much."

Ellice stared at the floor. Her face was prematurely old, her young skin shriveled on one side of her face and stretched on the other. Nervous fingers tugged at her apron. Jo recalled hearing the doctor who came to visit the orphanage once a month tell the nurse that Ellice's soul was scarred more than her face. She thought she understood what he had meant. Inside or out, they were all scarred. Jo leaned over and kissed Ellice's forehead. "Think about talking to Mr. Driscoll," she suggested. "Ellice, the world must know our story. Mr. Driscoll says it's important that people remember what has happened to the Armenians."

Ellice pressed her lips together and nodded.

"Are you finished peeling the potatoes?" the cook asked as she stood in the doorway of the pantry.

Both girls turned. "Yes, ma'am," Jo answered. "They're all in the pot and ready to cook."

"Then you can go. I expect your Mr. Driscoll will be here soon enough. Shoo!"

Jo smiled and nodded. She turned quickly and hurried toward Miss Spring's office. She truly hoped that Mr. Driscoll would not be late. If Ellice would talk to him, he could write another installment of his series.

Mr. Driscoll *was* late, but only fifteen minutes late. And he announced that he had rented a proper carriage and reserved a table at the Adonis Restaurant.

"Am I late?" he asked, knowing that he was.

"Just a little."

"And where is Miss Spring?" he whispered conspiratorially and grinned.

"She was called to chapel. She said I could go when you came."

"What a pity to miss her." He laughed and winked and took her arm. "I'm going to wine and dine you. I bought a present, and I have the story, all printed in the paper with a big picture of you right on the same page. You're famous, you know."

"Let me see it," Jo begged. "Oh, do let me see it."

"Not till we're at dinner. Come on now, if its good, it's worth waiting for."

They left immediately and Jo sat in the back of the carriage proudly, feeling the rough tweed of David Driscoll's jacket on her bare arm. Was he as handsome as Krikor Berberian? She decided that he was. She also decided he was a good man, not like the men who had hurt her mother, sister, and aunt. It took a special kind of man to love with purity. She felt certain Mr. Driscoll was pure.

While they waited for the appetizers—large ripe black olives, bread, and hommis, a soft mixture made of chickpeas and spices—Mr. Driscoll unfolded the paper and handed the page to Jo. "Careful," he cautioned. "I only have one copy right now. Next week I'll have more, one for you and one for Miss Spring. But this came by special messenger this morning."

Jo unfolded the paper and stared at her picture. She blushed, wondering if she always looked so very sad. But Mr. Driscoll had told her not to smile, and besides, the picture had been taken before she really knew him, long before he had begun to make her laugh with his stories of little people who played pranks and did magic.

She read the story slowly. Her own part was much as she had related it to him, though part of it was a lie, she thought. Mushgin had not covered her eyes, though she wished he had. In the dim light of the Kurdish torches, she saw her mother and sister raped and beaten. She saw man after man fall on their screaming, struggling bodies, she saw them stabbed, their throats finally slit when the men were finished. Then the horses had been turned loose to trample the bodies into the ground. They were the horses of her dreams, with twitching nostrils and gaping mouths. Her father, Mushgin's father, and her grandfather Apel had died being dragged about by the Kurds' horses.

"You okay?" David Driscoll asked. "Hey, you're supposed to look happy. This is a celebration. You're famous, and I'm pretty sure we're going to find your uncle."

Jo looked up and blinked back her tears. "I am crying for joy," she lied. Then added truthfully, "It would be wonderful if you could find my uncle. I must get to the United States, I really must. It is what my father wanted. I have to go and make him proud."

David nodded. It was her determination that made her different. He'd talked to kids in Athens and to others here through Jo, who acted as his interpreter. Some of his interviews were with young men who wanted only to grow strong to fight the Turks and avenge their people; others wanted only to go home, to try to recreate their lives. Some wanted to go to Russia, where most of the surviving Armenians were; still others were only the shells of children, living with poverty and bad dreams. But if Jo had bad dreams, she kept them to herself, and certainly she had perseverance. Her command of English was absolutely astounding, except of course she knew little slang, and sometimes she used slightly stilted language. He smiled to himself. He was teaching her slang and she learned quickly. Yes, he thought, this kid was different. She had a goal. She felt that she could honor her family by following through with her father's dream.

"Ready for your promised present?" he asked with a wink. He reached under the table and withdrew a box.

"Is that big box for me?" Jo questioned, wide-eyed. Every Christmas, each orphan received a package with a toothbrush, a washcloth, a towel, and a pair of slippers. But this was the first real present she had been given since her father gave her *Little Women*.

"Here, open it." He thrust it in front of her and Jo struggled for a moment with the string, then the paper. She lifted the top of the box and gasped. It was a dress, a pale blue dress trimmed with lace! It was a real dress, not a dull scratchy uniform.

"It's beautiful!" Jo stuttered. "I've never had a dress this beautiful."

"Glad you like it. You can wear it when you go to the good old U.S. of A."

"Are you so sure I'm going?"

"Sure, I'm sure."

"Do you think I can be a writer?"

He smiled. "Of course, but you know there are lots of different kinds of writers."

"I think I want to be a journalist, like you. I want to be able to use the newspapers to help people."

Journalist. It was such a grand word, David thought, looking into her dark eyes. So European. In Europe he was a journalist, in America just a plain old reporter. "Why the hell not?" he asked, lifting his glass of red wine to her. "When you're old enough, you come to Chicago, kid. I'll help you get started. Look, your words are already in print. You can do it, I know you can. You come to Chicago and I'll make you the best damn reporter in the Windy City!"

Jo's eyes filled with puzzlement. "The Windy City?"

"Another name for Chicago. The wind blows off the lake and around the buildings. It howls! Of course, some people say they call it the Windy City because of the politicians. They blow too!"

Jo smiled but didn't understand. Sometimes he used words in a way she couldn't fathom.

"I mean politicians make promises they don't keep, they talk a lot, but their words don't mean anything. We call that blowing, like the wind blows."

"Oh, I see," she said brightly.

"Ah, here comes our feast!" David poured more wine into his own glass. "Can you help me write some more stories?" he asked. "The people I work for want more articles in the series."

"Of course, but will Miss Spring let me?"

"Sure. Miss Spring is about to be kept very busy counting donations. I think she'll let you do anything I ask. I'll just butter her up a little."

Jo giggled. She recognized it as another of his expressions. "Spread butter on her?" she asked, wide-eyed.

David roared. "No, just blow at her . . . like the wind!"

Miss Spring sat behind her cluttered desk. Her face was pink, and when she talked, her hands moved animatedly, revealing her pleasure and excitement. "There are so many good Christians in America!" Miss Spring's eyes were misty as she looked at the piles of letters on her desk. "A child sent a dollar for the starving Armenians, and a businessman from New Jersey sent two hundred dollars! Dear Mr. Driscoll, I can't tell you what all these donations mean to our orphanage! And we even have letters offering to adopt children—especially Josephina, since it was her picture that first appeared. Of course, adoptive families have to be screened very carefully, and the authorities definitely prefer that Armenian children go to Armenian families."

"Understandable," David agreed. He had been in Salonika for two and a half months now. He'd done five stories, and had instructions to write two more to finish the series and obtain sufficient material for the book. Jo had come up with a corker, a little girl named Ellice. She was ten, and her family had perished in a fire deliberately set by Turkish troops.

He'd even hired a photographer, a middle-aged Sephardic Jew whose studio walls were lined with photos of wealthy Jewish families, a student drama club, and a portrait of a rabbi bedecked in long robes. David didn't like the photographer, Haim Haviv, but he had to admit the man was good at his work and his pictures were an important part of the book, which was now a certainty. He supposed that Haviv had also taught him something. He had made David realize that Salonika was a kind of publishing mecca, and that there were no less than ten publications in Ladino. That, as it turned out, was an irritation of sorts. Haviv and his German

camera were always busy providing pictures for local
publications. It irritated David because he paid better,
and he paid in U.S. dollars. He was, nonetheless, Haviv's
last priority.

Ellice flashed across his mind. He decided he wouldn't
use her picture, since Jo had asked him not to. "She's
very shy, and while she has agreed to be interviewed,
you mustn't take her picture."

David's thoughts jumped back to the photographer,
who always kept him waiting. Hardly the way the author of a series that had been nominated for the prestigious Winford Journalism Prize should be treated.
Of course, none of that mattered as much as the
extra money he'd received for syndication rights.
The series also had another impact. People were demanding that Armenian widows and orphans be allowed
to emigrate.

"Hammer on that angle," Mike Hamilton advised.
"It's always a feather in our cap to force action on an
issue like resumption of immigration. Especially as most
of the immigrants will be going to Boston or New York
and not coming here to Chicago." That comment summed
up one of Mike Hamilton's most endearing qualities.
He understood the public and was duly cynical. Just as
I am, David thought. The natives of the good city of
Chicago loved prodding Washington—writing to their
congressmen about resumption of immigration gave them
a "good" feeling, as long as none of the immigrants
moved next door to them.

"Mr. Driscoll, you are a very fine man. I can't tell you
what your stories have accomplished." Miss Spring looked
at him benevolently, almost worshipfully. "And you
know, you've made that little girl very happy. Of course,
she's very special anyway. I noticed that the first time I

ever met her. She's got ambition, and a real talent for
languages."

"She's a great kid," David agreed honestly. "You
know, we think we've got a lead on her uncle. The
paper's following it up."

"Oh, that's wonderful news!"

"Don't tell her yet, I wouldn't want her to be disappointed if it doesn't pan out."

"My lips are sealed." Miss Spring lifted her bony
finger to her thin lips and blinked her eyelashes. David
nodded and thought: My God, she's flirting with me. It
wasn't the first time he'd noticed her flirt, and he would
have put an end to it, but unfortunately, he had to
continue to flatter her. He still needed access to Jo in
order to finish off his interviews.

"You've got quite a tan," Miss Spring gushed. It was
actually the first time she'd allowed herself to say anything personal, and he noticed that her mouth twitched
with nervousness.

"I've been spending some time at the beach. It's a
good place to think."

"Well, it makes you look . . . uh, healthy," she
stammered.

He smiled warmly. He would have to take her to
lunch or dinner or something. Fortunately she was too
repressed and too shy to become a real problem. Well,
what the hell, she worked hard and she needed some
kind of excitement. "Can you have dinner with me next
weekend?" he asked politely. "You've been such a help,
I'd really like to show my appreciation."

Miss Spring's face turned an even deeper red. "I'd be
delighted," she stuttered. Then, as if on cue, she began
again to shuffle through her mail. But, he noted with
discomfort, her hand was trembling.

David walked by the water and watched as the small craft at anchor in the bay swayed in the gentle breeze. He stopped at the sea wall and paused to look at the so-called White Tower. It would need a good white-wash before it could really be called white, he observed. Still, it was the most famous landmark in Salonika. He shrugged and walked on, wishing that his headache would go away.

It was Saturday, August 16, and without a doubt Saturday was the deadest day of the week in Salonika. Both the large Jewish population and the Moslem population observed Saturday as the sabbath and it seemed as if most of the stores and restaurants were closed. Still, he readily admitted he too needed a day of rest.

The last forty-eight hours had been less than triumphal, and he acknowledged the fact that he felt somewhat depressed. On Friday he had taken dear Miss Spring out for dinner. Much to his chagrin, she wasn't as shy as he'd thought. Indeed, her flirtations increased with each glass of retsina. Silly woman, he hoped her headache was as bad as his.

She appeared at his hotel decked out in a flowered print dress that looked as if it were homemade in Poplar Bluff out of a Purina flour sack. Of course he knew full well that many farm people used the print sacks to make clothing, but imagine bringing such a thing to Greece. Besides, the style of the dress was woefully out-of-date. It made her look even older than he supposed her to be. And she had also worn a hat, a hideous picture hat with a garish red flower stuck in its ribbon band.

Miss Spring blushed and giggled her way through the first course of dinner while he nobly attempted to explain the various dishes. He couldn't quite get over the idea that she had actually been in Greece longer than he and had never tasted Greek food. Her small-town reluctance to sample the unknown made him more daring, and he boldly recommended the retsina, which he himself had never drunk. He remembered thinking that surely she was a teetotaler so it didn't matter what he ordered. No such luck. Not only did she drink, she liked the retsina.

"It's so unusual," she cooed.

"When the Turks occupied Greece, they used to put resin in the wine and make the Greeks drink it," he told her. "It was a punishment, but the Greeks grew to like it, so they made it their national drink."

"You astound me, Mr. Driscoll. You know so much! I'm even taken aback by your knowledge of the Scriptures. You're really very well educated."

"Thank you," David answered as he drained his glass. She was being generous. He gave himself full points for being self-educated, and he knew that his years as a reporter had certainly broadened his knowledge and outlook. The truth was, he knew a little bit about a lot of things, and could discuss all of them with a certain glibness. But he was by no means well educated. He'd left Hannibal when he was nineteen and come back to Chicago. He had held a variety of jobs till he was twenty-nine; then he had gotten his break on the *Journal* as a junior reporter. Still, he was lucky. He had worked with a good bunch of guys, and their conversations ran the gambit. He hadn't liked Benny Hecht much at first because he was younger and had a better job. But for a Jew, Hecht turned out to be an okay guy. He was smart, and he wasn't formally educated either. In fact, he wasn't even very street-wise in the beginning. Hecht and D. W. Griffith hung out together. They were so

naive they actually lived in a brothel for months before
they found out it *was* a brothel. The two of them were
the laughingstock of Kings Restaurant.

Those were great days, David reminisced. Carl Sand-
burg was on the Chicago *Daily News* and crazy Ring
Lardner was over at the Essanay Studios on Argyle
Street writing movie scripts for the likes of Wallace
Beery and Gloria Swanson. All the writers, reporters,
poets, novelists, playwrights—the whole bunch of them—
used to go to Kings and shoot the shit. They talked
politics, poetry, and sex. No, he wasn't formally educated, but he had a degree from Kings Restaurant.

He remembered that he had learned to type on the
first model of the Remington ever built—he even knew
how to set type. Golden days, David thought. Days
when you really apprenticed to become a reporter.
Days when you got your education on the streets. But
things were changing. More and more of the new reporters being hired by the big papers had graduated
from the journalism school at the University of Missouri—it was the first journalism school in the United
States—or they were coming out of Northwestern, the
closest thing the Midwest had to Harvard. Northwestern was turning out young eager-beaver newsmen who
were heavy on book knowledge but who didn't really
know a damn thing. Mind you, apprentices were still
being hired. A man could still go from a copy boy to
editor. College boys, he thought of them scornfully.
Fate hadn't been kind enough to allow him to be born
into a family that could afford to send him through
school. When he looked up from his thoughts, he noted
that Miss Spring had drained her glass of retsina and
was holding it out for a refill.

Three glasses of retsina later and she was giggling
girlishly and talking about Poplar Bluff. "I love chil-

dren," she confided. "I used to teach school in Poplar Bluff. I always wanted children." She leaned over meaningfully. "I've never met a man like you," she whispered.

David remembered that he smiled weakly at her. He was thirty-seven, he assumed she was at least forty, perhaps older. Not that the thought of older women bothered him. In fact, he rather liked his women older, provided they were lookers.

The rest of the evening with Miss Spring was an unmitigated disaster. He knew his palms were sweaty, and he was uncomfortable to the core. He couldn't drink too much because he had to see to it that Miss Spring got back to the orphanage, and he had to continue to be nice because he needed her continued cooperation. At the same time, he had to avoid verbal or physical entrapment. As the hours passed, it became evident just what Miss Spring had on her mind, and nothing could have interested him less.

Finally, at nine-thirty, David managed to load a somewhat flustered, frustrated, and tiddled Miss Spring into a carriage. He deposited her on the steps of the orphanage, but when he reached out to shake her hand, she kissed him on the lips. It was a furtive, darting kiss, more of a peck really. David could not shake the image of a caged canary at her seed ball. Poor Miss Spring. The paper in the bottom of her cage definitely needed changing.

David leaned against the sea wall and stared out at the ocean. "I'd feel better if I'd been able to bathe," he said aloud. The damn water in Salonika came from wells, and whenever it got hot, there was a water shortage. The toilet in his hotel wouldn't flush, and the pipes were nearly dry. They yielded only a dribbling stream of rusty, tainted-smelling liquid.

Wash. Yes, he wished he could wash. No wonder old Lady Macbeth and her hand scrubbing was such a powerful literary symbol. No doubt about it. You could wash your sins away—at least you felt better if you tried. He recalled the rest of the evening. It was both the best and the worst.

He hadn't returned to the hotel, but rather had run directly to a Greek nightclub, where he listened to the melodic strains of the bouzouki and drank more than he should have. The club suited his mood. It was dark and smoky, the atmosphere heavy with the pungent odor of Greek and Turkish tobacco. There were a few women in the club, but they were professionals. Groups of Greek men sat at tables and talked animatedly, while the orchestra sat in a long row, stony-faced and playing intently. It was a different culture and a different country, and as far as you could get from Michigan Avenue. But something about the men in conversation reminded him of Kings Restaurant, which he had been thinking about earlier. He felt suddenly lonely, and he longed for the past. Good Irishman that he was, he was practically crying in his warm sour beer when he was joined by a woman who called herself Allya.

Allya had golden skin that looked soft and pliable, olive eyes, and rounded full breasts. Her dress was low-cut, and the cleavage she revealed made her voluptuous figure delightfully obvious. She was a prostitute—no respectable woman would be alone in a bar in this part of the world. But it didn't matter, he'd slept with prostitutes for years. He liked them—no entanglements, no broken promises, no crying fits or arguments. You simply paid, and they disappeared, leaving your life much as they entered it.

He took Allya back to his hotel, even though he knew it would be morning before he could fully avail himself of her services. He fell asleep holding her in his arms and crying about his mother's death, the loss of the companionship of his cronies at Kings Restaurant, and about the men he'd seen choking on poison gas in the trenches. He cried about anything and everything that made him sad. And she had seemed understanding and even tender. Allya ran her fingers through his hair and crooned to him in a language he couldn't understand, and was indeed too drunk to even recognize.

In the morning he awoke next to her smooth naked body. He staggered from the bed and drank all the water in the carafe. He then returned eagerly to the bed.

She moved sensuously for him, holding her own breasts and lifting and dropping her hips in a smooth circular motion. He had taken her hands and put them on his own aching member while he kissed her dark nipples, licked her smooth skin, and touched her intimately while she groaned beneath him, her body moist and inviting. Unable to restrain himself, he fell on her none too gently and took her with unrestrained passion. She was young and beautiful and seemed compassionate. He rarely found those qualities in a woman of the evening. For a short time he felt as if he were in love with her. She moved beneath him as if she had enjoyed him. He, in turn, breathed in her ear and fondled her rounded buttocks.

When he was spent, he held her close. "I love Greek women," he told her. It was then he discovered she spoke English.

She looked at him sadly. "I'm Armenian," she said simply.

He immediately thought of Jo. "Armenian?" He repeated the word dumbly. "Why aren't you in one of the refugee camps?" It was a stupid question.

She sat up and covered herself with the sheet. Her face seemed contorted, her eyes penetrating. "What do you think happens to us when we are too old for charity?" she asked him. Her olive eyes were like hard jewels, and her full lips were set. "There are lots of Armenian prostitutes! We all lost our virginity in the Turkish camps! How else should I earn a living? How else should I survive? I've lost everyone, my whole family was killed! Do you think I like selling myself? If my father were alive, he would kill me because of what I do. But I don't want to die of starvation or be sent back to Turkey, where I'd be murdered. I must do this. I have no choice."

He felt ill. He paid her more than she asked, and when she left, he fell across the bed and retched. He couldn't shake the idea that Jo might end up the same way. He couldn't shake the idea that somehow he had violated Jo by sleeping with an Armenian who had, by force of circumstance, been turned into a whore. Up till the moment she had wailed at him, he had thought she enjoyed him—in fact, he had always thought all whores enjoyed their work.

David turned away from the sea wall and the view of the White Tower and began walking again.

"Hell," he swore under his breath. He'd let this kid get to him, he'd let them all get to him. It was time to go back to Paris and get cracking on some action stuff, or maybe an exposé. But he vowed he wouldn't leave without saying good-bye, even though he dreaded encountering the amorous Miss Spring. He admitted that he felt disgruntled with himself, maybe even a little guilty because of the Armenian prostitute. I'll leave the kid some money, he decided. It was the least he could do.

"Immigration to Resume! Hope for Thousands of Widows and Children!"
by David Driscoll.
August 15, 1919. Exclusive to the *World*.

Three

Dear Diary,

David Driscoll is coming tomorrow to finish up his last story. I am overjoyed that he's coming, because he hasn't been here for three days now. But I am afraid too. He told me that there were lots of offers to adopt me. But the truth is, I really want *him* to adopt me. I want him to take me to Chicago and teach me to be a writer. I want to work with him and be his collaborator. What a wonderful life that would be!

David is a good man, I can tell. Even Miss Spring thinks so. He is full of ideas and dreams. He's so like Papa. I prayed and prayed and it's as if God sent David so I could keep my promise and make Papa proud of me. Oh, I do hope that when he comes tomorrow he will tell me he is taking me with him. He told me he had a surprise. It would be wonderful if that were the surprise.

Goodnight, diary.

Jo Gregorian

Jo closed the book and extinguished the lamp. Through the open window a mild breeze blew in off the sea. Jo imagined the fluttering curtains to be angels' wings on which she traveled back in time. Warm days, soft evening rains, and cool evenings were the pattern this time of year. She inhaled deeply, smelling the aroma of the wet earth. How often had she lain on her pallet at home and smelled that wonderful odor? Dew on warm soil. It made the earth seem alive and newborn.

She and Mushgin were skipping home from school. It was late summer, and a dainty rain had fallen overnight, washing the flowers and bathing the leaves.

"Come home with me, Mushgin! Grandmama makes hommis every Monday and we can have some on hot pita bread. She'll say no at first, but if you look sad and hungry, she will say, 'Well, go to the pantry and get some!' Then she will complain, 'I hardly get it off the stove and you children eat it! You certainly keep a body busy.' " Jo could almost hear herself imitating her grandmother.

"I ought to go home, my father wants me to help clean the ovens and I do have to study. My math is not as good as yours, Josephina," Mushgin confessed with a frown.

Mushgin was short for a ten-year-old. He wore great thick glasses that made him look wise, and he had thick curly hair and a habit of sucking on his lower lip. Jo knew he liked to be with her because the other boys teased him about his glasses and called him a sissy because he wouldn't steal fruit from Mr. Agajainian's fruit wagon or fight in the street as they did.

"Come on, you can study later," Jo urged. She took Mushgin's hand and pulled him along till they stood outside her house. As soon as they were across the threshold, Mushgin's will melted. He loved to eat, and indeed was a trifle plump. He smelled the hot pita bread and protested no more.

"Mushgin, Mushgin." Jo whispered his name into the darkness. The last time she had seen him was a year ago in Athens. He was thin and nervous. His glasses had been lost, so he couldn't see so well, and he squinted. He had held her and cried and cried. "I don't want to go to Syria! I want to stay with you! Josephina, you are all I have. You are my family now."

"You must go, Mushgin. You must go and find a new family. We must both find new families. If we don't look to the future, we will betray our parents' wish for our survival."

Mushgin had sniffled and held her closer. "I'm going to get strong," he whispered. "I'm going to get even, I'm going to avenge my father's death."

She remembered shaking her head, but she also remembered the quiver in his voice. Jo wondered if Mushgin had meant what he said.

"Josephina?" The door to her room opened a crack and Jo looked up to see Miss Spring's fuzzy head framed in the ray of light.

"Yes, ma'am."

"Are you asleep?"

"I was just going to sleep."

Miss Spring smiled. "That's good. You have a big day tomorrow. Mr. Driscoll is coming, and I'm certain he has exciting news for you."

"I wish I knew what it was."

"It wouldn't be a surprise if you knew. Josephina, may I ask you a question?"

"Yes, ma'am."

"Does Mr. Driscoll ever say anything about me?"

Jo looked at Miss Spring and wished she could see her expression in the shadows. She thought a moment, and decided that she should be careful. "He says you are a very fine lady," she replied.

Miss Spring smiled, and Jo could see her teeth in the dim light. "Isn't that nice," she said, closing the door quietly.

It was August 25. David's story, dated the fifteenth, detailed the facts concerning the resumption of immigration to the U.S.

David whistled through his teeth, and the farmer slowed his wagon, allowing him to drop off the back. He was half a kilometer from the orphanage and he fairly skipped along, singing and humming as he went. Damn, it was a beautiful day! Hot damn! Everything had fallen into place. He felt as great today as he had felt lousy on Saturday. He grinned and thought of Mike Hamilton's oft-made comment. "You're the most up-and-down guy I've ever known," Hamilton had observed. "You go from the depths to the heights with no in between." The first time Hamilton had made the comment was about a week after David had left the *Journal* and joined the *World*. He had fallen into a deep depression, wondering if he had made the right decision. He drank too much, was unable to sleep, and found his work suffered. Then he stumbled on a big story. He'd gotten a byline, and he became euphoric. High and low, he was always one or the other.

"There's no denying I'm up today," he announced as he approached a cow grazing by the side of the road.

In addition to his story on immigration, he also had a telegram from Mike Hamilton. It bore an important message. The kid's uncle had been found and he'd agreed to take her. What a coup! Now, David thought happily, he could leave Salonika before Miss Spring somehow managed to rope and brand him. Most important, however, he could leave with a clear conscience. The kid would get to America and wouldn't end up in some damn cathouse in Greece.

"I've done one hell of a job," he said as he lightheartedly stopped for a bit of conversation with the cow. "Hear that, bossy? I've done one hell of a job! The government is going to welcome Armenian refugees, the kid's going to live with her uncle, and I'm going to have a book published." He ambled on. "Pretty good for a guy on vacation," he yelled back to the cow, who went on chewing her cud without concern.

David straightened his tie and paused as he approached the gates of the orphanage. It felt great not to have to let the kid down.

"Oh, dear Mr. Driscoll!" Miss Spring gushed. "Do come in and sit down. I've ordered tea, and Josephina will be here in ten minutes. I thought you wouldn't mind if we had a few words alone."

"I'd be delighted." He smiled and kissed her hand.

"I can't tell you how much I enjoyed our dinner. I learned so very much! You know, Greek food appears to be quite wholesome. I've begun a whole new diet plan for meals here. Do you think grape leaves and whatever is stuffed into them are as healthy as tinned American peas?"

He smiled in spite of himself. "I'm sure they are."

She sat down and arranged her dress, then folded her hands in her lap. Her cheeks looked rouged and fairly glowed under a layer of powder. He wondered if she'd been into the retsina again.

"You're such a fine man, so handsome. Tell me, dear Mr. Driscoll, have you ever thought of marriage?"

David looked at the floor. He conjured up his most troubled, most sincere look. "To tell you the truth, dear lady, I have."

"But you aren't married, are you?" Her tone took on a certain edge. My God, he thought, she's going to propose.

"No, no, I'm not married. But that's because there is an impediment." He emphasized the word "impediment" and tried to look unhappy.

"Oh dear."

"I have faith, dear Miss Spring, and that faith forbids carnal knowledge. I've taken a vow of celibacy."

"You're Catholic?" She sounded shocked to the core.

"I confess. I'm a Jesuit, an ordained priest. As I'm sure you know, our order goes forth into various professions, but those of us who are ordained cannot marry."

She looked thoroughly bewildered. "My goodness," she whispered, as if to admit she had been thinking the unthinkable. "A priest. I never would have guessed. Of course, there are a lot of Catholics in Chicago." It was a wonderful non sequitur. She was doubtless anti-Catholic to her good Midwestern Bible Belt roots, but the realization that she had been tempting a priest was simply too much for her. Beneath her rouge, her cheeks were flushed, and she was truly flustered. She actually jumped when Jo knocked on the door. "Oh, thank goodness," she stuttered.

He couldn't have put it better himself. Jo came in and stood near him.

"Should she call you Father?" Miss Spring said, frowning.

"Father?" Jo questioned. Her face lit up the room. He was going to adopt her. He was going to take her to America!

"I don't think that's necessary," David objected.

Miss Spring stood up. "I think I should leave you two alone. It's not my surprise, after all."

David nodded in relief. He had no desire to bring the kid into his bold-faced lie.

Miss Spring made a hasty exit and David sat down in her chair. He could congratulate himself on one score.

Miss Spring was too shocked to be hurt, and she had swallowed his absurd story hook, line, and sinker.

"Are you going to adopt me?" Jo blurted out. "Oh, Mr. Driscoll, please adopt me! Is that why Miss Spring asked if I should call you Father?"

David frowned and reached out, putting his arm around her slim shoulders. "No. I'm sorry if you misunderstood. I'm afraid that was a little joke."

Jo's eyes flooded with tears. "You're not going to take me to America? I have to stay here?"

"No and yes. Hey, look, we've found your uncle. What's-his-name, Garabed. He's going to take you. You're going to Boston on a big ship, and you're going to live in a nice place with your family."

"I want to go with you. I want to work with you." Her large eyes seemed even larger, and he damn near said: Why not?

"Look, Jo . . ." He squeezed her shoulders in a friendly bear hug. "I'm a rover. I have to travel a lot. I never settle down—that's the reason I'm not married. I can't take responsibility for bringing you up. You have to go to your uncle and lead a normal life."

She was staring at the floor. David squeezed her again and kissed her gently on the cheek. "You're a smart kid, and a real pretty little girl. You're going to grow up to be a knockout, you know. You're going to make it. Listen, if you ever need anything, you get in touch with me at the *World*. I'll help you get started, I'll help you write. But that's all in the future. You've got some growing to do first."

Jo lifted her eyes and stared into his. "Do you promise?"

"I promise."

She straightened her shoulders. "Tell me why Miss Spring asked if I should call you Father."

He grinned impishly. "Promise not to tell. Promise it will be our secret?"

"I swear."

"She wants to marry me," he whispered. "I told her I was a priest."

Through her tears, Jo burst out laughing. "That's naughty."

Garabed Gregorian hunched his heavy shoulders and leaned over his syrupy black Armenian coffee. It steamed back in his face, fogging his thick glasses. His expression was unsmiling, and he breathed heavily, his fleshy cheeks puffing in and out like those of a large lizard.

"You should be happy," his companion, Nassredin Ajemian, told him. Nassredin was as thin as Garabed was heavy. Both men were about fifty, both conversed in Armenian and punctuated their speech with grunts and hand movements.

Garabed's bushy brows lifted. "Why?" he asked.

"You're famous! Look, your picture was in the American newspaper! People have sent you money in the mail. Your niece is coming to America!"

"They didn't send enough money for me to go to California," Garabed complained. "That's my only dream. I want to go to California and buy a vineyard. I want to spend the rest of my life sitting in the warm sun, watching as my grapes ripen. They say the soil is so rich a man doesn't have to work. Once the planting is done, nature does the rest."

"They said the streets of America were paved in gold," Nassredin replied sarcastically. "If they are, why do I work such long hours? Why did my wife die and leave me with four children? Why do I live in this hellhole!" He rolled his eyes heavenward as if to appeal his position. "Even the climate is a misery! It's only September, but it's already cold."

"At home a man of my position would not have had to work!" Garabed grimaced. "My family was wealthy! But here, here I am treated as if I were some lowly peasant. And look at Tartarian the trader. A disgrace. In Armenia he *was* a peasant, but here he lives like a king, while we of the upper class labor like common field hands. It's that way all over America. Peasants run this whole country. It is upside down. The poor become rich and the rich become poor."

"But now you have a good job with the Armenian Benevolent Society. You sit behind a desk! And all because your niece was in the American newspaper!" Nassredin peered into Garabed's eyes. He knew that Garabed always thought life was better elsewhere, while he himself felt only bitterness at what seemed the broken promises of the New World. But in a sense, Garabed was right. America was upside down. Nassredin's sister, Annya, was a fine example of the law run amok. Annya had married a wealthy American who had died and left her a fortune. In Armenia, Annya would not have inherited the money. He would have. Of course, he would have been expected to provide Annya with the necessities of life, just as Annya would have been expected to care for his house and children. But not in America. Annya was rich. She had moved away to the fashionable suburbs of Worcester, and came only once a week to visit him. She arrived with a flourish and behaved like Lady Bountiful, bestowing small gifts on his children. Not that he himself was poor, though he never let on how much he had. The truth was, he hoarded money and then pretended there was none.

"I don't make much money at the Society," Garabed

grumbled. "Not enough to feed another mouth. And where will I put her? I have only one room and one bed. I live in a tenement. I share a bathroom with eight others now. But you, you are much better off. You have a shop, and above the shop an apartment."

"I'm a poor shoemaker," Nassredin said with a shrug. "A poor shoemaker with three children and no wife to raise them."

Garabed shook his head. "America is too crowded. I long for Armenia, for the hills and the mountains, and for the warmth of the golden sun. But it's all been taken away, we can never return home again."

"Still, you will have your niece. She's family. She can cook and keep house for you, Garabed. She can support you in your old age."

Garabed spit and ground it into the dusty floor with the toe of his shoe. "A woman! I would rather it was one of my brother's sons that had survived. What am I to do with a young girl? And worse yet, in a few years I'll have to find her a husband. I haven't the money for a dowry."

"But people sent you money."

"I'm saving that for my vineyard. I suppose if we can move to California it will be all right. She can work in the vineyard and I'll find her some young farmboy with a strong back."

Nassredin nodded, and tugged at his heavy beard. "To change the subject, whom will you vote for in the election? Will it be Alchian or Bedrosian?"

"Alchian, of course! How can you even ask? Would I vote for a member of the Ramgavar party? I want Armenia returned to the Armenians! We must have a community leader who will support this."

Nassredin leaned across the table and squeezed Garabed's shoulder with his hand. "I knew we thought alike," he whispered. "But we must keep our politics to ourselves." He winked slyly. "You know how it is. The community has so many factions, I can't let on anything without fear of losing customers. Politics is one matter, business is another."

Garabed sipped at his coffee and looked around the tiny room. It was hardly more than a hole in the wall. There were no more than ten tables, each surrounded by four chairs. The little coffeehouse was below street level, but two steamed-up windows looked out on the sidewalk. They bore the name of the coffeehouse in Armenian. Here and there were copies of the Armenian newspaper, and on the shelf near the door were a few books. "A poor recreation of home," Garabed muttered as his eyes roamed the gloomy off-green walls.

"Perhaps we should be grateful," Nassredin suggested.

"Grateful? Grateful to toil all day behind a desk shuffling papers to make a few dollars? Grateful because people sent me money? Grateful for having some nosy writer find my niece, whom I can't even support? What have I to be grateful for? I would only be grateful if I could go to Fresno and buy my vineyards. I'd live in a big house. I'd hire people to do all the work."

"Perhaps it isn't as you imagine it."

"Of course it is. It is a little Armenia. They say even the climate is the same."

"Perhaps you would be happier if you learned to read in English?" Nassredin suggested. "I'm thinking of learning myself."

"I'm Armenian," Garabed insisted. He doubled his fist and hit the table. "I was born Armenian and I shall die Armenian! I'm not giving up my language. If people want to talk to me, let them learn Armenian. Imagine knowing only one tongue? I speak Armenian, Turkish,

and Russian! As you do, my friend. But they call us
illiterate!"

Nassredin smiled. "You will never change, Garabed."

Garabed nodded his agreement. "I do not want to
change," he said.

———

Springtime in Paris might be romantic, David Driscoll
mused as he walked through the Jardin des Tuileries,
but November was quite the opposite. It was damp,
cool, and cloudy. The best he could hope for was a few
hours of tentative sun in the late afternoon. Today even
that was denied.

Low, ominous clouds moved across the eastern sky, a
brisk wind shook the bare branches on the trees, and
the ground squished beneath his feet. But he had to get
outside now and again, even if it meant walking in the
cool drizzle and braving the wind. And weather aside,
Paris was made for walking. No point within the city
limits was farther than six miles from the square in front
of Notre Dame Cathedral. Paris was not at all like
Chicago, which sprawled over miles and miles, coming
to an undistinguished petering-out in the middle of a
cornfield.

David stuffed his hands in his pockets. "Make the
most of it," he muttered. "This is practically your last
day in Paris."

I've had enough anyway, he admitted to himself. He
was tired of conferences, committees, and meetings.
Politicians had a way of droning on. Wilson pontificated
on the virtues of a League of Nations to prevent future
wars. But hell, his proposed League would have no
teeth. Nationalism was stronger than ever. Nations,
especially those that had triumphed in the war, were

not about to give up one ounce of their sovereignty. Certainly the United States wouldn't. No, the "Little Professor" was barking up the wrong tree. He persisted in pushing his pipe dream, and the old men who led Europe nodded in agreement, eager to push themselves into positions that would seem important, even if in reality they were totally unimportant. Yeah, it was all so much blabbering. The internationalists versus the nationalists, but when states themselves are still divided from within, David knew it could never work. And in fact, he doubted international government could work in a totally ideal world, whatever that was.

"Conferences aren't my meat," he muttered as he kicked a small pebble with the toe of his shoe. And it was true. He was bored, utterly and completely bored. The war had been great. Every day there was a new story and a new adventure. It hadn't been pretty, but hell, it made for great reporting. Greece had been sensational too. He'd returned to Paris with a top-notch story under his belt, a book that was being published, a great suntan, and he felt invigorated. But after a few weeks he was again bored. Paris was just as he had left it. The politicians were just where he had left them. It was impossible to go on writing about nothing day after day after day. They ought to have special correspondents to cover meetings, people with infinite patience, people who didn't crave action and drama as he knew he did. But the only action was in French politics, which he admitted he didn't understand and cared less about. That, he assumed, went double for his readers. The *World* duly reported international news, but it had to be international news that affected the U.S. of A.

David crinkled his face as the first of the afternoon raindrops hit his nose. He drew up the collar on his rumpled trench coat and walked out of the park that ran nearly parallel with the Seine. He headed for the bridge that led to the Left Bank and the Boulevard Montparnasse, even though it was a long walk. He smiled and waved as he passed a group of acrobats vainly trying to attract a crowd. Paris was full of street entertainment. It was one of the aspects of the city he liked, one of the attractions he would miss.

There were four possible choices of destination. He could drop by the bookstore Shakespeare and Company on the Rue de l'Odeon, go to the café Les Deux Magots, drop by the restaurant La Quatrième République, or go to visit Evette, a sometime model who also worked as a prostitute.

Shakespeare and Company was not only a bookstore but also a meeting place for all sorts of writers. Some were journalists, like Ernest Hemingway, who covered Europe for the Toronto *Star* but who had literary pretensions. Some were snotty academics who spent all their time discoursing on matters philosophical, and others were just hangers-on. More reporters, however, gathered at La Quatrième République on the Rue Jacob, just below the Place Saint-Germain-des-Prés. He decided to go there. La Quatrième wasn't the Kings in Chicago, but he liked it. It was filled with Americans arguing politics, discussing world events, and wallowing in French culture. They are a lively group, David conceded. Just what the doctor ordered for a slight case of depressive writer's block. And, he thought, after a time he would go and avail himself of Evette. Yeah, that was the ticket. A little brew and a farewell screw. Then just maybe he'd be able to finish his latest assignment.

David shivered. It was getting cooler and damper. He needed a hot meal and some good French table wine. He began walking faster; then, as the rain fell harder, he hailed a cab, thinking about his destination

with humor. La Quatrième République drew its name
from the fact that France was living under the Third
Republic of President Poincaré, a man who typified
French stubbornness in terms of the Germans and how
they should be treated. The owner of the restaurant
believed that France would soon need a new constitution, that matters could not go on as they were. He
therefore celebrated his future vision by calling his
bistro the Fourth Republic.

Like all such restaurants La Quatrième was filled
with bare wooden tables and straight-backed chairs.
But the decor on its walls was sheer artistic madness.
Cubist art decorated every surface, and there was even
a set of painted false stairs. So good was the perspective
that those who consumed too much wine often mistook
them for real stairs and stood stupidly in front of them
before discovering they were trying to climb a mural.

All else aside, the food was hot, good, and cheap.
Hors d'oeuvres, pâté, stew, salad, bread, and wine
came to only thirty cents American. David entered the
bistro and looked around. A group of literati sat gathered at one end of the room. They were not hard to
spot. They had that starving-writer image even if they
weren't thin. He turned his head away and looked to
the far end of the room. Spotting his fellow reporters,
David headed toward them.

"At least you know enough to come in out of the
rain," Dick Farnham of the London *Times* said as he
patted the empty chair next to his. Farnham was in his
mid-thirties, a tall scarecrow of a man, sharp-featured,
thin, myopic, and effeminate. He peered at David
through his thick glasses while simultaneously lifting his
hand toward the waitress, silently ordering another carafe of wine. "Have one on me," he said without smiling. "And congratulations."

"On what?" David sat down, straddling the chair in one swift movement. He fumbled for a cigarette, and in disgust crumpled his empty pack of Camels. "Got a fag?" he asked. It was British slang for "cigarette," but of course Dickie, as he was better known, was British.

Dickie Farnham produced a pack of English Ovals and proffered one. "On your book. I heard this afternoon that it's won the Winford journalism prize. Listen, we even reviewed it. American books don't get reviewed very often, I can tell you. Not in the *Times* anyway." Farnham drained his glass just as the waitress set down more wine.

David smiled. "Did it? How's that for communication? I haven't even been sent copies yet."

"It didn't take long to write, did it?" Dickie asked, a cool, belittling sarcasm in his voice.

"They just put together the articles," David admitted. Hell, if it had taken three years, would that have made it better? he silently asked himself. He lifted his glass and drained it, watching as good old Dickie sipped. He held up the menu and pointed to what he wanted. The waitress nodded pleasantly. It was only three in the afternoon. He had a story to write, but he doubted it would take more than an hour to pound it out, and he didn't have to send it out till morning. He decided to spend an hour with the boys and maybe two hours with Evette. That would leave him plenty of time to meet his deadline.

"I should be off after I finish this one," Dickie announced. "I've got a full afternoon ahead of me, and a smashing interview with David Lloyd George first thing in the morning."

"Good for you," David replied without looking up. Dickie's announcement was only his way of letting it be known that he wasn't going to pay for another carafe.

"I hope you're enjoying your moment of glory," a cold female voice hissed. David nearly jumped; he hadn't heard her come up behind him, and he turned, his mouth partly open, to face Maggie Adams.

He was going to say "I was surprised" or "Sure, I am enjoying it." But that was before he realized it was Maggie. She stood there, her long arms at her sides, her pretty face frozen, and her eyes unblinking. "Good afternoon," he said instead. Then added, "Maggie Adams, meet Dick Farnham."

Maggie didn't even turn toward Farnham, she simply continued to glare at him. "Any friend of David's is no friend of mine," she said nastily.

"Oh dear, that is a good exit cue," Dickie said as he slid off his chair. "Do sit down, madam. I'm just leaving." He plunked his money down and winked at David. "Intimidating, old man. Very intimidating," he whispered.

"Do you want to sit down?" David asked, lifting his eyebrow. He wondered just why he had found her so attractive in Vienna. She didn't seem at all attractive now.

"No, I do not want to sit down. I just want to tell you what a low, miserable, wretched excuse for a human being you are," she said loudly.

David frowned at her. He felt decidedly uncomfortable. It was a public place, and other patrons were staring at them. Two of his buddies at the adjoining table had stopped talking in order to eavesdrop.

David just stared at her. Her tone was not only reproachful but also filled with hate. It was a far cry from the tone she had used when she eased out of his arms and said, "No, not just yet. We don't know each other well enough."

"I'm all those things, honey." He was trying to make

a joke out of her words, trying to belittle her. But he knew his face was red and he knew he felt like a naughty child. David poured himself another glass of wine in order to look nonchalant. The waitress, who was certainly the soul of discretion, brought another carafe without a word. "Do you want a drink?" he asked Maggie.

"I don't want anything from you, or with you. You stole my story, my book, and my title, you . . . you washed-up lush!"

Her dark eyes narrowed and he could see that her knuckles were white from gripping her purse strap. "I wrote my own story," he replied defensively.

"From my idea. What's the matter, don't you have any ideas of your own?"

"You can't copyright ideas," he answered.

"You don't deserve that prize, you exploitive bastard! I hope you choke on your liver pâté." With that she turned and stomped away.

David's three friends at the table in the corner clapped as she left the room. "Ought not to allow broads in bistros!" one of them shouted.

"Certainly a shrew worth a screw," Dan Watson called out. "Come on, David, my boy. Come on over and let us buy you a drink."

David ambled over and sat down.

"Women belong in bed, not behind typewriters," Ed Creighton muttered. "Say, David, what did you do to send that one into a tizzy?"

David refilled his glass from the bottle on the table. "I wouldn't marry her," he lied as he drank the entire glassful in one long gulp.

Watson laughed. "But did you lay her?"

David forced a grin. "Sure. Want to know a secret? She's got no tits."

"Bits for tits." Watson laughed. "I'm a leg man myself."

"I'll get the next bottle," David offered. In spite of his brief encounter with Maggie Adams, he felt warm inside. What a bitch, he thought. Still, her ravings would have no effect. The guys in the press corps always stuck together. He pushed his assignment to the back of his mind and mentally canceled his visit to Evette. He decided to get just plain drunk.

What the hell? He was leaving Paris day after tomorrow and he would be home in Chicago by mid-December. In spite of Maggie, he still felt good. He'd done a good job for the *World* in Europe and he now had a book to his credit. Certainly they would make him a columnist and he would get a substantial raise. With pleasure he imagined his picture heading his dreamed-of column, "Around the Town," by David Driscoll.

———————

"Oy vay!" Mama Krakow proclaimed. "Such a big place! Look, the buildings are like trees." She jostled her youngest son's shoulder and pointed to a huddle of tall buildings in the distance. Mama Krakow was of an inderminate age. Her head was always covered, and her dark skirts fell to the floor. She had nine children, ranging in age from nine years to twenty-two. Her husband, a dour man, also dressed in black. He had a long beard, and throughout the voyage, night or day, he never removed his skullcap.

The Krakows were a Jewish family from Poland. They were the largest family among the steerage passengers. Mama received her name because she mothered everyone in spite of the fact that none of the other passengers could understand Yiddish. Still, her instructions were always understood. She ladled hot soup into bowls and forced them on the ill, urging them to eat lest they die. She bathed those with fevers in cool water, and she shook her finger at the ship's officer till he relented and allowed the steerage passengers time on deck.

Jo looked off into the distance just as Mama Krakow's son did. Through the fog, she could see the buildings, and her excitement increased in spite of her fatigue.

"So, this is America," Marcella said with resignation.

"This is the home of Louisa May Alcott," Jo added. "She's the famous writer who wrote *Little Women*."

Marcella shrugged. "You know everything."

Jo smiled. "If only I did," she answered in French. Marcella was French and Italian. She spoke no English, and like Jo, she was traveling alone into the unknown. But Marcella was in her twenties, a tall leggy girl with long raven-colored hair, round dark eyes, and olive skin.

The steerage passengers had emerged from below deck like creatures of the netherworld, Jo thought. The steaming tugs attached themselves to the ship to guide it into port.

Her first sensation was neither pleasure nor joy; it was the biting damp cold of February in Boston harbor. The wind swept in off the foggy sea and blew fine ice pellets of snow.

"I'm glad I'm not staying here," Marcella commented. "It's far too cold."

Jo shivered and pulled her shawl tighter around her. "You aren't staying?" she questioned. It was odd. In the three weeks they had been at sea, the steerage passengers had lived intimately, sharing sickness, sleeplessness, anxiety, and even hunger. She and Marcella had talked endlessly about their reasons for coming to America, and about their past. But till this moment

Marcella had not mentioned her plans. Jo had assumed Marcella's relatives lived in Boston like her uncle.

"No. My uncle lives in Chicago. He has arranged a factory job for me there," Marcella explained.

Jo turned toward Marcella. "Chicago!" she said in surprise. "That's where I want to go. It's where I will go as soon as I can."

Marcella smiled. "Then we shall see each other again."

Jo opened her satchel and searched for her pencil. "You must write your uncle's address for me."

Marcella took the pencil and the scrap of paper Jo offered. She scribbled the address and Jo watched, feeling a surge of envy. Why couldn't her uncle live in Chicago? Why did she have to live in Boston, so very far away from David Driscoll and the newspaper he practically ran.

"What kind of factory?" Jo queried.

Marcella shrugged again. "They make hairpins," she replied. "But of course, it is only a beginning. I don't intend to work in a factory for long. I want to live in a fine house, drive a long car, and have jewels and furs. Everyone in America does, you know."

Jo nodded, though she did not believe that everyone was so fortunate. Indeed, in the last few months her dreams had been tempered by apprehension. From the very day David Driscoll left Salonika, nothing had gone as she had expected.

Her uncle had written her saying that passage had been arranged. But his letter was cold and offered neither love nor affection. He wrote only of the injustice done to the Armenian nation, and he wrote of his desire to go to someplace called Fresno in California.

"If only I remembered you," Jo had said over and over as she read and reread his letter. Her uncle Garabed had left Armenia in 1900, before she was born. Her father had seldom spoken of him, though he was usually mentioned in family prayers. Garabed Gregorian—his face was as unknown to her as the streets of Boston.

Before receiving the letter, she had thought he must be like her father. But after receiving it, she knew he was not. A letter from her father on such an occasion would have been filled with warmth. Her father welcomed strangers to his home more readily than her uncle seemed to be welcoming her. And then there were his puzzling references to Fresno. Did this mean he intended to leave her or take her with him?

At first Jo had pushed her concerns about her uncle to the back of her mind. Her uncle had been in America twenty years; surely he was well-off and she would be no financial burden. And she was going to America! It was where her father had wanted to go. Everything, she told herself again and again, would be all right. She would be able to go to school. She would study writing, and when the time came, she would go to Chicago and David Driscoll would help her.

Jo had traveled from Greece to Paris by train in December, accompanied by Miss Spring, who had decided to take a short vacation from her work at the orphanage. They had traveled first class, and Miss Spring was quick to point out that the Missionary Society was pleased to pay her fare since her story had been instrumental in raising so much money. At the time, Jo had never thought to question Miss Spring's comments on the matter.

But once in Paris, Jo was turned over to an Armenian family recruited by the Armenian Benevolent Association to look after her till final arrangements could be made for her passage. She remained with them for nearly two months. It was not a pleasant two months. They had five children of their own to feed and clothe, and they lived in one room. Uncle Garabed cannot know what this is like, Jo tried to convince herself. He couldn't have guessed that there was seldom sufficient food for all, and surely he would have been shocked to learn that she slept on a pallet in the corner of a crowded room and listened to the sounds of rats inside the walls as they skittered about, a four-legged army threatening at any time to invade and attack the heavy sleeper.

Finally, when her passage had been arranged, Jo learned she was to travel steerage. The trip was horrible in spite of Mama Krakow and her benevolent care. It was horrible in spite of the fact that she and Marcella had become friends. It was like an inverted Tower of Babel. The passengers lived in communal squalor, they grew sicker with each swell of the waves, and food and water were rationed.

How could her uncle allow her to travel in such circumstances? Why had he not sent more money? Jo felt bewildered.

The vessel was secured to the dock and a long gangplank was pushed into place.

"We're going ashore," Marcella said enthusiastically. "This will be good-bye for us, Josephina. We'll be separated."

Jo hugged Marcella, even though she could feel the crush of others pushing against her now. "We'll see one another again," Jo told her friend.

"We won't know one another, we'll be in such fine clothes."

"I hope you'll be happy," Jo said sincerely.

"You too, little Josephina. You too."

Jo watched for a second as Marcella disappeared into the anxious crowd. Although Marcella was over twenty, it had seemed as if they were the same age. Jo bent over and picked up the box which held all her belongings. She followed the others down the gangplank and onto American soil.

Jo inhaled and felt the stabbing pain of the freezing air in her lungs. She was proudly clad in the blue summer dress David Driscoll had given her, and the cold easily penetrated the thin cloth. She held her box in front of her, but nothing seemed to keep out the cold as the scraggly line of immigrants was herded across the open space. It had been cold on deck, but they had been huddled together. Now the wind whipped around each one of them individually.

She had seen snow in Paris, but it was light and fluffy, finally turning to slush in the city's streets. At no time had there been more than a few inches. Here she could see the snow piled high, pushed away from the docks to form mountains that lined the sides of buildings and roadways.

February 5, 1920. A month after my fifteenth birthday, and my first day in America, Jo thought. Her fingers felt numb, and she walked faster, trying to keep up with the others.

The inhabitants of Babel shrieked out their shock as they walked through the snow. They waved their hands and gripped their coats and jackets, they held their children close, they muttered curses. France, Greece, Italy, even Armenia knew no such cold. Jo could not imagine that even the snowcapped peak of Mount Ararat in winter was as cruel as this damp cold.

Uniformed officers herded them like goats in long lines across an open expanse of roadway, then pushed them into a barnlike warehouse to be processed. But nothing was immediate. They stood for nearly an hour before they were put in long lines.

"Two ships docked this morning," someone revealed.

The rumor spread rapidly, and people groaned and complained.

"Name?"

Jo reached the long counter after two hours. The immigration official was middle-aged. He looked bored with his papers and irritated with those who had passed before her.

"Josephina Gregorian," she replied clearly.

"Papers . . ."

She handed him the sheaf of documents issued to her in Paris.

He looked up, his dull eyes studying her. The family before her had shrugged when he'd asked for their papers. He'd tried hand motions and shouting, he'd rustled papers. Finally an interpreter had been summoned. "You speak English?"

"Yes, sir."

He actually smiled. "Thank God," he muttered. "Where were you born?"

"Constantinople, Turkey."

"Nationality?"

"Armenian."

He nodded and checked the documents. Jo knew full well her answers agreed with the papers.

"You're fourteen?"

"I was fourteen when the papers were issued. I turned fifteen on January first."

"Oh, yes. I see it here." His chubby finger poked the location on the document. "Your uncle is taking you?"

"Yes, sir. He said he would be here to meet me."

He took out a stamp and stamped a number of papers. "You're a smart kid," he allowed. "If he's meeting you, he'll be in the other half of this building. You just go through that door. Here, here are your papers." He paused. "If anything happens and he isn't there, come back. I'll see you get some help."

"Thank you," Jo answered politely.

He smiled again. "Better tell your uncle to get you some warmer clothes."

"Yes, sir." She gathered her papers up and replaced them in her small satchel. She walked across the warehouse, listening to the others as she went. She looked around, but Marcella was nowhere to be seen. The officials, Jo decided, were not so pleasant to everyone. It made a difference if you spoke English.

She walked through the door. Beyond a rope, a huddle of people waited restlessly, talking among themselves. They studied each face that emerged. In the corner, a man hugged a woman and two children cried loudly.

"Who are you looking for, kid?" a man with a bullhorn asked. He was wearing the same sort of uniform the immigration official had worn.

"Mr. Garabed Gregorian," she answered.

He bellowed the name through his bullhorn, and Jo watched as a small, stout, ill-dressed man pushed his way forward through the crowd. He held his hand up like a schoolchild with the correct answer.

The official nudged her forward beyond the rope. "Can't stand here," he grumbled. "You'll block the entrance."

"Uncle Garabed?" Jo asked hesitantly. He didn't look at all as she had imagined him. Her father had been tall and lean; his brother Garabed was short and fat. Her father had soft brown eyes; her uncle's eyes were small and dull. Her father had thick wavy hair; her uncle's head was nearly bald. But more upsetting than his physical characteristics was his expression. He didn't smile, nor did he hold out his arms to welcome her. He looked bored and impatient.

"Josephina?" he asked, raising a bushy eyebrow.

"Yes, Uncle."

He eyed her appraisingly. "I've been waiting for many hours."

"I'm sorry. It took a long time," she answered, and forced herself to hold back tears. Waiting? She had been waiting since 1914 to be reunited with one of her family.

"We must hurry." Garabed prodded her with his hand. "We'll miss the last train to Worcester."

"Worcester? I thought you lived here, in Boston."

He shook his head impatiently. "No, Worcester. It's a smaller town. There are many Armenians there. We all live together in the same neighborhood."

"I speak English, Uncle Garabed. You can speak to me in English."

He grumbled beneath his breath, "I don't speak English."

Jo stared at him in utter disbelief. He'd been in America a whole twenty years! He didn't speak English? She couldn't quite believe it.

He took her arm and propelled her across the room. "There's no need for me to learn a foreign language. All my friends are Armenian," he explained curtly.

They crossed a windy street and took a streetcar. Then, after a short and silent ride, they left the streetcar, and Garabed led her down a steep flight of steps and onto a narrow tiled platform. A long fast train sped by on the opposite platform.

"Is that the train to Worcester?"

Garabed shook his head. "This is a subway. It goes to the North Station."

Jo digested the information. Paris had a subway, but

she had never been on it. A train appeared on their side of the platform and they got on. It lurched forward and was propelled through a dark tunnel.

Jo clutched her satchel and put her box on the floor. She pulled her dress down over her ankles and shivered. "I think I shall need warmer clothes," she suggested in a small voice.

"I will get some used ones from the Armenian Benevolent Society. Clothes are expensive, you know."

Jo didn't answer. She felt curious, lonely, and somehow angry. Clearly her uncle was *not* well-off. And just as clearly he had made no attempt to become an American. He reminded her of one of the older and most conservative elders of the village—a man about whom her father had complained endlessly.

The subway came to yet another screeching halt and they emerged into a station filled with bustling people. Her uncle led her to a window and there purchased two tickets. They again went out into the cold, this time onto one of many long platforms. The wind whistled down and around the great trains that waited to leave. To Jo they looked like giant steel animals belching steam and dirty, sooty smoke.

Garabed led her to the train. He shoved the tickets into Jo's hands. "Ask him if it is the train to Worcester." He pointed rudely to a uniformed conductor.

Jo asked, and received a curt "Yes."

Garabed climbed aboard first; he did not even turn to help her up or offer to take her box.

Jo followed her uncle down the long aisle and sat beside him when he selected a seat. The train was not unlike the one she had traveled to Paris on, and she thought of the dining car that Miss Spring had taken her to each evening. Jo closed her eyes; she felt a gnawing hunger in the pit of her stomach. She hadn't eaten well on the voyage, nor had she eaten all day.

"I'm hungry," she blurted out.

Garabed grumbled. "It's a short trip. There's food at home."

Jo nodded and stared at the blue-cushioned back of the chair in front of her. Her uncle was like a stone, and she hadn't been prepared for that. America? She hadn't yet seen anything, but it was clear the first thing she was going to see was a small town and an Armenian community. She hoped against hope it would not be like the community in Paris.

The train edged out of the station and traveled slowly between low brick buildings. As it left the city, it picked up speed and traveled through heavily wooded areas. Jo looked out the window, but darkness enveloped the countryside. Still, beyond the trees there always seemed to be lights. It was not difficult to tell that the area was densely populated. Time and again the train came to a jolting halt in some town. But all Jo could see were the outlines of buildings near rivers. Time and again the train passed over steel bridges, below which black water wound its way through an unseen valley.

"Are there many factories here?" Jo asked.

Garabed wrinkled his face. "Mills, shoe factories."

"There must be many jobs," she concluded.

"For peasants skilled with their hands."

Jo frowned at his answer. His tone was one of disgust at the thought of manual labor. "You do not work in a factory?" she questioned.

"Of course not! I work with my head. I told you, I work at the Benevolent Society. But one day I shall own vineyards and employ peasants."

Jo bit her lip. He sounded angry with her questions.

She dared not mention her belief that America had no peasants. Nor did she mention that she had thought his work at the Benevolent Society was merely a hobby of some sort.

"Of course you will have to work," he announced.

Jo turned toward him, feeling suddenly rebellious. "I want to go to school," she said firmly.

"What for? You are a girl. Besides, you will have to earn your keep. I used to live alone, but now I've been compelled to rent a two-room flat. It costs more."

A two-room flat! Jo felt the tears forming again. She would have no privacy. She wouldn't be able to study writing. But this was America, this was the land she had dreamed of for so long. "I will earn my keep," she said stubbornly, "but I must go to school too."

Garabed didn't look at her. "There are some classes at night," he muttered. "Some Armenians go at night."

Jo wiped a tear off her cheek. Disappointment, weariness, and hunger combined into a sweeping feeling of defeat and misery. David, she thought to herself, would help her. Somehow, some way, she must find him.

"Stop crying," Garabed demanded. "What have you to cry about? You're out of the refugee camp! You're in America now. You should be happy. You're a lucky little girl."

"Shoot-out in North Side Speakeasy!"
by David Driscoll.
April 5, 1922. Exclusive to the *World*.

Four

Jo lifted her dark blue woolen skirt and gingerly stepped over a large puddle. The snows of February had melted, giving way to the rains of late March. Spring, like a bashful actress, hid just behind the curtain of late winter, afraid to step out, afraid to make her debut.

Jo turned the corner of Gold Street onto Assonet. This block and the next two constituted the Armenian section of Worcester's lower-class immigrant neighborhood. The stores, the tiny restaurant, the bakery where she worked, the shoe shop, and the coffeehouse all had their names proudly painted in Armenian script. Farther down the street, Italian names replaced Armenian, and then the neighborhood gave way to the shanties where the Irish lived. Here in upstate Massachusetts, Jo had learned, the Irish were the most disliked of the newcomers. They were Catholics in a Protestant stronghold.

Last election day, the wealthy mill owners kept the Irish laborers working till after the polls closed, thus depriving them of their vote. Jo had become aware of the prejudice not only from listening to people talk but also from reading the papers. She was a voracious reader, and gradually she had come to understand the politics of New England.

She learned that Boston politics were controlled by the Irish, whose numbers had swollen the voters' list, but that the population of upstate Massachusetts resisted the influence of the city, clinging to themselves and nastily holding back the Irish immigrants.

The buildings in the lower town had a uniformity. Row on row of three-story joined-together gray clapboard houses lined both sides of the treeless street. There were shops at ground level, and above the shops tiny apartments and rooms. Each of four or five apartments shared a communal kitchen and bathroom. Behind the dull dwellings, clotheslines were strung from one building to another. In the winter the wet clothes froze and hung like rigid scarecrows; in the summer they fluttered like proud flags. Overalls and workshirts, uniforms and housedresses, they portrayed the status of their owners with faded glory.

At the foot of the street, the mills in the gulch by the Blackstone River belched filthy black smoke, and fine dusty soft ashes rained down, turning the new-fallen snow gray within minutes and coating the puddles with scum. Jo thought of Worcester as a gray town, populated by gray unsmiling people who toiled long hours in the mills and factories. The town's chief products were rugs and shoes, but the ashes came courtesy of the iron foundry. When the air was still, the lower city smelled of burning coal and the chemicals used in tanning. It was a loathsome odor, pungent and at times sickening.

Jo often wrote about Worcester. She tried to describe it, to make it live in words. It was industrial, it had wretched slums, and the slum dwellers lived in abject poverty. Beyond the slums, the three-story clapboard houses gave way to small independent homes with tiny yards. Many of Worcester's French population lived in that area. They formed a human barrier between the wretched and the wealthy, whose homes dominated the hills beyond the railroad tracks.

That was the other Worcester. It was a community of stately, graceful white houses with tall brick chimneys. They were clean homes with large airy rooms, with expansive manicured lawns and flowers in the summer. Beyond those homes were hills and forests, and streams so clear you could see the fish swimming at the bottom, darting in and out of jagged rocks.

But for Jo, the most important place in Worcester was the Worcester Public Library. It had every kind of book you could imagine, and newspapers from Boston and New York. Unhappily, there were no newspapers from Chicago. Jo longed to see a Chicago paper, to search for stories by David. David Driscoll must be very important by now, she imagined. Perhaps he was no longer at the *World*, perhaps he had his own paper. She pictured herself in Chicago. She saw herself as a reporter, writing for the publisher, Mr. David Driscoll.

Jo shook her head as if to summon reality. She did not allow herself to daydream often. She reminded herself that daydreams were a luxury. What mattered was to devote all her spare time to study. She read as often as time allowed, and following the advice of other writers, she listened to other people's conversations.

She strained to listen to the wealthy women in the library when they spoke among themselves. She loitered on the way home from school at night in front of the pool hall and listened to the men swearing and cursing. She overheard complaints and praise, hopes and dreams, fights and lovemaking. She made up conversations in her head, she practiced slang in her thoughts. Daydreams were an escape, but Jo knew her only real escape lay in her ability to absorb, and to recreate what she had absorbed on paper.

Jo slipped down the alleyway next to the bakery. She always entered through the back door so that she could put on her crisp white apron before going to the front of the shop. A bell in a nearby church pealed the hour of six A.M. She was just on time.

Jo opened the back door, knowing that Mr. Karpazian, the baker, was already there. She inhaled deeply, smelling the fresh pita bread in his ovens.

Working in the bakery had its compensations. Unlike her uncle, Mr. Karpazian was a generous man. He always gave her free food, and the aroma of baking bread combined with the familiar odor of cumin reminded her of her childhood. But she hated the work. No, she corrected her thoughts. She didn't really hate the work, she hated the fact that Mr. Karpazian paid her meager salary directly to her uncle, leaving her nothing of her own.

"Have a piece of warm pita," Mr. Karpazian invited. He offered her a piece every morning. "You are my taste tester," he always joked. "Ah, Josephina, you have such a long day! You work too hard for such a pretty young girl."

She smiled at him. He looked as a baker should: round, fat, and jovial. "I feel fine," she replied. But he was right, she did work a long day. She worked in the bakery from six in the morning till four in the afternoon. Then she hurried home and cleaned and cooked for her uncle. At seven in the evening she attended school. On weekends she tutored the children of Nass Ajemian, helping them to master English. And often she wrote letters and résumés for Armenians who could not write well in English. Nass, like the baker, paid her uncle directly. But sometimes those who asked her to write résumés paid her directly. Garabed always asked her for the money, but at times she held out, carefully giving him only a portion of it while putting some aside for herself. It's not stealing, she told herself time and again. It's my money, I earned it.

"Is it good?" Mr. Karpazian asked, interrupting her reflections.

"Delicious," she answered.

Jo didn't wait to be told what to do. She immediately began lifting the heavy metal trays of bread, taking them to the front room. There she would divide them into lots of a dozen and wrap them in brown wax-paper bags. After that she would lay out the pastries, lay out the hommis in a tin, and dust the shelves that held some of the tinned food. A few of the tins, the ones which held the grape leaves, came from California, from Fresno, where her uncle longed to relocate. Others came from an Armenian cannery in Boston.

Each and every day Jo followed the same routine. She knew it by heart, for there was never any variation. She would have finished all the preparations by nine. After nine, she would wait on customers while Mr. Karpazian directed his culinary talents to fulfilling special orders for rich Middle Eastern pastries. One of his best customers was Annya Casement, Nass Ajemian's widowed sister, who lived on the other side of town in a great white house on the hill. She had married an "American," to everyone's shock, and when he died, he left her a wealthy widow.

Annya was virtually the only Armenian Jo could think of who was "Americanized," as the others called her. Nass didn't seem overly fond of his sister, and Garabed belittled her, saying she had forsaken her heritage and now wallowed in the shallowness of America.

But Jo felt Annya was right. She herself vowed to become "Americanized" as soon as possible. Garabed and Nass lived in the past. They were still foreigners in a land they had lived in for twenty years.

Two years, Jo reminisced. She had just turned fifteen when she arrived in February 1920. Now, in April 1922, she was seventeen. She had experienced two years of disappointment, drudgery, and loneliness. America, at least what she had seen, was not as she had thought it would be. Her uncle was not the man she imagined. Still, she felt that beyond Worcester and beyond the confines of the Armenian community, there was another America, just as there was another Worcester on the other side of the railway tracks. That "other" America belonged to David Driscoll and to her dreams, dreams she knew she could not realize unless she found a way to leave.

Garabed Gregorian was a strange, somber, and even bitter man, Jo had discovered. He spent long hours at the coffeehouse with his few friends. He was consumed with Armenian politics, Armenian traditions, and religion. He hardly seemed aware of the fact that he was in America. He never traveled, never made any attempt to find out what was going on, never tried to speak the language of his adopted country. And he was a ne'er-do-well. He considered himself too good for manual labor and continued to eke out a living at the Benevolent Society. His clothes, and hers, were donations brought to the Society for the poor. Garabed did not hesitate to appropriate the charitable donations and he complained endlessly at the cost of keeping her. But Jo knew she cost far less than he collected in her wages. She paid for their small rooms and for their food, not Garabed.

Garabed saved. He scrimped every cent and hoarded it to buy his imagined vineyards in Fresno. He believed he would not have to work, that he could live his life in ease, taking from the land. Fresno was a place that filled his thoughts, becoming at once an excuse for not improving himself now and a reason for his frugality. And he was strict, far stricter than Miss Spring had ever thought of being. He muttered about the place of Armenian women, and proclaimed the need for Jo to have a dowry, even though Jo protested that she didn't want to marry.

Garabed didn't favor her studies either, or at least not until he discovered that her ability to write English could result in added earnings. Then he gave in and allowed her some time to attend classes, pore over her books, and go to the library. Still, Garabed gave her no encouragement. He was not impressed when she passed her placement tests with high marks; he showed little interest in the fact that she would obtain her high school diploma in June.

Jo wrote often in her notebooks. Then she hid them beneath her mattress so Garabed would not find them, not that he could have read them in any case. Garabed might hoard money, but she hoarded her writing, waiting for the time when she might sell a story.

"Spread some hommis on your bread," Mr. Karpazian urged. "It's fresh, I ground the chickpeas early this morning."

Jo gladly spread out the rich hommis on the pita bread.

"You daydream," Mr. Karpazian observed with a smile.

"Of finishing my education," Jo confided. High school was not enough; she wanted to go on to college.

"That's good! That's good!" He rubbed his hands on his apron and grinned. "Education is important. My son is studying to be a lawyer. He lives in Boston and attends Boston University." Mr. Karpazian quickly opened a drawer beneath the counter and withdrew a picture of his son, Miran. He was broad-shouldered, had thick hair, and sported a heavy mustache. He looked a studious, severe young man.

"He will one day be a prominent lawyer, Josephina. What do you want to be?"

"I want to write," Jo confessed.

"Good." He nodded his head up and down. "We are a very literate people, Josephina, very literate. We read many books and there are many fine Armenian writers."

Jo blushed slightly. "Don't tell anyone," she asked. "It's a secret."

"Whom would I tell? The loaves of bread? Your secret is safe, but will you show me some of your writing?"

Jo pressed her lips together. Mr. Karpazian spoke some English, but she knew he did not read it. "I write in English," she confessed, feeling a trifle apologetic.

"Only in English?" He looked sad, then added, "What will happen to our language if our children write only in English?"

Jo looked down. There wasn't really any answer she could give. She couldn't say, "I don't feel part of your world," or "I want to be truly American." She couldn't explain. She hadn't met another Armenian who felt as she did. Perhaps Annya did, but she had never really talked to Nass Ajemian's sister. But for Jo, the past was a nightmare; she only wanted to bury it. Her family would always be remembered, but Armenia, the Turks, what had happened—it was over. Armenians were scattered. How could they continue to be a nation? Speak their language? Keep their culture? It all seemed impossible.

"Others will write in Armenian," she finally said. Mr.
Karpazian only nodded before he turned away and returned to his baking.

———————

Nass Ajemian slouched in his worn blue armchair, a
copy of the *Hairenik*, the daily Boston Armenian paper,
held in front of his face. At fifty-two he was a tall, thin
man with a balding head, a thick pointed beard, and
darting eyes.

Nass Ajemian's moods were usually divided between
depression and boredom. He never knew which came
first, or which he felt more severely. Lately, he had felt
neither, and the new feelings which flooded over him
confused and elated him. "Beneath the surface, there is
fire," he mumbled to himself.

His wife, Savan, had been fifteen years younger than
he. A plump, vivacious woman who worked ceaselessly,
Savan was his helpmate and companion. She had borne
him four children. Three healthy fat babies and a fourth
who was small and sickly.

Savan had died within hours of the birth of their last
child. At first the doctors thought the child would die
too, but he did not.

The death of his wife had left Nass to rear his children alone in an alien land, to run his shoe-repair shop
without assistance, and to care for his home above the
shop with only the help of his widowed sister, Annya.
But Annya had been more fortunate than he. She had
borne no children, and her husband was wealthy. Now
she selfishly lived across town in her own good-sized
home and spent her inheritance with abandon. Not
once had she suggested the children come and live with
her, and of course there was nothing he could do.

Annya was a widow. She was independent. But still, she did come once a week with her maid to supervise the cleaning of his house, and she often brought cooked food that needed only heating before it could be eaten.

How might his life have been different if Savan had lived? It was a question he often pondered. It was because of Savan that he had begun saving money, and in spite of her death, he continued to save. He supposed that had Savan survived, they would have moved to a better house. He also supposed he would have learned English and that he would have expanded his business.

Nass looked around his flat. In spite of everything, he knew he was better off than many. The children were healthy and well-dressed, the flat had comfortable furniture, and there was even a new electric refrigerator. It was certainly not his circumstances that troubled him, but rather his desires.

"It's warm out," Josephina was saying to his children, Martha Ajemian, age twelve, George, age ten, Abraham, age six, and Quincy, age five. "I think we could take our books out back, we could sit under the tree and study there."

Nass smiled behind his newspaper. He was proud of his children. Each bore the name of a President of the United States, except Martha, who was named after the first president's wife. They were a good lot, and they worked as hard as he did. Savan had been the one to insist they be given patriotic names, just as Savan used to push him to "fit" into the scheme of life in Worcester.

But when she died, everything changed. He sought solace from his Armenian friends. He stopped trying to learn English. He spoke Armenian at home, and the children learned it. Now they had trouble in school, which was why he had hired Josephina. The children

loved Josephina and looked forward to the days when
she came to tutor them. He leered at her from behind
the corner of the paper. The children were not the only
ones who looked forward to her visits.

It was his fault that they needed tutoring, he acknowledged. He hadn't learned English well enough to
talk to them. He barely knew enough to converse with
his customers. Before Josephina came, the children had
been sullen and unhappy, he remembered. But Josephina
had changed all that. They adored her, they learned
quickly, and her tutoring was well worth the money he
paid Garabed for her services.

"Best get your sweaters," he heard her suggest. "It's
warm, but there's a cool breeze. Spring is deceptive,
it's not yet as warm as summer."

So motherly! Nass smiled. The children scampered off
to get their sweaters. Ah, little Josephina! She'd come
two years ago and he had watched her grow and change.
At fifteen she had been tall and gangly, a scrawny
young girl with huge, beautiful eyes and thick hair.

At seventeen she was hardly recognizable as the little
waif who arrived that night two years ago. She had put
on weight, but not too much. Her waist was tiny, her
hips rounded, and her breasts full. She had long legs
and graceful arms and hands. Her eyes still dominated
her angular face, but one could not help but notice her
perfect mouth, high cheekbones, and luxuriant hair.
She was certainly taller than most Armenian women,
and her facial structure spoke of some distant Tatar
ancestry. Josephina had blossomed like a rare flower.
She had gone from girl to woman before his very eyes.

"You don't mind if I take them outside, do you?"

She had caught him staring at her from behind the
paper. He felt his face flush. "No, of course not," he
quickly replied. He focused on the newspaper, wonder-

ing if she had seen his thoughts in his eyes. Poor Josephina, he lamented. Garabed Gregorian was his friend, but Garabed was certainly no company for his ward. Moreover, Garabed couldn't, and probably wouldn't if he could, give her anything. Garabed was possessed of a single desire, but he failed at everything and was unwilling to work hard to achieve his goal.

If you were mine, he thought, stealing a last glance at Josephina's swinging hips as she herded his children outside, I would spend all my savings to buy you a nice house and proper clothes. I would be loyal and faithful. I would treat you kindly and respect you. He frowned slightly as she disappeared. He was over fifty and she was only seventeen. Still, such marriages were common. Women needed the protection of marriage. And what could a girl like Josephina do? Garabed was too much of a miser to provide a proper dowry. And, he added on a more practical note, she did know English. Not only would she be a good mother, but he wouldn't have to pay a wife for her tutoring services. She could make even more money tutoring others, as well as work in the shoe-repair shop by his side.

Nass heard the back door close and laid the paper down in his lap. For months he had been admiring Josephina, and to himself he now admitted that his admiration had blossomed into lust. He found himself daydreaming about not only marriage but also the consummation of marriage. He watched her, and imagined undressing her. She would make him young again, and he longed for that feeling, for the throbbing, absorbing sensations he now only vaguely remembered.

Josephina was seventeen, a marriageable age with the consent of her guardian, he thought. Not until today had his desire for her taken such a practical form.

Now, with little hesitation, he vowed to speak to Garabed as soon as possible.

Nass leaned back in the chair and imagined how pleased she would be. Of course, it didn't really matter whether she was pleased or not. Even in America a woman didn't achieve independence till she was twenty-one. Strange country, he contemplated. In Armenia a woman would always belong to her guardian; age played no role. "But she won't object," he said aloud. After all, she must feel the desire to be married, and she must know that Garabed will never part with the money for a dowry. Nass closed his eyes and began to think about the new inn in Fall River. He would take Josephina there for their honeymoon. What more could a young girl wish?

———

Garabed Gregorian hunched over the round wooden table in the crowded coffeehouse. He held his ever-present pipe in one hand, and with the other he traced small imaginary circles on the table's surface. He concentrated his gaze on his moving fingers in order to hide his thoughts. It was not good to look a man in the eye while bargaining; a flicker of the eye could reveal satisfaction with an offered price. Garabed feigned disinterest, pretended not to listen to Nass.

Nass Ajemian felt annoyed that Garabed wasn't at least looking at him. He was not being a friend, but was playing the game of the Arab horse trader. "Are you listening?" Nass finally said with some irritation.

"Sh! Keep your voice down," Garabed advised. He glanced around the *srjaran*. The room was hot and airless, its two windows shut; humidity from the steaming coffeemaker clouded them, blocking out even the afternoon sun. Smoke from the customers' pipes filled the room with the heavy, pungent aroma of Middle Eastern tobacco. "This is a private conversation; no one should overhear us. A man's business is his own," he added.

Nassredin nodded, though in fact he didn't care who heard. It would come as no surprise to his friends and neighbors that he wanted to marry, just as it was no mystery that Garabed was a skinflint miser who would drive a hard bargain, placing money above concern for Josephina. Fortunately, he told himself, he would be good for her. He would worship her, give her everything, and deny her nothing. He thanked heaven that he had found his courage before some unscrupulous young man approached Garabed to ask for Josephina in marriage. "I've given marriage long hours of thought," Nass reiterated—he had lost his train of thought. He felt uneasy. "I know there's a great age difference . . ."

"She's very attractive. She'll attract many fine suitors." Garabed smiled slyly as he fully grasped Nassredin's mood. Nass was desperate for Josephina. He was at once a lovesick calf and an old bull pawing at the ground in anticipation. Josephina, by the same token, was no ordinary prize. Her education gave her commercial value, and that meant she could provide Nassredin with added earnings.

"I'm sure she could attract many suitors if she had a dowry," Nass observed. "But among young Armenians, who would marry her without a dowry?"

"Perhaps the son of the baker, young Karpazian. Josephina tells me that Karpazian speaks endlessly of his son and shows her pictures of him. Now, what does that sound like to you? Frankly, I expect Karpazian to approach me at any moment. There aren't so many eligible young Armenian women in Worcester. Certainly there are none with Josephina's talents. With or without a dowry, she is a woman of value. Certainly she would have a special value to a young lawyer. I don't know, Nassredin, I feel I should think carefully about your proposal."

Nass frowned. To his knowledge, young Karpazian had been away at school for three years. He had never even met Josephina. "I think Karpazian would want a dowry," he insisted. "And who is to say that such a young man won't marry an American woman? He's been away living in Boston, so he's been exposed to American women. Perhaps he might find one who could help further his career."

Garabed grunted.

"For that matter, Josephina might marry a man who isn't Armenian. You wouldn't like that," Nass suggested.

"I wouldn't allow it," Garabed said quickly.

"She might run away. This is not Armenia, Garabed. Who knows what can happen? You could end up with no control over her. The laws are different. I have no control over Annya, and the same thing could happen with Josephina. You know I'll care for her, Garabed. Give some thought to her happiness and her future."

Garabed finally looked up. His small eyes narrowed, and Nass knew he was about to make a proposal.

"She may not have a dowry, but she has earning power. She's educated. In a few weeks she graduates from high school."

Nass shrugged. "So what are you suggesting?"

"She's worth something."

"I should pay you?" Nass tried to sound surprised, though in fact he had expected Garabed to make just this offer. He looked steadily at Garabed, who again fingered the table. Garabed was cagey, not one to miss his desire and sense of urgency. Well, no matter. The only question now was: How much?

"I've always wanted to go to Fresno," Garabed began. "I need so little, a few hundred dollars for my fare, and I could leave. I have the money saved for the vineyards. All that holds me back is the fare."

Nass pressed his lips together and thought of Josephina. He daydreamed about her ample fine high breasts, her thick dark hair, her fully lovely lips. Two hundred dollars seemed so little. And when they were married, they would be free of Garabed. He wouldn't be there to leech off them. "All right," he said slowly. "I shall make such a bargain."

Garabed's face broke into a rare grin. "I will want to leave right away. Josephina can live with your sister till the wedding. Is that agreeable?"

Nass wondered if it was. But surely Annya would allow it. After all, if he were married, she would be free of all moral obligations toward him. "Yes," he said, though he knew it wouldn't be easy to convince Annya.

Garabed nodded. "We'll draw up the papers. You come to the Society tomorrow. We'll have them properly witnessed."

"When will you speak to Josephina?"

"When the papers are signed," Garabed replied without hesitation.

———

Jo climbed the stairs to the two rooms she shared with her uncle. Her shoes left damp footprints on the surface of the worn wood. Her hair, wet from the sudden spring thunderstorm, clung to her forehead and fell in wet ringlets over her shoulders. She struggled for a moment with the key, silently cursing the dim light in the hall.

Garabed didn't usually come home till six. She assumed she had plenty of time to clean up and fix the evening meal before leaving for school at seven.

"Is that you, Josephina?" Garabed's voiced boomed from the second room of the flat and she jumped, startled to discover his presence.

"You're home," she said, half-expecting him to announce he was on his way out again to the *srjaran*. Indeed, she hoped that was his intention. It was hard to clean and cook when he was about. He followed her around, complaining about his day, making suggestions, and reminding her of her duties.

"Come in here," he requested.

Josephina stopped in the doorway of her uncle's room, and her mouth opened in surprise. Four corrugated cardboard boxes were on the iron bedstead, two already tied, the other two obviously being filled. Garabed's drawers were open, his belongings strewn about in untidy piles.

"Don't stand there gaping like a goose. I'm packing— can't you see that?"

"Packing?" She felt a numb sense of foreboding. Why was he packing? Where was he going? Where was *she* going? A vision of her mother putting precious belongings into sacks flashed across her mind. There were soldiers on the doorstep shouting, and Mama looked around in bewilderment for her most precious belongings. Jo had followed her example and taken her beloved book, stuffing inside it a picture of her family. The picture had been lost, but the book survived. Jo stared at Garabed, and she felt herself tremble.

"I'm going to Fresno," Garabed announced. "I'm

going this very night! I'm going to buy my vineyards and start my new life!"

"What about your job?" she murmured.

"I've resigned."

Her mouth opened and closed. She felt incapable of sound.

"You'll have to pack too, of course. You'll be leaving this flat as well."

"Am I to go to Fresno?" she whispered hoarsely. Was he taking her farther away from Chicago? Were they going to live alone on some isolated farm in the middle of nowhere? Where would she go to school? How would she finish? She was about to graduate, and that was singularly important to her. How could he take her away now?

"Of course not! I can't afford to take you. You know that. You're going to stay with Annya Casement . . . for a short while."

"Annya Casement?" Jo felt a slow-growing panic.

"Yes, Nass's sister. You'll stay there till your marriage."

"Marriage? To whom? Uncle! What have you done?" she half-wailed as the foggy picture of her future began to paint itself in her mind.

"To Nass. He has asked for your hand in marriage and I have consented. The papers are signed. You are a minor, you are an Armenian. You will marry Nass Ajemian and that is settled."

"I won't!" Jo screamed, and was surprised to hear the power of her own voice.

Garabed turned angrily. "You will do as you are told! You're lucky to have a man like Nass. He's a fine man. He'll care for you and make you a good husband. Do you think I can look after you forever? Do you think I have the money for a dowry? Well, I do not, so you are lucky to be marrying at all!"

"I won't marry him," Jo said, knowing that tears were filling her eyes. "He's old! I won't. I want to be a writer! I don't want to get married!"

"You will marry—the undertaking has already been signed. I have given you to Nass Ajemian in your father's name! Your father's honor is at stake. We have our ways, Josephina. We have our traditions."

Jo stared at him uncomprehendingly. She shook with the anger of her own outburst. She fought the tears that formed in her eyes. "I won't!" she screamed again.

But this time Garabed did not hesitate. He was in front of her in a single step, and the flat of his hand struck her hard across the face, stinging her skin and causing her to falter backward. "You will do as you are told! You are a woman! How dare you speak to me that way? Fancy ideas! That's what's been put into your head. Fancy ideas, American ideas!"

He raised his hand and stood glaring at her. Jo tried desperately to steady herself. In a moment Garabed would hit her again if she didn't appear compliant. She nodded and looked down, trying to compose her thoughts and deal with her fears. It was necessary to think rationally. She would have to go to Annya's house tonight. She would have to buy time. She would have to make a plan. Arguing with Garabed was futile.

"Go pack," Garabed demanded, turning his back. "I put some cartons in your room. Nass is coming in two hours to fetch you. Really, Josephina, you will get used to the idea, you will see what a good arrangement I have made under the circumstances."

Jo whirled away from her uncle. It was hateful, it was all hateful. How dare Garabed give her away in her father's name? How dare he threaten her with her own father's honor? Her father never would have done such a thing. He would never have compelled her to marry such an old goat. Honor? What did Garabed know of honor?

Once out of Garabed's sight, Jo let her tears flow freely. What kind of plan could she possibly make? She had little money, and didn't know where David Driscoll lived. It was possible he wasn't even in Chicago. Jo bit her lip till it almost bled. In America, the land of freedom and opportunity, the land she had yearned to come to, she had known nothing but one hardship after another. Now, in this supposed land of freedom, she was practically being sold into a life of slavery. Jo trembled as she began slowly to pack her few belongings. She opened her drawer and took out the dress David Driscoll had given her. For a long moment Jo stared at it. Then she crumpled it in her hands and sobbed softly into it. "There will come a time," her father had once told her, "when you will have to put the dreams of childhood aside and become a woman." Jo shook her head slowly. She had lost her childhood long ago in a mountain camp, and now her whole future as an adult was threatened. "Oh, Papa, what should I do?" she moaned in a whisper. "Help me find a way."

David Driscoll contemplated his two years back in the Windy City with cynicism and anger. He'd been bored in Europe, he was bored here. "You're a permanent malcontent," Mike Hamilton told him. "You've got a good job. What's the problem?"

David drank another straight whiskey. He stared at himself in the mirror. He was forty and he looked closer to fifty. He was back on the police beat, like a dumb rookie reporter. Thirteen damn years of writing and he was nowhere. Hecht, who was ten years younger, not only was writing plays but also was a sought-after feature writer. Sandberg had become a poet, and half the guys that used to hang out at Kings were out in Hollywood writing flicks and getting laid by starlets. And where was he?

The answer was depressing. He was covering one predictable gangland murder after another. What kind of reporting skills did you need? His last big story was on a bust at a brothel. He got an exclusive because he was there getting laid at the time. And though it hardly compensated for his low salary, he did write off against expenses the $98.50 the broad and his bail cost. When his case came up, he was discharged. "Just a reporter doing his job," the judge decided with a grin.

David shifted his weight on the bar stool. He perched with one foot touching the filthy sawdust floor, the other resting on the rung of the wooden stool. I love this dump, he thought as he looked at the decaying charm of the decor. O'Malley's had mirrors behind the bar—gilt-edged mirrors with peeling paint. The walls were decorated with several fake figureheads such as were once attached to the bows of Viking ships. These figureheads were mermaids, large carved-wood mermaids painted with huge pink-tipped tits and long sinuous green tails.

There were twelve thousand speakeasies in Chicago, but this one, O'Malley's Hideaway, on the Near North Side, was his favorite. Its fake front was a religious bookstore that featured assorted prayer books, candles, bookmarks, and statues of the Holy Family. One entered the speakeasy by identifying oneself to the manager of the bookstore. He pressed a button and a full-length painting of the Virgin Mary that graced the back wall slid aside, revealing an Irish bar par excellence. It was owned by one Sean O'Malley but was "managed" by the boss of the North Side, Dion O'Banion, whose flower shop was next door. Both the flower shop and the innocent front of O'Malley's Hideaway faced Holy Name Cathedral. This was Irish territory; O'Banion owned the North Side lock, stock, and cathouse.

Big Jim Colosimo, once a white slaver, bootlegger, gambling kingpin, killer, and bulbous son of a bitch, had owned most of the rest of Chicago and its outlying areas. His influence had stretched from Joliet to the terrible little steel towns of Gary and Hammond along the Calumet. But Big Jim had met his maker in May 1920, six months after David's return from Europe. Big Jim was, David had written, a victim of his own success. Nonetheless, his empire lived on, run by his not-so-trustworthy former aide and probable killer, one Diamond Jim Torrio, and his protégé, Al Capone. They worked with such charmers as Harry "Greasy Thumb" Guzick and Frankie "Millionaire Newsboy" Pope.

Yeah, David thought, Prohibition had done a lot for Chicago. His own conservative estimates showed that between them Torrio's gang and O'Banion's netted close to four million a year on booze, three million from gambling, and two million from the cathouses. And I'm a fair contributor, he drunkenly acknowledged. Except I don't gamble.

"You're quiet tonight," Blackie O'Halleran from the *Sun Times* observed as he slowly drank his whiskey.

"I'm not relaxed yet. Besides, I was thinking," David slurred. "Do you realize that if the feds busted one speakeasy a night, it would take them thirty-three years to clean up just Chicago?"

"Does that include Sunday busts?" Blackie asked with a curious grin.

"Sure," David replied as he drained his glass.

"Come, come, you weren't just thinking of that, my friend. You're morose, I can tell."

"Why not? I've been writing the same damn stories day after day. 'Raid on Speakeasy!' 'Body Washed Up on Shore!' Shoot-outs here, there, and everywhere. Crime and corruption, corruption and crime. Who gives a shit? And what really makes me sick is that local stories don't get a byline. Hell, I've been thirteen years in this business. I deserve a byline!"

"Sure, because you were a big war correspondent, right?"

David filled his glass and drank it all in one gulp, wiping his mouth unceremoniously on his sleeve. "I wrote a book and the book won a prize. I should be doing a column, and I want a damned byline!"

"Tell it to your editor," Sammy "The Nose" McGovern shouted from his stool up the bar.

"My editor, his editor, and the publisher are nothing but a bunch of capitalist lackeys. Reporters are locked in, handcuffed, muffled," David announced loudly.

"He's going to start with that socialist crap again," Blackie predicted for the benefit of the five other reporters who stood at the bar.

"Nothing wrong with socialism," David said, waving his finger. "Look at John Reed."

"You look at him. He's dead." They all laughed.

"I mean look at the relevance of his reporting. What's relevant about reporting crime and corruption day after day? Hell, as long as Big Bill Thompson is mayor, the police are in Diamond Jim Torrio's pocket. And as long as Prohibition exists, there's going to be crime. That's capitalism for you. Prohibition is nothing but a way to sell more booze for more money."

"Well if socialism means an end to Prohibition, I'm a

socialist," Blackie proclaimed, waving his glass in the air.

"I want to do features," David muttered.

"Well, do them," Blackie suggested.

"You're drunk," David said, knowing he was too. The pitiful truth was, he was dry. He couldn't think of a subject. Every time he faced a blank piece of paper, he felt sheer dread and panic. He didn't have either the guts or the energy to look for stories. He just waited for them to happen.

He reached over and filled his glass from the bottle, staring at the amber liquid. At least O'Banion had good whiskey brought in from Canada. It wasn't watered down, and it wasn't brewed in some wop's basement and filled with rat droppings. A lot of the press hung out at the Sheepshead Tavern, a real dump in the shadow of the revered fortress of the Chicago *Trib*. Its spattered floors, uneven wooden tables, and dirty brown paint reflected the feeling of poverty reporters so loved to cultivate. Poverty made them feel like real honest-to-goodness writers. It also had wop booze with rat droppings. Hell, you could go blind drinking that sewage.

Blackie nudged him in the ribs. "Big night," he whispered. "Did you notice the boys in the corner?"

David turned a little sideways and squinted. Fingers Casey and Jake Cohen were huddled together. Cohen was O'Banion's lawyer, a mouthpiece, as the slang went. "No matter how you feel about them," O'Banion was known to advise, "if you want a good lawyer or doctor, get a Yid."

"They've been here before," David said with a shrug, turning back to his unfinished drink.

"I got a feeling," Blackie said, shaking his head like a Gypsy fortune-teller. "Something's up. Maybe a big meeting."

"So what else is new, me boy?" David shrugged.

"Mmm." Blackie raised his eyebrow as the painting slid away and two more men came in. O'Malley's wasn't usually this crowded so early in the evening.

David didn't turn, but looked in the mirror instead. Blackie was dead on, and he felt a cold chill of fear fill him. It mixed with his finely honed sense of self-preservation, and an inner voice warned: Get the hell out of here.

One of the newcomers was Nick Genna, a division boss for Torrio. The other one he didn't recognize. But Genna was out of his territory, no question about it. "I gotta piss," David said, ambling off his stool and heading for the men's room. He took five long steps, and waved casually as he disappeared into the dark hall. Then, instead of going into the men's room, he cautiously opened the door of a storage closet and slid in. Darkness enveloped him. He was aware only of a damp mop to one side, a huge bucket, and a mass of rags on the floor. He shivered slightly and crouched behind the bucket. He began counting.

He hadn't gotten to 150 before the heard the blast of the guns—handguns first round, then Tommy guns. Genna and his friend hadn't been alone. The guys with the heavy artillery must have been waiting for the first shot as a signal to storm the sliding door.

David could hear the yelling through the walls, then he heard someone stomping down the hall. The someone shouted in Italian and David knew they were shooting at the men's room. They fired so many rounds that if anyone had been standing at the yellowed urinal, he'd have looked like a piece of hard European cheese filled with holes. Vaguely David wondered: If you were shot while pissing, did you finish pissing, or stop in mid-stream?

David stopped breathing as the assassins paused in the hall. He himself began pissing involuntarily and he felt the warm stream of liquid run down his leg. Mercifully, it made no sound as it hit the bunch of soft rags on the floor.

Running. They were running to beat the band. In the distance David heard the sirens wailing. Relief swept over him, but he waited till he heard the noise of the Chicago cops coming through the door. *The Charge of the Light Brigade*, he thought. And always they came *after* a gang killing. They knew. They had to know when a big wipeout was coming. The sons of bitches, he thought. They just waited till it was over. And by the same token, he would wait till they were inside and well into their investigation. The idiots in blue were likely to burst in the door and shoot anything that moved. If there were survivors, you could count on the cops getting them.

David edged out of the closet and down the hall. He opened the door that led into the bar a crack. Cohen and Casey were spread out facedown in a pool of blood. Blackie and O'Malley were dead too. Blackie was crumpled like a rag doll at the foot of his bar stool, his last drink still clutched in his hand. O'Malley was facedown across the bar, his hand still gripping a whiskey bottle. David almost smiled; at least the lads knew what was important to take along to heaven.

The other five reporters and two other patrons had also been shot. Only three of the seven looked as if they had a hope in hell of making it.

"Who the fuck are you?" a blue-shirted cop shouted as David flung open the door. The cop nervously pointed his gun at David, and David's hands went up automatically. "Reporter. I'm a reporter for the the *World*," he said nervously. "My press card's in my pocket."

The cop relaxed. "Okay," he said, motioning David to produce his identification. David fumbled for his card and the cop examined it. "You witness this?"

How to get killed, David thought. Admit to a Chicago cop that you can finger a killer. If the cop was on the take, you were as good as dead instantly. If he wasn't, the mob would get you before you could get to court to testify. David shook his head. "I was out back being sick," he lied.

"You didn't see anybody?"

"No one."

"You know those two in the corner?"

David nodded. "They come here all the time."

"But you didn't see who took them out."

"I told you, I was in the alley being sick."

The cop nodded.

"Mind if I use the phone?" David asked.

"Be my guest."

David took out his pad and pencil and glanced down at his trouser leg. It was wet and he felt stupid. Still, he hadn't been stupid. He was still alive. He dialed the city desk and prepared to dictate the gory details. It was another ready-made story. Another sensational shooting. Another gangland murder in yet another speakeasy. Another day in Chicago, David thought.

Five

Jo moved quietly and quickly around Nass's small apartment. She was aware of his eyes on her. They seemed to follow her every move as she swept, dusted, and cleaned the four-room apartment over the shoe shop.

"Soon enough you'll be my wife," Nass announced from his worn blue chair. "Then you won't have to go home to Annya's in the evening. We'll be together all the time."

He leaned forward and smiled, leering at her over the top of his newspaper. Marriage. Jo shivered at the thought. She had prevailed on Nass to set the date for their nuptials late in June so that she might finish school, but it was already June 12 and the days seemed to be flying by. She would have her diploma on the fourteenth. Then, she had decided, she would put her plan into action.

Her first reaction to her uncle's command to marry Nass had been fear. And for the first week after he left, she had cried every night.

Next she had to face the discussions regarding the marriage with Annya and Nass. Her first defense had been to postpone the date of the wedding, but the peace the delay brought was short-lived.

Next she began to formulate an exact plan. She had gone to the library and studied the map of the United States. Chicago seemed to be so far away! Then, in a moment of bravery, she had ventured to the rail station and discovered that a ticket via New York City would cost $32.50. She deemed it best to go via New York so that if Nass came looking for her, he would think that was her destination. Still, $32.50 was a fortune. All she had managed to save in two years was thirty-seven dollars. The trip would take all her money. And what if she couldn't find David? What would she live on? Where would she go? Her turmoil returned, and guilt and fear overcame her once again.

"You're preoccupied," Nass said, coming up behind her.

Jo jumped. She hadn't heard him. Sometimes he walked like a cat, especially when he wore his soft sheepskin slippers.

"I was thinking about my examinations," she replied.

"I'm sure you'll do well," Nass said reassuringly. He slipped his hairy arm around her waist and bent over to steal a kiss. Jo felt herself go rigid. She wanted to scream as he pressed his wet lips to hers. She recoiled at his touch. He was utterly repugnant to her.

"Come, come now, my little dove," Nass whispered. "Move your mouth a little for your husband-to-be. Soon I will cover you with such kisses, awaken you, as a good husband should."

Jo shivered and pulled away. He had not tried to kiss her lips before. It was revolting. "This isn't proper!" she said indignantly, trying to cover her revulsion with outrage.

"It is because you don't realize how much I love

you," he pleaded, looking almost wounded. "Here, here, come with me, Josephina. Come and let me show you something." Nass took her hand and pulled her along into his room. "You're a young girl, you think you will have to spend your life living here . . . No, no. Nass Ajemian is a man of honor, a man of some means. I will show you." He bent down to the bottom shelf of a small bookcase that stood next to his bed. He carefully pulled out his worn copy of the Armenian Bible and from behind it withdrew a shoe box. He undid the string that held it. "See, my little dove. I have money here. I save and save, I have been saving a little each week. When there is one hundred dollars in the box, I take it to the bank. Now there is only seventy dollars, but soon I can make another deposit."

Jo bit her lip, not knowing what to say.

"Of course, I did give your uncle two hundred to seal our bargain, but there is more, much more. I intend to buy us a fine house! My little dove should have a fine house!"

Jo turned to face him. Her eyes studied his face uncomprehendingly. "You paid my uncle?" Jo could scarcely believe his confession.

"He insisted, but that's a matter of no importance."

"It's important to me! He sold me!" Tears of anger filled her eyes. Honor! How could Garabed have spoken of honor! Indeed, how could Nass speak of it! She felt infuriated. All these weeks she had vacillated—torn between protecting her father's honor, feeling sorry for Nass, and preserving her own life. But now, at this moment, she knew her decision to leave was more than selfishness or her own personal conviction. Papa would have been furious!

"It's not important," Nass repeated with a shrug. He was scowling somewhat, and he shook his head. "You are ignoring my promise to you. My promise to see to it that you are cared for properly."

Jo brushed her cheek with her sleeve. "I don't love you," she said firmly.

At first, his dull eyes filled with sadness, but his chin remained resolute. Then in a moment his expression grew hard. "Love before marriage is for Americans. It's an absurd idea. It causes nothing but trouble. My mother never even saw my father before their wedding! A woman learns to love and respect a man who cares for her. You will learn, Josephina, you will learn."

Nass shook his long finger in her face, and she trembled with her own fury. She wanted to bolt now. She wanted to leave this instant. But there was nowhere to go, and she knew that temper would not solve her problem. She couldn't go anywhere till she had her precious diploma in hand. Jo stared at him. What was she to say? Let him think he has won, she decided. "Perhaps you are right," she allowed.

Nass smiled. "Think about your fine house with the green lawn and the trees."

Jo nodded and rubbed her hands on her apron. "I must hurry," she told him. "It's time for dinner, and I have to get to school."

"Another moment, my dove."

He restrained her with his hand, then roughly pulled her into his arms. "No," she said, looking at him and feeling her own growing panic.

"I want you so!"

Nass buried his face in her neck, nuzzling her with his coarse beard. She felt his hands roaming her back, squeezing her. His breath in her ear was short and fast, his neck and face were warm. "No!" His hand grasped for her breast, and for a moment he held it, rubbing it roughly while making strange grunting sounds. "No!"

Jo pushed against him with all her might. "This isn't proper!"

"Papa! Papa!" Nass's youngest child called from the front room.

Nass let go of her suddenly, and she pushed herself away. His face was red, his mouth partially open, and his eyes looked at her hungrily. "Soon," he said, looking at her steadily.

Jo turned and hurried out of his room. She could hear him replacing the shoe box behind the Bible, and in that moment she made a decision.

"Dave Driscoll, meet Ted Kahn. Kahn, this is Driscoll. He's one of the old hands at the *World*. Started out as an ambulance chaser, covered Europe for us during the war, and now he's back on the police beat. If you need contacts, come to Driscoll."

With those few short words, Mike Hamilton had introduced Ted Kahn. David felt like spitting. He thrust his hands in his pockets and ambled up Michigan Avenue past Marshall Field. He had fled the office at the earliest possible moment; he couldn't sit there and endure his fury a moment longer.

Ted Kahn—a Yid kid from Niles Center. He was tall, dark-haired, good-looking, and above all, young. He had that suave college-boy presence. Of course, he hadn't belonged to a regular fraternity, but he'd probably belonged to the Yid equivalent. "Speaks a couple of languages," Mike Hamilton had said with awe. "Graduated tops in his class at Northwestern, best damn journalism school in the country."

Journalism school. What a laugh. What the hell did some wet-nosed little snot from journalism school know

about reporting? Hell, the only good reporters came up
the way he had. They'd run their butts off delivering
copy, stolen photos from recent widows because the
paper was too cheap to send a photographer, or had ink
under their nails from the presses. They didn't need a
quiet place to write. They could write in a smelly,
dirty, noisy room. They could write with people yelling
at them, with the presses running in the cavernous hall
right outside the city room. They hadn't gotten their
stories out of the library, they'd gotten them on the
street. Journalism graduates made him sick! And this
Ted Kahn not only made him sick, he made him angry.
What the hell did the management of the *World* think
it was doing? He'd been there for years! He'd won a
journalism prize. He'd been loyal. And what was his
reward? He was covering every damned sleazy crime in
the city. And Ted Kahn, know-nothing Yid kid? Ted
Kahn had been given a desk, a partition, and an assignment that would carry a byline. He'd even been given
his own phone!

David stomped along. He kicked a tin can with ven-
geance and then stopped to look at a poster attached to
a wood fence that surrounded a construction site. It
advertised the Riviera Theater. Gloria Swanson was
appearing in *Her Husband's Trademark*. It was billed
as a "Luxuriant Society Melodrama," and the matinee
that began at two featured not only the flick but also
Larry Semon, the comedian, and the music of Balaban
and Katz. David glanced at his watch. He had time to
get to the Riviera, but it was definitely too late to get to
the ballpark. Anyway, the two Sox pitchers, Connally
and Acosta, weren't doing so hot. They had nineteen
wins to twenty-three losses and it all looked downhill.
He opted for an afternoon of Semon, Balaban and Katz,
and Gloria.

Yeah, he'd go to the theater and see if Gloria could numb his sense of outrage. Then he'd have a couple of drinks and go see Hela. She would at least soothe his nerves and satisfy his growing need to get laid.

David hurried along and paused only for a moment to look at the display of the new Paige-Lakewood touring car that filled the glass window of the Moran Car Company. It was a long, sleek red car with six cylinders. But the price tag was $2,195. He whistled through his teeth and muttered, "Out of my league."

Gloria only partially numbed his senses. Larry Semon was less than hilarious, and the music of Balaban and Katz gave emphasis to his dull headache. Still, three whiskeys did improve his mood somewhat, and having downed them in short order, he headed for Hela's four-room sixty-five-buck-a-month flat on the Near North Side.

If he had been the type who "chose" women, he wouldn't have chosen Hela Jerome. She was far from his ideal, though he wasn't certain what his ideal was. Generally he considered sex to be a biological necessity. You needed it less often than a shave, but more often than a haircut. And if you wanted choice, and no entanglements, you paid for it. That was his usual practice.

Hela Jerome was the exception. He had more or less fallen into his relationship with her. She was a leftover from the days of the Chicago Renaissance, as it was now grandly dubbed. A poet of sorts, she was a fiercely intense socialist, though he doubted there was any other kind. Having vowed not to marry—"Marriage is a passé type of relationship"—she was a member in good standing of the avant garde. She never allowed herself only one man at a time. "Sex," she often said, "is little more than an expression of friendship." Hela had a lot of friends, and she didn't charge.

Free, but not beautiful, David mused. She was tall and skinny, you could pack her tits in a pillbox, and she had dirty-blond hair and pale watery blue eyes. But when she talked, her eyes could be penetrating. They flashed periods, blinked commas, and dilated for exclamation marks. She was, in his estimation, the kind of woman who devoted all her energies to being "different." And she was. Hell, she didn't even want to have sex normally. She always wanted to be standing up, bending over, or in some other contorted position. But after a few whiskeys it didn't matter. Hela became a goddess and he didn't mind the athletics. Besides, before they got to that, they would talk. He could say anything to her, and her only response would be to blame his predicament on capitalism. Then she would launch into a long discussion of the ills of society. Ills, according to Hela, which were all caused by corporations. If all else failed to relax him and help him put Ted Kahn out of his thoughts, Hela's diatribe on capitalism and her long foray into Marxist dialectics would bore him into sleep. Marx, he decided, would surely succeed where Gloria Swanson had failed. Besides, he thought fondly, Hela was out-and-out motherly. And perhaps he could convince her to try it lying down tonight. He acknowledged the fact that he really didn't feel like standing up.

Twenty-four hours later, David lay on the sofa and studied the veins that crisscrossed Hela's tiny breasts. They looked like a miniature map of the rail lines coming into Chicago. He reached down and touched her nipple. It popped up, tight and erect. Hela's nipples never failed to fascinate him. They were inverted, nonexistent till he played with them.

Hela was still asleep, and totally oblivious of his hovering presence above her as he stretched out on the fuchsia sofa.

They had done it lying down, but Hela's dedication to experimentation hadn't allowed them to lie in a bed. Actually, he wasn't sure she owned a bed. They had done it on the floor with four great red velvet pillows stuffed beneath her stomach. The effect of the pillows was to lift her absurdly small ass into the air so that he could enter her from behind. Initially, he'd felt like a dog, but whiskey dimmed his thoughts and after a time he'd simply given in to his sensations. Naturally, the whiskey caused him to be slow and Hela loved it. She wasn't the sort to give up, no matter how long it took. When they'd finished, she'd fallen asleep on the floor amid the pillows and he had clawed his way onto the sofa. "Not one to miss a good night's sleep," he muttered as he toyed abstractedly with her other pop-up tit.

Hela's eyes snapped open, and she blinked once. "Do you know some guy named Thomas Carg?" Her brow furrowed, and she brushed his hand away and stood up, freeing herself from the pillows.

David shook his head. He really hated people who woke up instantly and started talking as if they'd never been asleep. "I need some coffee," he mumbled.

Hela threw on an outlandish orange-and-red Japanese kimono. Not that she was shy. She often paraded around her apartment stark naked. "I'll get some. I just have to warm it up."

David groaned. Hela made strong black German coffee. When it was rewarmed, it was so acrid the spoon practically stood up straight.

"Well, do you?" she called from the kitchen.

David shook his head as he pulled himself off the sofa. Hell, it was probably already eight o'clock. He had work to do. He was off the Saturday paper, but the Sunday paper had to be put to bed by noon, except of course for the first page. They always held that for fast-breaking stories. "Do I what?" he asked.

"Do you know who Thomas Carg is?"

David pulled up his crumpled pants and stuffed his shirt inside. He ambled to the door, opened it, and picked up the morning paper. "Can't say that I do," he called back. "What a hell of a news day!" he shouted. "The lead story is about a raid on a woman's poker party." "Broads Have a Full House!" the headline proclaimed. He smiled. Hela wasn't one bit loyal. She read the *Sun Times*, not the *World*.

David plunked himself on the sofa. Hela sauntered out of the kitchen bearing her poisonous brew. She handed him the steaming cup. It looked less inviting than the crud that floated on top of the Chicago River, but he was desperate and he'd drink it anyway.

"He's a bailman," Hela said.

David looked up. "Who?"

"Thomas Carg. He's one of those capitalist creeps who get the criminals out of jail."

"A bail bondsman," David corrected.

"Yes. Thomas Carg is a bail bondsman."

"And?"

"I just think it's interesting. I mean, I was thinking of an idea for a story for you."

David let the paper drop to his lap. He even took a sip of the muddy coffee. It looked worse than it tasted and he was distracted now anyway. Hela had a mind, at least she came up with good ideas now and again, and

God knew he was bereft of ideas, especially in light of his anger over Kahn's being hired.

"Go on," he prodded.

"Well, where does this Carg get the money? I have a friend who told me he's posted a million-plus in bonds this month alone."

David frowned. Obviously Carg got the money from the mobs. But was there a story? Maybe a connection to Big Bill Thompson, Chicago's corrupt mayor? In point of fact, David had never thought of going at a story from the bail bondsman's end of it. It seemed like a good idea. "A million, huh?"

"That's what my friend tells me."

"Who's your friend?"

Hela smiled. "Just a nice cop who watches my place."

David nodded. He might have suspected she had something going with a cop. Where else would she have gotten such good booze?

"I think I could put you onto some people who might know more," she offered. "Interested?"

"I'll look into it," he said, then added, "Don't mention me to your friend."

"I'm not stupid," Hela replied somewhat indignantly.

David reached over and patted her cheek. "Did I say you were?"

Hela smiled slyly and sat down next to him on the sofa. She leaned over him and brazenly took hold of his dick. "One for the road?" she asked, allowing her kimono to fall open.

David leaned back and closed his eyes. He could feel her rounded mouth and experienced fingers as she set about her work with dedication. So what if he was late for work? He really liked it this way, and Hela sure knew how to do it.

Ted Khan was putting the finishing touches on his coverage of the libel case brought against the Chicago *Tribune* by Mayor Thompson. It was a big story. The mayor was going after half a million and the skin of the *Trib*'s owner. And everyone in Chicago was asking one question. Would the redoubtable Colonel McCormick survive?

Ted smiled to himself as he reread his copy. Chicago was a great newspaper town. It might just be the only town in the world where the papers and their rivalry made their own news. Hell, anything that involved the Chicago papers sold like hot dogs and popcorn at Wrigley Field during a World Series. Not that Chicago had played a series since 1919, he thought ruefully.

Ted finished his copy and looked around for the copy boy. He eyed Driscoll in the corner, furiously typing out a story. What a guy! His shirt still had last night's dinner on it and his trousers looked as if they'd been through a mangle. Driscoll had a paper cup full of whiskey by his typewriter, and even though two cigarettes smoldered in his ashtray, a third hung from his mouth. He leaned over his typewriter intently and beat out the copy with two fingers.

Driscoll was, to Ted's way of thinking, the epitome of the old-time reporter. He knew his stuff, he had a nose for news. But Driscoll was not a careful researcher. He was essentially an ambulance chaser. A onetime great guy who was close to burnout because he couldn't lay off the booze. It showed in his writing. Still, Ted felt an admiration for the man. He represented an era. An era when news was straight reporting, an era when analysis hadn't entered the minds of editors, nor libel the nightmares of owners.

I won't end up that way, he thought confidently. No

one knew it, of course, but he'd already been tapped for the foreign desk. He would spend six months on the city desk, then he'd be going overseas. After that, he was going to be doing a stint as editor. His next two years had been laid out by management. He was on his way to becoming a columnist.

Ted stood up and stretched his six-foot-one frame. He casually picked up his copy and walked toward Mike Hamilton's office. His route took him past Driscoll's desk. "Hi," he said cheerfully. "I hear you've got a live one."

David looked up and scowled. "Maybe."

Ted shrugged. Driscoll didn't seem to like him very much, and he guessed that when you were forty and a twenty-five-year-old came in and got better assignments, it had to be rough. "Good luck," Ted said, feeling it wouldn't hurt to keep trying. Maybe he could take Driscoll for a drink. Maybe they could talk and become buddies.

"Come on in and close the door," Mike Hamilton said. Hamilton was smoking a cigar. When he wasn't smoking, he was chomping on the end of a cigar or a pencil.

"Christ, it's only June and it's hot as hell. This summer's going to be a scorcher," Hamilton commented as he casually wiped his brow.

"I just brought in my story."

"Just lay it down. I want you to look at Driscoll's draft copy."

"I thought he was working on it now."

"No, he's working rewrite. I sent it back. But here, you take a look at the draft."

Ted took the typewritten pages. It wasn't a long story, but it was clearly a blockbuster. Thomas Carg, a bail bondsman, was accused of having put up over a million in bonds in one month. It boldly stated that Carg had no assets to back up his dubious "line of credit." The story went on to hint that more would follow.

"What do you think?" Hamilton asked.

"It's an interesting approach," Ted replied.

"Do you think he's onto something?" Mike lifted a bushy eyebrow.

"It's a good teaser. I don't know, what did he tell you?"

"He told me his preliminary check of Carg's assets according to the tax rolls, showed that he's only worth a hundred and thirty-eight dollars. For the city to take a million in bonds against a hundred and thirty-eight dollars in collateral sounds messy as hell."

"But not unlike Thompson's boys."

Hamilton grinned. "Not unlike Thompson or his boys. But you know, Carg's a citizen. You gotta be careful what you say."

"Is the *Trib* trial upsetting the guys upstairs?" Ted asked.

"Yeah. Caution's getting to be a big word around here. Is this story libelous?"

Ted looked at it again. "Not if Driscoll chooses the right words. He has to say that the tax rolls *indicate* Carg only has one-thirty-eight in assets. He's going to have to ask questions instead of making allegations."

Hamilton nodded. "Okay, when the draft's done, I want you to take a look at it. Hell, you're the only one around here who has taken a course in libel. God, I hate this. Sometimes I long for the good old days when you could say what you damn pleased. Nowadays you can't even call a crook a crook. They've got better lawyers than the press."

Ted smiled. "It's really not so hard to say what you want, you just have to watch how you say it."

Hamilton grinned. "We'll try."

Jo barely breathed. Even though her small room in Annya's house was off the kitchen, and Annya was upstairs asleep, she moved around her room barefoot, afraid even the slightest sound might awaken her sleeping housemate.

What if Nass counted his money at midnight like some old miser? What if he discovered her note and the missing funds? He would come after her. He would call the police and she would go to jail like a common thief.

Carefully Jo tied the knot on the heavy bit of rope that bound the cardboard box with her belongings. She had her winter coat and her boots, scarf, and gloves. She had two wool skirts and a heavy sweater. She had two summer dresses and the uniform she wore at the bakery, and one other pair of shoes beside those she would wear.

In her satchel she had her tattered copy of *Little Women*, her own notebooks, her precious diploma, her immigration papers, and ten dollars. And inside her blouse she had pinned in a little purse containing eighty-five dollars. Some of it was hers, but she had taken seventy-five dollars from Nass, leaving a note in its place.

"Dear Nass," she had carefully written in Armenian, "I can't and won't marry you. I do not love you. I must do what my father would have wanted, I must follow the dictates of my own heart. I am not stealing your money. I shall send it all back to you with the same interest the bank pays. I give you my solemn word on this."

Would it be enough? She feared not. Nass had a terrible temper and no doubt he would be furious. Heaven knew what he would do.

I must take great care, Jo thought. She hoped her plan would work. She intended to take the train to Boston and then on to New York. From New York she would go to Chicago. No one had any inkling that she wanted to go to Chicago. It was so far away! She felt as if she were journeying to another world.

Jo put on her hat and tied it. She picked up her satchel and box and tiptoed quietly down the hall. She eased open the front door and eased it closed again. She ran like a frightened deer across the front lawn. Only when she reached the road did she take her shoes out of her satchel and slip into them. She hurried down the road. The milk train was due in thirty minutes.

Breathless, Jo reached the station only seconds before the train was due to pull out. She climbed aboard, knowing she could buy a ticket from the conductor. Happily the only passenger car was empty and she snuggled into a seat, putting her box underneath.

"An odd hour to be traveling, missy," the old black porter said sleepily. "This the slow train to Boston town."

Jo nodded. "It's an emergency, my aunt's sick."

"Nothing serious, I hope," he said, smiling. "I'll get you a little pillow so you can rest."

"I'll be fine. I'm not tired, really." It was an understatement. Her nerves were raw and she couldn't help searching the platform with her eyes. Would this train never leave? Oh God, what if Nass had discovered the theft? What if the police were on their way?

After what seemed an eternity, the train lurched

forward like an inebriated old man. It sputtered and jerked, then picked up a little speed, only to come to a dead halt at the crossing outside town.

The conductor came down the aisle. His uniform was wrinkled and he looked as if he'd just awakened. "Don't get many passengers this run," he muttered grumpily. "That'll be a dollar-fifty."

Jo paid the fare from the small amount of money she had in her satchel.

"You in trouble?" the conductor asked. He tilted his head.

"Her auntie's sick," the porter replied for her.

The conductor grunted and walked to the end of the car. There he spread out across the seats, and in moments his uneven snoring filled the empty coach.

Shrewsbury, Marlborough, South Sudbury, Waltham, Arlington, Everett, and Somerville. Each stop the train made seemed longer than the last. At each station Jo searched the platform for uniformed men, but none were in evidence. Finally, as a pale line of pink light lit the eastern horizon, the train clattered into Boston's North Station.

Jo hurried into the station. It was crowded with early-morning commuters, newsboys hawking the morning edition of the Boston *Globe*, and old women selling fruit and candies.

Two policemen sauntered toward her, their nightsticks swinging at their sides. Jo felt she was going to faint. It seemed her heart had stopped beating.

"Top of the morning, missy," the younger one said in a thick Irish brogue. The other tipped his hat, and Jo felt a surge of relief as they passed her.

She went directly to the ticket window and bought a three-dollar ticket to New York. The train was leaving immediately, so she ran all the way to platform thirty-six.

This train was faster than the first, and by two P.M. it had arrived at Grand Central Station. Without hesitation, Jo went again directly to the ticket booths.

"How much to Chicago?" she inquired.

"How do you want to go?"

Jo frowned. "Is there more than one train?"

"Yup. Look, I haven't got all day."

"I want the fastest. I want the cheapest seat on the fastest train."

"That'll be the *Wolverine*, Michigan and Central. Twenty-two hours, Grand Central to La Salle Street Station in downtown Chicago. You can go third-class coach for thirty-one dollars."

"When does it leave?"

The ticket man lifted his green-shaded cap and held his watch to the light. "Two hours, ten minutes. Platform twelve."

Jo smiled. "I'll take it."

The man withdrew the long ticket and punched it four times. "You can't use the club car when you travel coach, nor the dining car either. You better buy some sandwiches at Fred Harvey's over there." He pointed off across the station.

Jo nodded. Sandwiches. It made her realize how hungry she was. But she cautioned herself. She must be careful of money. She must be very careful. In the end, she bought three apples, one sandwich, and a bag of crackers. Vaguely she wondered what a club car was. There was so much she had to learn, so very much.

The smoke drifted like a fogbank off Lake Michigan as it filtered through the dim light cast by the tin shades that hid the forty-watt bulbs on the ceiling. With every chorus of "Lord, Lord," sung with great emotion by Sweet Mama Stringbean, the onlookers clapped along, some calling out "Amen!" or "Ain't it so!"

The audience was tightly packed around small rough-hewn wooden tables, though a few boards placed between large concrete bricks were used for benches, forming front rows at the foot of the slightly elevated stage.

The air was humid and reeked of perspiration, the overpowering odor of cheap gardenia perfume, and the sweet smell of burning grass.

Sweet Mama Stringbean, whose real name was Ethel Waters, was on another refrain now. David drunkenly banged on the table, beating out the rhythm while others clapped.

She finished the last verse and bowed her head as the audience clapped wildly. Sweet Mama strolled over to guitar accompanist Josh White and embraced him. As the applause died down, Fats Henry, the trumpeter, stood up and started playing the final number.

The crowd went wild. It was always "Saints" or "Dark Town Strutters' Ball" that closed the evening. Foot-stomping, knee-slapping, hand-clapping bodies swayed back and forth in their chairs. David was doing it all. Even the horseshoes tacked to the wall seemed to be vibrating, while the photos of various jazz bands who had played at Tearney's Auto Inn shivered with life. The whole place was throbbing.

"Saints" came to its loud finale with Fats Henry on trumpet and Willie Washington on clarinet dueling back and forth. Everyone who wasn't already standing jumped up hooting and clapping, yelling "More!" or "Do 'Jelly Roll'! Do 'Jelly Roll'!" The group played another minute or two, sweat poured down their faces, then they all stood up and gave it one final blast. The Saints had finished their march home.

Tearney's was one of David's favorite late-night hangouts. It was a black-and-tan place, the ultimate stop on the slum tour of Chicago's South Side. They called it a black-and-tan place because it was the only after-hours joint where blacks and whites mingled. The jazz was the best, but the booze was rotgut, so David drank slowly and mixed it with ginger ale. But he was drunk anyway.

Hell, who wouldn't be drunk? Who needed a Yid kid coming around your desk saying, "Change 'has' and write 'alleged'?" Well, fuck! He wasn't a lawyer. He was a reporter. What was all this crap anyway? What the hell was the difference between "has assets of only $138" and "is alleged to have assets of only $138"?

David pulled himself up off the wicker chair. He looked around the room, which was emptying out fast. What was it? Maybe three A.M., he thought groggily.

Tearney's was deep on the South Side. The area was packed with hookers, dens of white slavery, drugs, and bootlegging, and muggings were frequent. Still, people flocked to Tearney's like cockroaches to tenements. Standing behind his chair, David surveyed the crowd for any of his cronies who might be heading over toward the Near North Side. The streetcar wasn't running now and cabs were hard to get.

"Hey, Driscoll, need a ride?" came a loud voice from behind him.

David turned to see who made the offer. A big burly broad-shouldered man, maybe five-ten in height, stood there. He was dressed in a dark brown suit with a bright orange silk tie, and had a pockedmarked face. Still, he was smiling and he had an Irish brogue.

David was about to ask: Who are you? But two mus-

cular hands grabbed his arm and jerked him back a
step. Turning to see who had latched onto him, David
looked down into the face of a short, heavyset little man
dressed in black with a red tie. He had shiny black
patent-leather shoes.

Once eye contact had been made, the short man
said, "Mr. Driscoll, we'd be delighted to give you a lift.
Come with us."

Feeling a twinge of apprehension, David earnestly
looked for an acquaintance. "I have a friend here somewhere," he said weakly.

"Don't you remember us, Driscoll? We drank together in O'Malley's Hideaway one night. I'm Squeaky
Murphy, and this is my buddy Tiny Tim Malloy. Come
along, Driscoll, we want to buy you a few drinks and
have a talk."

David brightened up. They were Irish. Hell, after
the rotgut he'd been drinking, he could use some Irish
whiskey. All the better if someone else was buying the
drinks. He couldn't remember Squeaky or his friend, but
he had many a drinking partner that he never remembered. These guys looked like hoods, but then, there
were lots of hoods who drank at O'Malley's, rest his
soul. Besides, the Irish stuck together.

"I read your story today," Squeaky said smiling. "We
may be able to help you with some of the details. Let's
go someplace for a few drinks. Okay, Mr. Driscoll?"

David hesitated. Maybe he shouldn't go. His sense of
self-preservation was tugging at him. "How about Al's
down the street? We could just have coffee."

"We already have the pefect place, Driscoll," Tiny
Tim interrupted. "Good booze. Come on."

David looked around again, but there wasn't a familiar face in the house. Hell, on any other Saturday night
he'd have known half the crowd at Tearney's. Squeaky

nudged him. Doubtless the little bastard was packing a rod, David thought. It might be better not to irritate them. He allowed himself to be propelled along.

David noticed how much noise Squeaky's shoes made as they walked, and guessed that's how he got his nickname. They got into a large Chrysler Imperial. Squeaky drove, and Tiny sat in the spacious backseat with David. They burned rubber as the tires spun and they sped off into the night.

"Where is this drinking hole you're taking me to?" David strained to sound nonchalant.

"Gary," Squeaky said, grinning.

"But there are just as many good places here in town," David protested. "Why go to Gary? It's a stinking one-street steel town," David slurred nervously. Hell, there *was* something wrong. He could feel it as surely as he could feel himself sobering up.

"This one's on us, Driscoll. You'll never forget this place," Tiny Tim added menacingly as he stared at David.

David raised his eyebrow and tried to hide his fear. The car sped along the deserted streets. They passed factory after factory, and then the long low strings of slum housing.

They passed the stockyards, and the stench of rotting flesh and blood filled the car. Within minutes the odor of the stockyards gave way to the familiar smell of the steel mills. They belched fire and smoke night and day, filling the black sky with an orange glow.

Gary, Indiana, Main Street USA. A long line of neon-lit whorehouses, strip joints, and dubious restaurants punctuated by the occasional gas station. They passed the Red Angel, where Stella Hart did her act. She was the one who shot milk from her tits at the audience and

smoked cigarettes in unusual places. She was an old
worn-out whore discarded by her pimp.

They pulled up in front of a neon-lit dump called the
Pink Palace, a run-down two-story clapboard building.
The smell of sulfur and smoke that blew in the car
windows as they pulled up was starting to make David
feel nauseous, or was it his premonition of what was
about to happen? They got out of the car and went to
the back of the Pink Palace. There was one small light
over the door and a peephole in the center. A typical
speakeasy, David thought. Hardly any need to hide. No
fed in his right mind would try to carry out a raid in
Gary on Saturday night.

Squeaky knocked two short, one long. The peephole
opened and closed, and the door creaked open.

The barroom had about twenty black enameled tables, each with a doily and candle in the center; the
floor was bare. The bar was lit by a couple of overhead
bulbs. There were only a few customers, mostly hookers and their pimps.

The three of them went to the bar and Squeaky
ordered a "special" bottle and a glass. He filled the
glass and gave it to David.

"Drink up, Driscoll," Squeaky commanded in a serious tone.

David looked at the glass of booze and then at Squeaky
and asked, "Aren't you fellas joining me?"

Tiny Tim patted the revolver inside his jacket and
smiled. "We heard you like to drink, Driscoll. Drink.
Drink every drop of it. Now, no sipping. Chugalug,
Driscoll. Down the hatch!"

David flinched. Shit! They were going to poison him.
But he picked up the glass. "Sure, okay," he said oblig-
ingly. He took a swallow, choked on it, and spit out the
rest. "This is swine syrup! What are you guys trying to

do? I thought you wanted to talk to me about the bail-bond story." Buy time . . . that was it, get them talking.

"Drink it, then we'll talk," Tiny Tim commanded.

Cold fear spread throughout his body. Christ, this stuff could blind him. Squeaky was filling the glass again, but this time Tiny Tim pinned his arms while Squeaky poured it down his throat. "Drink! It's the best way for the Irish to go. Isn't this what you always wanted, Driscoll? Unlimited free booze. Drink to old Killarney, me boy."

Catching his breath, David shook his head. The alcoholic swill dribbled down his chin. His stomach was in rebellion. He felt dizzy. "What the hell do you want from me?" he shouted in panic.

"About that bail-bond story, Driscoll." Tiny pulled David by the shirt collar down to eye level with him. He had his gun out now, and he twisted the piece into David's ribs. "We're friends of Murphy and French." Tiny spit the words into David's face.

David's heart did a double thump, and complete terror took hold of him. Oh shit, was Big Bill Murphy behind the bondsman's pull at city hall? That had to be it. It was Murphy and Fred "Frenchy" Mader. They thought he knew more than he did—or had up until now.

Tiny's eyes were little slits. "And we don't want you writing another story on bail money, me boy."

"I won't!" David nearly screamed. There were plenty of crusading reporters in Chicago, but he wasn't one of them. He wanted to live, and he couldn't stand the thought of pain. "I'll write a retraction," he said, tears forming in the corners of his eyes.

"That's good of you, me boy. But we know how to make sure you keep your promise."

They forced another drink down him. Then another, till the bottle was empty. David's terror gave way to a carefree drunken haze. Tiny Tim and Squeaky carried him into a small empty room. It was soundproofed with padding and newspapers packed around the only window. They turned up the tinny phonograph.

Squeaky held David upright while Tiny punched David's gut with all his might. David groaned and retched, throwing up all over Tiny.

The pain was more from barfing than from the blow.

"You son of a bitch! You got me all messy!" Tiny shouted. He was infuriated and he slugged David across the mouth. Blood oozed out the side of David's jaw. David felt a hot-cold flash and heard a crack and groaned again. His eyes were open, but his vision was blurry.

Squeaky turned David's slumped body around and hit him across the nose, knocking him to the floor. David let out another moan.

"We're real nice, Driscoll. Got you drunk first so you wouldn't feel this."

"The least one can do for a fellow Irishman," Tiny Tim added.

Then, with a powerful kick, Squeaky hit David in the genitals. David let out a wild scream of pain as he felt the crushing blow—alcohol was an imperfect painkiller. One . . . two . . . three times Squeaky kicked. David doubled up in agony, his hands between his legs. His last thought was: Please, God, let me black out.

"That'll teach him," Squeaky yelled.

"Let's get out of here," Tiny Tim suggested.

"Officials to Be Tried in Carg Case,"
by Ted Kahn.
June 20, 1922. Exclusive to the *World*.

Six

"Hey! Lady! Get the hell back from the curb!" A racing yellow cab with a black-checkered top turned the corner at breakneck speed. It was followed by two police cars with blaring sirens and a long sleek fire engine. Bedlam. Cars piled up bumper to bumper, women scampered for nearby doorways, and men cursed. Jo stood on the curb outside the La Salle Street Station, temporarily paralyzed by the confusion.

She was jostled by passersby, and from a stationary cab a fat, bald, cigar-smoking driver yelled at her. "Taxi! Hey, sweetie! Where you headed? I'm going your way!"

At her side, a tall brunette with a short haircut leaned over and yelled back at the cabbie, "You got plenty of gas?"

"Sure, honeybun!"

"Well, step on it!" she shouted back sarcastically. She turned to Jo casually. "You gotta watch the bums," she said between clenched teeth.

"What's going on?" Jo asked.

136

The brunette shrugged. "Probably just a two-alarm fire. That's enough to pile up traffic at noon hour."

With that the brunette turned and headed down the street.

Jo stood bewildered. She was filled with enthusiasm and apprehension. Her long-dreamed-of destination was a larger and more exciting city than she had imagined.

The train had passed through miles and miles of city. Houses row on row, low flat buildings, belching smokestacks, stockyards, and finally it had crept along the shores of Lake Michigan, slid into long tunnels, and come to a noisy halt in the station. Chicago was immense! It was sprawling and undisciplined, noisy and full of cursing men and made-up women.

Jo shook her head as if to clear it, and began walking briskly. It was just after twelve noon and the streets were pulsating with humanity. And what streets! Flat avenues lined with buildings. There were no trees that she could see. Chicago seemed to be a city of brick and glass, of concrete and wood. A hot, humid wind whipped around the corner of a tall building. Jo held her hat with the same hand she held her satchel. She carried her cardboard box in the other; its weight seemed to grow with each block she walked.

She rounded a corner and came to a small restaurant bearing the name Union Café. The tempting aroma of bacon and eggs floated out its open door. She paused and studied the sign that read "Breakfast All Day. Twenty-nine-cent special." She decided to have some breakfast. She had to sit down, she had to decide exactly what she was going to do.

Down the street, just beyond the restaurant, Jo saw a newsstand. She went there first and bought one copy of each Chicago newspaper. Then she returned to the restaurant and ordered the special breakfast, which consisted of five long pieces of crisp bacon, two eggs, toast, and hot black coffee.

Jo searched the papers for a story by David, but there was none. Should she go to the offices of the *World*? Or should she phone? Jo decided to phone. If she couldn't find David today, she would have to find a place to spend the night in this strange new city. It was already afternoon, so there was no time to waste.

"Is there a phone?" she inquired when the waitress brought her breakfast.

"Nearest pay phone's back in the station," the black woman behind the counter told her. She rubbed her hands on her stained white apron. "You new around here? You look like you're fresh off the farm, child."

"I'm not off a farm," Jo protested. "I'm from the East."

"Young girl like you ought not to be wandering around. Go back to the station, talk to the Traveler's Aid lady. The Traveler's Aid is part of the Young Women's Christian Association. She'll steer you in the right direction."

"Thank you," Jo answered, straining to see her own image in the yellowed mirror behind the counter. She certainly did look odd compared to the other women. Her hair was long; theirs was short. Her face was free of makeup; the others had ruby-red lips, rouged cheeks, long fluttery eyelashes. The waitress was right, Jo thought. She looked totally out-of-place and completely unworldly.

Jo finished her breakfast and walked back to the station. The woman was right about another thing too. Chicago was an unknown maze to her, she could become easily lost, and she shouldn't be wandering around.

She went to the first public telephone and called the *World*.

"Is there a Mr. David Driscoll there?"

The phone clicked and a gruff voice answered, "City desk."

Jo asked again.

"He's not here," the impatient voice on the other end of the phone replied briskly.

"But does he work there?" she persisted.

"He did. He's away and won't be back for a while, girlie."

"Do you know where he is?"

"Sorry, I can't give you that information."

"But it's important. I'm an old friend."

"Sorry. Look, lady. This is a newspaper, not an information bureau."

The phone clicked and Jo stood dejectedly looking at the gaping mouthpiece. Then she struggled with the phone book, looking to see if Marcella's uncle was listed. She couldn't find his name. Marcella, the girl she had met on the ship two years ago, was her only other hope. She was the only person besides David that she knew in Chicago.

She picked up her things and asked a passing porter where she might find the Traveler's Aid lady. He directed her to a woman in a gray uniform who was sitting behind an oak desk. On the corner of the desk was a round white lamp, and painted on it in red letters were the words "Traveler's Aid." Jo felt encouraged; she hadn't known such people existed to help strangers.

"I was told you might help me to find a place to stay," Jo said hesitantly. She had already decided not to give her real name. If Nass called the police, they might be able to find her, even in Chicago.

"There are lots of hotels." The woman seemed to be studying her. "Are you alone? Haven't you any relatives in Chicago?"

"No relatives," Jo replied.

"You're not a runaway, are you?"

Jo shook her head. "I'm eighteen," she lied. "I'm an orphan. I need a place to stay until I find a job."

"Plenty of jobs advertised in the papers," the woman answered. "Here, I'll give you the address of a respectable place you can stay for a few nights."

"I don't have much money."

"It's fifty cents with breakfast. It's a good Christian place. It's run by the First Baptist Church. You go there."

Jo nodded. Fifty cents with breakfast seemed all right. She vowed to skip lunch and dinner.

" 'Course, you can't stay there for more than a couple of days. It's a sort of hostel for young women. I'd send you to the Young Women's Christian Association, but they're full. You have to be very careful in Chicago, young woman. We're here to help young girls like you from falling into evil ways."

"I understand," Jo replied.

"Don't get many girls whose English is as good as yours. Mostly we get young immigrant women. Are you sure you're not a runaway?"

"I'm not," Jo insisted. "My only relative in America is my uncle and he moved away to California."

The woman frowned. "Aren't you American?"

"I'm Armenian," Jo answered. "I have my papers."

"Oh, well, your English is very good indeed."

Jo smiled. "Can you tell me how to get to the hostel?"

The Traveler's Aid lady nodded. She seemed happier now that she knew she was dealing with a genuine immigrant. "Here's a map of Chicago. Here, I'll mark the place. It's not so far. You can walk."

"I can't thank you enough."

"It'll be thanks enough if you stay decent, young

woman. There's a lot of evil in Chicago." The woman
shook her finger at Jo. "Don't go talking to strange
men, and no matter how broke you get, don't let some
man tell you he knows how you can make easy money.
You walk with God. You pray to Jesus. He'll look after
you."

"Thank you, ma'am," Jo replied.

"I can tell you're a good girl," the woman observed.
"You be careful. This can be an awful bad town."

Jo hesitated for a moment. Then she withdrew the
yellowed paper with Marcella's address. "Could you
show me on the map where this address is? It was given
to me by a girl I met on the ship to America."

The woman studied the address and then took the
map. With a red pencil she marked the spot. "Should
be in this block," she told Jo.

Jo thanked her again and left the station for the
second time. She followed the directions the woman
had marked on the map. "Awful bad town" was not how
Chicago looked to her. It looked big and wonderful. It
looked as if it were filled with interesting people. And
somewhere, somehow, she would find David. But until
she did, she had to make do on her own. She had to get
a job, find a place to live, pay Nass back, and start
writing. David had told her, "If you want to be a
reporter, Chicago is the place!"

Jo found the Young Women's Baptist Hostel and was
assigned a bed in a large dormitory. She was given a
green metal locker in which to put her belongings, and
the woman at the desk told her that she could buy
dinner for an additional quarter and attend church services in the mornings and evenings. She also kindly
pointed out the want ads in the paper.

It was one-thirty and Jo decided to first try to find
Marcella.

———————

"Stupid son of a bitch!" Mike Hamilton's doubled fist hit his desk. "If I've told Driscoll once, I've told him a hundred and twelve times to get backup and protection when he's on that kind of story!"

Ted Kahn leaned against the wall and nodded his agreement.

"One-man crusader! Damn. Well, we can't have one of our guys have the shit beaten out of him and then drop the story. He must have been onto something—I mean something big. What do you suggest?"

"I suggest you go talk to him in the hospital and find out what he knows. Then I'll follow it up."

"Then why don't you talk to him?"

"He's in rough shape and I think he resents me."

Mike Hamilton agreed. "I'll talk to him. Now, listen, and listen carefully. If you take this story on, you're going to have protection. I don't want any more heroics out of anybody."

"What about Driscoll?"

"Already had one 'inquiry' today. I think the bastards are looking for him. I'm going to send him downstate to a rest home for a time. He needs to dry out anyway. Now, hear this: I'm the only one who knows where he's going, and if anyone—and I do mean anyone—tries to wangle his whereabouts, the answer is, 'We don't know where he is.' I don't even want you to tell anyone he's gone downstate. Mum is the word on Driscoll. I don't want one of my reporters pulled out of the river wearing concrete overshoes. And you be careful."

Ted smiled. "I'm a big boy."

"I'll call Sam and set up your protection. I don't give a damn how big you are, or how tough. And tell Security to go on the alert. This wouldn't be the first city room to have a bomb planted in it."

Ted thrust his hands in his pockets. "You going to talk to Driscoll this afternoon?"

"Yeah, the sooner the better. I don't want him getting out of the hospital and going on a binge. You spend the afternoon going over his notes. And try talking to a broad named Hela Jerome. I'll get you her address."

"Hela Jerome." Ted repeated her name, letting it roll off his tongue. "Driscoll's lady?"

Hamilton shrugged. "Sometime lay. She's no lady."

"Sounds interesting."

Mike Hamilton laughed. "I hope you have better taste."

"Everybody goes slumming now and again," Ted answered with a wink.

Mike Hamilton stood up and stretched. "This could be a big one," he announced. "I sure hope it is. I'd hate to think Drsicoll got that beat up for nothing."

Jo walked hurriedly down Michigan Avenue, following the directions given to her by Marcella's disgruntled uncle. "She doesn't live here anymore," he had told her through the half-open door of his flat. "A disgrace! She's a disgrace! Some better life," he added. But Jo had persisted.

"You can find her at the Gaiety. It's just off Michigan. Here, I'll write down the street."

Jo trudged along purposefully. Disgrace or no, she intended to find Marcella. Besides, if asked, her uncle and Nass would have said she was a disgrace too.

She stopped short at the street sign and turned the corner, looking around. Then, in the middle of the block she saw the flashing signs. "Gaiety Theater" they proclaimed in gaudy green and red.

Jo paused outside and stared at the pictures. Rows of scantily clad girls with their legs raised seemed to be dancing. And there were also pictures of voluptuous women in low-cut dresses, and one of a tall girl in a white wig covered by nothing save ostrich fans. "Oh my," Jo said aloud. "Burlesque at Its Best!" the pictures were captioned, and underneath, a list of female names. Jo ran down the list with her finger and stopped short at "Marcella Deschamps, Exotic Dancer Extraordinaire!"

Jo inhaled and summoned her courage. She pushed through the theater door and walked into the empty lobby. Finding no one, she followed what seemed to be voices in the distance. Into the dark theater and down the long deserted aisle, she found herself headed backstage.

"Hey, where do you think you're going?" A male voice startled her in the dim light.

"I'm looking for Marcella Deschamps," she said, wondering if this were after all the right thing to be doing.

"She's the French dame, right? You a friend of hers?"

"Yes," Jo answered. "An old friend. I haven't seen her for years."

"Should be down in dressing room C. Just head down there." He pointed her off to the left. "Show don't start till seven," he said by way of explanation.

Jo hesitated before the door, then knocked.

"Come in," a female voice called out.

Jo opened the door. There before a large mirror sat Marcella. Jo scarcely recognized her. Her triangular face was highly made-up and she wore a powder-white wig and a low-cut gown such as were worn by ladies of the French court during the reign of Louis the Fifteenth. It was most indecent, as it exposed half her breasts. "Marcella?"

Marcella turned and, with a surprised look on her face, smiled radiantly. "Josephina! Little Josephina. But my, my, you aren't little anymore. You are a woman."

"I didn't think you'd remember me," Jo said, returning the smile. She felt suddenly intrigued. David had said a writer should be open to all experiences—"an observer of life."

Marcella stood up and hugged Jo. "But what are you doing here?"

"I've come here to live," Jo answered. "I've run away from my uncle. I want to write, Marcella. I want to live in Chicago and write."

"Oh yes, I remember. All the way across the Atlantic you were writing in your little notebooks. Ah, Josephina, how old are you now?"

"Seventeen. I have to go to school, and of course I have to find a job and a place to stay."

Marcella rolled her dark eyes playfully. "I'm an actress," she said proudly. "Or I will be soon. Just now I wear this and sing songs and dance. Sometimes I wear less, but it pays well and I'm getting experience with an audience."

Jo thought of her aunt Yeghsa, who was also a dancer and singer. Perhaps Yeghsa's costumes were more modest. But times had changed and this was America. "Can we sit down, Marcella? I need to talk to someone."

"Of course, Josephina."

"I don't know this city. I don't know where to start."

Marcella laughed lightly. "Oh, there are lots of jobs. I can find you a job. And you can come and stay with me. We women must stick together."

Jo smiled. "What kind of job?"

"Oh, with your figure, it would be no problem."

Jo frowned. "I don't want to take my clothes off," she said quite forthrightly.

Marcella laughed again. "Then you can work for the wardrobe mistress. Can you sew?"

Jo nodded. "I do that quite well. We learned in the orphanage."

"I'll speak to her this evening," Marcella told her. "You go and get your things. You come back here and I'll take you home after the show."

———

Glen Hollow was located on a grassy knoll below which flowed a small stream, one of hundreds of tributaries of the Illinois, which in turn flowed into the Mississippi. Its manicured lawns stretched for acres, then blended with the low brush, beyond which tall graceful poplars reached for the sky. On the lawn directly outside the main building, wooden white lawn furniture was scattered about, and halfway down the hill a glass-enclosed summerhouse, filled with plants, served as a refuge if one were caught walking in a summer rainstorm.

The rooms at Glen Hollow were small but neat. Each contained a single bed, a desk, a dresser, and a wardrobe. Bathrooms were shared, and the food was served in a central dining room. It wasn't spectacular food, but it was wholesome and nutritious. The watchword at Glen Hollow was "peace" and the entire place had a restful charm, even if it was slightly institutional.

David Driscoll pulled himself up out of his lawn chair and checked his watch. It was almost time for his meeting with the doctor. He began walking slowly across the expanse of lawn toward the main building. He'd been here only a few days, but he knew he would stay longer.

"You're a physical wreck," the doctor at Cook County General had told him. "You're an alcoholic, and you've taken a terrible beating."

David had fought the word "alcoholic." "Sure, I like to drink a little, who doesn't? That doesn't mean I'm addicted."

"You're addicted."

"Aw, shit. Everybody takes one now and again."

"You can't live without it."

"Sure I can."

I'm not like my father, I'm not, David insisted to himself. But the days in the hospital proved him wrong. In addition to mending from his beating, he got the D.T.'s. After two days, he was begging for it, and then he knew the doctor was right. Mike Hamilton came to visit him. He pumped him for every detail of the story he was covering. Then he told him he had to go to Glen Hollow. "First, you need to recover fully from the beating. Second, we have to get you out of town for a while. Third, my friend, you aren't any use to us this way. We need you sober." The whole affair, David contemplated, was a real kick in the ass.

Admittedly, he'd been glad to wake up alive. He'd been roused by some broad named Sally. He only vaguely remembered looking into her sagging cleavage through the dried blood around his swollen eyes, but he'd been grateful when she wiped his face with cool damp cloths. Then she had him loaded in an old Packard and driven to Cook County General. There, after four hours in the emergency room, he was finally gone over. They'd kept him three days, put five stitches around his left eye, taped his broken ribs, set his nose. Then they had told him about his more severe injuries, those to his sexual organs. Put crudely, he could "get it up," but he could never father children.

But the blow that caused him the most anxiety was his discovery that Ted Kahn had taken over his story. Not just taken it over, but been given a byline to boot. Now he was at Glen Hollow, aware of his bitterness over Ted Kahn's meteoric rise in the world of journalism and his own sense of defeat. He didn't blame Mike Hamilton. Hamilton didn't, after all, own the paper. It wasn't his fault that the boys upstairs insisted on hiring college kids. Mike Hamilton had told him, "Come back sober, you got a job." Mike Hamilton, David decided, had his best interests at heart.

He recalled his father's instructions: "When you hit rock bottom, you should be able to hear your own head thud." David heard that thud, thus he had agreed to treatment.

He pushed open the door to Dr. Eugene Rosenfeld's office. Rosenfeld looked like a Midwestern version of Freud himself. He motioned David to sit down, and he took up right where he'd left off yesterday.

"There are probably more men than you think who have the same problem you do, Driscoll."

David snapped out of his thoughts and looked at Dr. Rosenfeld, the psychiatrist who had been assigned to his case. "I can't have kids and I can't write," he replied with acknowledged self-pity. "I'm burned out, sterile, and I can't look at a blank piece of paper without wanting a drink."

Dr. Rosenfeld half-smiled. "Honesty's important to treatment. I suspect the difficulty with your writing came first. I'd like to deal with it first."

David nodded. It was going to be a lot of bull. No doctor was going to discuss talent or his own feeling that he lacked it. They were going to spend hours making him "feel" better. But what the hell? His room overlooked a valley of wildflowers and trees. His bed was comfortable and the food was good. Reluctantly David admitted he was just plain tired. So tired he was going to stay and submit. And frightened. He was frightened, and he admitted that too.

"Tell me about your panic," Dr. Rosenfeld suggested. "Tell me when it began."

Began? As far as he knew, he'd always had it. He'd wanted to be a writer as far back as he could remember. But he never seemed to know what to write about. He had gone into journalism because, in a sense, the ideas were ready-made. You wrote about events, there was no need for great originality. Or at least there hadn't been in the beginning. But there were guys who started out with him—they'd gone on, progressed. They had started out doing just plain reporting, but they had ended up doing analysis, features, or they had columns. Some had become editors, others went on to write plays or books. He'd had one moment of glory—a moment achieved by a book that wasn't even his idea in the first place. But when he had come home, he again found himself chasing ambulances. Younger men were coming into journalism, guys like Ted Kahn. It seemed to David as if they were taking the good stories away. As surely as he sat across from Dr. Rosenfeld, he knew that Ted Kahn was going to be a big name in journalism. Kahn was going to succeed and David was going to fail. *The faster I run, the farther behind I get,* David thought to himself. And now he had taken a beating, he had nearly been killed. And was anyone grateful? Not on your life. The big thanks he got was to be cast aside. A pat on the shoulder and a "come back when you're better." "It began when I realized that journalism was essentially exploitative," David said to Dr. Rosenfeld. He knew even as he said it, that he sounded like Hela.

Well, he might not be able to write, but he knew he could entertain a psychiatrist.

"Exploitative?" Dr. Rosenfeld prodded, a serious expression on his face.

"Yeah, you exploit people's emotions. I wanted something else. I wanted to write like John Reed or Ben Hecht. I wanted to write about social issues. I wanted to achieve something."

"And what prevents you from doing this?"

"The way newspapers are run. We can't offend our advertisers, you know. And who do you think buys ads? I'll tell you, it's all those exploitative corporations." Hell, he was talking to a doctor, and he was actually quoting someone else. Was this really the way he felt? He wasn't even sure anymore. He felt like a used piece of carbon paper—his whole mind was a copy, his originality nonexistent.

"But others have succeeded in dealing with social issues," Dr. Rosenfeld observed as he rubbed his Freudian beard.

"Only after they had a name for themselves and the papers couldn't afford to ignore them."

"And just how did they make their names?"

David fell into silence. He felt perspiration breaking out on his brow. He wanted a drink and he wanted it badly. He felt like screaming: Because they write better than I do! Because they have ideas! But he couldn't say it out loud. He could hardly admit it to himself. So he didn't answer the doctor. He merely shrugged. After all, Dr. Rosenfeld was a Yid like Ted Kahn. Yids, it seemed, could all write. They all had college degrees. They were all intellectuals, or so it appeared to David.

"I can only help you if you let me," Dr. Rosenfeld intoned.

David nodded. No doctor was going to understand

him, of that he was certain. Still, he had to see the doctor only twice a week, and he felt he could shoot the bull and make Rosenfeld feel like he was making progress. And Glen Hollow was pleasant. It was, to David, a sort of womb where he could curl up and hide. "I'll let you," he told Rosenfeld. "I don't enjoy feeling this way, you know."

Mike Hamilton's office was a tiny glass-enclosed cubicle in the center of the city room. His desk was piled high with papers, and the shelf behind his desk was overflowing with assorted reference books.

"You did a good job finishing off the Carg story," Mike Hamilton observed.

Ted said, "Thanks." Hamilton was not one to give out compliments. He was a tough old bird who'd been in the business a long time. He'd seen newspapers change, but he'd been able to change with them. Ted knew that once upon a time it was all bold headlines and sensationalism. Now it was research and hard work. But it was also luck. It still helped if you were in the right spot at the right time, and poor old Driscoll had that kind of luck. If only the guy had been more willing to accept help, if only he had allowed someone to assist him in developing his story and aid in the investigation of the details. If he had let Hamilton in on the full extent of his story, the paper would have had him protected. Poor devil, he'd tried to go it alone, and his famed luck had run out. He'd taken one hell of a beating. But the bastards had been arrested, and Ted felt good about that. The state's attorney, William Crow, had taken on the case, and Carg and his miserable lying

associates at city hall would all be sent to the state
prison at Joliet. There was no doubt about that.

"You'll be moving onto the foreign desk soon, Kahn.
Tell me, are you looking forward to that?"

"Yes, I think so. But I like City Desk. I might not if
Chicago were a dull town, but it isn't."

"To say the least," Hamilton agreed with a grin. He
had decided sometime ago that he liked Ted Kahn.
Kahn worked hard, he never complained. But the guy
couldn't have had an easy time of it, Hamilton often
thought. He had to have determination; if he didn't
have that, the guys upstairs wouldn't have selected him
for rotation and the position of responsibility he would
eventually have. Kahn was being trained to be a columnist and analyst. To achieve that, you had to have
writing talent plus originality. You had to have an eye
for the essential information and you had to have the
educational tools to do good solid research.

"You've come a long way from Niles Center," Hamilton hedged. Nile River was a suburb of Chicago. It had
a large immigrant Jewish population.

"I've been lucky."

"Luck didn't place you first in your class at Northwestern. To be frank, not that many Jews get into
Northwestern in the first place."

Ted smiled. He appreciated Hamilton's honesty.
"You're right, they don't." It was an upper class school.
Every bit as much as Harvard or Princeton, except of
course that it was Midwestern establishment. He thought
for a moment about his parents, Ava and Joseph. They
had come to the United States when he was five. They
had come from Munich to start a new life, and it would
take as many words as were in the Sunday edition of
the *World* to list their sacrifices.

For four years the three of them had lived in one room. Both his parents had worked. His mother had originally come from Poland, and in her own way she was an educated woman. She had been trained as a midwife, though she was not allowed to practice her profession under American law. So, unable to find other work, she had become a domestic servant in the home of the Hendersons, a wealthy Chicago family.

His father had been a tailor, but as he did not speak English, he had gone to work in a factory. They scrimped and saved. Everything went into a bank account for his education. He went to fine schools, while his parents shared a bathroom and kitchen with five other families.

At Northwestern he had worked part-time, and every summer he had done manual labor. He hadn't been asked to join a fraternity, he'd existed outside the social structure of the school. Was there a day when he hadn't experienced raw anti-Semitism? He couldn't remember one. Twice he had been beaten by fraternity boys whose initiation rites included tarring and feathering a Jew. They hadn't succeeded, but he hadn't escaped unscathed either.

He had experienced anti-Semitism on the job as well. More often than not, he worked alongside the Irish, who joked about him and told him he was strong "for a Jew." For a long while he had thought the whole world was anti-Semitic, but then he gradually began to meet people who didn't care. Mike Hamilton didn't care, nor did the Hendersons.

As he grew older, and as he proved himself academically, his mother's wealthy employers had taken an interest in him. Jason Henderson was on the board of directors of the *World*. He'd read some of Ted's stories. After graduation he sent him a letter and offered him the chance to "prove himself." Ted had taken up the challenge, and the result was his present job at the *World*. "I can only give you the opportunity," Henderson had told him.

Ted had started out with the *World*'s Sunday supplement, and within two months he had been called upstairs and asked if he was willing to go on a three-year rotation training program. Willing? He had jumped at the opportunity.

"I've got a story here," Hamilton said, interrupting his thoughts. "You write well, Kahn. Not all the guys that are hired upstairs do. You've proven yourself. I want you to take a crack at this one."

"I'll give it my best," he said, leaning over Hamilton's desk to take the file Mike held out.

"It's a little touchy, involves hazing practices at Northwestern. Somehow I thought you might enjoy doing some background."

Ted felt for a second as if Hamilton had been reading his mind. "What brought on the interest?" he asked.

"A serious injury during hazing week. Just poke around a little. I think you'll get into it."

Ted nodded. Secret initiation rites. As a story it had real possibilities and he already knew a lot about it. The fraternities at Northwestern had a full week of initiation, and while there was a lot of foolishness, there was also a lot of just plain sadism. Young men were lined up naked in the snow and made to bend over for hours while they were beaten with long wooden planks. Once, last year, they had dunked a kid in the frozen water of Lake Michigan till his skin turned blue. Ted could never understand why the freshmen submitted to the cruelty of hazing; he guessed that the urge to "belong" was stronger than many assumed. "I might be biased,"

Ted told Mike Hamilton. "I once had a run-in with some frat boys during hazing week. You know, the frats don't just make the initiates suffer, sometimes the boys are told to beat up others."

"Jewish students," Mike Hamilton replied without looking up.

Ted nodded.

"I'm not entirely opposed to bias," Hamilton said with a grin. "Sometimes it's a good thing. Anyway, I don't approve of hazing. It's a dangerous practice and it can scar a person for life."

"I'll get right on it," Ted promised. And I'll enjoy it too, he thought silently.

The inhabitants of the rooming house on Erie Street were unlike any people Jo had ever known. Without exception, they worked at the Gaiety Theater.

Harry Haskill was the master of ceremonies and sometimes raucous comedian. He was short and middle-aged, had a balding head and a ready smile. "A real bottom-slapper," Marcella called him. Then she added cheerfully, "But completely harmless."

Buffy Barron was a clown. He wore a white face, darkened eyes, and a round red mouth. When he cavorted onstage, he withdrew yards of colored scarves from his neck, sleeves, and from under his round hat. He danced flatfooted, and nightly a cream pie was thrown by Harry Haskill, hitting Buffy square in the face and causing the audience to laugh.

Angel Jay and Ricky Moran were dancers. They tapped their way through a long routine to the tune of "Daisy, Daisy." Though they weren't married, they shared a room on the top floor.

Karen Marshall, Louise Koch, and Mabelle Mar were all strippers. It was Mabelle, whose stage name was Wabash Lil, who danced with the long white-feathered fans. As her act reached its torrid conclusion, she was all but naked beneath the fans. Still, the house lights were dimmed, and she appeared as only a ravishing silhouette with upturned breasts, uncommonly long legs, and rounded buttocks.

Marcella both sang and danced. Her deep voice and slight French accent gave her act a seductive air. Her costumes, Jo thought, were the most beautiful. Artfully made from drapery material, they had hundreds of glass beads, rhinestones, and gold and silver sequins sewn into them. Up close they were gaudy, but out in the audience they appeared rich and real.

"Theater," the aging wardrobe mistress, Miss Theodora, said, "is a study in illusion." She too lived in the house on Erie Street, as did the flighty Antoine, who did makeup and hair design.

"Show people aren't rich," Marcella told Jo. "At least not when they're starting out, as we are. You can share my room, but you'll have to pull your own weight. All the household chores are shared between us. Miss Theodora makes up the schedules."

Jo reveled in her new life. The house on Erie Street was a home, and its inhabitants became her instant family. They all left for the theater at the same time and returned home exhausted. They ate together and relaxed together. But most important to Jo was the fact that she worked from 10 p.m. till one in the morning, giving her ample time to attend classes at the University of Chicago in the mornings.

And she had what she had not had since she left the orphanage. Friends. Real friends who helped one another and from whom she could learn. Each day, the house on Erie Street was an experience, and each night, the theater was a hubbub of activity.

It might all have grown tiresome had it not all been so new and exciting. Then too, everyone was always working on a new act, and every two weeks or so, Harry had new jokes and there were new dance routines and new costumes. Time, it seemed to Jo, flew by.

"Darling," Antoine said one morning at breakfast, "you must let me do your hair. Such a pretty girl! But you do look a sight! All those little ringlets! I don't want to sound like a bitch, darling, but they're simply *not* you."

Miss Theodora ran her hand through her pused hair and laughed. "Nor are your clothes! Good Lord! We send you off to university every morning looking like the poor little match girl. As if there weren't enough material around to run up some decent suits! You know, fine fabric is everything. Now, let me see . . . I think a simple straight cut worn with some overblouses, and of course the jackets should have the new three-quarter-length sleeves."

"Let's make a proper fashion plate of her," Antoine suggested, warming to what he now saw as true creative challenge. "We can comb the robber's market for some good leather purses and shoes. Then we'll run up some of those new long scarves. Accessories are everything!"

Jo blushed. "I don't know if I should let you do this."

"Let me! But of course you'll let me!"

"Writers should have flair," Marcella commented. "Do it, Jo. Let them make you over."

"I'm not a writer yet. I'm a seamstress and a student."

"Listen to her! She wants to be Cinderella!" Antoine waved his hand. "Darling, I don't know where your handsome prince is, but I can certainly be your fairy godmother!"

The others at the table erupted in loud laughter, and Jo smiled, not understanding.

"I'll explain later," Marcella said slyly.

Jo pressed her lips together and tried to imagine herself with short hair, smart clothes, and makeup. She couldn't quite conjure up the image, but the idea of change appealed to her. "All right," she agreed. "Do what you want."

Antoine clapped his hands gleefully. "Oh, I feel like Michelangelo with a block of marble."

"I'd say you have a lot to work with," Harry Haskill put in.

Jo looked down at the table. She hadn't understood the laughter, but she did know the story of Cinderella. Prince Charming. She thought of David and wondered where he was. She had called the *World* several times now, and always the answer was the same: "He's on a leave of absence. We don't know his whereabouts." Well, with or without David, she had to make a future for herself. Perhaps, she contemplated, that future should begin with change. Her little-girl clothes were indeed unsuitable for Chicago. Her hair was childish, and surely a little makeup would improve her looks. Perhaps, she reasoned, she would feel more like visiting publishers and trying to market her stories if she looked more sophisticated. "When shall we begin?" Jo asked Antoine.

He clapped his hands again. "No time like the present! I'm going to cut your hair so it just covers your ears in the front, with the back a trifle longer. Parted on the side, I think." He had come to stand behind her, and

he moved her hair around, pushing it up with his hand.
"Yes, that's good. It should wave ever so slightly just
above the left eye. You'll have to get your ears pierced
of course. Your face was meant for earrings, darling,
simply made for them!"

PART II

1923–1925

"Bandits Hurl Three Over Cliff!"
by Ted Kahn.
A report from China. May 3, 1923.
Exclusive to the *World*.

Seven

Jo put down the morning paper and took a sip of lukewarm coffee from the blue-bordered china cup. Mornings were always quiet in the house on Erie Street, since its inhabitants were theater people who lived by night and slept until noon. But Jo allowed herself no such luxury. She rose at seven on weekdays, took classes from nine until eleven, returned home to nap for an hour, and then went with the others to the theater in the evening. She and Miss Theodora worked on costumes from 10 P.M. to one in the morning, though not steadily. There was time for chatter, time to catch all or part of the various acts and to partake in the backstage goings-on. On weekends Jo devoted herself to studying. In addition to her classwork, she read all the newspapers and attempted to write in their particular style.

She lifted the paper again and read Ted Kahn's story from China. It concerned bandits who had captured some American missionaries and were holding them for ransom. The American Navy had sent one of its ships, the *Sandusky*, to attempt a rescue.

Mr. Kahn's stories were so full of background and

detail, she felt as if she were an eyewitness to events when she read his accounts.

Jo finished reading about warlords and pirates, and perused the rest of the paper. New York State had just voted "wet" and told the federal government to enforce Prohibition itself. Another story involved a former U.S. naval vessel, the *Yanklon*. It had been caught running rum from the Caribbean.

"Nose in the paper again!" Antoine reprimanded cheerfully. "I want you to write for it, not spend your life reading it."

"I'm not ready yet," Jo replied. "One more course, the one that starts next week. It's the journalism course. When I've taken that, I'll start looking for a job on a paper."

"I think you're ready. I like your stories." He poured himself some coffee, lifted the cup daintily, and raised his eyebrow as if he had offered a challenge. "You have to put yourself forward, blow your own horn. Look at Marcella. Do you think she's satisfied romping about stage titillating men? Certainly not. She goes out on auditions all the time. One of these days she'll find a better opportunity. She'll leave the Gaiety just like that." He snapped his fingers for emphasis.

"But I just can't go around to city rooms. I have no experience," Jo protested.

"Posh! And how do you expect to get experience? Not sitting backstage and sewing all night. Nothing ventured, nothing gained. Personally, I should think they'd hire you just to look at you."

"I don't want to be hired for that reason."

"There you go again, all purity. Fiddlesticks. Who cares why they hire you, as long as you get the opportunity to strut your stuff?"

Jo looked at Antoine and then back at the paper. He

was quite right. In the year she had lived on Erie
Street she had grown comfortable. Too comfortable.
She had paid back Nass, and found a way to continue
her education. She had written a great deal, but her
efforts were read only by her friends.

"Put on your black-and-white silk suit, the one with
the three-quarter jacket and that smashing black overblouse," Antoine suggested. Then added, "And wear
the spectator shoes. Marcella's got a yard of pearls
upstairs that would complete the effect perfectly. Look
here, in this fashion magazine from Paris. Here's a
picture of Gabrielle Chanel. I swear her suit is almost
exactly like yours!" He smiled impishly. "You go out
this very morning. You march yourself right down to
the *World* and every other paper in town and try to
find a job. If you wait for your Prince Charming—what
was his name?—David Driscoll, to turn up, you might
wait a very long time."

Jo considered Antoine's advice. Then she nodded
slowly and said, "I'm going to be terribly nervous."

"Stage fright," he muttered disdainfully. "Darling,
you can do it. Have faith in yourself. And remember,
you're a princess." He smiled and cocked his brow.
"And do let me fix your hair before you go. Remember,
no matter how poor you are, you should never, but
absolutely never, lower your standards."

———

Jo stood nervously outside Mike Hamilton's glass-enclosed
office, painfully aware of the stares of the men in the
city room. Two had whistled when she came in; the
others just blatantly leered, eyeing her from head to
toe.

From just outside the city room, the horrendous

noise of giant presses could be heard. The glass of Mike
Hamilton's windowed office vibrated slightly, as if there
were a long, slow earth tremor. And the smell was
incredible. Cigar smoke, cigarette smoke, and ink all
mingled to create a stifling environment. In spite of her
nervousness, the overpowering odor, the noise of the
presses, and the wanton looks of the men, Jo felt a
sudden exhilaration. This was the *World* as David Driscoll
had described it to her. This was the newsroom she
longed so much to be a part of. Jo stole a glance at Mike
Hamilton, who was on the phone. Should she mention
David Driscoll? She decided not to. She had been told
time and again he was on a leave of absence.

"You can come in now," Hamilton growled.

Jo opened the door and slid into the office, surprised
how suddenly quiet it was when she closed the door.

Hamilton didn't stand. He too eyed her, though not
lecherously. His look was more one of curiosity tinged
with slight hostility. "What's your name? I lost the
scrap of paper with your name on it."

Jo inhaled. A new life demanded a new name.
"Gregorian" was too long and too foreign. "Jo Gregory," she answered, trying to look confident.

"Hmm . . . that's right. When the secretary brought
it, I thought you were a man. Well, as you can see, this
is a busy place. What can I do for you, Miss Gregory?"

"You can give me a job." She was taken aback by her
own assertiveness.

Mike Hamilton frowned. "Doing what?"

Jo inhaled. "I want to be a reporter. I know I can't
start out that way, but I can perform other duties. I can
proofread. I have very good grades in English. I can
type a little." She leaned over his desk. "I want to work
here," she said earnestly. "I think this is Chicago's best
paper."

Mike Hamilton leaned back and looked as if he might laugh. He stuffed a fat cigar in his mouth and lit it with a flourish. "Proofread, huh? You know, papers have a certain style. Anyway, we've got enough proofreaders. Besides, we don't just hire people coming in off the streets."

"I want the opportunity to prove myself," Jo said, feeling suddenly stubborn.

"Look, toots, a looker like yourself wouldn't last ten minutes out there." He waved his hand, referring to the room beyond his glass enclosure. "I can tell by the way you're dressed that you're a lady. Ladies and newsrooms don't mix." He tried to smile. It wasn't always true, of course. Jessie, his own wife, had been a reporter, and a damn good one. Still, Jessie was tough. She'd grown up in the business. But this girl didn't look tough. Of course, he gave her points for having initiative. Plus five for initiative, minus ten for her looks. If he hired her, the guys in the city room might never get around to their work.

"All I want is a job," Jo persisted. "Give me some copy to proofread, let me show you what I can do."

"Proofreading doesn't pay a helluva lot. I can tell by the way you're dressed, you're making more now."

Jo shook her head. "I work at the Gaiety. I don't make much now."

"The Gaiety!" Hamilton said in amazement. It was a rib-tickling burlesque! He squinted at her in disbelief. Did the girls at the Gaiety look this way with clothes on? He made a guttural sound in his throat. "And why do you want to be a reporter instead of a hoofer?"

"Because I don't hoof, I write," Jo answered, feeling a growing irritation.

Mike Hamilton glanced at his watch. The proofs for the noon edition were due soon. However much he was amused by this girl and their conversation, he had work to do. "Look, toots, I have to get back to work. Tell you what, take this copy and edit for me. Then come back this afternoon. Say, around four."

It was hardly a yes, but it wasn't a no. Jo felt almost elated. "Thank you," she said, smiling and taking the copy.

Mike Hamilton grunted. "You got nothing to thank me for," he muttered, wondering why he had committed himself to giving her a chance. Still there was something intriguing about this resolute young lady. He shook his head. If she worked at the Gaiety, she probably wasn't that much of a lady, he reminded himself. Still, that was part of her enigma. She did appear to be a lady. "You can do the editing at that table over there," he said pointing to an empty table. "Then just leave it there so I can check it over. Four," he added, repeating the hour she should return.

Jo nodded and took the copy. She sat down at the table and began editing the copy. When she finished she left it on the table as instructed and headed toward the elevator. She could hardly feel her feet touching the terrazzo floor as she walked. Had that been her? She had surprised herself. Now she wondered excitedly, would she last till four o'clock?

———

David walked briskly along Michigan Avenue, whistling "Dark Town Strutters' Ball." He had been back in Chicago a full week, and he didn't even feel tempted to seek out a speakeasy.

"Goals and hard work," Dr. Rosenfeld had advised. "Keep yourself so busy you don't have time to think about drinking, but don't lose sight of your long-term goals."

David looked back on his year at Glen Hollow with mixed emotions. At first he had resisted Dr. Rosenfeld, played the old boy along, really. Rosenfeld's flights into Freudian analysis amused him, and he kept telling the doctor what he thought he wanted to hear. But gradually, as his alcoholic haze lifted, and as rest, relaxation, and good food took effect, Dr. Rosenfeld began to make sense.

"You're a cynic," Rosenfeld told him. "I can't treat a cynic, but I can give you practical advice that will help to make you functional. You drank because you thought you were a failure, then you became a failure because you were drunk. Your original belief that you were a failure was an illusion brought on by fear of being one. But when you began drinking, you turned your illusion into a reality. Laugh at me, Driscoll, or with me. It doesn't matter. I told you months ago, I can't help you if you don't want to help yourself. You have to work at success, and you have to forget your perception that you're a failure. You have to set limited goals and work toward them. When they're achieved, you can go on to a new goal."

David went on whistling. He thought of good old Dr. Emil Coue. "Day by day in every way, I'm getting better and better," he said, quoting Coue, who was currently America's sage rage.

Rosenfeld's comments revealed that he understood David had been pretending, and from that moment on, David had paid more attention. It was a turning point of sorts. Toward the end of his stay at Glen Hollow, Rosenfeld had him writing. He received two rejection slips, and sold the third story to *Liberty*. Rosenfeld helped him deal with the rejection notices, and he

helped him deal with success. Rosenfeld told him that
success was usually harder to accept than rejection.
"Especially if you don't feel you deserve it," he had
commented dryly.

David supposed that was his trouble. He was hell-
bent on failure because he felt he didn't deserve success. He smiled at his own image in the window of
Marshall Field. His trial was over. He felt cured; he
was learning to take one step at a time.

David inhaled the cool humid air. The traffic along
Michigan Avenue hummed along, the city looked good,
damn good, he thought. And he felt optimistic. He felt
rested and healthy, he felt able to tackle the rigorous
schedule he had set up for himself.

Mike Hamilton had agreed to take him back and he
was due to start work in another three days. He'd be on
the city desk, of course, and he'd probably be back on
the police beat. But he felt reconciled to it. He'd also
vowed to write his book on Chicago journalism prior to
the war. "And it's going to be the best damn book
ever," he muttered under his breath.

Added to those two activities, he had arranged a
third. At the behest of an old friend, he had agreed to
take over a class in journalism at Chicago State University. The pay, he reasoned, would help get him back on
his feet, and certainly it would help keep him occupied
and off the streets at night.

"You can't really teach journalism," he had argued
with his friend. "Writing is instinctive. You know how I
feel about journalists going to school to learn how to
write. Hell, the best and probably the only education is
doing the job."

Marty Jackson had agreed. "But the money's good.
And you never know, you might find a natural writer
among your students. Look, I did it all last year and I

really enjoyed it. I'd do it this year, but Helen and I were just married and I don't want to be out three nights a week."

So David had agreed. It felt good to do old Marty a favor by taking his classes, and he knew that even if he didn't believe you could teach writing, it would give him something to think about besides the daily grind at the paper. The classes were scheduled to start in a few days. Tonight his students would be registering. But he wasn't needed for registration, so tonight he was free.

David walked on and turned a corner. He decided to stop at the Brass Ring on Wacker Avenue. He ordered a cup of coffee and sat down in one of the red leather booths.

He carefully unfolded the morning edition of the *World*. If I'm going back to work, he thought, I'd better start reading the rag again.

He read the lead story by Ted Kahn and his lips pressed together. Hamilton had told him Kahn was on the foreign desk and touring the Orient. He was in China now, but he would be going on to Japan to do a series. When he got back, he was being put on National and would probably end up in Washington. "Bastard," David muttered. Somehow Kahn had ingratiated himself to the boys upstairs. The son of a bitch would probably end up being sent upstairs to the fifth floor, where he would make policy. Of course, he would have to do a stint as an editor first. Right out of school, right up the ladder of success. People with more talent and more experience were simply passed over. David cursed again under his breath. Then he pushed Ted Kahn out of his mind as he recalled Dr. Rosenfeld's advice. "Don't get tied in knots over other people's success and seeming advantage. You see to yourself, and forget real and imagined insults." He and Rosenfeld had had a dandy argument over that bit of philosophy, but in the end David had agreed that envy wasn't a positive emotion.

"David?"

David looked up into Hela Jerome's pale blue eyes. She was standing by his table looking like some sort of Nordic Gypsy. She was decked out in a long brown woolen skirt, a red blouse, and she was draped in a shawl. Her protruding cheekbones made her seem even thinner than he had remembered her, and her huge bangle earrings heightened the impression. Hela's pale skin was sallow and her eyes seemed slightly sunken.

"Have a seat," he said. He could hardly say: "Go away, you're my past and I don't want to be reminded of it," though that's what he wanted to say.

Hela sat down. "You've been gone. I tried to call you once."

David nodded. He'd been told a woman kept calling, but he hadn't thought it was Hela. She didn't seem the type. When something or someone disappeared from her life she always seemed to take the disappearance for granted.

"It's not nice to ignore old friends." She smiled a bit too coquettishly.

David shifted in his seat. He felt suddenly confined by her presence and he was aware of the thin line of perspiration that broke out on his brow. She was going to try seducing him, and she was, after all, the last woman he had slept with.

"There's booze in the back room," she announced. "I'm surprised to see you drinking coffee."

"I've reformed."

Hela arched her brow. "I find that hard to believe."

"Booze isn't good for me."

She smiled enigmatically. "There are other things, better things, really."

David stared at her. That was it. That was why she looked so worn. He glanced at her thin arms. The blouse had long sleeves, but he would have placed a bet that there were track marks on her veins. Not that drugs were anything new in Chicago. Hell, coke and heroin were part of Chicago's seamier side, had been for years. They went with white slavery, illegal booze, and gambling. Well, he might have been a boozer, but he wasn't on drugs and never had been. They were one vice he didn't have. "Hela, are you taking drugs?"

"I like sensory experiences," she said, staring into his eyes. "Journeys to other worlds."

"That's garbage. You'll kill yourself."

She leaned back and laughed. "Aren't we sanctimonious."

"I mean it. Besides, it's expensive."

"There are ways to make money."

David shook his head. Not only was she on drugs, she was selling herself too. Good old political Hela. She'd become a hooker. He stood up and emptied the change in his pocket onto the table. "I gotta get going." Hela wouldn't be a good influence, he had quickly decided.

"I was hoping we could get together, for old times' sake."

"No," he said, almost feeling bad.

"If that's the way you feel." She looked away and he grabbed his jacket and departed. Seeing Hela left a bad taste in his mouth for two reasons. She was part of his ill-spent past, and she was washed up. Hela was a living example of what could have happened to him. She was on a down escalator. He hurried back outside and headed toward the lake shore. Perhaps, he decided, he would go for a walk in Grant Park.

He walked till he came to the park. Then he sat down on a wooden bench and lit a cigarette. The clouds over the lake were clearing, and it looked like tomorrow might be sunny. Poor Hela, he thought. Still, he had to admit that having encountered her, he felt stronger. She was his first temptation. "I'm going to write," he said aloud. "Dammit, this time I'm going to succeed."

———————————

Jo looked around the city room and marveled at the changed atmosphere. By four, many of the ill-dressed men who had been working that morning had left. In their wake, a pall of smoke floated above the long tables, desks, and covered typewriters. The presses were still; like giant beasts, they rested till midnight, when the morning edition would be printed.

"C'mon in." Mike Hamilton signaled with a shout and a wave of his hand. "Have a seat."

Jo sat down even though she wanted to get right to the point. Hadn't she waited long enough? But Mike Hamilton was on the phone again.

He covered the mouthpiece with his hand and looked at her. "Between shifts," he said by way of explanation. "Quieter now. I'll be right with you."

Jo nodded and folded her hands in her lap so he wouldn't notice they were shaking. If she got a job at the *World* she would leave her job at the theater. She would be able to take the journalism course offered at night.

"Fine. OKay." Hamilton hung up the phone and looked at her. "Why do you want to be a reporter?" he asked without preface.

"Because I've always wanted to write and I've decided this is the kind of writing I want to do."

Hamilton frowned. "You did all right. You will have to learn the right markings but, you have a good use of language. You've got a lot to learn and you are only a kid. How old are you?"

"Eighteen."

"Why don't you go to college?"

"I've completed one year. If I get this job, I'll be able to finish at night."

"Why don't you finish in the daytime?"

"I have to support myself. The job I have now has nothing to do with writing."

He scratched his chin and withheld the fact that he'd really liked her work. He couldn't tell her she was too young. He himself had started out at the age of fifteen. "This is a violent town. And this is a rough business. You got any experince dealing with hoods?"

Jo shook her head. "No. But I'm not naive. I've seen violence."

He stared into her dark eyes and couldn't help thinking that she seemed older than she looked. He resisted the desire to ask where a pretty young girl had seen violence. "I can't offer you much," he said, becoming the consummate bargainer. "But I'm willing to give you a chance at proofing. Thirteen dollars a week on a month's probation."

Jo smiled. "I'll take it."

Eyes like bright shoe buttons, Mike Hamilton thought. "You'll have to deal with those guys out there, you know. Think you can handle them?"

"I think so."

"Okay. Let's see you in here at seven A.M. sharp on Monday."

"Will I have the opportunity to advance?"

"One thing at a time. Let me put it this way. You'll have to make your own opportunities. In the meantime, you'll start learning the ropes on Monday."

"I can't thank you enough." Jo stood up and brushed out her skirt.

"Sure you can," Hamilton barked. "Just do a good job."

Jo hurried home feeling lighthearted. Antoine would be overjoyed, since it was he who had pushed her out the door in the first place. Marcella would be happy too. In fact, they would all be glad for her. That was the way they were. Each reveled in the others' successes. They were a kind of family.

Some months ago, when Buffy Barron, the clown, had left to go out to the Coast and work in films, they had had a big party for him. Harry Haskill had filled fifteen huge balloons with water, which had been dropped from the third floor of the house, splashing to the sidewalk below. And Harry had sent Buffy off with a final cream pie in the face, laughing: "This one is all yours, no audience or anything!" They had all drunk champagne till dawn, Harry told stories, and they had rolled up the carpet in the living room and danced.

Jo flung open the door of the house. She had Antoine's name on her lips when she heard the shouting from the living room.

"You can't go! It is absolutely out of the question! What are you thinking about?" It was Antoine, and his voice was loud, nervous, and high-pitched.

"I am going!" she heard Marcella reply in an equally loud voice.

Jo went into the living room and paused momentarily in the doorway. They were all there. Harry was staring at the carpet, and Angel Jay and Ricky Moran, the dancers, were holding hands and sitting on the couch. Karen, Lousie, and Mabelle were all standing. But it was Marcella and Antoine who held center stage.

"Well, here's Jo. She's your friend, maybe you'll listen to her, if you won't listen to me!" Antoine said petulantly.

"Go where?" Jo asked, looking at her friend.

"To work for Mike DeVaccio at the Crystal Palace," Marcella replied. "He's offered me a good job for more money. And God knows, more people go to the Crystal Palace than come to the Gaiety."

"It's a pit, and he's a mobster!" Antoine intoned.

"His girls usually have two jobs," Harry Haskill put in. "One onstage and the other in his bed."

Mabelle of the many fans shook her head. "I wouldn't do it, sweetie. He's a rough customer."

"Marcella, you should think about this," Jo suggested.

"I don't want to think about it. It's an opportunity. I get to do a solo and a song of my own."

"But if he is a mobster . . ."

"No *if* about it," Antoine grumbled.

Marcella stood straight, her hands on her hips. "I think you are all just jealous! This is my big chance and I'm going to take it!"

Jo looked at the floor. Marcella had always been a dreamer. Even on the boat coming steerage to America, she had talked of being rich and of being an actress. And certainly she was beautiful enough to be one. She was also beautiful enough to be taken advantage of. Headstrong and beautiful, it seemed obvious that she was headed for trouble. "Marcella, please don't do anything hasty."

"You too? I hoped you would be happy for me. Well, I'm sorry you're all not happy for me, but this is my decision and I've made it." She turned toward Antoine angrily. "And what do you know? You're only a hairdresser!"

Antoine flushed and stomped his foot. "I obviously know things it's going to take years for you to find out!" He turned and fled the room.

Jo looked after him, then turned back toward Marcella. "You don't have to leave the house, do you?"

She nodded. "Mr. De Vaccio insists all his performers live together."

"It's a whorehouse!" Antoine screamed from the other room.

"Is it?" Jo pressed.

Marcella's expression remained unchanged. "I really don't know," she answered. "But I can take care of myself."

———————

Jo fled the city room at promptly five-thirty when her shift ended. Bedlam! She had known the word for years, but only just looked it up. It was derived from the name of a seventeenth-century British insane asylum and it aptly fitted the city room.

The city room was noisy, confusing, dirty, and its inmates were a collection of diverse and sometimes weird men. Jeff Clayton, who was on the police beat, was a cursing tobacco-chewing man in his thirties. He swore constantly, and no fewer than five times he had passed her desk and whispered loudly, "I want to go to bed with you. I'm in love. I know it's love."

Chubby Windsor rewrote the teletype stories. His knowledge of geography was appalling and he shouted out his questions for anyone to answer. "Got a wire datelined Strasbourg. Where the hell is Strasbourg?"

"Depends on the year," someone had answered

sarcastically. But the joke was lost on Chubby. He didn't realize how often Alsace-Lorraine had changed hands.

Axel Dan McGrath was the sports reporter. He was an incessant gum-chewer and odds-maker. He bet on everything. His favorite expression was "Five will get you ten." Within an hour of her starting work, he had sauntered up to her desk, and pointing to her head, said loudly, "Five will get you ten, she's a virgin!"

Sammy the Cheese covered sex scandals, pornography, and sexual murders. He spoke a language all his own and was blunt and vulgar. He had tugged on her dress, winked, and said, "I'll bet that dress set you back more than a few fucking bucks."

It was Axel Dan McGrath who was assigned to show her the paper. "This is the city room," he began, sounding like a grade-school teacher. "The stories get written, proofed, and edited here." He then walked her around showing her the various departments. "International, local, national, sports, entertainment, and the women's page." Blithely he introduced her to the various editors, most of whom were on the phone at the time and only nodded and waved.

Then he guided her down a long hall. "Bet you can't guess what this place is called." He swung open the door to a room where for all the world it appeared that five old men were playing paper dolls. "Layout," he muttered. "See, they're laying it all out. Everything except the form with page one. That's done last for fast breakers."

She knew she must have looked puzzled, because he ran over and swept up a huge piece of newsprint. "This is a form—four pages, see. The form with pages one and two and pages nineteen and twenty is set last so we can move things around for late stories, and five will get you ten there'll be a late story."

Next he took her to the composing room, where the type was set, and after that he took her into the room where the giant presses rolled out the papers, then out back to where the papers were folded and loaded on the delivery trucks.

On the way back to the city room, he pointed to the top floors of the building. "Management," he muttered. "They sign paychecks, authorize expenses, and count their money."

"Is there a library?" Jo queried.

Axel Dan screwed up his face, then answered, "Oh, you mean the morgue. It's in the basement. All the old papers, a lotta books, and this weird old broad who looks after them. Never been there myself."

Jo turned the corner and walked through the park. The days were getting longer and warmer and she sat down on a bench. Usually she was at the theater this time of day. But now that was over, and she would be returning to an empty house on Erie Street, empty at least until one A.M. Jo stretched, enjoying the silence of the park. Tomorrow her journalism class would start.

Briefly she thought about Marcella. It would be lonely without her. "Don't worry about me, Jo." Those were Marcella's last words as she left, her belongings loaded into a taxi while Antoine stood on the steps making grim predictions about her future. "Promise you'll call me," Jo urged. And Marcella had agreed. "As soon as I get settled, we'll go out for lunch."

"She's lost," Antoine lamented. Then he had actually sat down and cried, pouring out his feelings for Marcella. They were not the feelings normal men had for women, but Jo knew they were genuine. Antoine, in his own strange way, loved Marcella.

Jo stood up and stretched. "Well, they didn't eat me alive," she said, thinking of the men in the pressroom.

Tomorrow is bound to be better. She shrugged and began walking toward home. After a year living with theater people, she was no longer capable of being shocked.

———

Jo hurried toward the el. Her class started in less than an hour. She paused at Blind Simon's newsstand, where every morning she bought copies of all the Chicago papers.

"Missy, what you doing here this time of day?" Blind Simon greeted her with a toothless grin. He always knew her even though he couldn't see.

"I have a new job," she said happily.

"How come you always buy all the papers, missy? One not good enough?"

Jo laughed softly. "I'm studying to be a reporter."

"No lie!" Blind Simon exclaimed, slapping his knee. "I'll tell you, missy. I'll save all the old editions for you. No charge. The boys, they come and pick 'em up when they deliver the new ones, but those old boys ain't going to miss a couple of old papers. They go for pulp anyways. Old Simon, he'll get you your papers, you're a good customer. You buy one new one a day, and all the others is yours tomorrow for free."

Jo patted his arm. "Thank you. You're very kind."

"Ah like to see young folks with ambition. Ah like to see 'em get ahead in this world." Blind Simon wobbled his head and giggled. "You pretty, missy."

"How do you know?" Jo said, a tone of amusement in her voice.

"I can hear pretty," he said confidently. "You want some stories to report, you come talk to me. Ain't no end to what an old blind man hears standing on this

corner! And jus' 'cause I'm blind don't mean I'm deaf
and dumb too. So you come on by, you come by here
and I'll tell you some stories. Real good ones, too."

"I'll do that," Jo promised as she bid him good-bye
and hurried to catch the el.

Jo walked toward the nondescript building on the
city campus of Chicago State University, where her
journalism class was to be held.

She pulled open the heavy door and walked down
the dimly lit corridor, following the numbers to room
128. She could hear other classes in progress, and she
passed other students searching out the right room.

She hurried along, aware it was nearly seven. She
paused at the door, and seeing it was the right room,
entered. It was the typical classroom. Tall green-shaded
windows flanked one wall, desks were scattered in uneven rows, and the room smelled like all classrooms,
musty and old with the lingering odor of floor cleaner.
She slid into a seat in the back row. There were eleven
others already seated. Two were young, and the remainder seemed middle-aged. And, she guessed, some
were immigrants. Possibly they had been writers in
their country of origin and hoped to acquire the necessary skills to continue their careers in America. It was
sad, really. Most of those in night classes would never
attain the language skills to write in English, even
though they might master the language verbally. She
counted herself fortunate that she had begun her studies so young and that all during her years in the orphanage she had been exposed to Americans and to the
language. She knew she could write in English, and she
hoped that she, like Joseph Conrad, could write well
enough to publish her writing. *Little Women* was her
most beloved book, but Conrad's *Lord Jim* was her

inspiration because the author had grown up speaking Polish. Conrad had more than mastered English, he had become one of the most respected writers in the language.

The door of the classroom again opened and Jo looked up from her notebook to see a man in a rumpled gray suit enter. Jo nearly gasped aloud. It was David Driscoll!

He perused the class and smiled. He looked at her, but he didn't really seem to see her. Jo felt like jumping up and screaming, "It's me, don't you remember?" but she contained herself. It had been years. She had grown and changed. And of course, her hair was short now. But, she observed happily, he looked exactly the same, except that his sandy hair was flecked with gray, which she thought made him look more distinguished. He began talking, and he asked the class to take notes.

Jo scribbled in her notebook, but she couldn't keep her mind on what he was saying. As soon as the class was over she would go up to him . . . their friendship would be renewed. He would help her and, she reasoned, all this good luck was coming because she had taken the first step and helped herself. David would be proud when he learned she already had a job on the *World*.

Days in Salonika returned to her, days spent in the warm sunshine, days spent talking with David Driscoll. She thought of Miss Spring and the terrible trick he had played on her, and she smiled. Poor Miss Spring, she had had such a crush on David.

David started out talking about headlines. He told them he would show them how to write a proper story. "Always written from the bottom up," he explained. "So if something happens that is more important, the story can be easily cut for the later editions. Essentials first, details later. Think of a well-written story as a

pyramid. Let's say you're covering a fire. Your headline—
we just call it a head—is going to read, 'Fire Destroys
Suspender Factory.'"

A few class members laughed, and David continued.
"Next you're going to write your first paragraph and it's
going to contain *where* the fire was, *when* the fire was,
and if possible, *what* caused it. For example, 'Fire
broke out in the Stretchy Suspender Factory at 75
Wacker Avenue, at two A.M. Sunday. Arson is suspected.' Now, your second paragraph is going to have
all the *whos*. Who was injured, who the factory belonged to, and who if anyone rescued the cat on the
fourth floor. The next paragraph will have any other
pertinent details, references to other similar fires in the
area, and so forth. Now, what happens is that the whole
story might appear in the paper's first edition. But if
there are other, more important stories, it will be cut
and only that vital first paragraph will appear in later
editions." Jo felt satisfaction in the fact that she had
already noticed that was how stories were written. She
often bought several editions of the *World* so she could
see how the various items were edited down. She noted
that a forty-line story could be cut to ten lines in the
paper's second edition

She watched David's expression as he talked. He had
such character. His eyes were so kind, and when he
talked, he moved his hands expressively. David Driscoll
was just as she remembered him—strong and confident, a good man—and she felt better just being in the
same room with him.

"Next week, we'll be writing a story. Then we'll
criticize it in class."

Jo glanced at the clock on the wall. The hour had
flown by. The students were getting up. They moved

toward the door, some nodding to David Driscoll as they left.

Jo hurried forward. "Mr. Driscoll," she said, standing right in front of him. "Mr. Driscoll, don't you recognize me?"

David stared at her. The young woman in front of him was an absolute knockout. She was dressed stylishly in a navy-blue dress trimmed in white. She had a crisp professional look, yet at the same time she appeared soft and vulnerable. Her dark hair was bobbed, and natural waves framed her angular face. It was her eyes, however, that held him. A smile crept around the corners of his mouth. "Jo?" he said questioningly.

"You do remember!" Her face broke into a smile, and she threw her arms around him. "I phoned you when I got to Chicago! I phoned every week for a year. They said you were gone, they wouldn't tell me where you were!" She was almost crying.

David held her for a moment, then released her. He smiled warmly at her. Who could have imagined his little Armenian waif could have grown up to be such a beauty! And, he admitted, he was glad to see her. She had brought him phenomenal luck once before, and now he felt a sudden surge of optimism.

"What are you doing here?"

"It's a long story," she said, still leaning against him.

"Hey, we've got a lot to talk about," he said, squeezing her arm. "Come on, I'll buy you something to eat and we'll get reacquainted."

Jo watched as he stuffed his notes into a beat-up-looking briefcase. "For starters, how old are you now?"

Jo smiled. "Eighteen."

"What happened? Did your uncle move to Chicago?"

Jo shook her head. "He moved to California. I ran

away. He sold me to a man . . . that is, he took money and promised me in marriage."

"What?" David felt outraged.

"I didn't marry him. I ran away. I've been here a year."

"On your own?"

"Yes, working as a seamstress at the Gaiety till a few days ago."

"Where do you work now?"

"I just got a job as a proofreader on the *World*."

David's face broke into a grin. "Well, well. I start back to work there Monday myself."

Jo almost jumped for joy. "We'll be working together!"

"Yes, but I'll tell you all about it." He took her arm and she felt truly secure. They walked down the hall and out of the building into the cool damp night.

"There's a café down the street," David told her. "Let's go there and talk."

"You don't know how glad I am to see you. David, did you mean it? Will you help me to become a writer?"

David squeezed her arm. Hell, had he promised that? So far, he hadn't done very well helping himself. "It's a tough business," he said, attempting to put her off. Christ, how very like him, promising to help some kid. He felt a little agitated, and he knew it was the thought of responsibility. Well, he'd take her out for coffee, shoot the breeze. Still, getting rid of her wouldn't be easy. She was, after all, working at the *World*. This, he knew full well, was no time to be taking on someone else's life. He was just getting back together himself.

They entered the garishly lit restaurant and David guided her to a booth. He ordered coffee and sandwiches and studied her.

"I have some samples of my writing. Will you read them?"

David smiled. God, she had a one-track mind. "Sure, but I'm a cruel critic."

"I want you to be, otherwise I won't improve." She opened her bag and withdrew a sheaf of papers. "This story is about the Gaiety. The other is about a girl I know. I met her on the ship coming to America."

David took the stories. "I'll read them when I get home."

Jo looked up as the waiter brought their coffee and sandwiches. "I am hungry," she said, relaxing. Sitting here across from David Driscoll, it seemed as if Garabed and Nass hadn't even existed. Even her last year in Chicago seemed like a dream. It was as if they were back in the sidewalk café in Salonika.

Joe nodded. "Tell me about you," she said sincerely. "I want to know everything that's happened to you."

David looked down at the table. No you don't, he thought to himself. He summoned his bravado. "Things have been great. I'm writing a book."

"That's wonderful!"

She glowed and he felt almost inspired by her utter and absolute faith in him. "I'll tell you about it," he promised. "Come on, child, eat. You look as if you're not well fed."

Jo took a bite of her sandwich. Her stomach was churning with excitement. She had found David, and things were the same. I won't lose you again, she thought to herself. We're going to stay together. We belong together.

"Bandits Prepared to Negotiate Release of
Americans!"
by Ted Kahn. A report from China.
May 4, 1923. Exclusive to the *World*.

Eight

David Driscoll's apartment consisted of a living room, a
small bedroom, a kitchen-in-the-wall, and a tiny bathroom.
It was continually cluttered with stacks of books and
papers, overflowing ashtrays, and unwashed coffee cups.

He let himself in and glanced at the clock. It was
twelve-thirty. He tossed his jacket, shirt, and tie on a
chair with abandon and went into the bathroom for a
quick shower. As he dried himself, he examined his
steam-obscured image in the mirror. "Now you've done
it," he lectured, shaking his finger. "You can barely
take care of yourself. How can you help that child?"

Reluctantly he admitted that he'd enjoyed the evening. Still, he chastised himself for having bitten off
more than he could chew. "She's too fond of you, me
boy," he told his mirror. "And having someone care for
you is a responsibility. One you can't shoulder." He
shook his head. She *would* want to be a writer. Didn't
everyone? He looked back on years and years of casual
conversations. "Oh, you're a writer," people invariably
gushed. "I write poetry," or "I've been thinking of
doing a novel," or "Listen, I have a great idea for you."

Writing, even reporting, was the profession of the few and the hobby of millions. In all these years, David acknowledged, she's the first person I ever offered to help. But he knew it was a mistake. He'd probably read her stuff and end up telling her there wasn't a hope in hell of her making it. He'd advise her to go to secretarial school. He'd tell her to find a job more suited to a woman. Then he thought, realistically, that he wouldn't be able to do that. He wasn't the type who could be honest with people, because he was so seldom honest with himself. He'd lie to her and hold out hope, but either way, taking on a protégée would probably not benefit either of them. He shrugged with resignation. There wasn't much he could do except lead her on. He was going to see her every day at the *World*. Vaguely he wondered why Mike Hamilton had hired her. Still, going after the job on her own did show initiative. Maybe somehow it would all work out and she wouldn't turn out to be a millstone around his neck.

David donned his nightshirt and headed for his unmade bed. He punched up the pillows and climbed in. He reached over to the night table and lifted up the sheaf of papers Jo had given him. "Might as well read it now and get it over with," he said aloud, feeling that the writing of a novice would surely cure his insomnia.

But her two stories didn't put him to sleep. They woke him up. They filled him with admiration and a rare feeling of discovery. Adrenaline raced through his veins, and a whole range of plans and ideas flooded his mind.

"I'll be damned!" he exclaimed as he watched a perfect smoke ring curl into the air. Beside him, Jo's neatly written stories lay on the bed. It was two in the morning. "Who'd have thought it?" He nodded his head in satisfaction. They weren't just good. They were great.

They were smoothly written, her characterizations were terrific, and they packed a wallop which nearly brought tears to his eyes. Hell, if she could write like that, she was a natural.

But they weren't newspaper stories. They were magazine material, and his first thought was the *World*'s Sunday magazine supplement.

But Jo couldn't get them published. She was unknown, and unknowns didn't get published in the mag sup, as it was called.

Nevertheless, her stories were the clincher. He would definitely take the *World*'s newest proofreader under his wing. Having her around could be a big help. For a while, until she was ready, he would have to rewrite her material, spruce it up. Still, with her kind of raw talent, she could do magazine pieces and he could rework them and sell them. Together they could make a tidy penny. And, he told himself, the poor kid needed help. She had come to him and asked him. She was his pupil. It was the least he could do.

David butted his cigarette and extinguished the light. They could make a great team, he decided. They had made a great team in Greece and they could do it again. She was beautiful, and beauty opened certain doors. She would have a female perspective, and added to his own male perspective, that could be useful. Her face floated across his mind. No emotional entanglements, he warned himself. If they were going to work together, it ought to be all business. Yeah, until he got completely back on his feet, she could provide him with raw ideas and he could rework them and help her earn some extra bucks. Maybe later, if things worked out, he would speak to Mike Hamilton and see if he could get her promoted to cub reporter. With lots of luck and hard work, she might make it. Luck. He thought about luck, and that brought Ted Kahn to mind.

David rolled over on his side. The kidnapping of the American missionaries had turned out to be a piece of luck for the Yid kid. The story had been front-page for five days now in three of the five Chicago papers. But hell, China was in turmoil. Stories like that were bound to fall practically in your lap. It was like covering a war. You didn't really have to dig all that much.

He smiled. With a little luck, maybe Ted would get himself kidnapped by a bunch of Yangtze River pirates. Maybe they'd throw *him* over a cliff as they had threatened to do with the American missionaries. What the hell? If the boys upstairs wanted a Ted Kahn, they'd just go out and hire someone else just like him. Maybe they'd hire someone even worse.

David tossed, and for the first time in months he thought how good a whiskey would taste. "Forget it," he said aloud, thinking of Hela. Talk about a dissipated, ruined broad. No, drinking wasn't good for him. "Don't want to end up like Hela," he said, turning into his pillow.

He tossed again onto his back and thought some more about Jo. If they were going to work together, she would have to live nearby. There was a flat for rent downstairs, he remembered. Yeah, that would be good. Abstractedly he reached over and patted her story. "Yeah, honey, I'm going to go off and sell you tomorrow. Old David and Jo are going to make it together. You're just what the doctor ordered. A beautiful, young, talented good-luck charm."

———

The Victoria Hotel was located in the middle of Shanghai's British concession, an area bounded by Chung Shan Tung Street on the east, Hsi Tsang Chung Lu Street on the west, and Yang-ching-p' Ang Canal on the south. The canal separated the British and French concessions.

Ted Kahn sat in the bar of the Victoria Hotel and slowly sipped the classic British colonial drink, a gin and tonic. The Brits knew what they were doing. Quinine water lowered the body temperature, and it was a real thirst-quencher and cooler in the hot humid heat that had settled over the city.

He wiped his brow with his handkerchief. It must be near ninety outside, with humidity to match, he thought. But the Victoria was a mecca for the tired and weary. Its large overhead ceiling fans droned continuously, circulating what air there was. A reporter could always find good diverting conversation in the Victoria. Everyone in China's international press corps ended up here. It was like a microcosm of the world.

He stared into his drink and found he rather regretted the fact that he would be leaving China tomorrow. His stories, he felt, had only scratched the surface of events. What was happening here would affect the world for years to come; of that he was certain. But the paper was insistent. The Far East was not a permanent assignment. It was a tour of exotica on the way to a job behind an editorial desk.

"I hear you're leaving us, old man," Dickie Farnham of the *Times* observed as he sauntered up to the bar and straddled one of the elegant hand-tooled leather stools.

Ted nodded. "Off to Japan tomorrow."

"Nice country. Not as interesting as China."

Ted smiled knowingly. China *was* more interesting. He had interviewed war lords, stalked opium dens, interviewed Sun Yat-sen, and watched a revolution in the making. And here in Shanghai he had made contact with the CCP, the growing Communist party, which had now joined the Kuomintang to create a unified national revolutionary movement. Rumor had it that Borodin was on his way from Moscow, and Ted felt regret that he wouldn't be here to see how the Bolshevik would be received.

"Great city, Shanghai," Dickie praised.

"But not terribly Chinese," Ted observed.

"Good heavens, no. I always call it China on the Thames."

Ted laughed. Shanghai was located at the mouth of the Yellow River, and its bridges and the architecture of its commercial district were certainly British to the core. From a distance it did in fact bear a striking resemblance to London.

"I like cities with bridges and water," Dickie said, sipping his pink Singapore sling. "How a city uses a body of water to beautify it, says something. Don't you think? I mean, you can have parks and bridges and the like, but you have to have a sort of total architectural cohesion."

Ted thought of the polluted water in the Chicago River and commented that it wasn't very inspiring.

"Pity," Dickie said dispassionately. "Paris is my favorite city. I love its bridges and parks. The Seine is part of the city. Its heartbeat really."

"I've never been to Paris," Ted admitted. He knew he would be going, of course. In fact, he would have been sent to Europe first had it not been for the Washington Conference on China that had just ended. The conference, which attempted to settle the interests of

France, Britain, the United States, and Japan in China, had created renewed interest in the country, thus making the goings-on in China front-page.

"Say, I always meant to ask you, Kahn, is Driscoll still with the *World*? We were in Europe together, you know. Covered the war and were in Paris together afterward."

Ted smiled. So Dickie Farnham knew Driscoll. It wasn't surprising. One of the unique aspects of a journalist's life was the cadre of acquaintances who kept turning up around the globe. Bars that journalists frequented were the same the world over. Walk into one, find someone you hadn't seen for years, and start talking as if no time at all had elapsed. He'd seen it happen, and he knew it would happen to him too. The foreign press corps had a real camaraderie. There was competition among them, but they also stuck together if there was an emergency or if one of them were arrested or attacked. "Driscoll's on a leave of absence," Ted replied.

"Good reporter, but an odd chap," Dickie observed.

"I don't know him well," Ted answered, "but I know he's been around."

"And around and around." Dickie laughed. "I knew him just after his book won that prize. Now, there's a dandy story for you!" Dickie slapped his leg and laughed loudly.

"I knew he'd won a prize," Ted said, not really wanting to hear Dickie's gossip.

"But did you know he stole the idea from some woman who was writing a book with the identical title? She caught up with him one night in Paris when we were having a drink. Gawd! I thought she was going to castrate him, she was so mad."

Ted raised an eyebrow and simply nodded. Driscoll

wasn't his friend or his enemy. He hardly knew him. But he did know that most of the boys on the paper respected Driscoll more than Driscoll seemed to respect himself. He was an old-timer, he'd come up the hard way, he was a street reporter, and it was said that he had good gut instincts.

"But don't get me wrong, I like him, really like him. And when you get back to Chicago, say hello for me, give him my best."

"Glad to," Ted replied. He finished off his drink and stood up and stretched. "I think I'll take a walk," he announced.

"Why not go over to the club, play a little tennis."

"Too hot," Ted answered. Go to the club indeed. Ostensibly his press card could get him in, but they would know he was Jewish and they wouldn't be friendly. Besides, he didn't know how to play tennis. It was a sport learned in private clubs, and Jews and blacks weren't allowed into private clubs in Chicago. Street hockey and kickball were what he played. But his best sport was survival. A good game for a kid growing up on the South Side.

"Most people spend their last night in Shanghai in a brothel. After all, Shanghai has the best brothels in the world," Dickie suggested.

"When you come from Chicago, you don't go to brothels for entertainment," Ted joked. "Shanghai may have the best, but Chicago has the most."

"Well, I suppose a man with your looks needn't pay for sex in any case," Dickie said with a giggle.

Ted shrugged off the compliment and decided it was definitely time to hit the road. Dickie Farnham was the perfect effeminate product of the British public-school system, or at least he was its stereotype. That he pre-

ferred young men to young women seemed embarrass-
ingly obvious.

Ted reached over and shook Dickie's hand. "Nice
knowing you," he said.

"Thanks," Dickie replied. "We'll run into one another again."

No, he would not go to the kind of brothel Dickie
had in mind. Ted walked out onto the busy street and
climbed into a waiting rickshaw. He would go and say
good-bye to Marika, a ravishingly beautiful girl he had
met through a Chinese friend. She was raven-haired,
brown-eyed, and had the body of a goddess. Marika's
mother had been Russian and her father Chinese. Now
she lived with a man she called her uncle, in a house
that surrounded the most beautiful garden Ted had
ever seen. The House of Cha'n Wang was not the usual
brothel, but the girls who lived there, including
Marika, were for hire. They served their customers an
elegant meal and entertained them with melodious flute
music. Then they bathed with them and walked in the
garden. There, without haste, they allowed themselves
to be seduced. The House of Cha'n Wang was as far
from the portside whorehouses as a man could get.
It was a place of Oriental charm and quiet. It was
the kind of place you couldn't find anywhere else in the
world.

Ted leaned back and closed his eyes as the aged
coolie expertly guided the rickshaw through the throbbing traffic and pedestrian-filled streets. He could all
but smell the pomegranate blossoms in the garden and
taste the perfumed sweetness of the lichee nuts Marika
would serve him just before she parted her kimono to
reveal her perfect breasts and ivory skin. Then, to the
music of a distant flute, they would make love slowly in

the Oriental way she had shown him. Ted opened his
eyes as the rickshaw came to a halt. Yes, he thought
ruefully, he would indeed miss Shanghai.

————————

Jo stood in front of the theater where Ben Hecht's play
A Thousand and One Afternoons in Chicago was playing.
David had asked her to meet him here after work.

She searched the faces of those approaching the theater. David was late. But she didn't mind.

"Jo!"

She whirled around to see David. He was dressed in
a light summer suit, his trench coat thrown casually
over his arm.

"David," she said with a smile, holding out her hands.

He took them and squeezed them. "Good news." He
winked. "Have I got a surprise for you!"

"Tell me," she urged.

"You were always impatient, child. Come on, let's
have a bite to eat. I have to talk with you."

He pulled her down the street and into the Piggly
Wiggly. He led her to a pink booth and sat down. "I'm
starved," he announced.

"David, tell me your news."

Jo's eyes widened and he stared into them. They
were large dark pools in a perfectly sculptured face. "I
read your stories. Listen, I really liked them. Now,
don't get me wrong. They needed a lot of work, that's
why I've kept them so long."

"But you liked them?"

"So much that I did some work on them and took
them up to the magazine supplement. They may buy
them."

"What?" Jo's eyes grew even larger.

"Yeah, that's what I said. Buy them."

"Oh, David, that's wonderful. I mean, I didn't expect . . . I don't know what to say."

"Well, there is one hitch."

Jo frowned. "What?"

"Well, you know, you're unknown. Listen, I hope you don't mind. I did revise them and I sold them under my name. I thought we would split the money, if that's all right with you."

"Of course it's all right! David, I'm thrilled."

Their food came and David began to eat immediately. "I have a sort of proposition to make you," he offered.

Jo smiled. "I'm listening."

"Well, your job proofreading doesn't pay much. I thought we could form a sort of partnership. See, you'll have trouble getting stuff published under your own name until you've earned a byline. Now, if you did the drafts, and I rewrote them, and we sold them using my name and split the money, we'd both make some extra and you'd be learning."

"That's a wonderful idea," Jo said, reaching across the table to squeeze his arm. It was just as if her childhood dream had come true. She and David were going to work together. They were going to be partners.

"There's an empty flat in my building. I think you ought to move in there. We should be close enough to work nights."

"A flat of my own," Jo considered. She would certainly miss her friends at the house on Erie Street, though she had to admit things were not the same without Marcella. Besides, now that she worked days and they worked nights, she hardly saw them. And David had a point. Even though they worked together all day at the *World*, they certainly couldn't get together there. She had piles of work, and he was often out of the office covering a story. Evenings were the only possible time to do extra work.

"It's forty-five dollars a month, and hell, it's in a good neighborhood. The furniture's not even bad."

Jo felt as if she were going to float away with happiness. They were going to live in the same building and work together. Her decision didn't take long because she knew it was time to move on. "I'll do it," she announced. Then, touching his arm: "You know, David, you've made my dreams come true."

David flushed. "Don't get mushy, child. It's not for you, it's for us." He squeezed her hand and winked.

Jo laughed. "Why do you always call me 'child'?"

"Because to me that's what you are, a very lovely child, one that needs to be protected."

"I don't really need to be protected," Jo replied. "I want to make my own way in the world."

"And you will," David promised. He resumed eating his sandwich with vigor. He felt better than he had earlier. She hadn't even thought of objecting when he told her he had sold the story under his name. In fact, now he felt downright benevolent. *I made her a promise to make her a reporter. I made it without thinking, and it's probably the only promise I've ever kept in my whole life.* "How are you finding life in the city room?" he asked.

Jo laughed lightly. "It's a challenge."

"You're good-looking," David said. "Are the boys giving you a rough time?"

Jo blushed. It was the first time he had ever commented on her looks. "They did the first week. By the time you came back, they had calmed down a bit."

"They like to shock young girls, but they're harmless."

"I think I can take care of myself," Jo replied confidently.

David smiled. "You have to realize that most of the guys just don't think a woman can do the job. This is a rough town. Some of the crimes are pretty scary."

"I read the papers," Jo said with humor.

"Yeah, but how do you react to carnage?"

Jo's expression turned suddenly serious. "I've seen my share," she said softly.

David looked away for a second. "Sure you have. Sometimes I forget about your background."

Jo nodded. "Sometimes I do too, though not often enough. David, take me to see Ben Hecht's play. I want to celebrate our partnership."

He grinned at her. "Sure. Child, did I ever tell you I started out with Hecht?"

She shook her head.

"Well, it's quite a story!" He reached over and took her hand. "Let me tell you about the old days," he began.

Harry Haskill, his balding head shining under the bright light of the overhead lamp, lifted a glass of champagne in toast. "Here's to our little Jo," he announced, tears forming in the corners of his round blue eyes.

"And her new life as a writer," Antoine added. He turned to Jo and smiled. "You know, you really must insist that Driscoll fellow let you publish the stories under your own name."

"He will," Jo answered, "when the time is right and I've earned my own byline."

"I've heard *that* sort of thing before," Antoine pressed. "You mustn't let him take advantage of you."

Jo touched his arm. "It's sweet of you to care, but David would never do anything to hurt me. I've known him a long time, and he's always helped me. If he thinks this is the best way to begin, well, I'm sure he's right."

Antoine shrugged in defeat. "You won't ignore us, will you? You won't be like Marcella and never come around at all."

"No, I won't. I'll come whenever I can." She thought briefly of Marcella. Since the day she had stomped out of the house over Antoine's objections, she had not returned. Calls to her new telephone number went unanswered, it was as if she had been swallowed up. "I hope she's all right," Jo said thoughtfully.

Antoine looked away. "How can she be?" he said seriously.

It was a painful subject for him. He was like a mother hen and Marcella was his most beloved responsibility. "Perhaps I'll go and see her next week," Jo said hesitantly.

Antoine turned quickly. "I don't want you to go near that . . . that den of iniquity. She's living with mobsters— wicked, evil people."

"I can take care of myself. Maybe David will come with me."

"Well, you can't go alone."

Jo nodded. She could go alone and probably would. But this was no time to argue with Antoine.

"This is supposed to be a celebration, dearie," Mabelle Mar reminded Antoine. "And here you two are over in a corner discussing heaven knows what! We haven't so much time. Rehearsal begins in less than an hour!"

"Don't get your fans in a dither," Antoine snapped. "I have every intention of sharing our Jo with everyone."

"Then let's finish the champagne," Harry suggested with a wave of the bottle.

"You'll get too drunk to go on," Angel Jay suggested.

"Never!" Harry roared. "And even if I did get drunk, I could always snap Mabelle's garters. Always good for a laugh."

"I'd snap you right to Hammond," Mabelle retorted. "Anyway, in my new act, I don't wear garters."

"Or much of anything else," Antoine added dryly.

Harry patted Jo's hand. "I hate it when people leave. But when they leave for success, something in me likes it." The others—Angel Jay, Ricky Moran, the strippers, Karen and Louise, and Miss Theodora—all agreed.

"I have a long way to go before I'm a success," Jo told them.

"But you're on the road," Ricky Moran put in. "That's what's important."

"The cab's here to pick you up," Antoine announced as he peeked through the lace curtains.

"So soon?" Jo looked around the room, searching each of their faces and smiling her farewell.

Mabelle positioned herself against the white wood pillar that divided the living room from the hallway. "Come around and see us sometime," she said throatily in her best imitation of Mae West, the ruling burlesque queen.

Antoine raised his eyebrow. "Perhaps *something* can be done with you after all," he allowed. "But you'll have to have new lines."

Mabelle laughed and kissed Jo on the cheek. "We will miss you," she said sincerely.

They all hugged and kissed her, and Jo made no attempt to stem the flow of her own tears. Antoine picked up her suitcase and bundles and carried them out to the waiting cab. "Stay in touch" was all he finally said.

Jo kissed him on the cheek. "I will," she promised.

———

Mike Hamilton's glassed office in the middle of the city room reeked of stale cigar smoke and rotting orange peels. Hamilton had a passion for oranges and he ate three or four a day, tossing the peels into his wastebasket, where they fermented, causing the small room to smell like a garbage heap at high noon.

Behind his desk was a shelf of reference books, including *The Chicago World Style Manual*, which he had written. Its back-page supplement dictated the way in which the names of foreign cities would be spelled. "Consistency is all-important," Hamilton proclaimed. Thus the *World* always spelled the capital city of Japan "Tokio," while the New York *Times* spelled it "Tokyo."

On the wall above the bookshelves was a chart with hastily scrawled notes. These notes, David well knew, were not pertinent to the running of the *World*, but were, instead, the phone numbers at which Hamilton's bookie could be reached, Hamilton's numbers in the daily baseball pool, and a record of any and all bets he had placed at the track.

Hamilton's desk was one of the wonders of the newspaper world. If some organization gave out awards for a mess, David's own apartment would win first prize and Mike Hamilton's desk would come in a close second. The edges of the desk were piled high with papers, which included the proofs of yesterday's *World*, half-finished stories, penciled diagrams of front pages, and snippets of headlines. The middle of his desk was bare, or would have been if that had not been where Hamilton put his feet. He was in his traditional pose: feet up, his chair leaning back precariously, and the phone receiver tucked under his ear while he held the phone and shouted into its mouthpiece.

David pulled up an empty chair and sat down.

"Get a picture of the body!" Mike shouted impatiently. "Faceup! Lying in the morgue, if necessary. Damn, Higgie, how many times have I told you a gory murder story is nothing without a picture, and if you can't get the whole body, for Christ's sake, get a photo of the parts, maybe an arm or something." He slammed down the receiver. "Rookies," he muttered. "Jeez, I really don't want to hear that he can't get a photo because there was mutilation. Mutilation's a gold mine!"

"Got a sec?"

"Sure. How you feeling, Driscoll?"

"Still on the wagon. Okay, I guess."

"It's nice having you back, Driscoll. Your copy yesterday was good stuff."

"Thanks."

Mike rubbed his chin. "Did you come in here to tell me you've been moonlighting—writing stories for the magazine supplement?"

"You know?"

"Sure. I've even read the two you've submitted. They're going to buy them. Christ, Driscoll, I didn't know you knew so much about burlesque."

David shrugged. Mike Hamilton was referring to one of Jo's stories, "Behind Burlesque." "I get around," he offered.

"Listen, I don't care how many supplement stories you write, as long as you get your assignments for me done."

"There's no problem there," David replied, flicking

the ash off his cigarette into Mike Hamilton's ashtray. "There is one more thing I wanted to speak to you about," he hedged.

"Shoot."

"It's that kid who proofreads—Jo Gregory."

Mike Hamilton didn't look up. "Yeah, she's okay. I didn't really expect her to last, but she's doing all right."

"How do you find her work?" David pressed.

Mike lifted his eyes slowly. "She's good."

"She's in my journalism class," David revealed. "Frankly, I think she's got some talent. I'd like to see how she can do on rewrite. And by the way, I interviewed her for the story on burlesque."

Hamilton screwed up his face. "She's only been proofing for a couple of weeks, Driscoll. Do you really want me to go out there and tell those guys who've been writing for fifteen years that some little chick who was hired to proofread two weeks ago is going to do their rewrite?"

David shook his head. "She could do mine. I mean, I'd like to help her."

Hamilton raised his eyebrow. "Driscoll, she's a kid. Admittedly a good-looking one. You're too old for her."

"That's got nothing to do with it!" David replied too quickly, his Irish temper starting to flare.

"Well, up till now I've not known you to be a benefactor to young writers," Hamilton retorted.

David inhaled and leaned over Mike's desk. "There's a reason," he whispered. "Listen, I'm not supposed to tell anyone, but I'm going to tell you."

"What's going on?" Hamilton demanded.

"Jo Gregory is not her real name. It's Josephina Gregorian. She's the Armenian refugee the paper went to bat for back in 1919. Remember?"

"That's reaching back." Mike Hamilton scratched his head. "No kidding, the same kid?"

"No kidding. She doesn't want anyone to know because she doesn't want to discuss it and she doesn't want anyone to feel sorry for her. Anyway, she moved to Chicago, and I ran into her in my class—guess it was a couple days after you hired her."

"Small world," Hamilton agreed. "And that's the reason you want to help her?"

"Yeah, that's it. The beginning and the end."

"Well, I suppose it wouldn't hurt if she did some rewrite for you—say, two hours a day."

"That's enough."

"What the hell," Mike said, almost cheerfully. "Anyway, if it doesn't work out, I won't be around to deal with it."

David frowned. Hamilton's offhand announcement caught him completely off guard. "You leaving the *World?*"

"Hell no. I'm being booted upstairs in a couple of months. Now, that's a secret, David me boy. Don't let me hear it as scuttlebutt on the city-room grapevine."

"That's great!"

Hamilton nodded. "Nothing all that big. Just assistant general editor."

"Who is taking over City?" David felt a sudden surge of anticipation. Hell, he was the one with seniority, in spite of his leave of absence.

"Kahn's being brought back from the Orient. He'll have it for a while anyway."

David felt as if a concrete block had hit him. "Jeez," he muttered as his stunned senses recovered and he was suddenly filled with both jealousy and anger. Kahn taking over City? He was actually going to be working for a Yid Kid College boy?

"You don't like him, do you?" Hamilton queried.

"No."

"He's a good man, Driscoll. He's well-educated, and now he's had the experience. You know, Kahn admires you. The two of you ought to be able to hit it off. Give it a try. I mean a fair try, just like I'm going to give your friend Jo."

David pressed his lips together. "Okay" was all he could manage to say. Then he added, "It's not happening tomorrow. I'll get used to it."

David turned and left Hamilton's office. He'd masked his deeper feelings, but he was seething inside. He should have gotten the job of city-desk editor. "Damn," he swore. He didn't need this kind of setback.

David leaned back against the blue sofa in his apartment. "So that's the deal," he told Jo as he butted out his cigarette. "Two hours a day you'll be doing rewrite for me, and the rest of the time you'll proof."

"How can I, David? I can't rewrite for you."

"Sure you can. Listen, what I'll be doing is giving you notes. You'll work them up for me, sort of get them in order and prepare the story."

"That's not rewriting."

"I know that and you know that. What I want is for you to have the time to write under pressure in the city room. Who the hell cares whether we call it rewrite or work-up?"

"Is that fair to Mr. Hamilton? He did give me a job, and I want him to be satisfied."

"I already talked to him. Let me deal with that, will you?"

"If you're sure it's all right."

David stood up and walked across the room to where she was sitting. He leaned over and hugged her. "Listen, kid. Anything I say is all right *is* all right."

Jo nodded silently.

"Hey, look, I've got other good news. So good, I think we ought to celebrate, maybe go to a play or something. I heard from Mike today that the supplement is going to buy both stories. We're going to be splitting at least a hundred and fifty bucks. How does that sound?"

"Oh, David! Why didn't you tell me that first?"

"I thought you would be happy," he said confidently. The phone rang and David reached over casually to pick it up. "Driscoll here," he breathed into the receiver.

Jo watched as he listened intently.

"Well, I was going out," David said wearily into the phone's mouthpiece. He listened again, then took his battered notebook out and started making notes. Jo watched as the expression on his face changed, going from uninterested to involved in seconds. "Spell that," he urged the caller. Then, after another few seconds of his silence: "Thanks," he said, hanging up.

"Story?" Jo asked.

David pressed his lips together. "What was that guy's name? The one who lived in the house with you and did your hair?"

"Antoine—Antoine Beaufort. Why?" It was like an alarm spreading through her. "Why?" she repeated.

"He's bought it," David said coolly. "Found beaten up and knifed."

Jo's hands flew to her face to muffle her own scream. "Oh God! No!" She half-sobbed the words.

"I thought it was just another fag who had bought it, but then I realized it was that guy."

Jo felt ice cold and she knew she kept shaking her head in denial of what David was saying.

"I know you liked him, but this is important—I need you to help me with the story, since you knew him. Come on. Get your coat."

"I can't . . ." Tears were streaming down her face even as David was tugging on her arm.

"You can and will. Come on, Jo. Friend or no friend, you're going to have to harden up. I told you once, this is a rough business!"

She allowed herself to be pulled along by David, more because of her confusion than her willingness to go.

"Maybe you can help find the murderer and bring him to justice," David was saying.

What he didn't say was that from Hamilton's description on the phone, this sounded like one of Chicago's more gory murders. He propelled her down the corridor and then down the stairs. "You're going to be okay," he kept saying.

Jo's mind flooded with thoughts of Antoine on the ride to the morgue. Who would want to kill him? All she could think of was the fight over Marcella's leaving.

Nine

"Great story, Driscoll! You're well on your way back to the front page!" That was what Mike Hamilton had said about the three stories published in the *World* magazine supplement in July. David was even more elated over the coverage of Antoine's murder. It was front-page for four days, and he got his byline. It was Jo's doing, David acknowledged to himself. The supplement stories were hers, and it was her friendship with Antoine that gave the stories on his murder poignancy. It turned out that Antoine had gone to find Marcella and tried to persuade her to come back to the Gaiety. Marcella's new boss had taken Antoine's persistent pleas badly, and Antoine had been killed. Of course it was a pro job and no one could prove a thing. To top it off, Marcella had disappeared. Antoine's death and Marcella's disappearance had shaken Jo, but David decided she had come through it with flying colors. She had written like a real pro.

And the stories had brought changes. Mike Hamilton was so impressed he'd moved David into Features and given him a regular byline. The boys in the city room gave him a new respect.

David put down the morning paper, which had screaming two-inch jet-black headlines that read: "President Dead in San Francisco."

"Talk about dumb luck," David commented to Jeff Clayton, who now worked the police beat. "Imagine just getting off a clipper from the Far East and landing in Frisco just in time for the President's death."

"Uncanny timing," Clayton agreed. "But you gotta hand it to Kahn on one score. All the other papers were screaming that Harding's illness of a couple of days ago was nothing but a cold or an allergy and that the old boy was on his way back to health, wealth, and the mediocrity that's been the hallmark of his administration. But not Kahn. He kept nosing around and sending in less-than-optimistic bulletins. And damn, he was right. Everyone else was caught off guard, but we weren't."

David grunted. Nose to the ground or not, he wasn't giving Kahn an inch. He looked up and caught sight of Jo. What a gal. She bustled around all day, they stayed up till midnight writing with him. He frowned. It wasn't really altogether fair that he'd gotten the promotion and she hadn't gotten anything. Not that she had complained. She never complained. In fact she seemed grateful to be in the same room with him. "Still, I've got to do something," he mumbled.

"What?" Clayton said, leaning over.

"Nothing. I think I'll go talk to Hamilton."

"Yeah, hit him now. He'll be gone in a few days. I heard Kahn will wind up the story in Frisco and travel east with the body. When he gets back to Chicago, it's good-bye Hamilton, hello Ted Kahn."

David shrugged. He didn't want to think about it. He stood up and ambled off toward Hamilton's glass cage.

Hell, he was doing features; maybe Hamilton would buy the idea that he needed an assistant.

"Mike . . ." David said cheerfully. At least Hamilton wasn't on the phone.

"Yup."

He was engrossed in rereading the front page. "I think we ought to do a side bar in tomorrow's edition—something sort of man-on-the-street. You know, what the local yokels thought of Harding and how sad they are now that he's kicked the bucket," Hamilton suggested.

"Sounds good." David lit a cigarette. "Got a question to ask you."

"Ask."

"What do you think of Jo? Everybody else likes her. You know, I've had her working on rewrites and she's good."

Mike Hamilton put down the paper and folded it. "Obviously I like her. I hired her. She's a good worker, I'd have to be blind to ignore the fact that she brightens up the place, and she's got a sense of humor. But she's not ready for reporting yet."

David summoned himself. "I disagree, at least partly. See, I think she's ready to start breaking in. I mean, hell, Mike, a woman can get into places a man can't. They have a certain touch . . ."

Hamilton's face reddened and he fairly leered. "A certain touch? Come on, Driscoll, don't give me lines like that. And about the only place a woman can get into easier than a man is the ladies' room."

"Sorry. What I meant was, widows and orphans prefer talking to women reporters."

"Yeah, most women write good sob stories. What do you have in mind?"

David butted out his cigarette. "I could use an assistant."

"Hold on a second," Hamilton said. "Driscoll, you're not making it with this kid, are you?"

David turned and scowled. "No," he said flatly.

Hamilton shrugged. "Well, you can't blame me for asking. I mean, you do take quite an interest in her . . . shall I say 'welfare'?"

"I'm strictly a Good Samaritan. Scout's honor. I told you before, it's because of the stories I did on her when she was a child."

Hamilton nodded. "Good. Wouldn't want to come in late one night and find the two of you on a desk or anything."

"Shit," David said under his breath. "Let me show you something she wrote just recently."

He went back to his desk and rummaged through the bottom drawer. He had some of Jo's stuff, not the better stories, but some that were good enough. He wasn't going to show Hamilton the better stories. They were magazine material and had potential sales value.

He went back to Hamilton's office and dropped the sheaf of papers on his desk. "Here," he prompted.

Hamilton was on the phone again. He looked up and pointed to a pile of papers and indicated with his finger where David should put Jo's work.

Hamilton waited till David had ambled back to his desk, then took his hand off the receiver and continued his conversation with Ted Kahn. "Can you get an exclusive with Harding's widow?" he queried.

"I've already got the appointment," Ted answered, his voice crackling across the long-distance lines.

"It was a godsend that you just happened to be in San Francisco."

"I'd have thought someone from National would have been traveling with the President."

"It didn't seem very important at the time," Hamilton admitted. "By the way, Driscoll's been turning out some good Sunday-supplement stuff. His stories have really improved. He's been put on Features, with a byline, and rumor has it he's about to get a rookie assistant."

"Good, glad to hear he's back among the living."

"Listen, as long as he stays off the sauce, he's a good man."

"Let's hope he stays off it."

"I think you'll find it less difficult to work with him now. Some of his resentment seems to have dissipated."

"I didn't know you noticed it."

"It's my job to notice things like that. Now, get back to your story, and have a nice trip home with the coffin."

"Thanks. By the way, I brought your wife a Japanese kimono."

"Don't soft-soap me." Hamilton laughed into the phone. "Have a good trip, Kahn."

He hung up the phone and picked up Jo's story. He read it quickly, then doubled back and read it again. It wasn't bad. She was hardly ready to write on her own, he decided. Still, he could see a raw, instinctive talent, and something told him she would be doubly good on tearjerkers. He shook his head. There was a little too much alliteration in the first few lines, and in places she was overly dramatic. But those were small problems, and with practice she'd learn how to write a catchy lead. He put the story facedown and peered through the nicotine-stained glass of his office into the city room. At first he had thought Driscoll had something going with the little broad, but that didn't seem to be it. He seemed to be genuinely trying to help the kid get started. In fact, his attitude to her was downright fatherly. Mike Hamilton shrugged. Well, if Driscoll wanted to play Henry Higgins to some Eliza Doolittle, it was okay with him, as long as he didn't push too hard, too soon, and allow an amateur to start doing stories.

———

Jo looked around her small two-room flat with satisfaction. It was far nicer than anyplace she had lived since she was a small child. And it was hers. She had privacy, something she had never had before.

The window in her front room overlooked Eleventh Street, and though she was three stories up, she could always hear the hum of the traffic below. The room was furnished with a sofa and two chairs, a table, a desk, a bookcase, and a false fieplace. On the mantel she had placed her copy of *Little Women*, and next to it she had added four other books purchased at a used-book store.

At the far end of the room, to the left of the door, was a kind of fold-out kitchen. Metal cupboards opened up to reveal a sink, two gas burners, and a tiny icebox that held a ten-pound block of ice.

The other room was smaller and held only a bed and a dresser. Its window was blocked by the brick wall of the adjacent building.

Jo collapsed on the sofa and kicked her shoes off. For two hours in the morning she had been down in the newspaper morgue looking up references for David; then she had returned to a monumental pile of stories that needed proofing. David was gone from the city room when she returned, but that wasn't unusual.

Jo reached for the phone and dialed the number of the house on Erie street. Harry Haskill answered.

"It's Jo," she said. "I just thought I'd call and ask if there was any word from Marcella."

"No," he answered solemnly. Harry had been as devastated as she by Antoine's death and Marcella's disappearance. Jo thought gratefully that she had gained her own strength from him. He had cried half the day, and then gone on that night performing his comedic role to perfection. "Laughter and tears," he told her, "go together. Comedy is just the other side of tragedy."

"I keep thinking she'll turn up and call you," Jo said.

"One day she will," Harry replied, trying to sound confident.

"I hope you're right."

"Come by and have dinner with me Sunday," Harry urged. Jo agreed and then hung up. David would be home soon, she thought. He would certainly bring notes for her to work up. He had been out covering a story most of the afternoon.

Jo pulled herself up off the sofa and went into the bathroom. If she hurried, she would have time to wash up and change.

———

"A promotion! To your assistant!" Jo threw herself into David's waiting arms and he waltzed her around the front room of her apartment while he sang "When Irish Eyes Are Smiling" in his fine tenor voice.

She laughed and hugged him. "I didn't know you could sing!"

"Tonight I feel like singing," he replied. And, he admitted, his spirits were high indeed. Even the fact that Ted Kahn was on his way back to Chicago to assume his new position of city-desk editor had slipped temporarily to the back of his mind. Jo's enthusiasm and her happiness further bolstered his mood. He began to feel he could accomplish anything and that the two of them were going to do great things together.

"I've sold another story to the Sunday supplement," he revealed.

"For the same amount of money?"

"Yup. What do you think, should we celebrate?"

Jo beamed.

"How about the theater, then a late-night snack?"

"Gloria Swanson's new film?"

"If that's what you want to see. Look, I have to go upstairs first and pick up my mail. You get dressed, and I'll be back for you in thirty or forty minutes."

"All right."

"Then it will be a big night." He winked and left.

David bounded up the three flights of stairs to the sixth floor. It felt good to do something for someone, he decided. Especially for Jo. He smiled to himself as he turned the key in his apartment door. The memory of the warm glowing look in her eyes remained with him.

He stopped at the table by the door, where Mrs. Coppola, the building superintendent, had left his mail. He stared for a moment at the telegram, then ripped it open.

Congratulations on promotion to feature writer. Looking forward to working with you. Best regards, Ted Kahn.

David stared at it and then swore under his breath. "Two-faced son of a bitch!" It sounded so "nice." But it wasn't nice. It was like turning the knife in an open wound. David felt certain it was Kahn's way of reminding him that he'd soon be his boss. Kahn, David was convinced, was out to get him.

He slumped into the chair and crumpled the telegram in his hand, tossing it with abandon toward the
wastebasket in the corner.

He opened his billfold and looked at the check for
one hundred dollars from the Sunday supplement. He
stared at it, his eyes turning glassy, his head beginning
to ache. It wasn't *his* story that he had sold. It was Jo's.
But the story bore his name, not hers. Of course he had
worked on it, but not really that much. Her writing was
maturing; it needed less work. I *am* doing it for her, he
reminded himself. She probably couldn't get them published under her own name. She wouldn't have a job if
it weren't for me; she wouldn't have a place to live, he
rationalized.

"She's satisfied," he said aloud. as if to convince
himself. She looked at him with only worship in her
eyes, and God knew he was trying to live up to whatever she saw in him. Inexplicably, tears started to run
down his cheeks. "I have to make the child happy," he
said almost irrationally. And reluctantly he admitted
she was important to him. Perhaps the only really important person in his whole empty life.

David closed his eyes. His mood of carefree abandon
had done a one-hundred-degree turn. Visions of his
father danced in front of him. The ever-charming man
with the glib tongue and the power to enchant, the man
who died in obscurity and poverty, the man who was
buried in a graveyard for the indigent. He could see his
mother too. She stood there grasping his own boyish
hand while tears streamed down her cheeks. "You're
going to do me proud, David," she had said. Implicit in
her comment was the fact that her husband hadn't done
her proud, that he was a failure. In David's mind, his
mother's face became Jo's face and he muttered to
himself. He wondered if he loved her, then reminded

himself of the age difference between them. But I can take care of her, I can help her. Wasn't that what he was doing?

"David?" Jo opened his door a crack and stood on the threshold expectantly. Her dark hair was brushed back, but soft curls caressed her forehead. Her lovely dark eyes looked at him affectionately, and she smiled warmly. She was dressed in her best clothes; she was waiting for him. "You didn't come back, and now we'll miss the beginning of the film."

"Sorry," he said, standing up. "I had some bad news."

"Oh dear, and on today of all days." She walked over to him and hugged him. "I hope it won't ruin our evening."

I love her, David thought. And if I try to express it, I'll ruin everything. "It won't," he said, trying to reassure her. "Look, we'll go to the theater, then I'll buy a bottle of wine and we'll come back here and celebrate. No, not wine, champagne!"

"Pink champagne," Jo added.

"If the bootlegger has it. It'll tickle your nose." He reached down with his hand and touched her nose. She crinkled it and laughed.

David straightened his tie and grabbed his jacket. Yeah, he would buy a bottle of champagne from Corky Mulroney, the bootlegger, and maybe a bottle of whiskey too. He'd been dry for over a year. A little celebration wouldn't hurt.

———

Ted Kahn folded his six-foot, one-inch frame into Mike Hamilton's well-worn leather chair and stared out the smoke-stained glass windows into the city room. He half-smiled to himself. Most of the guys out there didn't think he had taken a long time to get to this cubicle, but to him the journey seemed long indeed.

He contemplated his first years in Chicago. They hadn't been pleasant. His family had emigrated in 1900 when he was seven. He couldn't speak English then, and the other children taunted him unmercifully.

His family had fallen on hard times, partly as a result of the language barrier, partly because his father could not find work as a tailor in a city that machine-produced the clothing he had once laboriously made on his ancient sewing machine. They lived in a tenement, without heat or hot water. Ted's earliest memories were of his mother crying at night as she lay awake terrified of the rats that skittered behind the walls.

By the time he was nine, he was considered big for his age, and bigger yet for a Jewish boy. In a sense, he had his stature to thank for his survival. The streets were rough, his daily walk to the George Washington Elementary School was a walk through taunts, torments, and sometimes physical attacks. "Jew boy" rang in his ears. Those gibes and Chicago's occasional gang warfare lingered in his thoughts. If the big Polish kids didn't call him "Jew boy," they called him "Christ-killer."

When he was ten, he began working summers. "Your studies come first, my little bubelah," his mother insisted. She clung to her Yiddish, though in time, for his sake, she mixed it with English.

"I don't want you should have to work. I want you to go to school. You should be in a proper yeshiva," she lamented. But the school wasn't as bad as his mother thought. The teachers were strict and the lessons were hard.

"Mama, we need the money," he had insisted. "Look, Mama, I'm as big as any fifteen-year-old. If I work, I can save money."

"Only in the summers," she finally relented. So he had begun his long procession of jobs. The first summer he carried bricks in a brick factory. He worked from seven till seven. He worked till he thought his back would break. But certainly he worked no harder than his parents.

Later, he worked in construction. He worked with Irishmen who taunted him just as his classmates at school did. But he persisted, and partly because of his physical prowess, he earned their respect, or at least their silence.

His mother cried when he came home with a bloody nose. She wept when he appeared with a black eye. She complained and cursed when he came home with dirt and grime under his nails, blisters on his hands, and a sunburn blistered back.

"What kind of thing is this for a good Jewish boy?" she would ask. "We come from generations of scholars, what kind of thing is this?"

And then the war started. He'd been at Northwestern then, and though he spoke perfect English and was the university's top scholar, the taunts began anew. This time not because he was Jewish, but because he was a German Jew, born in Munich. Yet he knew that those of German and Polish heritage were the most anti-Semitic people in Chicago. Or so it seemed to him. Not that the Irish weren't; it was simply that they didn't have a history of Jews in their country, and besides, their most virulent hatreds were reserved for the English. He had learned early that if you could outdrink an Irishman, and if you were strong enough to close his mouth with your fist, you achieved instant respect. Not so with the others. Theirs were whispered hatreds. Hatreds that stemmed from fear and smoldered in the environment of their own poverty. Yes, he knew they

were afraid, though he didn't understand why. Surely it
was the ghettoized victims of European pogroms that
should have been afraid. But that, Ted realized, was
not the way it was. Jews were hated because they were
different. They spoke a different language, longed to be
somewhere else, worshiped a different God. Forced to
settle in alien lands, they huddled together and created
a world of their own.

Ted shook his head. That was it, of course. He belonged to two worlds. He belonged to the world of his
parents, where hard work, scholarship, and perseverance were the respected traits; indeed, they were seen
to be the way to combat prejudice.

"Don't talk back to them," his mother always said.
"Don't fight. Don't listen to them." But he couldn't do
that; he couldn't do it because he belonged to that
second world. He wanted more than the ghetto, whether
it be a real ghetto or a self-imposed one, whether it be
economic or intellectual.

He clung to his mother's lessons on scholarship, hard
work, and perseverance. But he rebelled against other
aspects of his Jewishness.

He had cast aside kosher eating in his teens, he had
traded his yarmulke for a brown felt hat in his early
twenties, and certainly his choice to be a newspaperman
was not what his mother truly had in mind when she
encouraged him to be a writer.

When she had introduced him to her employers, she
had hoped he might be given a better summer job, a
job that would enable him to earn money while escap-
ing the construction pits. She prayed to get him away
from manual labor and into an office where he could
wear a suit and work behind a desk. She was stunned
when he chose to make reporting a career.

"What kind of writing is this?" she asked. "You should

be writing books of poetry, essays, philosophical books, biographies even."

"But a career it is," Ted said, standing up and stretching. And he thought: I love it. It's part of that other world, it's alive and it's vital.

He peered through the glass. Driscoll's latest story was on his desk, and it was good. His eyes fell on Jo Gregory and he smiled. Hamilton had mentioned her, but this was the first time Ted had seen her. If nothing else could be said for Driscoll, he certainly had good taste. She was absolutely stunning. Vaguely he wondered if she was tough enough for this business. He made a mental note to have a talk with her.

He walked over to the glass and tapped on it. Higgie, the photographer, looked up and Ted pointed to Driscoll. Higgie tapped Driscoll on the shoulder, and when he looked toward the cubicle, Ted motioned to him. "Time to take the bull by the horns," he said aloud to himself.

David Driscoll walked toward the office and paused in the doorway. "Did you want me?" he asked.

"Sure, come on in, Driscoll. Have a seat."

"I have a story to write," David said defensively.

"And I think we should have a little chat."

"With tea and crumpets or what?" David slid into the chair.

Ted looked him right in the eye. "I know you aren't terribly fond of me," he allowed. "Frankly, I'm not sure why, but since you aren't, and since we have to work together, I'd like to clear the air, get your complaints out in the open."

"Maybe I don't like Jews," David said coldly.

"And maybe I don't like the Irish," Ted snapped back. "But I'm prepared to make an exception. Frankly, the fact that I'm Jewish and you're Irish hasn't got a damn thing to do with how we do our jobs."

"Granted, but I don't like interference," David said.

"I haven't interfered yet. And I won't unless you write something that's unacceptable or libelous. As long as you do your job, there won't be any problems."

"Maybe I don't like a college boy making those judgments. I've been in this business longer than you—I'm forty-two, you're twenty-eight, remember?

"You make it hard to forget. Okay, I don't know everything, but you don't either. Look, Driscoll, you don't have to believe it, but I came to this paper respecting you. I still do. I'm glad you're selling stories to the supplement, and from what I've read, your features are good. Maybe it's not fair that I'm in this office instead of you, but life isn't always fair. The business is changing, and you have to be willing to change with it."

"Touching," David said sarcastically. "Look, Kahn. I'll do my job, you do yours, is that fair?"

"That's all I want," Ted said, feeling exasperated and knowing he had not broken through Driscoll's antagonism.

"Good. Can I get back to work now?"

Ted nodded. He didn't bother to extend his hand. Driscoll was just bitter enough to have bitten it off.

"People don't just want facts. They want color and humanity," David stressed. "Now, when you write a sob story, you gotta use the right kind of language. Say you're dealing with a dead girl. You have to say things like 'Her dark hair fell over her shoulders in ringlets, her eyes were wide and questioning, her full ruby-red lips were parted in a final plea . . .' Heap on the adjectives. Stories don't come to you. You have to go

out after them," David added. "Look, I want a real
tearjerker for tomorrow's feature. Something heartrending. Go down to the South Side market, really early in
the morning, and see what you can find." He had
paused then and surveyed her carefully before he continued. "And try not to look too la-di-da. It's a poor
section of town, and if you expect anyone to talk to you,
you can't look as if you live on the North Side."

It was four-thirty, still dark, and, Jo realized, surpris-
ingly cool for late August. It was a predawn cool, and
the ever-present wind carried a hint of dampness, even
though it was still too dark to see if it was overcast. Jo
inhaled. Yes, she felt certain it would rain. She pulled
her kerchief a little tighter just as she felt the first drops
of drizzle on her nose.

Trucks and carts littered the street as boxes of produce were handed out to a chain of workers who loudly
passed them along a human conveyor belt, carrying
them into the back of the market. It was a lively yet
strange scene. Drivers shouted for others to move along.
Short paunchy Italians waved their fists in the air as
they broke open crates and raked through cabbages and
potatoes. The refuse—tops of carrots, turnips, and rotting potatoes—was tossed in huge barrels with a curse
for its uselessness. A slightly sickening array of odors
filled the air. Yesterday's rotting vegetable matter mixed
with the smell of fish and the blood of freshly slaughtered meat just brought in from the stockyards.

Jo watched and waited. But for what? Why had David sent her down here at this ungodly hour to watch
the city's food being unloaded? "Stay there and keep
your eyes open," he had instructed. "You'll know the
story when you see it."

Jo huddled in a doorway and shivered slightly, waiting for the first rays of light to penetrate the dark sky.

"Beat it!"

Jo started at the sound of the angry order and turned to face a woman of indeterminate age. She was a small stooped woman with greasy tangled brown hair and hard narrow dark eyes. Her stained dress hung on her, and her worn jacket had one pocket torn off.

"I beg your pardon," Jo replied.

"Well, ain't we the lady," the woman replied, making a face. "I said, beat it! Those barrels is mine."

Jo squinted at her. The lights from a nearby truck illuminated her face slightly. She was a mulatto woman, Jo decided. "What do you mean they're yours?" Jo asked, pointing to the barrels.

"They's mine—what's in them is mine. This is my territory. You want turnip tops, you go somewheres else. This corner's mine."

"I don't want what's in the barrels," Jo replied.

"Then whatcha doing here?"

"Just watching."

The woman spit on the ground. "Watch all you like, but you touch what's in them barrels and I'll tear your hair out," she threatened.

"I won't go near them," Jo replied. She fumbled in her purse, searching for her pad and pencil. "Darn!" she swore. The pencil was broken.

"What you doing there?" the woman asked. Her belligerence was obvious, and Jo took a step away from her, holding her purse protectively.

"I ain't no mugger," the woman said, scowling.

"I didn't think you were. Why are you here? What do you want that garbage for anyway?" It was, she decided, time to take the offensive.

"Turnip greens ain't no real garbage. White folks,

they throws out more than they eat. Look, Miss Priss, I got five younguns to feed, and I don't make a whole bag of cash scrubbing floors nights, so I come down here to get the greens. This is my corner, but I'm not alone. Lots of us come down here. Food's food, and who cares if its got a couple of rotten spots on it, or even a worm or two."

Jo nodded and silently cursed her broken pencil. The woman's language was worth quoting; she only hoped she could remember her words. This, she thought, was why David had sent her here. He had sent her to see what he called "Chicago's underbelly." He was always saying, "There's a whole other world out there, one most people don't see." Jo studied the woman for a moment. She didn't seem so angry now, but Jo sensed she was proud. Too proud to accept money or even breakfast. "I want to talk to you," she said boldly.

"Thought that's what we was doin'," the woman replied.

The truck pulled away, and the men who had been unloading the produce disappeared into the giant warehouse. The woman moved quickly away from Jo and hurried toward the barrels that lined the sidewalk. Jo followed cautiously and stood a few feet away as the woman poked and prodded with a long stick, withdrawing her treasures and stuffing them into a paper shopping bag.

"Got to get it while it's fresh, before the vermin at the bottom of the barrel get their nibbles," the woman advised as she withdrew a wilted cabbage with brown outer leaves. "See, just peel it away a bit, and I got the makings of a good soup here."

Jo waited and watched. The woman filled two bags from four of the barrels, then turned and began walking down the street. Jo hurried after her. "Do you come every day?"

"Three days a week."

"Could I come home with you?"

The woman stopped short and stared at her. "Why? Ain't you got nothing better to do?"

"I'm a writer. I want to write a story about you."

The woman swore under her breath. "So's people can feel sorry and give charity?"

"No. So people will know more about how others live. I want to know more about you. I won't even use your real name."

The woman spit again. "Good thing. I've done forgot what my real name is, honey. You want to write, you write. Come on, I'll show you something, I'll show you things your pretty eyes done never seen."

"Do you have a husband?" Jo asked as they climbed the stairs of an ugly South Side tenement.

"Oh yes. I got me a man, how else you think I got kids? He doing time on a chain gang down in Louisiana. Don't figure we'll ever see him again."

She opened the door and ushered Jo into a dingy dark room that reeked of urine and dampness. "I come up North four years ago with the younguns to find me a better life," the woman said, shaking her head. "But it's worse here. It's hard times here, and it's unhealthy." She flailed at the darkness and Jo shivered as she heard the skittering of mice. She braced herself as the woman lit the lamp. There were, she thought, even refugees in America. She wondered if her father had known about them.

Hours later Jo sat at the small desk in her apartment and worked on a feature about the garbage lady.

"Readers have to be made to cry," David had told

her when he read the first draft. "This is just a bit too much of a cry for justice. I want to see more about the rats, the hunger, the crying kids. I want you to describe the woman's haunted eyes and quivering lips."

"It seems wrong to exploit people like this," Jo countered.

"The hell it is. What do you think forces politicians to change laws? I'll tell you, it's a lot of crying citizens. Now, look, this woman is only one of hundreds in this position. When you write the story, you have to make that clear. You have to use one pitiful specimen because you can't rouse any sympathy for a crowd."

He was right, of course. He was always right. Sometimes he tore her writing apart and chastised her for not using words that were emotionally laden. He paced up and down in back of her, making her work faster and telling her she had to learn to write under pressure.

"When you write -30- under a story, that's not meaningless, toots. It means thirty minutes to press time. It means pressure, and it means perfection. Once the presses are wet, the front-page stories have to be ready to go. Wet presses cost money. Nobody waits—you gotta be able to write standing up, sitting down, in noise, in craziness, and in all kinds of confusion. You gotta think on your feet and move! And remember this: There are five other papers in Chicago. To make money, we have to sell more. To sell more, we have to have the fastest, lastest news. We have to have the most sensational stories. More gore, more death, the biggest disasters, that's what sells, that's what keeps us working. If a ship sinks and one paper headlines '100 People Killed' and we headline '101 Killed,' we'll sell more."

She had argued, but he told her she was too academic.

"When I read that story, I want to cry or curse or

gasp. This is a sob story, so make me cry, lay it on," he had countered.

Jo started at the knock on the door. She pulled her blue bathrobe around her. "Who is it?"

"Just me," David's familiar voice answered.

Jo opened the door. "I wasn't expecting you tonight."

David grinned and semi-lurched into the apartment. "I was researching a story, but I finished early."

"You've been drinking," she said. David, she acknowledged, drank quite a lot, but he had explained that sometimes he had to: it was necessary to drink with people in order to get information from them.

"Celebrating," he said with a grin. "Celebrating the beginning of a good story. Look, child, I've got all the facts here, but I have to finish my feature story for tomorrow, so I don't have time to work them up. How you coming with the 'City Scape' piece—the one you latched onto this morning."

"I'm almost finished."

"Good. You think you could take my notes and work this up?"

"Tonight? I've been up since three A.M."

"Yeah, should put it to Kahn tomorrow. Little bastard."

Jo raised her eyebrow. "I think he's really quite nice."

"Then you're not a very good judge of character," David slurred.

"I think you're drunk," Jo said without rancor.

David waved his finger at her. "Don't mother me, and I may be a little tipsy, but I still know a good story when I smell one." He withdrew his notes from his pocket. "Can you read my writing?"

"Of course."

"Then just be a good girl and work these up. Old

David will go upstairs and have some black coffee and get to work on tomorrow's feature."

Jo smiled. "Sure," she said, kissing his cheek lightly.

"You're a good kid," David allowed, "a really good kid, and I take advantage of you. Still, you gotta learn to work long hours. Reporting isn't a nine-to-five job."

"So I'm finding out. Now, go on, go get some coffee."

David waved and headed for the stairs. Work? Coffee? Why drink coffee when he still had a half-finished bottle under the sink? Yeah, the hooch at O'Malley's had dimmed his mind, but his own good stuff would clear it. O'Malley's had sure gone downhill since the boss bought a one-way ticket to the promised land, he thought ruefully. "I'll finish my feature in the morning," he promised himself. "All things in good time," he muttered.

———

Ted Kahn leaned against the floor-to-ceiling bookshelf in the Book Nook and watched the girl at the cash register. It was Jo Gregory. She was dressed in a light ivory suit with a wide collar and a long straight skirt. The collar and cuffs were trimmed in a rich dark braid that matched her little helmet-style hat, her leather bag, and her shoes. His eyes fell admiringly to her trim ankles, then rose slowly until they settled on her short, loose hair. He smiled to himself. In all the time he had worked on the paper, he had never run into another employee in the Book Nook, or any other of his bookstore haunts for that matter. He watched as Jo opened her purse and paid for two books. She was some looker, and for some reason she looked better today than she did on most working days. For one thing, she was dressed to the nines. He conservatively estimated that

her suit must have cost at least twenty dollars, and he
wondered how she could afford to dress so well on her
salary. Maybe, he thought, Driscoll kept her. He shook
his head as if to dispel the thought, which he found
oddly unpleasant.

Hands in his pockets, he gave up his vantage point
and strode to the cash register. "Hi," he greeted her
with a broad smile. "I didn't know anyone else on the
World read."

Jo turned to him and smiled. "Oh, I didn't see you."

He silently conceded that her eyes were simply magnificent, and he wondered how old she was. "Come in
here often?"

"Almost every Saturday afternoon."

"Me too," he said. "You look all dressed up. Are you
meeting someone?"

She blushed slightly and shook her head.

"Pity to be all dressed up and have nowhere to go.
How about catching a matinee with me?"

Jo looked into his eyes and tried to compose herself.
For some reason, she felt flustered and slightly tongue-
tied. "I'm afraid I have work to do later," she told him.

"Well, how about a coffee, then? Come on, you can't
say no to that."

He winked at her and she felt her face grow warm.
He was flirting with her and she couldn't think how to
respond. "I guess I can't," she gave in. He waited while
the clerk put her two books in the bag; then he took her
arm and led her out of the store. Jo felt the strength of
his arm against hers and she gave in to the mild pressure as he guided her across the busy street. She was
five-foot-six, and her head was more or less level with
his shoulder. He was wearing a summer suit, and she
couldn't help thinking that he looked a bit like a college
boy dressed up. His face was youthful, and his thick

dark hair was totally unruly, which added to the illusion. He had a strong square jaw, and something in his stride and manner reminded her of Krikor Berberian, the young warrior she had idolized in her childhood.

"What did you buy?" Ted asked casually as he opened the door of the coffee shop for her.

"Oh, just two novels. *The Rise of Silas Lapham* by Howells and *Sister Carrie* by Dreiser. Have you read them?"

"Sure. Are you taking a course on the pitfalls of industrialization?"

"No," she answered, laughing lightly. Ted pulled out a chair for her and she sat down.

He leaned across the table. "That's a lovely suit. The color goes well with your hair."

Jo blushed. "Thank you. I made it."

"Made it? You mean you sewed it?"

Jo laughed again. "Of course. Clothes are expensive. I don't make that much."

"I know," he said, raising his brow slightly. "Maybe we should do something about that."

Jo looked down at the checkered tablecloth. "I don't know exactly what to say. You are my boss, more or less."

"More than less," he replied jauntily, then added, "but this is my day off too."

The waitress came and Ted ordered two coffees. "Driscoll's your boss too. Does it bother you to have coffee with him?"

Jo shook her head. "No." She wanted to add: Because he treats me like a student and you treat me like a woman. But she couldn't say that even though it was what she suddenly felt. His eyes seemed to be devouring her, and though she found him extremely good-looking, his flirting made her feel ill-at-ease. Then too,

Ted Kahn was much closer to her own age. David was over forty, and Ted was not yet thirty.

"Well, don't be ill-at-ease with me either," Ted said. "Just because I find you devastatingly attractive, slightly mysterious, and generally intriguing is no reason for you to feel uncomfortable."

He winked again and Jo wasn't certain if he meant it or whether he was teasing her. In spite of her life at the Gaiety, her own experience with men was close to nil. Of course the men in the city room all teased her, but she knew they didn't mean it. Ted, on the other hand, looked almost serious, and she felt suddenly panic-stricken by his boldness.

"I'm not really mysterious," she countered.

"Sure you are. How many women go to school nights? How many want to be journalists? You work hard, I've watched you. Most women want to get married and have children."

Jo shook her head. "No, that's not what I want."

"You mean that's not what you want now. You're young, you'll change your mind."

"I don't think so. I'm determined to write."

He pressed his lips together and nodded. "Are you tough enough for this business?"

"I think so," she answered, thinking of Antoine.

The waitress came with their coffee and Ted studied Jo. Maybe it was just as well that she was rejecting his advances. He was city editor and he supposed it wasn't a good idea to get involved with the staff. Still, he felt drawn to Jo and he knew he wanted to get to know her better. "Driscoll treat you all right?" he queried.

"David's very good to me," she answered without hesitation. "He helps me with my writing."

Ted nodded. He wondered what else Driscoll helped her with. She appeared ladylike and reserved, but she was a looker and he couldn't imagine that Driscoll could ignore that. He was too much of a womanizer. Ted smiled at his own condemnation. Hell, he was a womanizer too. "How are you at research?" he asked casually.

"I like it," she answered.

He reached across the table and squeezed her hand. "I'll keep that in mind."

Jo knew her mouth opened slightly as his warm hand covered hers. She felt herself shiver, but she couldn't move. It was as if she were absolutely paralyzed. He lifted his hand and checked his watch. "I've got to run, otherwise I'll miss the matinee. Sure you won't come?"

"I really can't," she stumbled.

He took out some coins and put them on the table. "See you," he said as he casually got up and left, waving to her from the door.

Ten

Ted Kahn looked out across the city room with growing irritation. Then, for the third time in as many minutes, he checked his watch. It was ten-thirty and all the stories for the afternoon edition were on his desk, except Driscoll's daily feature. He cursed. Driscoll, of all people, knew this edition went to bed at noon. The feature had to be in typeset by ten.

He tapped his fingers on his oak desk and then without hesitation strode to the door and opened it. Jo Gregory was at her desk, pencil in hand and a pile of papers in front of her. She was wearing a plaid skirt and a little white blouse with a tie. Her dark blue jacket was casually slung over the back of her chair. "Jo!"

Jo looked up and then stood. She hurried toward Ted Kahn's office. "Yes."

Her large dark eyes were questioning and he couldn't help thinking she looked troubled. "Do you know where Driscoll is?"

Jo averted her eyes. "He was working on a very important story the last time I saw him." It was the best

she could do under the circumstances. She hadn't seen
or heard from David since last night.

"Great," Ted grumbled. "This edition goes to bed in
an hour and a half, and Driscoll hasn't handed in today's feature column. As of this moment, his space
allotment is empty. Do you have any idea what that
means?"

Jo stared at him. She had assumed David had dropped
off his copy earlier. Her mind raced. David usually left
notes in his top desk drawer. Could it be there? Then
she thought about the feature she had written a few
days ago. The feature about the woman she'd met at the
produce market. She had rewritten it twice, and she
wondered if it was good enough. But how could she
tell? David hadn't read the final draft, and certainly he
hadn't seemed satisfied with the first draft, which he
had read in the afternoon. Jo looked again at Ted Kahn's
angry face. Surely, she rationalized, at this stage something was better than nothing. "I have one of his features, but I'm not certain it's in final draft," she lied.

"Well, bring it in here," Ted said anxiously.

Jo darted to her desk and back. Should she give Ted
Kahn this story before David had read it? Even though
David seemed to be making few changes to her stories
lately, she felt nervous and self-conscious as she handed
Ted the feature she had prepared for David.

"You look like a ghost," Kahn said as he took the
sheaf of papers she handed him.

"I didn't sleep well last night," Jo said hesitantly.
David didn't like Ted Kahn, she knew, though she
couldn't imagine why. Perhaps Ted Kahn didn't like
David either. Thoughts of David losing his job ran
through her head. She had no choice except to turn
over this feature, she told herself. Surely giving Ted

this story was the best way to protect David, who was, as far as she knew, out covering another story.

"I'll get right on this," Ted told her. "Look, go back to work and try to find Driscoll."

Jo nodded and went back to her desk. She sat down and anxiously began calling the numbers David had casually labeled "In case I'm needed." She felt a strange combination of elation, fear, and anger. Elation that she'd written a story on her own and had the courage to hand it in, fear because she knew David might well lose his job, and anger that he hadn't at least called in to say where he was.

Ted slumped into his chair. Pencil in hand he began reading. He nodded to himself, and made a few editorial changes. It was a heartrending story, a perfectly good feature. If it was ready, why hadn't Driscoll handed it in? He reread it again. There was something about the style . . . something almost feminine.

Abstractedly he looked up and saw that Jo was on the telephone. His eyes returned to the story and then he looked up again. Was it possible that she had written it? Something didn't ring true. It didn't sound like Driscoll. Then he thought with more concern: Nothing Driscoll had done lately sounded like him.

Ted stood up and walked to the door again. "Jo!"

Jo darted to his office like a nervous bunny. Her large dark eyes looked even larger than usual, and her expression was tense.

"I'm not an ogre," he said, smiling.

Jo looked at him uncomprehendingly.

"Look, the story is fine. I'm sending it to be set."

The relief that flooded her face was so obvious that Ted nearly said: Your story is fine. But he restrained himself. He hardly knew her, and he didn't really know what her relationship with Driscoll was. For all he knew, they were lovers, though he hoped not. And he had no proof that what he was thinking was true.

"Have you found Driscoll yet?"

"He's on his way in," Jo said in a near-whisper.

Ted nodded. "Care to grab a bite of lunch with me?"

"Yes, all right," Jo floundered. Her mind was a million miles away. She had told David on the phone that she had handed in her story, and his only response had been a sleepy "Swell, that's okay, don't worry about it. Had to give him something."

What in heaven's name was he doing home in bed at this hour? He should have been in the office by eight at the latest. Home had been the last place she had expected to find him, but she had phoned his apartment out of desperation.

Ted Kahn was putting on his jacket. "You want to get your coat?"

"Coat? Oh, yes." She picked up her jacket. Why did he want to go to lunch with her? What on earth were they going to talk about? She didn't want to talk about David, for fear of getting him into trouble.

"You're not eating," Ted Kahn commented as he looked at her relatively untouched roast-beef sandwich.

"I guess I'm preoccupied."

He smiled. "All writers are preoccupied. Are you working on something?"

"Yes, but it's not very good yet."

"Is David helping you?"

"Yes, he's very kind, you know."

"Have you known Driscoll long?"

"For years," she answered vaguely.

Ted raised an eyebrow. "What are you, eighteen, nineteen?"

Jo inhaled. It was like an inquistion. "Eighteen, almost nineteen. I've known David since I was a child."

"Ah, a friend of the family."

"Yes," she lied. "He's always been like a big brother to me."

Ted nodded and bit into his sandwich. He guessed that meant they weren't lovers, and somehow that knowledge was encouraging. Driscoll had seemed all right for a while, but in the last few days he seemed to be headed downhill. It would be a pity if he took anyone with him. "Have you got a boyfriend?"

Jo stared at the tablecloth. His line of questioning was further unnerving her. "No," she said firmly. "I only care about writing."

"Could I see some of your writing?"

She felt like saying "You already have," but she kept silent. "Sometime."

Ted Kahn sipped his coffee and thought. If he was right and she had written that story, and probably others, there was one good way to find out. He could take her away from Driscoll and give her a story of her own. It might, he reasoned, be worth the gamble just to find out. "I've been thinking about giving you an assignment," he hedged.

Her magnificent eyes looked up in surprise. "You're teasing me."

"I never tease. Give me a couple of days. I want to find the right kind of story. I won't have you writing right away, but I'd like to see you do some basic groundwork."

Jo actually smiled. "You know, I read all your stories from China and Japan. I felt as if I were there."

"Flattering the boss?"

She blushed again. "No, I didn't mean to do that."

He studied her for a long moment. She sure wasn't

like the other women trying to break into journalism. They were hard as nails. Jo was soft and hesitant, anything but strident. Yet he felt she had a kind of inner strength and single-mindedness. And he certainly couldn't fault her on the way she handled the guys in the office. She just laughed at them, and now she was laughing with them.

But there was her relationship with Driscoll. She must owe Driscoll in some way; that was the only explanation he could think of. And, he admitted, not only did he want to find out what she owed Driscoll, but he also wanted to get to know her better. "Why don't you wrap that up and take it back to the office," he suggested. "I have to get back, the proof pages will be in by one."

"Fine." Jo carefully wrapped her sandwich in her napkin. "I have work to do too."

" 'In Xanadu did Kubla Khan, a stately pleasure dome decree; where Alf, the sacred river, ran through caverns measureless to man, down to a sunless sea.' " David waved his hand expansively, indicating the city room. "Your Xanadu!" he exclaimed. "Hi, Kubla Kahn, I heard you missed me."

It was two-thirty, and David Driscoll stood in the door of Ted's office, a broad, jaunty, confident smile on his face. An impudent smile, Ted thought. The smile of an evil leprechaun. Of course, Driscoll was challenging him. "You missed your deadline, Driscoll."

"Yeah, well, sometimes more important matters take precedence. Anyway, you got my story, didn't you?"

"Driscoll, your daily feature goes on page two. It's supposed to be on my desk by ten, rain or shine, in sickness or in health. Your feature goes in a fifteen-inch column. As I know, you know, the A and B wire

stories are already in the paper. So, my man, if your
space allotment is empty, we have to fill it with stories
off the C wire. You know what kind of stories, Driscoll.
'Woman Finds Two-headed Calf in Kansas.' The *World*
is the second-largest paper in America. Our readers
don't expect, or deserve, fillers on page two. I don't
want this to happen again."

"I don't need a course in elementary journalism. I
teach one, you self-righteous son of a bitch!"

David leaned over, and Ted could smell the strong
odor of whiskey on his breath. He contemplated firing
him, but for the moment held his tongue.

"Look, I've been riding a humdinger, I've got the
first part here. I have to talk to you about it."

"Pull up a chair," Ted invited coldly. If they'd been
playing football, he'd have called this a diversion.

David slid the story across to Khan. "Peruse it first,
then we'll talk."

Ted read the head: "Building Collapse Due to Faulty
Construction." The story had to do with bribery of the
city's fire inspectors and it seemed to be fairly well-
documented. It indicated that the fire inspectors were
being provided with booze, women, and money to issue
permits without actually inspecting the premises, and
that bribery was also going on in other city permit
offices. The headline referred to one building that had a
weak foundation, and there were hints that another had
burned down because of faulty wiring. The story was
well-written and concise, and Ted reread it twice, certain that it had been written by the same person who
had written today's feature. He was just as certain that
person wasn't Driscoll. "You want to follow it up?"

"Of course," David said with irritation.

Ted rubbed his clean-shaven chin and nodded thoughtfully. "Call girls involved, right?"

"That's what it says."

Ted stood up and walked to the door of his office. "Jo, can you come in here, please?"

Jo looked up, and seeing David in Ted's office, approached with apprehension. She came into the office and stood by David.

"I see this as a piece that might take a couple of weeks to iron out. For that matter, it could take months. We can run this first section tomorrow, but we can't do more until we've fully investigated. It's not fast news, it's exposé, and we'll need lots of backup research. Maybe affidavits, that sort of thing. Are you familiar with this story, Jo?"

Jo started to look at David. She had written it last night from his notes. But David spoke before she could respond.

"She's read it."

"Good. I want you to work on it together. Driscoll, you handle the interviews at city hall and check out the bank accounts. I think you should also try to find the bootlegger and get a list of his deliveries. You'll take the byline on this initial story and on all the stories related to your areas. Jo, I want you to interview the call girls when Driscoll finds them. I think a woman stands a better chance of getting information from them. You'll take a research credit on the call-girl sections. Okay?"

Jo wondered why David was utterly silent, when she felt like singing. She was going to get a story! Ted hadn't been teasing her, as she had thought. "It's all right with me," Jo said, glancing at David.

"Me too," he said, standing up. "Come on, let's get to work."

Ted watched as they walked across the city room. Driscoll was cool, that he had to allow.

*   *   *

"It's wonderful," Jo said in David's ear. "Now we'll share a byline."

"Sure," David responded. "It's good."

SKIMPY BATHING SUITS BANNED FROM BEACH!
One-piece, low-cut female swimming attire has been forbidden by a Chicago city police ordinance. Women's bathing blouses must have quarter-inch sleeves and their bloomers must be full and no shorter than nine inches above the knees. Stockings beneath the bloomers are mandatory.

Sammy the Cheese read the story aloud to the assembled men in the city room, and peals of laughter combined with shouts of "Now I'll never see her legs!" and "Hard to have your way with attire like that!"

"Our Jo would have looked good in one of those one-piece suits," Sammy declared with the appropriate leer.

"Will you model one for us in the city room, Jo?" Chubby Windsor yelled from his teletype machine. "We won't tell the cops!"

Sammy laughed. "Whoever heard of a woman exhibitionist being arrested!"

"You're all going to need a swimming suit if you don't get to work!" Ted Kahn bellowed from his office. "Windsor, get those late dispatches in here, will you?"

Chubby Windsor leaned over and scooped up the teletype paper that had tumbled out of the machine. He hadn't read the dispatches, but at this point it didn't matter. "Coming," he yelled back.

Jo rubbed her eyes, realizing how tired she felt. She and David had spent a week trying in vain to turn up some of the call girls involved with the bribes at city hall. In addition, the daily features still had to be done.

"That's the way it is," David declared with bravado. "Reporting is a full-time job, not a nine-to-five occupation." She could hardly disagree. David was handing her his notes and asking her to write the daily feature now. Moreover, he prodded her to keep turning out draft copy of magazine articles. Her days, she contemplated, were easily twelve hours long.

"Jo . . ." Ted Kahn came up behind her and she nearly jumped off her chair. "My, you are absorbed," he said with a wink. "Have you and David found any of the call girls yet?"

"David has a few leads," she hedged.

"Don't let him push you too hard. I told you, this is a research story. I'd rather have it right than fast. Besides, the story that just came in on the wires is going to wipe everything off the front pages for at least a week."

Ted handed her the wire-service story; it smelled of ink, and the paper was still warm: "100,000 Probable Death Toll in Tokio Quake—One Million Homeless— City in Flames."

"Oh, God," Jo said as she read the scant bulletin.

"We have a problem," Ted said, leaning a little closer.

"Can I help?"

"I think so. The truth is, we don't have anyone in Japan at the moment, but the *Tribune* does. He's a great fellow, one of their best reporters, a guy named Roderick Matheson. Now, if Rod is alive, he's going to get out a firsthand report and that's going to sell papers like mad."

Jo frowned. "We're going to send someone to Japan?"

"It's too late for that, but I have an idea. I'm going to pull you off everything you're doing—and I mean everything. Now, I won't pretend this is a plum assignment or that you'll get to write a story, but I am going to give you a chance to show me if you've got the right stuff to make a reporter. I need an accurate researcher, one who's willing to do a lot of legwork. Are you game?"

"Yes," she replied without hesitation.

"What I want you to do first is contact the State Department and get a list of every embassy-registered American in Tokio. That list is going to include Americans working in Japan, American naval personnel, embassy staff, consulate people, missionaries, and tourists. I want you to pull all the names from Chicago, and I want you to find their families and interview them. You'll have to find out about their fears and their apprehensions. You'll have to get them to contact you when they hear from survivors. I want you to start now. I want to wring the most out of our local stories, so get going, honey, and don't waste one single second. Use the teletype to get State in Washington. Chubby will show you how."

Jo hurried away toward Chubby. Her weariness seemed to have fled and she suddenly felt full of energy. Good coverage would mean help for the victims of the quake, and that was the plus side of the assignment.

Jo sent the first wire off to State and turned to Chubby. "How long do you think it will take to get an answer?"

"Couple of hours. These things take time."

"I'll be back," Jo told him as she quickly turned to leave. Her mind had suddenly fastened on an idea. When Ted had been in Japan, she recalled that he'd written a story on the Imperial Hotel in Tokyo. It had been built by sometime Chicago resident Frank Lloyd

Wright. As she recalled, Wright had proclaimed it "earthquake-proof." Jo headed first for the morgue to pull Ted's original story, then decided she would go after Wright for an interview. He was in town, that much she knew.

"Stories don't come to you . . ." David's words played in her mind as she searched the yellowed file copies of the *World*. No one had given her *this* assignment, but she felt certain Ted Kahn would use it, if she could pull it off. And certainly if she hurried, she could do the interview and be back in time to start running down the names on the list provided by the State Department.

Jo scribbled quotes from Ted's original story, then found the recent "Who's in Town" column that mentioned Wright was visiting friends in Oak Park. She hurried out of the newspaper morgue blinking in the sudden sunlight. I won't call, she decided. I'll just go.

Jo waited in the well-appointed study of the house in Oak Park. She was grateful for the fact that although she had been tired when she arose, she had taken the trouble to wear her light brown suit and autumn-gold overblouse. Her hat, gloves, and sensible shoes made her look like a reporter even if she was here of her own accord and about to conduct her first interview.

Frank Lloyd Wright was in his mid-fifties; he had a weathered face, thick white hair, and, Jo noticed, enormous strong hands that gesturered expressively as he spoke.

He removed his glasses and studied her press card. "Jo Gregory," he said in his flat Midwestern drawl. "Do sit down, Miss Gregory. What might I do for you?"

"I should have called first, Mr. Wright, but it was quite urgent, so I simply decided to take the chance that you would be here and willing to speak to me for a few minutes."

"When I give interviews to the press, my secretary usually makes the appointments in advance."

"No one else has been in touch with you, then?"

He frowned. "About what?"

"There's been a terrible . . . no, devastating earthquake in Toyko. The first wire-service stories just came in"—she glanced at her watch—"a little over an hour ago. They indicate that at least one hundred thousand people have been killed."

Wright looked down at the blue Persian carpet and shook his head sadly. "It's the construction, you know. The houses are practically built of paper, there's no foundation, no steel beams for support. And so close together, you can't imagine. Tokyo is like a house of cards, and when there's a quake, they just come tumbling down. That's what causes deaths, that and the fires that follow."

Jo scribbled furiously on her notepad. Then she looked up. "Mr. Wright, last year you gave an interview to one of our reporters who was in Japan, Ted Kahn."

Wright nodded. "I'd just finished the Imperial Hotel. If I do say so myself, it's the best work I've ever done. But it was a hellish job, absolutely hellish. Just couldn't get the workmen to understand the necessity for the proper types of beams and support."

"But you did. I mean, it is earthquake-proof, isn't it?"

"I'd wager that if every building in Tokyo has fallen down, the Imperial is still standing."

"May I quote you?"

"Certainly. Look here, young lady, if you're going to do a story, you'll need some technical details. Now, I have some information on the Imperial Hotel construction, and I have a paper on earthquake-proof construction." Wright had stood up and was rummaging through the desk. "Yes, here we are. You take these so you'll be sure to get the details right."

"Thank you so much."

"I like to further press accuracy." He grinned. "Strange no one else has tracked me down. Are you the early bird who's found the worm?"

"I think so."

"You do seem very nervous. Is this by chance your first story?"

Jo blushed and nodded.

"Well, first come, first served. Shall we make it an exclusive?"

"An exclusive?"

"Well, why not? I'll simply decline to talk to anyone else. Actually, I'm very busy today in any case."

"Thank you for taking the time to talk to me."

"Not at all, not at all. Go back to your paper and write that Frank Lloyd Wright says the Imperial is still standing."

Jo smiled and bid Mr. Wright goodbye. Mentally she was already writing the story. She wagered she'd have it done before the State Department answered.

"What's this?" Ted Kahn leaned over her desk as Jo paused between phone calls to those on the list provided by the State Department.

She looked up into his eyes and smiled broadly. "It's an interview with Frank Lloyd Wright. He gave it to me this morning. It's an exclusive."

"Bright idea. Why didn't you suggest it to me?"

"Because you would have sent a more seasoned reporter."

"Damn right, honey. I would have sent someone who knew how to do an interview."

The smile faded from her face, and she felt defensive. Sometimes the other guys called her "honey," but when Ted said it, it seemed to have sexual connotations. What's more, she knew the interview was good. "There's nothing wrong with that interview," she said firmly.

Ted laughed, and touched her shoulder. "It's sensational and it's going on page two. I suspect you'll get a byline as well. It's nice to know you have personal ambitions and initiative."

"What made you think I didn't?" Jo queried, still feeling irritated.

Ted shrugged and avoided the question. "It's getting late, and that's going to take you a long time. Shall I send down for some sandwiches?"

Jo started to dial another number on her long list. She nodded.

"Where have you been?" David questioned when Jo got home at midnight. "God, we've got three stories and two supplement articles to write."

"I can't," Jo said softly. "I don't think I can focus my eyes anymore tonight."

David was sprawled on her couch, a whiskey in one hand, a cigarette in the other. "Surely you realize there are deadlines to meet?"

Jo nodded. "Ted pulled me off everything to cover the earthquake—I've been running all day, David. I did an interview with Frank Lloyd Wright, and I've been checking lists from the State Department. I can't move."

David frowned at her. Her eyes were red and she looked dead tired. "Big story," he said sarcastically.

"What a great headline, 'Tokyo Destroyed, Chicago Man Breaks Arm.' "

"I don't think you understand."

"Don't understand? The hell I don't understand. Rod Matheson is in Tokyo and Khan isn't. We haven't got a story, so we're inventing one. And he's put you on it so you can't help me. I'm loaded down, and he takes you away so I'll fail." David gulped down his whiskey. "Frank Lloyd Wright? Boy, we in Chicago sure need to know about earthquake construction. We have so many."

Jo pressed her lips together. "David, it's an important story. I don't think Ted would give me an assignment to deliberately hurt you."

"You don't think! That son of a Hebe is out to get me."

Jo walked over to the sofa and sat down. "David, you're tired too." She meant "drunk," and she wondered what he'd been doing all evening while she was working. He didn't look well, he had been drinking heavily, there was no question about that. She was beginning to notice that he was always more belligerent when he drank. "I think you should get some rest," Jo suggested.

He looked into her concerned eyes and felt like crying. God! He was using her. In the beginning he had done a few rewrites on her work, but after her first month on the paper he hadn't done more than change a few words. Yet he still took the credit for the stories they sold to the magazine supplement, and he still took half the money. Now he hadn't written spit in weeks, and she was doing all the work. "Why don't you leave me?" he slurred. "Old Ted will take care of you. More your age too, and he sure is after you, there's no doubt about that!"

"What are you talking about?" Tears flooded her

eyes, tears that were as much a result of her weariness as her reaction to his sudden attack. "I wouldn't leave you. I wouldn't ever leave you."

"You ought to. I use you." He stared into his drink. "I've got writter's block. It happens sometimes. I've got the facts, I just can't work them up into a story!"

Jo reached out and put her hands on the side of his head. He looked as if he was going to cry, and she herself couldn't stop. "David, Ted isn't interested in me, and I'm not interested in him. I love you, I've loved you since I was a little girl."

"Love?" He looked at her through alcohol-dulled eyes. "I love you too, honey. Like a sister, is that good enough?"

Jo nodded. She could never explain it to him, or to any man, but it *was* good enough. It was love as she wanted it for now. Love on a plane above physical contact. They shared affection for each other. It was enough, it was beautiful. She leaned over and kissed him tenderly on the forehead.

"Sorry," he muttered. "But I need you. I need you till I can get back to writing. It's my book," he said, making reference to the book he had vowed to write but for which he'd produced only ten pages. "That's the whole trouble. I'm blocked, I can't concentrate."

"David, I'll get up early tomorrow morning and I'll put the daily feature together before I go in. Ted's put the exposé on hold, and the magazine articles will wait for a few days. David, just make the notes. I'll put them together."

He nodded dumbly and slipped into a drunken and troubled sleep on the sofa.

Jo covered him with a blanket and went into her small bedroom. She undressed, turned off the light, and fell into bed. For a few minutes she stared at the ceiling. Shaded neon light, partially blocked by the building next door, played on the walls, casting shadows, in subdued greens and reds.

Poor David, she thought. He seemed so frustrated and angry, but she thought underneath it was really bewilderment. His quick changes of mood, his confusion, even his heavy drinking must be caused by his block. I'll just have to help him, she vowed, closing her eyes. The only question was, when was she going to find the time?

———

The weeks of September flew by, giving way to October. Clouds blanketed Lake Michigan almost every day. Heavy and rain-laden, they reached toward the northern horizon. The cool autumn winds swept around the corners of the buildings, a warning of the horrific winter to come.

The Japanese earthquake had held the headlines of the city's dailies for the entire month of September. As it turned out, several hundred local residents had been in Japan. Jo's first set of stories involved the hopes and fears of their relatives, her second string of stories reported on the injured and the survivors, and her third round presented personal interviews with those who returned.

She also did two subsequent follow-up interviews with Frank Lloyd Wright, because true to his prediction, the Imperial Hotel was one of the few surviving buildings in the devastated city.

All the work was worth it, Jo thought. The people of Chicago donated hundreds of thousands of dollars to earthquake relief, tents for the victims to use as shelter, and vast quantities of medical supplies.

"You've done a terrific job," a pleased Ted Kahn told her. "And don't think that I don't know that this kind of story is ninety percent perspiration—chasing down lists of names, selecting individuals, making them real for the reading public. You've been a real go-getter, Jo. You're a natural writer and you're a fine reporter with a nose for the human side of a story."

Jo accepted the compliment in spite of the fact that his compliments caused her to feel embarrassment. Over the past month she had seen real evidence that Ted Kahn was well-organized and an excellent city-desk editor. He knew when to praise and when to chastise. He knew when to talk softly and when to raise his voice. She judged him to be extraordinarily well-balanced in his work. He had a solid knowledge of the technical aspects of production, as well as considerable creativity. Moreover, he worked hard himself, and in so doing, inspired those who worked with him and for him. This, Jo thought, was the secret of good management. If the boss was seen to be doing nothing, the employees felt free to laze about too. Buy when the boss was dead tired and putting in long hours of overtime, everyone did likewise without complaint. Mike Hamilton had been the same way, she thought. But Mike Hamilton was older, and he lacked Ted's youthful energy and drive.

Ted, she admitted, was also good-looking and charming. David believed Ted was interested in her, and he sometimes harped on that theme, much to her annoyance. Jo herself wasn't sure, but she did feel that Ted's praise for her work was honest and not inspired by personal motives to win her attention.

It was after seven in the evening, and the day staff had filtered away, though Axel Dan McGrath still sat at his cluttered desk marking up his racing form. The night staff, those who would finalize the early-morning edition had not yet come in. These were the twilight hours in the paper's day, the time when the usually frantic city room was deserted, its inhabitants having gone to a speakeasy or to dinner. The typewriters were silent, a breeze blew through the open windows and cleared away the day's smoke, and papers rustled beneath weights placed on them. Occasionally the teletype machine would begin typing out a dispatch of its own accord, sending a ghostlike reverberation through the silence.

Jo cleared her desktop and put her personal belongings in a drawer. She glanced toward Ted's office, and to her surprise, saw that he was standing in the doorway.

"Jo . . ." he motioned toward her, and shouldering her bag, she walked toward him.

"In a hurry?" he asked.

She shook her head, and followed him into his office.

Ted sat down and reached for one of his pipes. He leaned over the ashtray and banged the bowl against the glass side of the receptacle. Then he cleaned it out, using a pencil. "You leave a neat desk," he commented offhandedly.

Jo sat down and watched as Ted packed new tobacco from his pouch into the bowel of his pipe. He then lit it, and sweet-smelling smoke billowed into the air. "You want to talk about my desk?" she asked, a bemused expression on her face.

"Hardly. It's just that I so seldom get the opportunity to talk to you at all. Usually you run off with Driscoll after work, and during the day this place has all the peace and quiet of a riot."

Jo laughed softly. "It's nice now. This is my favorite time of day."

"I already told you you were doing a great job," he

said, "but I ought to offer you congratulations on another score," he added, looking into her eyes. "It's not easy being a woman in the city room. The language is rough, and the guys razz you a lot. But you seem to be able to take it. In fact, you've not only taken it, you've managed to remain every inch a lady, and that's even more difficult. Nobody's going to tell you, but in the last three weeks you've earned the respect of every guy out there."

"You're embarrassing me," Jo said slowly. "I only want to be a good reporter."

"You're well on your way."

Jo looked around furtively. Through the glass that enclosed Ted's office she could see that Axel Dan was totally absorbed, and she felt mildly relieved. Every time Ted took her aside, David complained. "He's showing favoritism toward you because you're an attractive woman." She argued, but to no avail. His accusations hurt her; she yearned for his approval, for his admission that she was doing a good job. But, she contemplated, she could never say that David's interest in her was motivated by her sex. He never attempted to seduce her; he always treated her with the greatest respect.

"Have dinner with me," Ted suggested as he relit his pipe.

Jo thought for a moment. David had said he wouldn't be back till late. She thought, and decided she wanted to have dinner with Ted Kahn, even though she knew it would cause an argument with David. She loved David, but surely that didn't mean she couldn't have other male friends. At various times other reporters had taken her to lunch and David hadn't complained. He certainly didn't complain when she went to the house on Erie Street and visited Harry Haskill. He only complained about Ted, but, she reasoned, he didn't have to know. "All right."

Ted nodded and looked pleased. "We can leave now," he suggested.

Ted watched as Jo went to get her coat. Every single day she perplexed him more, and increasingly he wondered about her relationship with the self-centered David Driscoll. He was now absolutely convinced that Jo Gregory had either written or rewritten every single story David had published in the last few months. Still, he held back from a confrontation with Driscoll, hoping that Jo would have her own confrontation and pull away from Driscoll of her own accord. She has ambition, he told himself. But she also has a feeling of strong loyalty to Driscoll. He wished he knew why, and he admitted that he wished it weren't so. This girl was getting to him, he decided. He felt strongly drawn to her even though he hadn't yet expressed himself.

Ted puffed on his briar pipe and watched the smoke rings curl in the air. His mother wouldn't like it, he thought. He could hear her now. "First you give up eating kosher, now you go out with a shiksa? There aren't enough nice Jewish girls in Chicago?" Then of course she would go on to lecture him on the sacrifices made for him. Papa wouldn't say anything; he wouldn't have to. He'd sit on the worn sofa and blink back tears at the very thought of intermarriage. Verbal guilt and silent guilt. No, his parents wouldn't be happy to know he was even mildly interested in a girl who wasn't Jewish. He watched as Jo came back wearing her tan coat. Mildly interested? No, he was more than mildly interested. She damn well looked like the kind of woman who could be both a wife and a mistress.

"Where are we going?" Jo asked as Ted's little black

Ford sped through the wide streets of the South Side
past low dull tenements, wagons full of merchandise
pulled by weary big-eared horses, and the smoking
chimneys of factories.

"To the Stockyards Inn," Ted answered. He turned
to look at her lovely profile and couldn't help thinking
that unless his mother was told, she wouldn't immediately know that Jo wasn't Jewish. Indeed, her thick
dark hair, her huge eyes, her soft golden skin, and her
most bedworthy figure all added up to classic Middle
Eastern beauty.

"That's a very expensive restaurant," Jo said in surprise. "I'm not dressed for a restaurant like that."

He half-smiled. She was wearing a soft champagne-
colored knit dress with gold earrings and a long gold
chain necklace. She looked stunning. "You look just
right. Besides, it's not that expensive. I've never been
there myself, and I've always wanted to go. Best steaks
in Chicago, or so they say."

They started to pass the endless miles of boarded
fence that marked the famous stockyards. Ted turned
slightly. "Did I ever ask you where your family comes
from?"

"Massachusetts," Jo replied slowly. No, she decided,
she wouldn't tell him she was Armenian. He would ask
her about the deportations and the massacres, and the
conversation would dredge up suppressed emotions and
memories. He would be sympathetic—wasn't everyone? She recalled a story in the paper only a few weeks
ago. "Washington Offers Sympathy to Armenians, But
No Action," its headline had read. The Russians had
taken over that part of her homeland that was now
within their territory, and some Armenians had protested and made representations to the U.S. government. Of course, there were others who had not. The

Armenian community was split, so split that there had
been an assassination of political leaders within the community. There were those who believed that Soviet
domination had to be accepted so that they would be
free to visit and communicate with their relatives. Others believed that Soviet Armenia should be free, and
they were violently anti-Communist. The fighting within
the community made her ill; in her view it accomplished nothing save further bloodshed. Furthermore,
Armenian immigration had been all but cut off by the
quota system. In the year she came, 1919, some five
thousand women and children had been allowed to
emigrate, but since then there had been only a trickle.
No, she wanted to forget the past. She had changed her
name before coming to work at the paper; no one
except David knew, and no one else had to know.

"Massachusetts," Ted repeated. "I mean before that."

Jo stared at the floor of the car. "Somewhere near
Russia, I think." Not quite a bare-faced lie. Her family
had come from Istanbul, but historically Armenia had
spanned the area that was now divided between Turkey
and the Soviet Union. The difference was, the Turks
had eliminated the Armenian population, while the Soviets had merely absorbed and suppressed them.

Ted turned the car down the road that led to the
Stockyards Inn. Not only wasn't she Jewish, she probably came from the Ukraine or maybe Ruthenia. Hard to
find an area of the world that was more anti-Semitic
than that which had once been part of the Austro-
Hungarian Empire. No, his mother and father would
not be pleased at all.

"I'm Jewish," he offered, just to test her reactions.

Jo smiled. "I know."

"I was actually born in Berlin, but my mother came
from Poland and my father was a German from Munich,

though a generation back, his family came from Poland too."

Jo turned to him in surprise as he pulled the car into a parking space. "I thought you were born here. I'd have never guessed you were born in Germany."

He laughed and playfully asked, *"Warum, meine Liebe?* Because I have no accent?"

"Well, you don't," Jo said with a smile. "Do you speak German?"

"Yes, and Yiddish, and a little Polish. But I was only five when my family came here. And speaking of accents, you don't have one either."

"Why should I?" she asked apprehensively.

"Most people from Massachusetts do."

Jo felt a surge of relief. He didn't know. Still, he was right. She certainly didn't have a clipped New England accent. Her tutor as a child had been a graduate of Oxford University, but in the orphanage she had been taught by Midwesterners, and that broad Middle American accent was the one that had stuck. In fact, she could easily have been a native of Chicago. "Oh well, I guess I've lost it," she replied with a smile. "I've been here for several years, you know."

An enigma, that's what she was. And how come Driscoll had known her for years if she came from the East? "You speak any Russian?" He could have said "Polish" or "Ukrainian"—her declaration that her family came from "somewhere in Russia" offered a variety of linguistic alternatives.

"A few words," Jo offered. "And I know the Cyrillic alphabet. My strongest language after English is French. Why?" She hated lying; her strongest language was Armenian, followed by Turkish, but she wasn't going to tell him, and she wished he would stop asking so many questions. It was like the day he took her to lunch.

"Languages can be an important asset in our business. French? Why French?"

"My father thought French was important." That much was true; it was important for an Armenian wanting to emigrate, and moreover, it was the second language spoken by most educated Turks. And thinking quickly, she added, "Worcester has a large French-speaking population, you know. The largest on this continent outside of Canada." She felt proud because she knew that was not a widely known fact, not even in Worcester. But it was true, and she well remembered the little Catholic church that served Worcester's French community. The French were, in fact, among Mr. Karpazian's best customers.

"Smart father," Ted said as he got out of the car and went around to open the door on her side. "Come on, let's go feast. I'm starved."

Ted took her arm and led her into the Stockyards Inn. Vaguely Jo felt a twinge of guilt. Would it be wrong to keep this evening a secret from David? Perhaps she was being childish. She decided she would probably tell him.

"Smells good," Ted said, looking around the large room. It was decorated in red velvet, had gleaming white tablecloths, and graceful chandeliers hung from the high ceilings. The waiters, all black, were dressed in spotless white uniforms with huge gold buttons. "Who'd have guessed this place existed in the middle of the stockyards," he said, squeezing her arm.

"I've never been in a place like this," Jo said in awe.

"And they say Chicago has no elegance!" He looked at her across the candlelit table and knew that his eyes revealed what he thought of her. Brains, beauty, and youthful enthusiasm—she had all three. But there was something else, something he couldn't quite define, an aspect of her personality he didn't understand. She appeared to be wiser and more compassionate than others her age. That dimension of her personality was revealed in her writing. He couldn't help wondering what mysterious experiences lay in her background that gave her that wisdom and compassion, and he wondered what lay behind her often sad eyes and serious expression.

11

Jo stood next to Ted Kahn on the steps of the Adler
Planetarium. It was a quiet, lazy Sunday afternoon, one
of many Sundays they had spent together over the last
eight months.

"It's pouring," she lamented. "We'll be soaked."

Ted shook his head and laughed. "No spring walk in
Grant Park today. How about grabbing a cab and heading over toward Michigan Avenue? I know a hole-in-the-
wall café that serves the best German pastry in Chicago."

Jo let him take her arm as they walked down the
slippery stone steps of the planetarium, both hovering
under her raised umbrella. "It's all wrong to leave the
peace of the night sky and come out into a spring
storm."

"Contrast—it's the stuff of life. I've always loved the
planetarium. Sitting back in those chairs relaxes me. It
allows me to let go and convince myself I'm out under
the stars, that I can nearly touch them." He turned to
look into her face. "How else can I spend a romantic
evening with a woman who won't go out with me except on Sunday afternoons?"

Jo caught the glint in his eye and blushed slightly, as she always did when he hinted that he wanted their relationship to be more than it was. "You know why it has to be Sundays," she replied.

"Because Driscoll sleeps it off on Sunday," Ted commented somewhat sarcastically. He whistled for a cab, and one pulled up in front of them. Jo jumped back slightly so as not to be splashed. Ted opened the door for her and she slid across the leather seat. He came in next to her and told the driver the address.

What he had just said was perfectly true. David did sleep most of Sunday, and it was the one day she set aside to see and know the city, to roam in bookstores and go to the museums. That's how she had begun seeing Ted. They had met accidentally one Saturday in a bookstore; sometime later he'd taken her to dinner, and then one Sunday, they met again. She had been looking for a used copy of Joesph Conrad's *Heart of Darkness*. They had talked, then he'd asked her out for coffee and they had talked some more. He'd been looking for *Lord Jim*, and it turned out they were both lovers of Conrad's work and style.

Gradually they had begun going out on Sundays. She enjoyed his company. Still, she hated it when he suggested there should be more. She hated it when he started talking about David.

"Want to take in a matinee next Sunday?" Ted asked, turning toward her. He smiled. "You have a raindrop on your nose."

Jo brushed her nose with her hand and laughed lightly. She could feel his leg against hers and could smell the sweet aroma of his pipe tobacco. At moments like this, she felt a strange and powerful attraction to Ted, but she fought it because it caused her to feel disloyal to David, who needed her so very much. She moved away from Ted, making more space between them in the backseat.

"You always keep me at arm's length."

"Ted, I can't get involved with anyone," she said softly, almost pleadingly.

He shook his head and held up his hands in surrender. "Just friends," he answered. "Scout's honor."

The cab glided to the curb and stopped. Ted paid the cabbie and helped Jo out. "Ever have fresh sweet apple strudel?"

Jo shook her head. "You love sweets and you eat too many of them," she admonished. Vaguely she thought how much he would like the kind of rich Middle Eastern pastries she knew how to make. Thin flaky layered crusts filled with honey and raisins.

"A passion for good chocolate and fine pastry runs in my family," he answered with a wink.

"I used to work in a bakery," Jo confided.

"Oh, you never told me that! I'm afraid that particular experience makes you even more desirable. Tell me, can you make strudel?"

Jo nodded. "I can even make marzipan."

"You're an angel," he whispered, squeezing her arm. "Too good to be true."

They sat down at a tiny table covered with a checkered cloth. "I'm afraid my ambitions don't include returning to the life of a baker."

He feigned a deeply disappointed expression. "Does this mean I'm never to sample your culinary skills?"

"You're teasing me."

"Not entirely, but I made a promise to restrict myself to being friendly, so I won't tell you how much I'd like to come to dinner."

Jo sighed. "Maybe sometime."

"When David's busy?"

"Perhaps," she answered, burying her face in the menu. Why did she always have such a good time with Ted? It had to stop. David was upset each time she went out with him. He ranted and raved at her; once, in a drunken fit, he had even called her a slut. "It's not so, it isn't," she had retorted. "There's nothing between us, nothing."

She thought of David and their relationship. More and more it troubled her. They worked on magazine articles and features. She continued to write them while David sold them. He was critical of her work and sometimes tried to belittle her. But he rarely changed anything. Increasingly his attitude annoyed her, and she felt angry that he still used his name on the magazine stories. Still, she put off talking to him about it because he continued drinking heavily and still complained of writer's block.

Not that there weren't moments of tenderness. Wonderful fun-filled moments when David was alive, happy, and full of charm. He took her out dancing, to theater clubs, and to jazz spots. He told jokes and stories that were truly entertaining, and for a while he seemed himself, he seemed the man she remembered knowing in Salonika. But David was a study in contrasts. He sometimes held her, he held her and wept with frustration because he couldn't write. Slowly, almost without realizing it, Jo knew she wanted more from their relationship. She began to suspect she wanted him to love her the way men should love women, and her own desires surprised and dismayed her simultaneously. Then, lingering on the periphery of her thoughts was the image of Ted Khan. She felt attracted to him too. She told herself she was drawn to his even temperament and that she admired his intellect. With David, life was a swirling turbulent whirlpool of conflict; with Ted she

felt at ease, calm, and yet sometimes she experienced
an undefinable excitement in his presence.

The waitress brought the strudel and coffee.

"You're very quiet," Ted observed.

"Lost in thought," she admitted. Then, returning to
the day's activity, "I really did enjoy the planetarium.
I've never had an experience like it. It was so real, just
like being in the desert and being able to see the whole
of the night sky."

Ted frowned slightly. "I've always lived in big cities
where the sky is invisible. When were you on the desert?"

Jo shrugged. "I didn't mean I'd been on the desert, I
meant that's the way I always imagined it would be,
you know, because the air is so dry and so clear."

"One day I'm going to find out you're the long-lost
daughter of an Arab sheik."

Jo laughed. "You're being silly." She glanced at her
watch. "Oh dear. It's almost four. I'm sorry, Ted, but I
do have to run."

Ted looked at his half-demolished strudel and nodded. "Next Sunday?"

Jo reached across the table and touched his hand. "If
you like."

Jo sat down in the empty el car and stared out the
sooty window. She shouldn't have accepted Ted's invita-
tion to the matinee next Sunday—she should have ended
it now. David, she told herself, would be angry. She
forced the thought out of her mind. On Friday he had
been buoyant and happy. She concentrated on that,
pushing away the other times—times when he was in
the depths of depression, times when he was morose
and cynical. At those times he drank to excess, drank
till the bottles were empty and until he couldn't stand
up. Sometimes when he drank, he was verbally abu-

sive; sometimes he was filled with self-pity. She hated
it when David drank, because he became another person, a person who was almost a stranger.

When he was abusive or unnecessarily biting in his
criticism, he came to her in the morning and begged for
forgiveness. "I'll stop," he promised. "I'll go back on
the wagon." Then he told her he loved her, respected
her, wanted only the best for her. He talked about the
reasons he couldn't set pen to paper, he told her he
needed her.

Love-hate. She loved David one way, and hated him
another. But she always forgave him, and when he held
her and promised it wouldn't happen again, she always
believed him and was filled with hope. It hadn't been
that long, she told herself. He needed to write; he
would be restored to his old self when he could write.

Jo arrived home and changed out of her damp clothes
into a warm bath robe. She lay on the sofa in the
semidarkness, imagining she was back in the planetarium looking at the stars.

"Jo!" David's familiar voice at the door roused her
from her thoughts.

She opened the door and forced a smile in spite of
the fact that he was carrying a bottle of whiskey. Still,
she hoped he hadn't started drinking yet, and in fact he
looked in high spirits. She knew that sometimes he
could drink and stay in a good mood. He did not, after
all, always fall into depression.

"I have it!" he said, encircling her waist with his arm.
"I've found a key!" He waltzed her around the room
and began singing. He was overjoyed, and with relief Jo
thought: it wouldn't matter how much he drank. He
would probably remain in a good mood.

"Have what?" she pressed.

"The key to the story that's going to blow this burg apart, sweetie! Remember, hey way back, remember the bribery story? Remember Kahn spiked it 'cause we couldn't find any of the girls?"

Jo frowned. It was a dead story. Ten months old. Ted had cast it aside because they hadn't been able to verify it. Still, if David had found a witness, one who would go into details, she was certain Ted would revive the story. "You've found something?"

Impulsively David kissed her cheek. "And it couldn't be better!"

"Tell me," Jo pressed.

"Found a girl . . . one of the call girls who has been used by the syndicate. She knows everything—how much was paid, what buildings were given lax inspections. Hell, there's a judge involved! A federal judge, at that."

"Will she come into the paper and tell her story?"

David leaned back on the sofa and put his feet up on the coffee table. He opened the whiskey bottle and took a long swig without bothering to ask for a glass. "Not for me, but she'll talk to you."

"Me? Why would she talk to me?"

" 'Cause she's your friend. Says she saw your byline and knows you work for the paper. Now, mind you, she hasn't said she would talk—she knows it's dangerous. But I think you can get to her, appeal to her better nature. You know, you can go and see her and push the woman-to-woman thing. She's the gal you used to live with, that cute little French broad. Marcella Something-or-other. Mind you, she's pretty banged-up. Somebody tried to bash her head in."

Jo felt herself pale. She stood up and reeled toward David. "Marcella?" she said in amazement. "Oh, David, no."

"Well, I'm not kidding. Started out as a hoofer and ended up working on the circuit for one of the mob bosses. I saw her myself. Somebody really messed up her face, but she still has her voice and memory. That makes her good for something."

Jo's hands covered her mouth. She felt like bursting into tears. "Don't talk that way! Marcella's my friend, she's—"

"Very valuable," David said tersely. "Look, I think you can go in and make her spill her guts to you, kid."

"Stop it!"

"What the hell is wrong? Where's my hard-nosed reporter? Where's the girl Ted Kahn puts so much faith in?" He looked and sounded irritated.

"David, I can't do it. If she names names, her life will be in danger. Look what happened to Antoine when he went after her. She's obviously been through hell. I can't put her through more. That's exploitative. I'd be using her."

David's face hardened. "Using her? For Christ's sake, how do you think I made it? I used you! Nice little girl in a refugee camp, no parents, witnessed a horror, saw her family killed. You were ready-made. And that, my dear, is exploitation. That's what this business is all about. It's about using people!"

"It isn't. It doesn't have to be that way. And you didn't use me, you really cared, I know you did."

"I used you then, and I'm still using you."

"That's because you have writer's block—"

"Don't make my excuses for me," David shouted. Then, almost dissolving, "I make enough of my own!"

"David, I love you, I want to help . . ."

"Love! Don't patronize me! Why the hell don't you fly into Ted Kahn's arms? I'm sure Teddy can give you what you need. If he hasn't already."

Jo felt herself begin to shake. His face was contorted with agony and anger. It welled up from somewhere deep inside of him like lava bubbling out of a volcano. She couldn't think what to say or how to answer. David was tormented. And it wasn't just her reluctance to talk to Marcella that had sent him from happiness into this tailspin, it was something deeper, something she didn't know about or didn't understand.

"Say something!" he bellowed. "Confess how you feel about Kahn. Tell me he makes love to you. Tell me you love him and want him. Tell me to get out! Don't just stand there staring at the carpet."

"I don't know what to say. I like Ted, I enjoy Ted. I love you—I know it's not the usual sort of love, it's something else."

"Damn right it's not the usual sort. If it were the usual sort, you wouldn't have your clothes on right now!"

Jo's lips parted in surprise. He had never spoken to her like this, and now she was certain he had been drinking before he arrived. She looked down, her face flushed, her eyes filled with tears. "I could take them off," she said in a whisper. "David, I do love you, I'd do anything . . ."

"Stop it! You're a child! I don't want you to do anything except talk to Marcella!" He covered his face with his hands. "I don't know what I'm saying or doing."

His features softened as rapidly as they had hardened. "I'm sorry," he muttered after a second. "But I still want you to get Marcella to talk and to sign the affidavits." He pressed his lips together. "Look, maybe we can make a deal with Kahn. Maybe the paper can provide her with protection and fork over some money so she can go someplace where she can have a decent life. Surely you want to help her? It's even possible we'll get the guys who killed that fag friend of yours, the hairdresser."

"Stop it! Antoine was a wonderful person."

David cursed. "Why can't I make you understand?" he shouted. "This is a big story. *The* big story!"

"I do, but if I write that story, I'll be profiting from Marcella's misery and Antoine's murder."

"If you don't like journalism, you should do something else. It's a blood business. It's all profit on misery. How much good news do we print, anyway? Didn't you profit from the victims of the earthquake in Japan? I know you didn't know them personally, but was that any different?"

"It doesn't seem the same. Besides, a lot of money was raised in Chicago for earthquake relief."

"And if you work it right, you could get Marcella off the streets and get a crooked judge locked up to boot."

"I want to think about it."

David took a gulp of whiskey. "Do that," he said firmly. "But don't think too long. Look, I'm tired, I'm going to bed."

Jo watched him as he lurched out the door, the whiskey bottle still in his hand. She leaned back and closed her eyes. She would talk to Marcella if protection could be arranged, she decided. She knew she would have to ask Ted in the morning.

Slowly her scene with David replayed in her mind. What had he meant by his comment about her clothes? Then she had made a fool of herself offering, and he'd rejected her. If David wanted a physical relationship with her, why didn't he say so? She shook her head wearily and thought again of Ted Kahn. The smell of his briar pipe and tobacco seemed to flood the room and she could almost feel his tweed jacket on her arm. Ted Kahn loomed in front her—tall, strong, and gently beckoning her toward him. In her imagination, he opened his arms and enclosed her, and she felt his strength and stability. Jo opened her eyes and shook her head. "David doesn't know what he wants, and neither do I."

At nine every morning, the editorial staff of the *World* had its budget meeting. "Budget" was the name applied to the meeting where space was allotted to various departments and stories. City Desk, National, and Foreign worked side by side, and usually there were few arguments. A foreign story might have local implications, as the earthquake had. The same was true of a story handled by national. The teletype was shared, and Chubby Windsor did rewrite for all three departments.

When there was an argument between the editors, it was usually an argument over the front-page space allotments. Yesterday, City had the headline and four columns on page one. The story was Jo's, and it was headlined "The Ladies at City Hall: Indictments and Enticements."

This morning, Ted wanted to continue her story, and he wanted it to remain front-page.

"You had the lead yesterday, Kahn," Ken Wilson, the editor of the national desk, argued. "Come on, it's a hot story, but it can move to page two. I've got the scandal in Washington. I'd like it up front."

"I want the city story to play front-page for another day," Ted said firmly. "Besides, the scandal revelations have been going on for months."

They had gone on arguing for an hour; then Mike Hamilton stepped in and settled it with a simple, curt, "The space goes to City. Next!"

Ted unfolded the paper and surveyed the proof pages with satisfaction. The story was a blockbuster, and it was Jo's byline.

Kahn glanced at Driscoll, who was slumped over his desk, phone in hand. He chastised himself for not taking the bastard on before. He'd certainly known for months that Jo was doing all Driscoll's writing, plus her own. But he'd let it ride, hoping she would of her own free accord stop propping him up. But now that Jo Gregory was a front-page property, he knew he couldn't wait for what might never happen. For whatever reason, Jo was too loyal to expose Driscoll. He himself felt no such compunction.

He glanced at his watch. The office was emptying out for lunch and Jo was out on assignment. Now, he reasoned, was as good a time as any. And certainly if he didn't catch Driscoll before lunch, he wouldn't catch him sober.

"Driscoll!" he shouted from his doorway.

David looked up, an annoyed expression on his face. He responded none too quickly. "What can I do for you, Mr. Kahn?" David asked sarcastically. "I'm on deadline."

Ted thought that Driscoll being on deadline was patently absurd. He couldn't produce anything because Jo wasn't here to write it for him. "You can come in and close the door."

"Oh, personal, is it?"

"Very."

David slung himself casually across the chair and stared at Ted. It was definitely a look that bore a challenge.

"I've been reading your features carefully for many months," Ted said slowly.

"And have you complaints?"

"Only one."

"Well, spit it out. I've got a story to work."

"You didn't write them," Ted said evenly.

David's face visibly paled and he straightened himself, puffed himself up, it seemed to Ted.

"What the hell do you mean by that!" David blustered.

"Exactly what I said. You didn't write them. Nor did you write a single one of the stories that have appeared in the supplement."

"Who did, the good fairy?"

"In a manner of speaking. Look, Driscoll, I know you don't like me, and up until now you haven't had a good reason not to like me. Today I'm going to give you reason. Jo Gregory wrote those stories and all your features. She's been covering your ass for the better part of a year. You think I'm young, gullible, and inexperienced. But regardless of what you think, I wasn't born yesterday. I can see the similarities in style and I sense the feminine touch. Those stories just aren't yours."

David blanched, but he didn't offer a denial. "What if they aren't?" he said, trying to sound casual. "The *World* is getting good copy. You've got no cause for complaint. Besides, a lot of the stories were my ideas."

Ted looked at him evenly. He felt like hitting him, but he gripped the desk and scowled. "Stealing someone's talent is the worst kind of theft. Driscoll, you're a cynical, burned-out drunk. And you're using that girl. I won't tolerate it. You're without ethics, and for all I know, without feeling. As for ideas, my friend, they're a dime a dozen. We don't pay for ideas, we pay for the men and women who can develop them. I know people who can't write their own names who have ideas. Ideas in and of themselves are not a salable commodity—you have to be able to bring them to fruition. As I said, you have no feeling for her; it comes down to that."

"I see you have plenty of feeling for her. You Yid bastard, I see through you! A knight in shining armor. Stand up for her, see she gets a good deal, and you think you'll be off to bed with her!"

Ted felt his face flush with anger. "If there's one thing I know about Jo, it's that she's a lady. I respect her."

David stood up. "You smart-ass rich Yid college kid! What do you know about the streets? What do you know about busting your ass getting a story? What do you know about the Irish and the prejudice we've had to endure? What the hell do you know about life? I didn't get put through a rich kids' school, you son of a Hebe. I learned journalism by inking the presses, running copy, and doing a damn good job. Well, I don't want to work for you. I don't want to work for this damn newspaper. I'm going away to write a book, and you can shove this job and your accusations!" David turned, spit on the floor, and stormed out of the office, slamming the door.

Ted inhaled and slumped into his chair. He shook his head. "Self-righteous bastard," he muttered. But it was all there, it was on the table like spilled coffee. Driscoll's bitterness still seemed to fill the office. It filled his ears. Prejudice against the Irish? Driscoll yelled one anti-Semitic phrase after another and then pleaded that he was a victim of prejudice? Rich? Not know the streets? Ted thought of his childhood and youth. Driscoll didn't know the half of it.

Ted Kahn shook his head. In fact, they probably had similar backgrounds, and he had no doubt they had similar experiences. Certainly his advantages in life were little different from Driscoll's. But advantages were only as good as what you made of them. Ted knew he'd made the most of one break he had received. Driscoll hadn't. He was self-destructive to the core.

Jo's head pounded, and her nostrils still seemed full of the anesthetic odor of Marcella's hospital room. It was a nightmare, and every time Jo looked at Marcella's swollen bandaged face, her mind traveled back to her own first day in Chicago. "There's a lot of evil in this town," the woman at Traveler's Aid had warned. Marcella, Jo thought, had found the evil. And so had Antoine.

Jo swung open the door of her apartment building and headed for the stairs. She ought to feel good that Marcella was leaving town with Harry Haskill and that she had received a new identity, money from the paper, and an opportunity to start over. But the idea that she herself had used Marcella lingered. Marcella's dream of becoming an actress had ended, and because it had ended, Jo's own dream of a front-page byline had been realized.

"David?" Jo tiptoed into her apartment and saw David's sleeping form on the sofa, curled in an embryonic position. An empty bottle of whiskey and a stained glass stood side by side on the coffee table.

Jo quietly opened her small closet kitchen and prepared a pot of coffee. Hearing her, David stirred on the couch, then, rubbing his eyes, pulled himself up.

"I didn't mean to wake you," she said hesitantly.

"I have to wake up to go to bed," he replied.

"You could stay there. I don't mind."

He touched the whiskey bottle and laughed. "No need to worry, I've slept it off. Drank that one for lunch."

She stood for a long moment and looked at him. "What's happened?" she asked.

"Ah, you didn't go back to the paper? You haven't heard?"

She shook her head.

"Kahn accused me of using you. Said you wrote all my stories. It's the truth, of course. I didn't deny it."

"Oh, David . . ."

"No need for an 'oh, David.' I quit. I resigned."

"You didn't?"

"I did, and I'm damn glad. I want to work on my book. I want to earn back my own self-respect. Look, you've made it. You're a name. I want you to write and publish your own stories and articles from now on. I went upstairs and talked to the people on the supplement. I told them everything. From now on, your credits are your own. I just want to devote myself to my book."

She looked at him in amazement. He seemed calm and he seemed sincere. "Are you sure?"

"I'm as sure as I've ever been of anything in my life. You stay at the paper, and don't stand there looking like the world has come to an end."

"David, I want to be with you."

"Who said you wouldn't be? I'll see you all the time. I do live upstairs."

Jo forced a smile. Maybe this would be good for him. Maybe if he worked on the book full-time he would be less given to swings in mood. Maybe, she reasoned, he would stop drinking if he felt he was under less pressure. She suddenly felt optimistic. "Will you still read my stories?" she asked, smiling. "I value your opinion, David."

He beamed and nodded. "Child, you're like a guardian angel, but David's used you, and he's not going to do that anymore. Sure I'll read your stuff, but it will go out under your name."

Jo poured a cup of coffee and walked over to him.

"Here," she said, offering it to him. "Have you got enough to live on?"

He nodded. "Sure. I've got a little salted away, and I have a small income from the farm in Hannibal. I'll survive, child." He stirred his coffee abstractedly. "Did I ever ask you why you stuck with me?"

"No."

"Tell me," he pressed. "My ego needs boosting."

Jo leaned back against the sofa. "You were there when I needed someone, so I'll be here when you need me. I love you because you don't make demands on me, because you make me laugh and you make me cry."

"You mean I don't make sexual demands on you."

"Yes."

David looked at her profile in the dim light. She was leaning back and her eyes were closed. She looked like an angel in repose. Tears started to form in his eyes. God, if only she knew how much he wanted to make sexual demands on her at this moment. His heart ached and longed for her. He could visualize making love to her, but he knew the reality would terrify him. He'd never had this kind of relationship with a woman before. She was no chippie, she was a virgin. And damn, she was just still too much of a girl. "You're young," he said hesitantly. "One day you'll want a man to make sexual demands on you."

She didn't answer him.

"I'm glad I make you laugh," he finally added. "Jo, I'll try to make you cry less often. I promise."

He leaned back too and put his arm around her slim shoulders. Her head rested gently on his arm and he could smell her hair. It was like a field of wildflowers in spring, fresh and comforting.

It's good, Jo thought to herself. Ted had forced David

into making an important decision, and she felt, considering the moment, that it was the right decision. David would be happy now, and with the pressures of the newspaper and its demands removed, he would be able to write again. She envisaged long evenings with him, happy evenings spent talking and laughing, going out, having quiet dinners. They would stimulate each other's creative talents. They would both be successful in their own right. David, she felt certain, would make it. And she vowed to help him, to take care of him, to ease his way in any way she could.

She imagined him as he was the first day she had met him. She thought of the happy hours they had spent in Salonika walking up and down near the ancient sea wall. She smiled to herself when she thought of Miss Spring and her crush on David.

Poor David, he was going through such a terribly bad period, but she would help him over it. He needed someone to care for him and about him. He needed her love. Jo closed her eyes and thought of Ted Kahn. Even though his argument with David had resulted in what she believed was a good decision, she felt miffed. Ted did hate David, and surely he had confronted him because of her. What right did Ted Kahn have to come to her defense in this way? What business was it of his? What indeed did he know about her relationship with David?

Jo stood framed in the doorway of Ted's office, her lips pressed together, her arms folded.

Ted looked up. "An avenging angel?" he said, lifting one eyebrow.

"I want to talk to you," Jo replied coldly.

"Good of you to wait till the city room is empty. Come on in, close the door."

Jo did as he asked, but she didn't sit down. "I thought you were a kind, sensitive person," she began. "I don't know how you could have done what you did! I was angry about it yesterday when David told me, but today was even worse. Everyone in the city room knows—they're all making jokes about David, they're all saying I did all his writing for him." She felt on the verge of tears—angry, frustrated tears.

"Didn't you? Even he didn't deny the accusation."

"You don't understand!" she countered.

"I understand that he was taking credit for stories he didn't write. I understand that he was stealing your talent and using you."

"David taught me to write. He taught me everything! And besides, the stories were based on his ideas."

"This isn't easy for me. I've gotten to know you, perhaps better than I should have, since you work for me. But I told him and I'll tell you. This is a newspaper, we don't pay for ideas, we pay for writers. There are people who get paid for ideas, but not in the city room of a newspaper. There's no shortage of what David calls ideas. We hire people to implement, to write."

Jo inhaled. "I know that, but you still don't understand. David has writer's block. He's troubled, he needs help."

"David needs to be shoved out the door and made to stand on his own two feet! You're not doing him any favors, you know. In fact, you're making him weaker."

"I love him and I'm trying to help him."

Ted stared at her. He hadn't wanted to hear her say that she loved Driscoll. He tapped his pencil on his desk. "You love him like a mother," he retorted. Then he looked up into her eyes. "What you need is a man, not a patient."

Jo's face flushed in anger. "Stay out of my private life! I know what I need and I know what David needs."

Ted pressed his lips tightly. "Just do your job and turn your assignments in on time. That's all I care about. You do what you want. You go home when your shift is over and you mother the hell out of David Driscoll. But you'll find out. You'll find out the hard way that life with a washed-up alcoholic writer is going to be a living hell."

Jo turned abruptly and opened the office door. "Just leave me alone," she said in frustration. "Let me make my own mistakes."

⸺

It had been thirteen months since David had left the paper. It had been thirteen months of ups and downs, of emotional turmoil, of promises, recriminations, and apologies. Jo's hopes soared with David's small victories and plummeted with his continued defeats. She couldn't count the times she had thought the war was over, only to discover she had been witness to another skirmish. No, "witness" was not the right word; she was an active participant, a soldier in David's battle for himself.

Jo knew her personal life was in chaos as she walked by David's side through his own version of hell, but she took comfort in her career. It was the rock she clung to.

From seven in the morning till seven at night, her pace was hectic. In fact, from a reporting standpoint, this spring had seen one sensational story after another.

On May 21 the *World* reported a crime that was so horrendous it left even the crime-jaded citizens of Chicago aghast. Little Bobby Franks, a studious dark-haired schoolboy at the Harvard private school on Chicago's South side, failed to come home after classes. Bobby Franks was the son of Jacob Franks, one of the city's wealthiest realtors. His parents had received a call that indicated the child had been kidnapped. But before the ransom could be paid, the police found the child's mutilated body.

The story was front-page for the remainder of May and the first week of June. It was, Ted Kahn said, "irresistible to readers . . . all the right elements." And he was right. First, the press played a large role in finding the killers, Nathan "Babe" Leopold and Richard "Dickie" Loeb. They were two young honor students from the University of Chicago whose reputations gave rumor to dark perversions. Furthermore, they admitted killing for kicks. One reporter from the *Tribune* had recognized the ransom note as being an exact copy of one that had appeared in a detective magazine. Two other reporters, Mulroy and Goldstein, from the *Daily News*, found the typewriter on which the note had been written. The police and reporters combined their efforts and the two young murderers were arrested on May 31.

The coverage had been sensational and unrelenting. Jo's own story, a long interview with the Franks family, had been nominated for a prize. Writing it was grueling because David had been ultracritical, advising her not to submit it. Then he was angry when it was nominated for a prize, but it wasn't really anger, it was jealousy, another example of his troubled personality.

Jo glanced at her watch. It was three-thirty. She pushed her way off the el and hurried across the deserted platform. Thank heaven it's not rush hour, she thought.

It was hot and muggy, one of those rare unbearable

days in late June. She turned and descended the stairs
to street level. A gust of humid wind blew her skirt and
she held it down with irritation.

She felt anxious as she walked rapidly along. "God,
come home!" David had wailed into the phone. "I'm
going to kill myself. I need you, come home!"

"He won't do it," she told herself firmly. David had
called her twenty, perhaps twenty-five times in the last
six months and said the same thing. It was a ruse. He
did it to bring her flying, he did it because he needed
attention. He did it to take her away from the paper,
which he now seemed to consider his "competition" for
her time and affection. "I know it, and I understand it,"
she told herself. But it didn't matter. She always came
flying home with a pounding heart. For all her logic,
she feared that there was always the possibility that he
was serious. She was frightened that one day the black
moods that so often took possession of David would
overwhelm him.

Jo reached her building and ran up the stairs. She
was torn between anger and concern, weariness and a
false energy born of her anxiety. She felt anger because
she was covering a story and it was always when she
was deeply engrossed that David used this terrible way
to summon her. She was concerned because she was
never certain what he might do, though on previous
occasions she had hurried home to find him passed out
dead drunk. And she prayed she would find him so this
time. But, she admitted, she was tired, bone-tired, and
relieved that Ted Kahn was out of town for a few days.
How many times in the last year had she left her job to
come home to David? Ted never said anything to her
because her stories were always on time, but his eyes
followed her and she knew he wanted to say something.

She had hurt Ted, she knew that too, and it added to

her emotional burden. But how could she leave David? Especially now?

"The road to hell is paved with broken promises," David had said only a few days ago. "I break all of mine, haven't you noticed?"

Yes, she had noticed. He had a routine now, and his swinging emotions followed it slavishly. First the unrestrained joy and optimism. "I wrote a chapter today! Best thing I ever wrote! God, I can hardly wait for you to read it!" He would waltz her around, take her out for dinner, be buoyant and funny. "I love you," he would tell her, "and I know what I've put you through, but I'm mending, Jo. I'm going to make it all up to you."

Then the recrimination. "I reread what I wrote, and it's garbage. I can't write, I'm a fake. I feel what I want to say, but I can't get it on paper. I have demons."

At those times she tried to encourage him, she begged him to let her see what he had written, but he would not. "Hey, I'm the teacher," he would reply. "You'll see it when its good, really good."

Then the slippage. He would begin drinking, and he drank not for hours, but for days and weeks. She cleaned up after him, cooked for him, covered him at night. She listened to him vomit and heard him crying. One night she discovered a pile of blank paper and knew he had written nothing.

Then he would sober up, swear off alcohol, and make another set of promises. "No more. I'm finished with it forever. Stayed dry for a whole year once, I can do it again."

Two, maybe three days, and then he would begin drinking again. He would threaten suicide and call her, beg her to come and be with him so he wouldn't do it. She would comfort him like a mother, and then the cycle would begin again. There were days when she

never wanted to see David again. Days when she wanted
to throw herself into Ted Kahn's arms and let him hold
her. And she knew his arms were waiting. She could
sense his feelings toward her and could see his affection
for her in his eyes. But she couldn't do it even though
she felt trapped and helpless. There had to be a way for
her to help David, there *had* to be.

Jo thrust the key into the lock of David's apartment.
"David!" she called out. There was no answer. She ran
through the three rooms, but there was no David. She
inhaled and forced herself not to be sick. He had been
ill in the sink, and a pile of garbage mingled with the
odor of vomit to create a horrible stench. She hurriedly
wrapped the garbage and rinsed down the sink. Then
she thrust open the window to air out the place. It was
hot, and things went bad easily in this weather.

Jo stopped to catch her breath. She had assumed he
was at home when he called. Perhaps, she reasoned
now, he was in her apartment.

She ran down the stairs, opened her own door, and
stepped inside. "David!" she called out. Again there
was no answer. She opened the bedroom door and
peered in. He wasn't there.

Jo sank down on the sofa and closed her eyes. Where
was he? What was he doing? Why had he called like
that and then disappeared? A thousand thoughts ran
through her mind. Perhaps this time he had meant it;
you never knew with suicides—she had read that.

She jumped when she heard a groan from the bathroom. "David!" She ran toward the bathroom and flung
open the door. Then she screamed.

He was lying over the edge of the ancient tub. His
wrists were gushing bright red blood, which mixed with
vomit. His face was ashen, and he was clearly unconscious.

Jo screamed again, but forced herself to grab a towel. She rapidly bound one wrist, then took a second towel and bound the other.

"Oh, God, let him live," she murmured as she staggered toward the telephone. "Please, if there's a God in heaven, let him live."

She dialed the police and gave the address. "Hurry," she pleaded. "He's lost so much blood!"

Jo glanced at her watch; it was nearly four, and he had called at three. Rush hour was starting . . . Oh God, how long would the ambulance take?

She went back into the bathroom and held his wrists, applying all the pressure she could to stop the flow of blood, even though she knew he had already lost a great deal and had most certainly severed a main artery.

This was no ruse, and she was flooded with guilt for even having thought it might be. All the other times he had called faded from her thoughts.

Jo closed her eyes, gripping David's wrists hard, and she rocked back and forth on her knees, crying and holding onto him. "Don't you dare die!" she begged again and again. "This is my fault, I didn't come soon enough. David, don't die . . . please, don't die!"

An eternity later, she heard the wail of sirens in the distance. They grew closer and at last she heard the ambulance attendants and the police storm through her door. "In here!" she called out. "Hurry!"

Two white-clad attendants lifted her by the shoulders, prying her loose from David. They bound his wrists and listened for his heartbeat.

They bundled David's unconscious form onto the stretcher.

"This way, I have a few questions," a young policeman said, gently prodding her away from the bathroom.

"I have to go with him," she pleaded. But the strong arms guided her along, and she was too weak to resist.

"Name?" the police officer said, holding his pad.

"David Driscoll."

"And yours?"

"Jo Gregory."

"The reporter for the *World*?"

"Yes."

"Gee, I read your coverage of the Bobby Franks murder. Somehow I thought you were a guy."

Jo looked at him dully. He was young, blue-eyed, and awed. "I'd spell my name with an E on the end if I were." It was such an absurd conversation. She felt removed from this world as she watched them strapping David on the gurney.

"Oh yeah, here's the razor," the young policeman commented as he bent over. "Were you here when it happened?"

Jo shook her head. "I just got home."

"He your husband?"

"No. He used to work on the paper, he's a writer. He lives upstairs."

"Just friends, right?" The young policeman winked. His expression betrayed his thoughts.

"No," Jo corrected. "*Good* friends."

"Well, I guess that's it. No foul play, just a suicide attempt."

"Can I go with him?"

"Afraid not. But they'll take him to Cook County General. Since this is an emergency, I'll drive you over."

"Thank you," Jo said, following him out of the apartment. She felt drained and ill, and most of all guilty. "I should have gotten home sooner," she kept saying again and again. Then, just as the ambulance attendants shoved the gurney into the vehicle, she asked, "Will he be all right?"

One of the attendants shrugged. "Lost a lot of blood. Fifty-fifty, I'd say. Pity you didn't find him sooner, lady."

The young policeman leaned across her and opened the door of his car.

Jo stared at the huge hospital and nodded. Her legs were rubber and she wasn't even sure she could walk.

"Sorry I can't go in with you," the policeman said. "I gotta go."

"You've been very kind," Jo said, staggering out of the car. She stood for a minute as he pulled away and out of the circular drive; then she hurried toward the entrance.

Inside the emergency room of Cook County General Hospital Jo found the legendary purgatory. It was filled with lost souls. It was noisy, confused, and disorganized. It was impossible to tell the medical staff from the patients.

It crossed her mind that she had read a story of Ted's on the famed hospital. It was the choice of medical students all over America as "the hospital to intern in." "Cook County and Massachusetts General," wrote Ted Kahn, "have in one day more variety of injuries and diseases than most hospitals have in a month, sometimes in a year."

Jo looked around and saw an overhead sign that read "Information." She fought her way toward the desk, where huddles of people babbled in at least five languages.

"Watch out! Watch out! You'll step on Harry!" an ill-dressed old woman shrieked at Jo, jostling her. The woman looked annoyed and angry.

Jo stopped. "Harry?" she said dumbly.

"My husband, Harry. Can't you see him? You're standing right in front of him!"

Jo looked where the woman pointed. It was an empty space. Clearly the woman was a mental case. "Sorry," she murmured, trying again to reach the desk.

Two women stood at the desk, alternately sobbing hysterically and chattering in Italian. An old man shouted in Greek at the top of his lungs while pounding the desk. On the floor behind the information desk, two young black men were lying on stretchers. They bled from what could only be gunshot wounds, and they moaned loudly.

Standing behind the desk, two beleaguered women attempted to field questions, at least those questions they understood. Jo literally threw herself at the desk. Leaning forward, she demanded attention. "David Driscoll," she shouted. "He was brought in just a few minutes ago."

Hearing English, the woman looked up. "What for?" she asked.

"He slit his wrists," Jo answered as quietly as possible.

"Driscoll, Driscoll, Driscoll . . ." She ran her finger down a list. "You his wife?"

"No."

"A relative?"

"I'm his friend, he doesn't have any relatives!" Jo's voice was sharp.

"Fourth floor. He's been taken to the fourth floor. You can ask up there, ask Dr. Grange."

Jo hurried up the stairs and headed directly for the fourth-floor nursing station. "Dr. Grange," she said, "I must speak to him."

A young man looked up from his charts. He was

dressed in a white coat spattered with blood. "Yes," he said, wiping his brow.

"David Driscoll—will he be all right? Will he live?"

The doctor moved from behind the desk and took her arm. "He's in critical condition," he confided. "We just can't tell yet. Sometimes patients recover when they've lost that much blood, and sometimes its too much of a shock and they go into a coma."

"Oh, dear God." Jo slumped against the wall.

"Miss, I think you should go home. I'll give you a number to call. You can check with us in the morning."

"Men from Monkeys? Teacher Accused in Tennessee—
Bryant and Darrow Square Off,"
by Jo Gregory.
July 12, 1925. Dateline: Dayton, Tennessee.

Twelve

Mike Hamilton's office on the fifth floor of the World Building was large, spacious, and overlooked Michigan Avenue. But in spite of its increased size, it was as cluttered as the small office he had left in the city room. Stacks of papers marked the perimeter of his oak desk, and in the center, he reserved the traditional space for his feet.

Ted Kahn sat opposite Hamilton. "Like it upstairs?" he asked.

Hamilton scratched his ear. "Not much different than downstairs, except I get the galleys later. And it's quieter. Oh, yes, and I have a secretary who keeps trying to straighten up. She moves everything and I can't find a thing. One day they're going to find her body hanging from the flagpole."

"I don't think I could work in this quiet. I need the presses humming." Ted grinned and decided not to comment on the secretary. But the truth was, Hamilton could never find anything before he acquired her. He lived in a tyranny of paper.

"Did you venture off your own turf to discuss the

292

merits of working in the city room? We're not strangers, you know. I mean, I do come down from this ivory
tower to appear at the daily budget meeting."

"Indeed, but it's not often that I come up here.
Frankly, I've come to discuss Jo Gregory."

"Ah, the lovely girl wonder. Young, a fine writer,
good researcher, clever interviewer, and very attractive."

"All that and more."

"And this is a problem for you?"

"In a way, yes." He hadn't decided how much to say,
even though he considered Hamilton a discreet man
who was also a personal friend. Was he going to say: "I
love her and she won't give me a second look and its
driving me crazy?" Or: "I can't go on working with her
because she's rejected me"?

"I'm not a mind reader," Hamilton prodded.

"Sorry, I was thinking of how to put it. The truth of
the matter is, I'm very fond of her. So fond of her that
I've lost my objectivity where her work is concerned."

"I can tell you her work is excellent."

"I'm glad you approve, but that doesn't solve my
problem."

"I'm not sure I understand. After all, you're going to
be pulled off the city desk in August when you go to
Berlin to take over the European desk. Can't you work
with no objectivity for two months?"

Ted shook his head. "I'm not doing her justice. I
don't give her the plum assignments because I don't
want to show favoritism and cause gossip. I think I
bend too far backward to avoid that accusation. I think
she needs to grow, and she won't grow on the city desk.
Hodgkins is taking over when I leave, and he doesn't
like women. She'll end up writing the society column
and doing celebrity interviews."

"You think I'd let that happen?" Hamilton queried.

"Maybe not, but I'd like to see her put on National. The Scopes trial is coming up in Tennessee and that's a good story for her. She already knows Darrow, and I think she could do a good job of covering our hometown boy fighting off the hicks in the sticks. It's also a good transitional story, because it belongs to both National and City. She'll technically be on National, but she knows how to write the local angles."

"Well put. Okay. I don't see any problem. I'll move her over to National. Tell her to pack her bags, I'll want her to leave by next Friday."

Ted stood up and stretched. "Thanks," he said, turning away. I'll tell her tomorrow, he thought to himself. Proximity, he decided, was a curse. He was too close to her, too close every damn day of the year. Maybe he'd forget about her if she wasn't around. Maybe he'd forget how he felt about her.

And maybe, just maybe, she would finally give up Driscoll if she was traveling. She sure couldn't baby-sit the bum from Tennessee. Driscoll! He felt like spitting. The stupid bastard had tried to kill himself. He was putting Jo through absolute hell and she simply wouldn't wake up and see him for what he was, a user.

Ted sauntered back into his office in the city room. Jo wouldn't be there; she was bringing David home from the hospital. God, she was playing mother again. He felt as if he wanted to shake her. How could an otherwise intelligent woman be so blind? "Some people are too damn good for their own good," he muttered as he slammed the door to his office.

Two months! In only two months he would be leaving for Europe. He was glad he was going to Europe, glad he was going to get away from the emotional pulls and throws of being around Jo. I need a change, he decided. And though reporting from Europe might not be any easier than handling the daily problems on the city desk, it would be different. In any case, he was looking forward to it, though sadly he wished Jo would give up Driscoll and come with him. "It's not in the cards," he said under his breath. "She's in love with Driscoll, and that's that." And what the hell was he holding out for anyway? She hadn't gone out with him since the day he'd fired Driscoll, and while they got along all right in the office, she had certainly kept her distance. Well, soon they could both relax. Soon there would be plenty of distance between them.

David sank into the worn green cushions of his sofa and put his feet up on the coffee table. He looked around his apartment. It was spotless, and the windows were open, allowing a warm humid breeze to blow in. "You're hovering over me like a mother hen," he said, chastising Jo.

She looked at him steadily. He was still pale, but he was smiling. "You scared me."

"I scared myself, child."

He looked older, more tired. But at the same time, he seemed placid. Perhaps because for the first time in months he was truly sober, she thought. Jo forced a smile. After all, this could be a new beginning for David. "I organized your notes by the typewriter. David, you need to get back to work, you really do."

"You're the one who needs to get back to work. It's nearly three, and you said you had a story to finish."

"I hate to leave you."

"You don't have to worry. There's not a drop to drink in the house and I'm out of razor blades."

"Don't joke . . . please don't joke about it."

He nodded silently. She looked stricken and her dark eyes were pools of sadness. "Sorry."

"You're right, I do have to get back to the city room."

"I'll be fine," he told her. He watched as she went to the mirror by the door and pinned on her large broadbrimmed hat. God, he thought, I love her and I'm dragging her down with me, down to the depths. I love her and I'm afraid to touch her. And he admitted that he felt jealous because she was going back to the paper.

She would be with Ted Kahn—a young, successful, and no doubt virile Ted Kahn. The very man he hated was the man who could give Jo everything. It's small comfort that she chose to stay with me, he thought. She's doing it out of gratitude or out of guilt. Maybe out of pity. The thought made him angry, and he felt his frustrations rising to the forefront even though he struggled not to wound her now. "Go on," he urged.

Jo came back to the sofa and leaned over. She kissed him on the cheek. "Please rest. I fixed some food . . . try to eat something."

"Milk and cookies," he said sarcastically.

"No cookies, but you need lots of milk. And the doctor said you need to eat liver to build up your blood."

"I hate liver."

"Eat it anyway." She turned and then she was gone. He leaned back and closed his eyes and swore when he heard the door that led to the hall close. The more she does, the more I need her, he thought. She's the best thing that ever happened to me, and she's also the worst.

Jo caught the el and hurried back to the *World*. She went directly to her desk and began working. As it was late afternoon, the city room was quiet, but she was on deadline for tomorrow's story. It was a background piece on Clarence Darrow, who had just left for Tennessee to defend Scopes in the so-called "Monkey Trial."

Jo worked steadily for two hours. She wrote, edited, then did a rewrite. It was a good profile, she thought. It went into Darrow's background, it even talked about the reasons he had chosen to defend Leopold and Loeb and why now he would fight the Scopes case.

"Jo?" Ted Kahn touched her lightly on the shoulder and she jumped.

"You startled me."

"I have some news for you. Can you spare a few minutes?"

Jo nodded and followed Ted into his office.

"How's Driscoll?" he asked, looking as if he really cared.

"I think he'll be all right. He lost a lot of blood, but he's recovering." She bit her lip and then looked up. "I do appreciate your not letting anyone know what happened. I wouldn't want David to be the talk of the city room. His friends wouldn't understand."

"It's nobody's business," Ted said firmly. "But that's not why I asked you to come in here. I have news for you. You're being promoted, transferred off City Desk onto National. You're being sent down to Tennessee to cover the Scopes case. Darrow's a hometown boy, so the Chicago papers are all sending their best people."

Jo stared at him. Implicit in his comment was a compliment, but go to Tennessee? How could she leave David? "Tennessee," Jo repeated in confusion.

"That's what I said. You'll have to leave by Friday."

"But David—I can't leave David now," she heard herself protesting, and she felt suddenly at war with her desires. David was a responsibility, but going to Tennessee and writing for Ken Wilson, the well-known editor on the national desk, was an opportunity. An opportunity most reporters didn't have so early in their careers.

Ted tapped his pipe on the ashtray, as if for emphasis. "You'll have to go. I know you don't believe me, but Driscoll will be fine. He might even be better without you to lean on."

There was an element of truth in Ted's words that she couldn't argue with. David needed time to get himself together, and perhaps time away from her was a good idea. Then she thought: Perhaps it's a good idea for both of us. "I'll go," she said softly.

Ted nodded in satisfaction. "Finish your backgrounder. You can pick up your tickets and expense money from Emmie in Accounting tomorrow."

Jo nodded and turned to leave.

"One other thing. Could we have dinner Thursday? Just a farewell dinner, before you leave for Tennessee?"

"Oh, Ted, I can't. David will expect me to spend my last night in Chicago with him."

Ted dropped his pipe into the green glass ashtray with a clunk. "I really have tried to be patient, even understanding," he said evenly. "I haven't complained when he phoned and you ran out of here in a panic. I would have complained if you hadn't been doing your job. But somehow over the last thirteen months you've managed your baby-sitting chores and your work, so I didn't say anything." His fist doubled, and he angrily brought it down on the desk. "What the hell are you trying to do, Jo? You're young, beautiful, and talented. Why are you wasting your life and your talent playing nursemaid to a burned-out suicidal alcoholic bum who uses you!"

"Don't talk about David that way!" she responded with fury, and she felt her face begin to flush. She

glanced around. It was late, so the city room outside
Ted's glass-enclosed office was deserted, the rows of
typewriters covered.

"Yes, you're free to shout," he said. "No one is here,
we can fight in peace."

"I don't want to fight. I want you to understand about
David and how I feel." She looked into his eyes, then
added, "Not that it's really any of your business. You're
my boss, but you act as if you had some claim to the
rest of my life."

"For a while I thought we had something happening," he replied. "I got to know you well enough to
know I wanted more. Call me an egomaniac if you
want, but sometimes I sensed you wanted more too."
Ted stood up and walked around the desk. He stood in
front of her, his expression hard. "I understand David
all too well. I understand that he's a no-good boozer,
that he's latched onto you and he won't let go. I understand that you're busy playing Florence Nightingale or
something. Who do you think you are? Are you trying
to save the world one person at a time? And do you
really think you're helping him? You're not, you know.
You're making him more dependent. You're part of his
problem." He felt his face grow red with frustration.
He'd said it all before, of course. But she just wouldn't
listen.

Jo looked at him, but she didn't answer. She hated
every word he was saying, but some of it was true. She
blinked back tears and looked down.

"Are you afraid to have a normal love affair and find
out what it's like to be a woman instead of a nursemaid?" Ted reached out and drew her into his arms.

Jo quivered as she felt Ted embracing her, pulling
her toward him. Her cheek brushed his jacket, and he
cupped her chin in his hand and lifted her face.

"Dammit, I love you," he said, pressing his lips to hers.

In spite of his harsh words, she felt herself responding to his moving lips. She gave in momentarily, feeling a flash of electricity between them. It was animal magnetism that drew her to Ted. He was right—there were times when she had wanted more. David's pale face flashed in front of her closed eyelids. She pulled away from Ted's strong embrace and steadied herself.

"Be a woman," Ted was saying. "Give him up. You need a man who can be a real lover, not one who needs you to lean on."

"I *am* a woman," Jo said defensively. "What makes you think David isn't a good lover? Why are you saying these things, why?"

"I think you feel obligated to him. I think you love me."

"You're arrogant! And I am David's mistress, I am!" she lied, defending David's manhood, and watched as Ted's face contorted with pain. Then she turned and fled his office.

Jo went back to her desk and didn't look up to see if Ted had left or was still in his office. She fought her tears, and she shook as Ted's words came back to her. Was she part of David's problem? And why wouldn't David make love to her? She had asked herself a hundred times, but there was no answer. Often he looked as if he wanted to make love to her, and sometimes she wanted him too. But David had never touched her, and now, she thought, she had foolishly lied. Did she lie to protect David or herself from Ted's accusations? She shook her head and brushed a tear off her cheek.

Maybe her relationship with David was as abnormal as Ted seemed to think. Maybe she should make an effort to find out.

David stretched out on his sofa, blew smoke rings in the air, then butted his cigarette in the overflowing ashtray and lit another.

Jo busied herself in the small kitchen. She had made salad and was now frying strips of liver and bacon.

"The smell of that liver is making me sick," David complained.

"You have to eat it," she insisted. Soon she would have to tell him she was leaving town. She paid little attention to the liver, and tried to work out just what she would say.

"Maybe we should eat out," David suggested. "I think I could stomach some eggs and sausage."

"David, you'll like the liver. It's very good fixed this way."

He grunted. "I don't suppose you could take a few days off?" He lolled over on his side and faced the open doorway of the kitchenette.

Jo turned, and she wondered if he saw the panic in her eyes. "I can't," she replied quickly.

"Work, work, work . . . all work and no play will make you dull. I wanted us to go up to Wisconsin, stay in a rustic cabin near a clear-water lake, someplace out in the woods. You know, you forget what a clear-water lake looks like when you live around here. Come on, Jo. Old Ted will let you take some time off, just butter him up a little."

Jo stared into the frying pan. His voice was heavily laden with sarcasm, as it always was when he mentioned Ted. "I can't," she answered.

"Why not? Doesn't Ted love you anymore?"

Jo turned off the small gas burner. She put the liver

and bacon on plates and carried them to the table, together with the salad. "Dinner's ready," she told him.

"You didn't answer me. Doesn't Ted love you anymore?" David rolled off the sofa and came to the table. He stood looking at her, his face tense.

"I don't work for Ted anymore," Jo answered. She looked at him steadily, waiting for his reaction.

David looked surprised. He had been baiting her for a fight; now he didn't know quite what to say.

"I was going to tell you after dinner," Jo informed him. " I've been transferred to National."

"You can't go to National!" David's face paled, and his eyes filled with panic. "That means you'll have to travel, maybe be away for weeks at a time."

"I have to go to Tennessee on Friday to cover the Scopes trial," Jo told him as she sat down.

David slipped into the chair and stared at her uncomprehendingly. "This Friday?"

"I'm sorry, David. I had wanted to discuss this later. It was very sudden, I didn't expect it."

"And of course you couldn't have turned it down." He looked at her steadily, defiantly.

"No, I couldn't. Frankly, I didn't think you would want me to turn it down. David, you'll be all right . . . maybe you'll even be better off without me."

He put some salad on his plate and didn't reply for several minutes. Then he said, "I've treated you badly, Jo. We see too much of each other, and I end up taking everything out on you. You're right, I will be better off. I need time to be alone and time to write. I need to be able to do things for myself. You go to Tennessee, and when you come home, I'll surprise you. I'll have finished a couple of chapters."

Jo smiled cautiously at him. He had been frightened at first, but seemed to have overcome his fear quickly.

She felt better already. Perhaps his attempted suicide had been a turning point. Perhaps now he would be able to write and gain back his self-respect. Certainly he would have moments of fear and bitterness, as he had just had. But, she told herself, the worst was over.

After dinner they sat and talked. David put his arm around her shoulders and she rested her head against him. "You're doing okay, child," he told her. "I'm proud of you, you know. I know I don't always show it, but I am."

Jo felt comfortable and warm. She closed her eyes and thought of the lovely nightdress in the box on her bed. "Wait here," she whispered to him. "Wait here, David."

Jo stood in front of her mirror. She tugged a little on the neckline of the low-cut nightdress and stared at herself, almost in disbelief. This was what women wore when they wanted to seduce a man. She had read stories and seen advertisements in the magazines.

It was a white gown with long ribbons; it clung to her and fell in pleated folds over her hips. The top was just low enough to reveal her cleavage. It was, the sales-clerk assured her, "most provocative."

Jo ran her hand through her hair; it was curly and loose, caressing her neck.

Ted Kahn was wrong. David was a man and she was a woman. She and David loved each other . . . hadn't they said so? I do love him, she insisted to herself.

She turned from the mirror and then glanced back again. Her memories would make her frightened when the time came, but David would be gentle; he was kind and he was her friend.

She walked into the living room. David was still on
the couch, his eyes closed.

David opened his eyes and sat up staring at her. His
eyes looked lustful, though he seemed to gaze at her
through a haze.

Jo ran to him. "David, please . . . I want to be a
woman for you."

"Child, you look beautiful."

"David, I'm not a child. I want you, don't you want
me?" She could hear the pleading quality in her voice
and she hated it.

David closed his eyes. She was a gift and she was
offering herself to him. Of course he wanted her! But
she was different from any woman he had ever had, so
different he wasn't sure he could bring himself to defile
her perfect, gentle virginal beauty. He opened his eyes
and knew that for the first time in his life he was crying
because he loved someone. He reached out and drew
her into his arms.

Jo snuggled against him. She felt his hands as they
slipped beneath her nightdress. He tenderly laid her
back against the pillows and explored her, though he
hardly seemed to be touching her at all as his hand
moved across the surface of her flesh.

David closed his eyes. She was exquisite to the touch,
her skin cool and soft. God, how he wanted her, and
yet he did not feel aroused. He felt awestruck, overcome with emotion.

He carried her to the bedroom with apprehension. It
was a dream from which he would awake. His lips
caressed her breasts, his hands roamed her still body.
She lay beneath him with her arms around his neck
while he kissed her, and he prayed he could satisfy her
without hurting her or altering her innocent beauty.

"You're beautiful," he whispered. "More than I ever

dreamed of, more than I deserve. Oh, Jo, I don't deserve you." The heart desires, but the body doesn't always obey. He'd been with a hundred whores and felt himself strong and virile. It was true that sometimes he was slow when he drank too much. But this was different. It was as if a glaring light blinded his fantasies, as if he loved her too much. He touched her intimately and felt her warm and moist, he heard the short, rapid breathing that expressed her readiness. I have to be able, he thought, cursing himself. He thought of a whore he had once had. A dancer with long strong legs and a lithe hard body. He thought of her turning and twisting and he concentrated on the image till he knew he was ready and able to enter her. Twice he lost the image, only to retrieve it from the corners of his mind. Then at last he came.

Jo lay curled in David's arms and fought thoughts of Ted Kahn. David had been gentle and kind. Her fears of sexual encounter had fled with the mild sensations she had felt when she looked into his worshipful eyes and experienced his gentle kisses. But what she had felt when Ted kissed her was missing. With David there was no electricity, no animal fever, no real desire. Jo blinked back silent tears and stared into the darkness of her small bedroom. David had made love to her, but which man did she really want?

Jo had watched the rolling hills of Tennessee give way to the more mountainous Ozarks of lower Missouri, then to the flatlands along the upper Mississippi, till finally the chugging steam-belching train was surrounded by the cornfields that characterized so much of Illinois.

In her lap she held a copy of yesterday's *World*,

dated July 24, 1925. It carried a black banner headline: "Scopes Convicted of Teaching Evolution!" Below the headline was a two-column story with her byline.

She had been in Tennessee for three weeks, and she had received only one hastily written postcard from David. All it said was, "Miss you, and I love you." She closed her eyes and leaned back, chastising herself for her immaturity. Ted had challenged her and she had made love to David to prove him wrong. Now she knew it was Ted to whom she was attracted, but it was too late. David loved her, and to leave him would be to destroy him.

Jo forced both Ted and David from her thoughts. She reread her story with satisfaction, and again she checked the time. In an hour the train would be rolling into Chicago's Dearborn Station.

"Jo!" She heard her name being called before she saw Ted Kahn pushing his way across the crowded platform.

"You didn't have to meet me," she said, allowing him to relieve her of her suitcase.

"I wanted to."

"Thank you, but I do have to go straight home."

"Hey, how was Tennessee? Did you get plenty of moonshine from the boys in the press corps?"

She smiled in spite of herself. "I was offered a lot."

"But you didn't have any."

"No." They were out of the station and into the sunshine. It was blistering hot, and she could feel the heat from the concrete pavement through the soles of her shoes.

"Notice how there's always a wind in the winter, and not so much as a breath of air in summer," Ted commented cheerfully.

She smiled at him as he opened the door of his Ford.

He was making small talk, his way of saying he was sorry for what had happened in his office three weeks before. He turned the car and headed into the traffic.

"Aren't we going the wrong way?"

"Yes. I'd like to park down by the lake for a few minutes. I have to talk to you."

"I really should get back—I have been traveling for twenty-three hours."

He swung onto Lakeshore, and suddenly there was a breeze. Then he pulled into Grant's park and drew up into a spot where the lake could be seen between the green lawn and leafy trees. "I won't keep you long, I promise."

She nodded silently.

"Jo, I've been given the European desk. I'm going to be headquartered in Berlin. I'll be leaving in a few weeks."

"Ted, that's wonderful."

"I've known about it for a while." His eyes devoured her and he put his hand on her arm. "Jo, I do love you. Come with me to Europe. Marry me."

Jo stared at him. His dark eyes were intense, and she could feel his hand gripping her arm. He was strong and solid, she knew that, and the electricity was there. She knew that too.

Ted leaned over her, his lips brushed her forehead, then her warm cheek, before he sought her lips, kissing her deeply. She felt his hands caressing her hair, then his lips kissing her neck. He was breathing heavily, so close she could feel his heart pounding.

"God, I love you, Jo. Come with me, say you'll come with me."

Jo closed her eyes, amazed at her own feeling of love and exhilaration, her own excitement as he caressed her gently.

"I feel like a fool parked in a car and making love in broad daylight," he said, kissing her eyelids. "I want you."

He kissed her mouth again, and she felt tears forming in her eyes. She was a child! She didn't know about men, and her own reactions were untested. Ted wanted her and she wanted him. At least she wanted him physically. But David loved her, and it was her fault. She didn't know what it meant, she couldn't think of what to say. Still, David was there. He absorbed her, and in her thoughts she could see him holding out his hands to her. Even as Ted kissed her, she knew David needed her.

Ted withdrew from the long kiss and looked into her eyes. "Come with me, marry me," he pleaded.

"I can't. Oh, Ted, I can't."

"Jo, I'm leaving. I want you to come with me."

She watched his eyes and reached up and lightly touched his cheek. "I'm flattered, Ted. But I can't, I really can't. David means too much to me."

"You're making a mistake. He'll take you with him. Jo, he's no good for you."

For the first time, Ted didn't sound angry, but resigned. She didn't answer, except to murmur that she had to get home. He moved away from her, his face set, turned the key, and stepped on the starter. "All right," he said. "I'll take you home to David."

Chubby Windsor was sitting at his desk next to the chattering teletype machine, staring mesmerized as it spewed out wire-service stories.

Axel Dan McGrath, wearing a brown felt hat with a racing form stuck in the headband, chewed gum furiously and pounded out a rousing description of the latest Sox loss. He was a marvel. Win, lose, or draw, he made the home team look good, and the game, no matter how boring, sound like a cliff-hanger.

The noise of clicking typewriters, mumbling copy editors, and cursing reporters filled the city room, while to the side, in the big warehouse room just beyond the wooden doors, the pounding presses rolled out the day's first edition, sending the smell of fresh ink and newsprint to every corner.

Jo looked around her numbly. This was how the city room had looked on her first day of work. Then she had had to fight the distraction of the sounds and the closeness of others. She had found it exciting, an adventure in an atmosphere of hyperactivity and tension. But today as she cleaned out her desk and prepared to move to the room where the national stories were written, she acknowledged she hardly heard the sounds. It was her own thoughts she had to fight, her own reality that threatened her.

She had returned home to a terrible scene. A scene so unexpected that she was sent into wave after wave of shock, her sensibilities shattered, her dreams crushed.

As clearly as if it had just happened, she could see the room as she opened the door to David's apartment, intent on surprising him. But her intended surprise replayed like a bad movie in her memories.

David had been in bed with a girl. And Jo could see herself now, standing there, framed in the doorway, her mouth open, her eyes wide. In her hands she held a Tennessee corn-cob pipe she had brought David as a gift.

The girl was a bleached blond with large blue eyes. She was wearing a red slip and black stockings, the slip well off one shoulder, exposing the curve of her white breast. David, naked and groping like an animal, was struggling with her. He was cursing and crying, dead drunk and raving mad.

Jo remembered screaming incoherently as she turned to run away from the scene. "I thought you loved me, David" was all she had said. It was a betrayal of everything she believed their relationship to be. The girl was obviously a prostitute, and David had looked like a hungry monster pawing her body as if he were looking for something.

Jo had staggered down the two flights of stairs and hurried into her own apartment, slamming the door and then slipping to the floor and sobbing. How long she had sat there, her back against the door, her face in her hands, she wasn't even sure. But at some time she got up and went to bed, even though sleep wouldn't come, and her thoughts closed in on her, causing wave after wave of misery to sweep through her.

The sun was coming up when she opened her eyes and saw David, unshaven and unkempt, standing by her bed. His eyes had dark circles under them, his mouth quivered slightly, and he was crying too.

He hadn't said anything at first, had simply sat down and taken her in his arms and held her against him. Then he spoke in a halting hoarse voice. "I didn't mean to hurt you, child. You don't understand, you don't understand anything."

"I forgive you," she remembered crying.

"Don't," he said harshly. "Jo, don't forgive me, that's the one thing I can't stand." He touched her hair, running his hand through it. "I'm not good enough for you. I never will be. I can't live up to the person you think I am, and trying will kill me. Jo, you gave yourself to me and I was wrong to take you. You were beautiful, like a dream, but I can't go on with you—I can't."

"But why that girl?" Jo prodded.

"Back to reality. Sex without entanglements. I can't have entanglements. Jo, I have to leave you. I have to sink or swim on my own."

"Leave me? No, David, please don't leave me."

"I have to," he had answered. Then he told her he was going home to Hannibal to write. She begged to come with him, but he insisted it wouldn't work.

Sadly Jo agreed. David was right. Ted was right. That afternoon, she took David to the train station.

She returned to work the next morning, but Ted Kahn was gone too.

"Left for Europe a couple of weeks early," Mike Hamilton told her casually. "Had some vacation time coming and decided to wander around the south of France before heading for Berlin."

"Is your copy ready? Ken Wilson says he's ready for it," the young redheaded, freckle-faced copyboy said.

Jo nodded her head as if to wake herself up. "Here," she said, handing him her neatly typewritten pages.

The young boy grinned. "Mr. Wilson says you're a good reporter with a fine career ahead of you. He said I should ask you for some pointers."

"Sure," Jo answered. "When you have time, I'll take you to lunch."

The blue eyes looked worshipful and the young boy blushed. "Can I help you carry your things to your new desk?"

She smiled and picked up a box, indicating the remaining box to him. "Please," she answered with a nod.

A new desk, a new job, she thought as she followed the lad down the hall.

He was fourteen, maybe fifteen. At twenty, Jo felt a hundred years older. Why did all the people she love disappear? Was that the way it would always be?

PART III

1926–1937

Thirteen

A soft fluffy white snow blanketed the parks, lingered
on windowsills, and turned to instant slush on the well-
walked busy streets of Chicago's Near North Side.

Jo hurried home from the paper. Mike Hamilton and
his wife, Jessie, had invited her for Christmas dinner at
seven, and there was barely time to bathe and put on
fresh clothes.

She felt tired but grateful that the *World* published
on Christmas Day. Christmas was the one holiday that
brought back memories of her childhood, and on this
day she always endeavored to be busy in order to avoid
thinking about the past.

Her life, she contemplated, had fallen into a routine.
She saw friends on Friday and Saturday nights, and
during the week she took classes at the University of
Chicago. Her current course on modern European history was taught by Professor William Dodd, with whom
she had become good friends. Apart from those diver-
sions, however, her career was paramount.

The situation on the paper since Ted's departure had
changed radically. In fact, the entire organization of the

paper was new. The *World*, once the private domain of
the wealthy aristocratic Hartley family, had been purchased by Global Enterprises, a large faceless corporation.

Mike Hamilton stayed on as managing editor, but
many others had left in the inevitable reorganization
shuffle. The reporters who had covered the national
desk were sent back to the city desk and rotated to
cover national and international stories in an effort to
streamline the staff. Ted Kahn, who had controlled the
European desk, was one who had left the employ of the
World. He'd gone to the Washington *Times* and was
now a syndicated columnist for a dozen papers.

But new management or not, Jo couldn't complain.
She was now a top reporter, and often she was sent to
cover fast-breaking stories on the West Coast or in the
South. The rest of the time she covered the city and
produced a regular bylined column entitled "Cityside."

Chicago, Jo believed, was a town of never-ending
opportunity. There were good theaters, a fine sym-
phony, excellent libraries, interesting restaurants, and
some of the nation's best-known stores. She often went
to the theater with Jessie Hamilton, and only a few weeks
ago she had gone with Jessie and Mike to the Blackhawk on Wabash and Randolph streets to dine and dance
to the music of Coon Sanders and his Night Hawks. The
Blackhawk was billed as Chicago's liveliest rendezvous.

Jo opened the door to her apartment and switched on
the light. There on the coffee table was a card she had
received yesterday from David. She picked it up and
reread it:

Merry Christmas, child.
Just a short note to tell you I'm well and not pickled
in a bottle. I've been doing some free-lance articles, not
really what I want to do, but they keep me busy.

Hannibal is, as always, peaceful and lovely. There's something poetic about the river. It's timeless, and living on its shores makes me feel immortal, able to orchestrate the changing of the seasons and control my destiny. There are no temptations here, no pulls, and few throws.

I read your stories with satisfaction, but I can't help thinking: Better you than me. I always hated Christmas on the paper. Traditionally it's the day to report fires. I don't know why, I guess it's all those candles on brittle branches. My trees are outdoors—they cover the bluff above the river. No fires, but maybe a blizzard. Take care, write when you have time.

David

Jo laid the card down and hurried into the bathroom. There wasn't time now for sentimentality or regrets. Dinner was at seven.

She drew a shallow bath and climbed in, smiling and thinking that David was right. Disasters were Christmas Day fare.

Yesterday, on the twenty-fourth, two deluxe trains had crashed into each other and thirty people had been killed. The Marines, under Rear Admiral Julian Lutner, had taken over Nicaragua, and there were no fewer than fourteen fires reported. The paper's front page was a mishmash of stories. A criminal disguised as Santa Claus was given the same amount of space as the Marines marching into Nicaragua.

Jo finished her bath and hurriedly dressed. Checking the time, she decided to take a cab rather than the el.

"Merry Christmas!" Jessie Hamilton embraced Jo warmly. Jessie was a lovely sixty-two-year-old matron who still had a slim figure. Her short hair was snow white and fashionably bobbed. Jessie was an active,

interesting, bustling lady whose thoughts, ideas, and
activities made her seem much younger. She was, in
every sense of the word, her husband's partner. She
knew the newspaper business inside and out.

"My parents were both reporters—they owned and
ran the Topeka *Gazette*," she had told Jo. "Goodness,
not only was I almost born under a printing press, I was
practically married next to one!"

Jessie pulled back. "Don't you look lovely." She smiled
and took Jo's coat and scarf. Jo handed her two neatly
wrapped gifts and a box of chocolates from Fannie
May's. Jessie accepted the gifts graciously and guided
Jo into the living room. "I have to go back and see to
the turkey before Mike ruins it. You just sit here. I'll
send him out to entertain you."

Jo watched as Jessie hurried back to the kitchen. Her
friendship with Jessie meant a lot to her because it was
close to a mother-daughter relationship.

In the past two years they had talked a great deal. It
had taken a long while, but Jo had finally told Jessie
about David.

"You know, my dear, when you're young, loneliness
and a feeling of obligation can seem like love. You
idealized David, but he couldn't live up to your ideal.
What you thought was love for David was really only
the love you felt for your lost family."

"I think I know that now, but I was so confused. And
then there was Ted. I loved him too, in a way."

"Ah, yes. That's young love. That's the thrill of a
sudden kiss, that animal feeling that you can't and don't
want to control. That kind of love has to have time to
grow. I think you and Ted would have been good
together."

"I hurt him badly. He's gone, and we'll probably
never see each other again."

Jessie had smiled. "Never is a terribly long time."

"I don't know what I'd do if I didn't have you to talk with," Jo had told her truthfully.

"Do you want to adopt me? My daughters are all grown and moved away."

"Yes," Jo had told her. "I need a woman to talk with. There are only men at the paper."

"Oh, I know. It's a wonderful place to meet a husband," Jessie said wryly.

"There you are, all alone. Here, let me give you some egg nog," Mike Hamilton offered as he strode into the living room.

Jo snapped out of her reverie. "I hope it's not too strong."

"*I* don't!" He laughed and handed her a cut-glass cup. "Have you heard from Driscoll?"

"Yes. He's doing well."

"Good thing he got out when he did. Old-time reporter like that couldn't have taken the new corporate image we're supposed to be developing."

"Can *you* take it?"

"I'm only a couple of years from retirement. I can't say I'm crazy about the new owners—whoever the hell they are—but I'm in a position where I can take my money and run."

Jo frowned. "I didn't know you felt that way."

"Well, it's a growing feeling. I had a bad day today. Still, I must say, if I were younger, I'd head out. I'd do what Ted's done. I'd go to Europe. The Versailles Treaty was a disaster, those Huns are going to pop their buttons again one of these days. Yup, Europe's an exciting place, Jo. You ought to think about it yourself."

"Are you two talking business?" Jessie came in with a plate of cheeses.

"No, we're discussing Jo's future. I've been saying she ought to go to Europe. I hear it from everyone: all the real happenings are in London, Paris, and Berlin."

"I love Chicago!"

"You need the stimulation that travel can bring."

Jessie smiled knowingly. "He's as tactful as a bull in a china shop. He's trying to tell you we had a card from Ted. He asked after you."

Jo turned toward Jessie. "How is he?"

"I'm not sure. Frankly, for a writer, he's not very forthcoming. I think you should write to him. Here, I'll scribble down his address for you."

"Now who's matchmaking?" Mike asked.

"Not matchmaking, darling. Just seeing to it that they get back into contact with one another." Jessie turned to Jo. "It wouldn't hurt to write."

"I suppose not," Jo said thoughtfully, taking Ted's address.

————

Jo returned home from Mike and Jessie Hamilton's feeling uncomfortably full from the large meal, and overstimulated from the evening's conversation.

She undressed and climbed into bed, though she was unable to sleep. For a time she thought of Ted, wondering how he really was and if he had changed. Dreamily she thought about the possibility of going to Europe. But of course such a move wouldn't be easy. There were few women in journalism, and fewer still in international journalism. On reflection, the only one she could think of was Louise Bryant, John Reed's widow. Jo remembered reading some of Bryant's articles, which were highly personal. Bryant was emotional and outspoken, a strong feminist who didn't hesitate to present her bias. Louise Bryant had just done an article on Soviet women since the revolution. Jo began to think about American women. In the six years since women had gotten the vote, not a great deal had changed, especially for young immigrant women who couldn't read English and were ignorant of the laws designed to protect them. They were still given in marriage according to the customs of their culture, were still exploited in factories, and were denied an education. Jo was thinking of the marriage laws in the various states, considering that she might write an article discussing the inequities. What was the marriageable age in Tennessee? Twelve or fourteen? She began planning the story in her head, drifting off to sleep in the process.

Jo tossed on her side restlessly, and she started when the phone rang, rousing her from the edge of a dream.

"Have we got a Christmas fire!" Bill Dane shouted over the phone. Dane was an assistant assignments editor. He was flippant and cynical, the kind of person who simply couldn't be serious. He was alone on the city desk Christmas night.

"Where?" Jo asked as she switched on the light and groped for her pencil.

Dane gave her the address. "It's a big one, a nightclub. God knows how many injuries and deaths. Can you get right over there, interview the survivors? You're the only one available."

"Yes. Do you have to sound so enthusiastic?"

"Enthusiastic! I'm in ecstasy! Hell, without this fire, I'd have to go with a puny little house fire on the South Side. What kind of headline is that for the morning edition? This is a real conflagration!"

Jo promised to go immediately and hung up. David had been cynical too. She was used to it.

*   *   *

She arrived at the scene of the fire forty minutes later. The building was still in flames, fire engines were arriving, and ambulances whirred through the night. A brisk winter wind off the lake fanned the flames, while the survivors, those able to stand, huddled under blankets, some still in obvious shock.

Jo edged up to the police barrier and showed her press card. The pink-faced officer allowed her through, though he warned her to go no nearer than the chalk line marked by the fire department.

Jo stared at the fire, then at the huddle of injured who were waiting for ambulances. One man with seared facial skin, moaned in pain. Two others writhed on the ground, unburned but obviously injured in their effort to escape the flames. Smoke mingled with the distinct odor of burning flesh.

Jo approached an attractive brunette dressed in the remnants of a silver evening dress. It was torn and hung in uneven shreds around her knees. One of the high heels on her dancing shoes was broken, and a jagged cut on her forehead oozed blood. She was wrapped in a blanket, but she still shivered and studied the entrance to the building with an expression that combined horror, anxiety, and disbelief.

"Can you tell me what happened?" Jo pressed.

The girl turned toward her, looked at her, but didn't seem to see her. "I paid nineteen-fifty for these shoes," she said vacantly. "I lost Tommy. They can't find him. They haven't brought him out."

The girl's eyes were large but expressionless. Her comment showed that she had confused the totally unimportant with the profound. Clearly she was in total shock. "Is Tommy your husband?" Jo asked gently.

"Fiancé . . . he pushed me toward the entrance . . . somebody hit him . . . they can't find him."

Jo glanced around and saw a stone bench a few feet away. It was partially sheltered by the overhang of the building it stood in front of. "Come over here and sit down with me." Jo guided the girl along, holding her elbow so she could walk on her uneven shoes.

"He'll come out in a minute. I have to stay here," she protested.

"We can see from that bench," Jo insisted. "Come on, you should be sitting down."

The girl slumped onto the bench, her face still turned toward the entrance of the burning building. Her eyes were glued on the door.

"Can you tell me what happened when the fire alarms went off?"

"No alarms," the girl said, gripping the coarse woolen blanket and pulling it more closely around her.

Jo frowned. "Are you sure there were no alarms?"

The girl nodded. "No alarms. Just smoke. Awful acrid smoke. We couldn't breathe, we couldn't see. Everyone started screaming and running. I ran . . . Tommy pushed me. No alarms, though. Just smoke, then flames."

Jo talked to the girl for a few more minutes, then moved on to others. Their stories were the same: they heard no alarms, and each of them mentioned the dense choking smoke.

That would be the introduction to her story. But, Jo suspected, it would also be the beginning of a long and tiring day. After she had talked to twenty of the survivors, she cornered a young fireman who had been relieved for a few moments.

"I've been told there's a lot of smoke," Jo said pointedly.

"You a reporter?" he questioned.

Jo nodded.

"We aren't supposed to talk to the press."

She was accustomed to that response from the fire department, which was under the same corrupt administration as all the other city departments. Lest there be a question of responsibility, they avoided talking to reporters. Jo smiled and touched his arm. "*All* reporters?" she asked a little flirtatiously.

He grinned back at her and she could see from his expression what he was thinking. What does a woman know? The police were like that too; they often spoke to her when clearly they had been instructed not to talk to anyone. "Well, for a pretty girl I could make an exception," he replied in a lyrical Irish brogue.

"Was there excessive smoke?"

"Where's there's smoke, there's fire," he joked. "But I will tell you this, honey: the room adjacent to the dance hall was filled with damp mattresses, and some sort of chemicals too."

"Is that where the fire started?"

"Maybe, maybe not. You can't quote me, you know. I won't give you my name."

"I won't quote you," she promised.

"Well, I will tell you this: the smoke killed more people than the fire. They'd have all gotten out if it weren't for the smoke."

"Was this arson?" she asked directly.

"Oho! Now we're on dangerous ground. You'll have to wait for the inspector's report."

But Jo hadn't waited. She had begun at city hall and ended up phoning every insurance company in the area. The building that housed the nightclub was old. The land on which it stood belonged to a small corporation that had already filed notice of intended demolition. And the building was heavily insured.

At eleven A.M. she had sent two of the office boys
down to the burned-out hulk. They had found and
stolen one of the alarms. By one P.M. the paper's own
expert had taken the alarm apart and declared it faulty.
By six Jo had finished her story. The nightclub had no
proper exits, the alarms were faulty, the wet mattresses
seemed to have been placed intentionally, the company
was heavily insured and would doubtless use the insurance money to construct a new building. The city certainly seemed to be implicated. Jo's own theory was
that bribery had been paid to the fire inspectors. She
shook her head. It was not unlike the story she had
done when Marcella gave evidence. Still, in this case
the wrongdoing went beyond mere corruption. Arson
seemed to be a certainty, and arson had led to death. It
was small comfort that as a result of her own investigation, the fire inspectors from the insurance firm had
launched a full-scale inquiry.

"Damn," Jo murmured. Forty-two people were dead
and one hundred and fifteen injured—all for the financial gain of some corporation that was doubtless a front
for the mob. She reread her story and walked toward
Mike Hamilton's office. He would have to okay it because it was the day after Christmas and no one else
with any authority was around.

"It's a blockbuster," Mike said as he put it down.

"It's a disgrace," Jo said. "I'm sure organized crime
played a role."

"Oh sure. Since the boys started getting into legit
businesses, you don't know who owns what. Hell, the
mob controls every cleaning establishment in the city."

"Is the story all right? Should I tone down the
accusations?"

"Hell no! There's nothing libelous in it. It'll run as a headline story tomorrow."

Mike Hamilton initialed the story and marked "-30-" on the bottom. "Thirty minutes to press," he said, smiling. "Good job. Did you get any sleep last night?"

"No."

"Well, go home and get some."

———————

Jo stood in the well-appointed outer office of Howard Forester, the new publisher of the *World*.

The office had high ceilings, muted Persian carpets, subdued blue draperies, and massive mahogany desks. Mr. James, who was Mr. Forester's secretary, flitted around nervously. He was a small, wiry man with thick horn-rimmed glasses and thin greasy hair.

"You're expected," he said, pointing to the oak double doors that led to the inner sanctum of power. Jo stared at the doors apprehensively. In all the time she had worked for the paper, she had never been summoned to these offices on the eighth floor, nor had the publisher asked to see her. Indeed, never to her knowledge had he asked to see any reporter.

Jo nodded at Mr. James, and opening the door, obtained her first glimpse of Mr. Forester. He was stout and balding, a Buddha in a blue serge suit, seated behind a great desk on a dais. He didn't look as she had imagined the publisher of the *World* should look, but rather like a lawyer or a business consultant.

"Miss Gregory?"

"Yes, I'm Jo Gregory."

"Take a seat, Miss Gregory." He motioned her to a chair, and the double doors swung shut. "I have sent for you so we can discuss your story of December 26."

Jo frowned. She hadn't the faintest idea why she was here. She had come in to work and simply found a note on her desk telling her to come to the eighth floor. On the way up, she had stopped on the fifth floor to ask Mike Hamilton what was going on. But his secretary said he was gone.

"The story on the fire at the El Morocco?" she inquired. Another of her stories had appeared in the paper that same day, but it was unimportant by comparison.

"Yes, that story."

"Was something wrong?"

"Not with reporting the fire, only with the way you handled it. There were certain implications . . . perhaps I should say, allegations."

He seemed to be studying papers as he spoke to her, and she found his lack of eye contact and cool manner unnerving and annoying. "It was approved before it went to press," she said somewhat defensively. Then added, "It certainly wasn't libelous."

"Yes, and the person who approved it is no longer with us."

Jo leaned forward, her mouth open slightly. Had Mike had an accident? Forester made it sound as if he were dead. "What do you mean?" she asked.

"I mean he is no longer in the employ of this paper."

"He left?" Jo could scarcely believe her ears. She had seen Mike yesterday, spent Christmas with him and Jessie—he had said nothing, save the fact that he was "hanging on till retirement." Was that what his secretary had meant when she said "he's gone"? Jo had taken it to mean "gone to lunch" or "gone for the day." "When did this happen?"

"He was dismissed at nine this morning," Mr. Forester announced dispassionately.

"Fired!" Jo bolted up from her chair and walked to the corner of Forester's massive desk. "Mike Hamilton has been with the *World* for years! He's one of Chicago's most respected journalists! You fired him? How could you? And why?"

Mr. Forester looked up coldly. "He was dismissed because he authorized your story, Miss Gregory."

Jo paled. She felt as if none of this were really happening. This pompous little man, Mike's dismissal—now she was being told it was her fault. "I don't understand," she said, trying to control herself. "My story has resulted in an insurance investigation."

"Yes. Frankly, Miss Gregory, we would fire you too, but you're an underling. The ultimate responsibility lies with the person who approved the story. You have been summoned merely so that I might warn you about future stories of this nature."

"What are you talking about?" She knew her voice was higher-pitched than usual. She could feel herself shaking with rage. "This is a crusading newspaper, it's our responsibility to unearth stories like that and bring the culprits to justice. My story was properly researched, verified, and written."

"No, it was not. It contained innuendo directed at Carboni Enterprises. Innuendo which has led to a great many unpleasant questions. Unpleasant and unwelcome."

Jo's mouth opened. "Unwelcome? Unwelcome to whom?"

"To Carboni Enterprises, which is a subsidiary of Global Enterprises, the major stockholder in this paper. Mr. Hamilton was dismissed because it is the ultimate responsibility of the managing editor to reject such garbage before it reaches the front pages."

Jo stared at him. All business, cool and calculating. Her Christmas conversation with Mike rang in her ears, a harbinger of today's events. They had joked about the mobs and legitimate businesses. Mike hadn't known then, but he surely knew now that Global Enterprises was just one such "legit" business run by the mobs.

And cool, calculating Mr. Forester was no more than a front man. A man with business acumen, with the looks of a lawyer, and the tongue of a professor. But behind the blue serge suit and the crisp white shirt, he was a mobster.

"What an effective way to silence a great crusading newspaper!" Jo stormed. "So much less messy than dropping a bomb in the city room like you and your kind did to the *Dispatch* last year."

Mr. Forester didn't even react, he simply raised his eyebrow. "I was afraid you might get emotional," he responded. "Ladies do not belong in this business. Though if you want a job, we're prepared to have you take over the 'Dear Harriet' column."

Jo inhaled. Did this idiot really think she was going to move into an isolated office next to the ladies' room and write the letters-to-the-lovelorn column? "Dear Harriet" indeed.

"It's certainly a job that suits a woman better," he added sarcastically.

"I quit," she said firmly. "I wouldn't work here if you doubled my salary."

"We won't," Forester said, almost laughing.

"When other reporters find out, they'll leave too."

"Possibly. But you see, my dear, you're really in the wrong profession to garner support. There are a thousand little people running around Chicago dying to see their names in print. Half of them would write for nothing—that's why writers will never have any power. Putting pen to paper is everyone's hobby, so it never makes much of a profession."

Jo whirled around. "You'll get yours!" she said, trying
to sound threatening. She stomped to the door and
swung it open, then turned to Mr. James. "Better leave
it open," she shouted. "It smells to high heaven in
there!"

———————

Jo surveyed her small apartment. It looked as if it had
been attacked by hordes of squirrels in search of nuts.
The contents of her bureau drawers and cupboards
were strewn out on the bed, heavy wooden chests and
boxes were piled in every corner.

She glanced sideways at the desk. She hadn't even
attempted to attack it yet, even though she knew that
sorting through her private files and all-important contact lists would take hours. Moreover, the desk was still
cluttered with piles of résumés and tear sheets—samples
of her bylined stories and articles.

"You'll have no difficulty finding a job," Mike Hamilton predicted. "You're young, free to travel, and talented."

Certainly most people wouldn't have called her two
months of free-lancing while job-hunting difficult, but
to her it seemed like a long, drawn-out affair. Day by
day her bank account dwindled, and she always felt the
fear that she might not be hired again. Day after day,
she faced a blank piece of paper in the typewriter as she
was compelled to find subjects for articles and write
those articles. Then there was the endless waiting for
her work to be acknowledged, and the even longer wait
till she was paid for it. Thus far she had sold stories to
Collier's and *McClure's*, to the *Saturday Evening Post*,
and to *Reader's Digest*. But life as a free-lancer was
precarious. She had rejections as well as acceptances.
"The rejections don't mean there's anything wrong with

the writing," Mike Hamilton advised her. "It only means what you sent wasn't right for that particular market."

"Where will you go?" Jo had asked Mike and Jessie. "To the *Tribune* or the *Sun Times?*" It was common knowledge that Mike had been offered good positions by both papers.

"Neither," Mike answered with a smile. "Jessie and I have money put aside, we own property in Indiana, and we're going to retire." He smiled. "Of course, I am an old war-horse. I might just start a small-town paper. Maybe I could give Bill White and the Emporia *Gazette* some competition."

"Do you know William Allen White?"

"Sure, knew him on the Kansas City *Star* years ago. The man's an inspiration to us all. Shows what you can do with a small-town publication."

Jo had hugged Mike. It seemed logical that he would retire, but she thought it was sad to leave the business after so many years with such a bad taste in your mouth. She was overjoyed to learn he had a secret ambition to start a small-town paper. As she studied his expression, she knew he would do it. Men like Mike Hamilton might talk about retirement, but they never actually did it.

Jo's farewell to Jessie was even more emotional. "You've been like a mother to me, Jessie."

Jessie, tears in her eyes, had hugged Jo tightly. "Life's dealt you some nasty blows," she'd said softly. "But remember, we women are tough. The nastier the blows, the stronger we get. You came to this town a girl, but you're a woman now and I think you've finally sorted out your emotions."

"Right now it's my career that matters," Jo had told her.

"You're going to be famous, Jo Gregory. I sense it. But don't turn your back on love. You can have both."

"I won't," Jo promised. Jessie had kissed her then, and Jo, for the first time since she was a child, felt a mother's love and concern.

She took Mike and Jessie to the train station with a heavy heart. And she thought as the train pulled out of the station that once again someone she cared about had disappeared.

With Mike and Jessie gone, and with her bitter experience on the *World* lingering in her mind, Jo made the decision to go to Europe. It was that decision that made her job search more difficult. Jessie, she decided, was right. She should travel and she should become involved in international journalism. But *Time* wasn't interested, and the *Saturday Evening Post* even less so. So she had written résumé after résumé and typed letter after letter until, through Ken Wilson, now an editor on the *Sun*, she was introduced to Sam Rattner, the editor of *Profiles*, *Collier's* leading competitor.

Not that Sam Rattner had been interested initially in establishing a European section for his journal. "Go to it," Ken advised. "Create your own job on that magazine. Make Sam realize how much he needs to be focusing on international affairs. Tell him you speak French. Get to it, girl, go in there and sell yourself!"

Jo laughed to herself. It hadn't been easy, but Sam eventually became convinced. Now in a few short weeks she would be on her way to Europe.

Jo collapsed into the one empty chair in her apartment. She reached over and picked up Ted's letter. She had written to him first; she had written even before she applied for any job. She shook her head sadly, it wasn't the letter she had hoped to receive.

The envelope bore one miserable-looking triangular postage stamp with pale ink and a picture of a farmer with a tractor tilling the rough soil. "CCCP" was written across the bottom. Ted was in the Soviet Union, and his letter held at least one strangely veiled reference.

Dear Jo,

I was surprised to hear from you—glad, but surprised. Rest assured, the same kind of people who now own the *World* run this country. Very efficient.

I'm glad you want to come to Europe and I know you'll find something soon. When you get here, I'm sure we can arrange to meet. I'd like to see a face from home.

Just now, interesting things are happening in my life. I have two new loves. One is a beautiful, delicate girl named Irena. She's a translator in the information office. I think you'd like her. My other love is radio. In addition to my columns, I'm going to be broadcasting soon. God, it's exciting. It's so fast. And the best thing is, the news doesn't get rewritten like wire-service stories do. It comes direct from the person on the spot, and that person is known, he has a voice and a personality and he can express a viewpoint. The wires don't work like that. Of course, you can express a viewpoint in a column, but columns take so much time to transmit. Radio is going to offer analysts the same speed accorded instant news by the wire services. Imagine, commentary before a story is four days old! Mind you, I know it will take years to stabilize radio journalism, but I love it, I really do. Now, listen, telegraph me when you get to Paris. You have the Berlin address. And remember, the end of the *World* is not the end of your world. Be glad you're not in Moscow—it's colder than Chicago, it's even colder than Canada.

Yours,
Ted

Jo refolded the letter and put it aside. It made her sad, and at the same time, strangely happy. Ted deserved a good woman, he deserved someone who could care about him. And he was full of enthusiasm for his work; that too made her feel good.

Her relationship with Ted, like her relationship with David, seemed to be resolved. What did I expect? she asked herself. I rejected him utterly and absolutely. Whatever he once felt, he's gotten over it, and that's for the best. When and if they met, they would be nothing more than old friends and former colleagues. But, she admitted sadly, she did still feel something for Ted. He lingered on the edges of her mind, a memory tinged with regret and guilt. If only she had met him after she had separated from David. If only she had been mature enough to realize that she and David had a mutually self-destructive relationship. If only she had been mature enough to sort out her feelings. But life, Jo concluded, was filled with "if onlys."

Life is an adventure, she told herself. It's filled with possibilities. The future was what she must look to and plan for. Jo stood up and stretched. She was wasting time in thought when there was plenty of packing left to do. Her things had to be out in two days, loaded on a train and headed east. She herself would follow, picking up the *Majestic*, a liner of the White Star Line in New York. This, she vowed, would be a historic event. She was going to sail out of New York harbor first-class on a ship that had formerly been the *Bismarck* but which had been reoutfitted as a luxury liner after the war. She planned to leave the United States in quite a different manner than the way she had entered it eight years ago. She thought briefly about that nightmare journey in steerage and wondered if she would be seasick above the waterline.

"Go to Europe," everyone advised.

"I'm coming," Jo said under her breath. "I'm coming, and I'm going to make something of myself." She carefully picked up her beloved *Little Women* and opened it. Her father's neat handwriting was on the flyleaf. "For Jo," it said. "Love, Papa."

"For you, Papa," she whispered. "I'm going to Europe, and I'm going to be a success."

Fourteen

Jo sat under the tilted green umbrella in the warm April sunshine. Paris in the springtime was as beautiful as David had described it, and very different from the Paris she remembered in the winter of 1919.

The trees were laden with fresh blossoms. The parks were overflowing with laughing children and street entertainers, and the sidewalk cafés were filled to capacity.

This restaurant, La Quatrième, was one David had frequented, and so she too often stopped by to have a coffee or a glass of wine in the patio adjacent to the busy sidewalk.

It was here, only three weeks after her arrival in Paris a year ago, that she had met Louise Bryant. It was a meeting that affected her deeply. She found Louise a soulmate in terms of her feminist ideas, but she also found her disturbing. Louise's early work and her ideals were an inspiration. But like David, Louise was extremely self-destructive.

"My friend David Driscoll had great admiration for your late husband," Jo told Louise sincerely. "He always believed John Reed's journalism to be relevant because Reed was so involved in what he was writing about."

"He loved Russia," Louise said even as she blinked back tears.

She seemed to take compliments paid to Reed's memory very personally in spite of the fact that she had remarried and had borne her second husband a child. Jo didn't mention her own views on the Soviet Union, nor the fact that Ted's letters and articles presented a grim portrayal of both the people and the government. Louise was too emotional to partake in an argument on the merits of Marxism.

"Some journalists fight for objectivity," Louise murmured. "Others, like John, fight to make a point, to win adherents. He made no bones about wanting to influence his readers."

Jo studied Louise Bryant. She was in her mid-thirties, though sadly, what was left of her youth was ravaged by her excessive drinking. She had a long narrow face, intensely expressive eyes, a straight nose, and thinnish lips. She was attractive but not beautiful. Yet there was an undefinable, compelling quality about her. Jo felt it grew out of her intellectual intensity. "Did you mind being sent to Russia to write about the revolution from the 'woman's point of view'?" Jo asked.

Louise laughed cynically. "I wrote *Six Red Months in Russia* from *my* point of view. I don't try to be objective, either. I don't believe anyone's objective. You might as well be open about it. I write to educate, to change minds. Writers who fool themselves—tell themselves they're objective—write mush. If readers want objectivity, then they have to go out and find opposing views, read them, and *think*. Take the Russian Revolution, for example. Americans wanted to know who the good guys were and who the bad guys were. But in reality, the so-called good guys and bad guys were both good and bad. There weren't two sides, there wasn't any black and white. The situation was intensely complicated, but all the average American wanted to know—in fact ever wants to know—is, whom do I cheer for?" Louise sipped her wine and warmed to her subject.

"It seems to me that the press has two major responsibilities, and they ought not get them mixed up. They should report happenings, and those happenings should be reported accurately. And they should try to influence readers, make this a better world to live in. Personal journalism is very important, personal analysis is vital."

Louise leaned over, and Jo could feel her strength. Yet for all that strength, Louise Bryant was not a single-minded person. She had not given her life to her career, she had allowed her personal passion to mix with her professional passion. She had given up writing for long periods of time to follow her late husband and to be with him under terribly difficult circumstances.

It was also painfully clear that Louise was miserable in her second marriage. She and her husband were separated, and though they hadn't filed for divorce, they lived on different continents. It was just as clear that part of Louise had died with John Reed. When she spoke of Reed, her face took on a glow, her eyes grew misty, and it was as if she were reliving a beautiful memory. Clearly theirs had been an obsessive love.

"I read your interview with Mussolini," Jo had told her. "It was an excellent personal portrait."

"It proves the power of wearing a skirt," Louise replied sarcastically. "It was the first interview he ever granted an American, and he wouldn't have granted it had I not been a woman. That's what makes women journalists so important. Men open up to them. They say things they wouldn't say to a man. And women are more sensitive to nuances than men." A smile broke on her thin lips. "Do you know what Mussolini did?"

Jo shook her head.

"He had me come right up to him. Then he ripped open his shirt and asked if I wanted to feel the hair on his chest. Machismo, they call it in Italy. He wanted to show me he was virile. I knew that he defined virility in terms of his appearance, in terms of the hair on his chest.

"Fascism is like that—a virile show with nothing underneath. No ideology, no real morality. Mussolini is full of what people shouldn't do. He hasn't the foggiest notion of what they should do. He's surrounded by low-life. It's dismal. The man has set back the advancement of Italian women by fifty, maybe a hundred years. He took the vote away from them, he lowered their pay, he's made it very difficult for women who are single and have children to support. 'Go home and tend your children,' he tells them. 'Go be obedient and follow your husband's orders.' As if all mothers were married, or as if there weren't thousands of Italian men who didn't desert their wives."

"Fascism is a rising force in Europe," Jo remembered commenting.

"So they say. But keep that story in mind. When you interview men, look at their personal characteristics. Watch everything they do. Try to get beyond the words their lips are mouthing."

Jo tucked Louise's advice away, and she also stored the warning she felt Louise's own person offered.

Jo sipped her drink and turned her thoughts briefly to Ted Kahn. For the entire year she had been in Europe, they had been trying to arrange a meeting. But Ted was heavily involved in both writing and broadcasting, and he was traveling constantly to Poland, Hungary, Austria, Romania, and Bulgaria. His beat was east of Berlin, while hers was Paris, the Riviera, Spain, England, and Portugal. A meeting between them had proved impossible, and now even their letters were infrequent.

Jo glanced at her watch. It was time to head home and prepare for her interview with Aristide Briand, winner of the 1926 Nobel Peace Prize. Briand was to be her May "profile" and it had taken her two months to set up this interview. She smiled to herself and wondered if Briand would have insisted on taking a male reporter to Maxim's for dinner. Well, she thought, draining her coffee cup, this interview need not involve conflict. Briand was an advocate of the World Peace Pact, an idea that was hard to oppose.

"My dear!" Aristide Briand strode toward her, his hands extended as if they were old friends. He took her fox-fur stole and handed it to the waiting hostess, then guided her into the exclusive, charmed atmosphere of Paris' most expensive restaurant.

As she walked, Jo was conscious of Briand's eyes on her low-backed burgundy velvet gown. It fit tightly on the top, swirling out into soft gathers below the hip. Her hair was held off her high forehead with a woven gold headband, and her jewelry consisted of a gold armband just below the elbow and three strands of a gold rope chain. The outfit gave her the much-coveted "slave" look brought into vogue by Hollywood films.

Jo's initial impression of Briand was that in physical appearance he looked as if he might be the lead singer in a barbershop quartet. He was of medium height, with broad shoulders and a heavy chest. His hair was untidy and flecked with gray. He had a luxuriant handlebar mustache that gave his otherwise undistinguished face a softness, and his mouth was slightly crooked, but its ugliness was redeemed by a winning smile and bright eyes. And his eyes were roaming. Quite clearly he was a ladies' man.

"This table, my dear." He pulled out the richly brocaded chair with a flourish and Jo sat down. The gleaming white tablecloth was augmented with heavy sterling-silver place settings that glistened in the soft light. A bouquet of fresh roses served as the centerpiece, and champagne was already chilling in a heavy silver bucket. Maxim's always fascinated Jo. No matter how crowded with the great and near-great, it always seemed quiet. Somewhere in the distance she could hear the muted sounds of violins.

Jo mentally reviewed her notes as the waiter uncorked the champagne. Briand was sixty-six, a lawyer, an academic, a statesman, and a politician whose views seemed distanced from ordinary people. He had served eleven times as premier of France and had held more than twenty ministerial posts. He was active in the League of Nations, but before that he had been associated with left-wing causes. On the surface he appeared to be what he was purported to be—a man of peace. A man whose passions centered on a unified Europe. But Jo wondered. There were events in his background that suggested a certain pragmatic self-interest. He had been a strong socialist, but when offered a ministry in 1906, he took it even though his fellow socialists considered the government to be bourgeois, and his acceptance caused a break with them.

"This is fine champagne," he said, smiling. "We are going to have a lovely evening, you and I. Tell me, my dear, how long have you been writing?"

"Four years. I began with the *World*."

"But you're so young! And, may I add, lovely." He leaned over the table and took her hand. "You know, I don't usually like the press. In fact, I loathe interviews. But what Frenchman would turn down the opportunity to spend time with so beautiful a lady?"

"You flatter me, but we haven't met before tonight. How did you know what I looked like?"

"Ah, my dear. News travels fast at Versailles. You interviewed Mr. Lloyd George recently and he spoke of you."

Jo forced a smile, remembering her interview with Lloyd George. He, it turned out, was also quite the ladies' man. He had spent much of the interview trying to seduce her, and for days afterward, flowers arrived at her apartment, together with invitations for lunch, dinner, and even a weekend in Switzerland. "Lloyd George is too kind," she said, somewhat tongue-in-cheek.

"Oh no! He didn't do you justice. But I shall thank him for insisting I allow myself to be interviewed by the American lady writer, as he called you."

"Then let me begin," Jo said, sipping the champagne. "You desire to bring peace by unifying Europe's discordant nations. That desire seems to be completely at odds with the rampant nationalism that is reawakening."

"Nationalism is evil. It caused the Great War, and if nations will not yield to internationalism, we will have an even more devastating conflagration. Mind you, the time has not come when I can advocate a united Europe openly. Peace must come first. But I do dream of it, I dream of one parliament, one customs union, a common market for all our goods."

He moved his hands expressively when he spoke, and Jo could not help wondering if he also envisaged a place for himself in this united Europe of his dreams. Perhaps, she mused, as its prime minister.

"I'm telling you about my dreams confidentially. I wouldn't want you to print a story about a united Europe. That's too radical an idea for now."

"I won't," Jo replied. But, she thought, knowing a man's dreams helped. "Could we discuss the peace pact?"

"I want all nations to sign it, to promise to outlaw war as an instrument of national policy."

"Mussolini doesn't believe peace can be achieved by signing a peace pact. He believes peace can be assured only by preparedness for war, a readiness to face an aggressor."

Briand waved his hand as if to brush away her comment. "He likes to play soldier. The Italians are essentially a peaceful people. I would be more worried if the Americans thought that way. It's a cycle, you see. One side prepares, the other outprepares the first, and soon both sides are armed to the teeth. They stagger under the load of their own armaments, then they trip into war."

"I can't argue with that. But the idea of a peace pact denies the reality of nations' relations with one another. If an aggressor arose," she said carefully, "one who had not agreed to the peace pact, how would that aggressor be dealt with?"

"Through mutual strength."

"Collective security," she suggested.

"Ah, yes. That's what I meant, collective security."

"But suppose there are two groups of nations—each with collective security. That was the situation prior to the war. There were many treaties. Each of the camps sought out the neutral nations to join their side. England sought out Russia by promising it part of Turkey."

Briand patted her hand. "Such complicated thoughts for a pretty young girl. Tell me, dear, what would you like for dinner? Fish, meat, perhaps some escargots to begin?"

"Fish," Jo replied, all too aware that Briand had made a major diversion and was patronizing her. Still, she would bring this story home. When you dealt with men like Lloyd George and Aristide Briand, you learned to play the game. She smiled sweetly. "I don't suppose you regard the Soviet Union as a problem?"

"No. Our problems are with Germany."

He meant France's problems, and essentially, in spite of his pronouncements, his emphasis on Germany revealed his own French nationalism. "But Russia could prove a threat to Europe," she ventured.

"A socialist country? No, I don't think so. They'll sign the peace pact, I'm sure of it."

His idealism was so obvious it almost made Jo smile. She couldn't help thinking of her father, who had signed the loyalty oath to Turkey and believed that in so doing he would be safe. Her profile would have to take on his idealism. "People must be made to think," Louise had said. "They may scream that they disagree, or they may cry out that they agree. But their participation is essential. They can't just accept everything they read like mindless vegetables."

"What about certain populations within nations? What about the Croats? The Serbs? What of the Armenians? How would such a peace pact protect minorities in the signing countries? How would it ensure their rights?"

Briand's expression clouded. "A difficult question. A nation, or a group of nations, cannot interfere with the internal matters of a sovereign state."

"Not even if a minority is being slaughtered as the Armenians were?"

He poured more champagne and signaled the waiter. He ordered baked snapper and gave specific instructions as to how it was to be prepared. When he had finished, he returned his attention to her. "I have an apartment at Versailles. Quite a magnificent view, really. Perhaps you would care to continue our interview there after our repast?"

"I would like that very much, but I'm afraid I have a previous commitment," Jo told him. She lowered her eyes as if she were embarrassed.

"Ah, I should have guessed that such a lovely lady would have an assignation. But forgive an old man, I don't only dream of uniting nations."

"About minority groups . . ." Jo pressed.

"Well, I suppose one would have to count on moral pressure."

Moral pressure. Jo might have laughed, but it would have been an ironic laugh. Moral pressure hadn't saved her people. She watched the look on Briand's face. He was thinking about a thorny issue he had not previously contemplated. "I suppose there ought to be some provision for certain basic rights. Rights for minorities such as you mention."

"If there are such provisions, do you still think the Soviets would sign? Last week an American reporter was deported for writing about Stalin's purges. Now they say there is mass starvation in the Ukraine because of forced collectivization."

"That story is not authenticated."

"Because reporters are not allowed to report freely," she retorted.

"The press—excuse my saying so, my dear—often exaggerates and spreads false information."

"The press did not start the war, and more often than not, their stories are only thought to be false. We must be free to report what we see and hear."

"Well, I certainly didn't mean the Fourth Estate was to be ignored."

Briand didn't like the press. She had heard stories about his intolerance for reporters. He was, however, known for his wit, though she had seen little of it this evening. She wondered if he confined his humor to his political colleagues. She decided he was a politician who played what she had dubbed the "Oxford Game." She called it that because the British seemed best at it. It was the ability to slay an opponent in debate, not with logic, but with sarcasm. Jo felt like being blunt. "You don't like the press, do you?"

"I think they hamper negotiations, when negotiations are, shall I say, sensitive. I believe news should be controlled—managed, if you like."

"But then the public won't know what's being negotiated. They can't react and their governments may take actions which displease them."

"It's not an ideal world, my dear."

Jo nodded. "But only in an ideal world would a peace pact be adhered to."

Briand lifted his glass to her. "I've been called an idealist, a socalist, a political opportunist, and no doubt many other names which I could not repeat in your company. I know my plan is idealistic. But don't you see, you must always start negotiations with the highest expectations, even though you may settle for less than the desired perfection. What's important is the act of getting negotiations started, of getting the various sides talking, and keeping them talking."

Jo wrote down his last quote and thought it would make a good lead for her story. "Thank you," she said, putting her pad in her purse. "That's what I wanted."

"May we now enjoy an elegant meal," he toasted, again lifting his glass. Then, smiling, "You'll see, my dear, the fish is absolutely succulent the way Maxim's prepares it. And after dinner we'll have some cognac. Perhaps you will consider visiting my apartment another time. The view is *truly* remarkable."

———

Dear Jo,

No one who has been to Paris can ever forget it. Your letter brought back both pleasant and unpleasant memories of the time I spent there.

You may enjoy it, of course, but I don't envy you the job of interviewing people like Briand. Covering endless boring conferences just isn't my meat. I like action, not words. I see Briand and his kind as super civil servants who are trying to make it on a higher level, the idea being that if one government structure doesn't work, you create another, higher structure. What you end up with is more paper shufflers.

I know you'll be glad to hear that I've pulled myself out of the depths of self-misery and found a job. I'm with INS—International News Services. We're a wire service owned by Hearst Newspapers. We're small but, I like to think, efficient. What we need is some stringers; we just don't have the staff to station reporters around the globe. How about it? The magazine can't take up all your time. How about being an INS stringer and supplementing your income?

If you say yes, wire me back and I'll send you your credentials and a list of the teletype offices at our disposal.

Love,
David

"Good for you," Jo said, putting David's letter aside. He was working! It made her feel good to think he was

well and that he'd pulled himself out of his rut and was
back on a news desk, where he belonged.

Jo leaned back and considered David's offer. Working as a stringer for a wire service would give her the
opportunity to do hard news again. Moreover, it would
give her more exposure and possibly open the door to
some syndication possibilities. She decided to accept
his offer.

Slowly she reread David's letter, trying to imagine
his face, trying to picture him working in a cluttered
office at INS. Louise had differentiated between "reporters of fact" and those who made and changed opinion. Perhaps, Jo decided, David was best suited to
being a reporter of fact. He questioned his own views
too much to play the analyst, and he was unwilling to
put in the long hours of research and reading that were
necessary to master each subject. The article writer was
a perpetual student; most of the work was done in the
library.

"He *is* better off without me," she whispered to
herself. Together they had formed a never-ending cir-
cle of dependency, each feeding off the other. She
knew she had used David to replace her lost family,
and David had used her to replace his lost talent. No
two people could live together happily until they had
learned to live alone, she concluded. Need, emotional
or otherwise, she decided, was not a good basis for a
relationship.

Jo pulled herself off the settee and walked over to her
desk. Beneath a glass paperweight was a letter from her
editor. He suggested she interview Emmeline Pankhurst
and her daughter Christabel. "We'll call it the forty-
year fight," he suggested. "Our female readers will eat
it up."

Jo leaned over and checked the calendar. Briand was

her May feature, and she hoped that the second Baron de Rothschild, who lived in London, would consent to be her June feature. That would put the Pankhursts into the July issue. If all went well and the baron agreed, it would mean two trips to London. The Pankhursts were not a problem; they both sought and eagerly gave interviews. It was only a matter of making an appointment. The baron, however, shunned reporters. His interview would be much more difficult to arrange. Difficult, but not impossible.

Abstractedly Jo picked up a copy of the *Herald*. It was one of the many papers that carried Ted's column. In this issue he talked openly about his recent deportation. The Soviets claimed he was deported because he had married and helped to smuggle out a Soviet citizen, Irena Mitka Mokhov, a translator at the information office. Ted himself claimed his deportation was the result of his stories on Stalin. Jo shook her head in resignation. Ted was married now, and no doubt that was the reason his letters had grown infrequent.

Jo folded the paper and sat down. Ted had been traveling between Berlin and Moscow for over a year, and before she had left Chicago he had written and mentioned Irena. Jo closed her eyes and tried to imagine what Irena looked like. Ted had written once and described her as being frail—somehow Jo could not imagine Ted married to a frail woman. Perhaps, she thought, Ted too has something of the savior in him. He had been so critical of David's dependency, she could not help wondering if Irena too was dependent. "How often do the strong attract the weak?" she asked herself aloud. Vaguely she wondered if two strong people could survive one another, or whether there was some human impulse to seek out those who needed care and nurturing.

Jo hurried back to her hotel, arriving at its portico just before the hard raindrops began to fall from the ominous summer sky. On her previous trips to England—one made shortly after she arrived in Europe, and the other only weeks ago—she had marveled at the seemingly endless acres of lush green grass, the manicured shrubs, and the ever prolific gardens with their carefully tended roses, marigolds, tulips, and irises. It did not, however, take long to fathom the reason for the greener-than-green lawns and the lush beauty of the gardens. It rained a great deal, and even in the middle of June the skies were prone to cloud over and the temperature plunge, making it feel like a damp fall day in Chicago. But no matter what the weather, this, Jo knew, was a memorable day.

She had nearly canceled this trip when she learned that Emmeline Pankhurst had died June 4. But then Christabel had urged her to come. "There's an important vote in Parliament," she wired, so Jo came to London in spite of Emmeline's death.

Christabel was eager to be cooperative, and together they decided that the article should be a memorial to Christabel's mother, Emmeline. The feature's cornerstone was the vote that Jo had watched this very day from the parliamentary press gallery.

"This," Christabel declared, "is the finest homage that could be paid to my mother. This is what she fought for. British women were first enfranchised in 1918," Christabel reminded Jo. "But that enfranchisement was limited to keep the vast majority of working women and poor women from voting. Its limitations were directed primarily at young women, because it was felt that young women would be more radical and more demanding. So the right to vote depended on marital status and on age. But today's vote enfranchises all women over twenty-one. There are no property or marital requirements. This is what my mother wanted. This is the beginning of true equality, because now we have a voice and our demands must be listened to."

"And what will British women fight for now?" Jo had asked, even though she knew what Christabel would say.

"For the right to marry whom we please if we are under twenty-one, for the right to higher education, for birth control, for equal treatment under the law, for equal wages. There is no shortage of issues to address."

Jo had smiled at Christabel's first priority. She thought of her uncle and of Nass Ajemian. The very year she had run away, women were granted the vote in the United States, but in many ways women still remained the property of their fathers, guardians, and husbands till they reached the age of majority. She had written an in-depth article on the marriage laws in the United States, which were still a hodgepodge, varying from jurisdiction to jurisdiction.

Christabel was right: there were many rights still to be attained. England's vote was historic, even though Emmeline's death cast a shadow over it. The struggle would continue.

"Jo!"

Jo was closing her umbrella when she heard her name and looked up.

"Are you sleepwalking?" Ted Kahn grinned at her and strode across the lobby, his arms extended. "God, what a surprise!"

He was taller than she remembered, and he had filled out a little. He was more muscular, and a wisp of his dark hair fell across his brow. He looked incredibly handsome and relaxed. His eyes fastened on her, warm and glowing. He looked truly glad to see her.

"You look beautiful," he breathed in her ear as he embraced her and kissed her on the cheek.

Jo shivered, then forced herself to pull away from him. "I thought you were still in Berlin," she stammered.

"I was till yesterday, and I'm going back tomorrow. I thought you were in Paris."

The feel of his hand on her arm made her tremble. Her long-suppressed desire for him seemed to bubble to the surface, and she was surprised that it still existed. "I came to London to profile the Pankhursts," she told him as she tried to regain her composure.

"It's wonderful! Ever since you got to Europe, I've hoped we'd meet." He glanced at his watch. "It's nearly four. I have to make a few calls, and I have an appointment at five. But it'll be a short appointment," he assured her. "Can I pick you up around eight for dinner?"

"You and your wife?" Jo looked at him steadily.

Ted shook his head. "Irena's in Berlin. Look, just because I'm married doesn't mean I can't have dinner with an old friend."

"Of course not," Jo replied quickly. "Eight is fine with me."

"We'll have to become reacquainted," he told her, and his eyes lingered on her face. It was a long, meaningful look. Then his expression changed, and he smiled broadly. "Do you have any idea how many used-book stores there are in London?"

Jo laughed softly and remembered the long rainy days in Chicago, days when they had gone from one bookstore to another, then had dinner in a small restaurant and gone to the theater. Her fondness for him rushed to her consciousness, and she kissed him on the cheek and squeezed his arm. "I'll be waiting for you," she promised. "We have a lot to catch up on."

Ted waved, then turned and headed away and outside to the taxi stand. Jo stood in the lobby feeling for a moment like Lot's wife. She had turned and looked back into the past, and this brief encounter with Ted had turned her to stone.

She forced herself to walk toward the elevator. She was being silly; it had been years. She was just glad to see him, that's what it was. And it was the same for him. The spark she'd felt was loneliness. What she had momentarily felt was a product of her imagination. It was the fact that they hadn't seen each other in so long. Ted Kahn was a happily married man, and she had her career and was settled comfortably in Paris. They would be friends, there could be nothing more, and there wouldn't be.

Jo wore a moss-green cashmere knit dress with a printed paisley scarf and alligator accessories. She hadn't brought an evening gown to London, and in this tiny secluded restaurant in Soho, there was no need for formal dress.

They ate rare roast beef, Yorkshire pudding, a crisp salad, and warm homemade bread. Ted ordered a rich red French wine, and they ate slowly and talked.

"Every great city has a Soho," he said, smiling. "New York has the Village, Chicago the Near North Side, Paris the Left Bank. Even Berlin has a Soho. It's a wild place, and Berliners are unique. You know, I love being there."

Jo laughed. "Fine for you to say. You speak German."

"You could learn enough to get by in short order."

"I like Paris," she insisted. "Besides, I can always visit Berlin."

"You have to live there to appreciate it." He leaned over the table and touched her hand. "But I'm glad you're happy. Pity about the *World*, though. It was a fine newspaper in its day."

"I miss it sometimes. It's harder to work on one's own." Jo laughed softly. "Sometimes I sit in my apartment and I think: I can't write in this silence. I have to have the presses humming. I listen to records, and then I can write because there's sound."

Ted nodded his agreement and sipped some wine. "Do you still have a—what shall I call it?—a relationship with Driscoll?"

Jo pressed her lips together. "We write. He's pulled himself together and he's doing all right."

"You loved him, or said you did. Why didn't you ever marry him?"

Ted's eyes were intense, and Jo was aware of a vague discomfort. But she decided there was no need to lie. "I loved David in a way you never understood," she said slowly. "At the time, I don't think I understood it myself."

"Make me understand now, Jo. Tell me the truth."

"Before I tell you, Ted, let me make it clear that I don't want sympathy. Sympathy is a patronizing emotion, and I must confess I find this hard to talk about. I'm going to try to explain something to you. David knows part of my story, but not all of it. There are things I've never told anyone."

Ted nodded, silently begging her to continue.

"I'm Armenian, Ted. My real name is Gregorian, not Gregory. I was the child David Driscoll found in a Greek refugee camp nine years ago."

"Armenian? I'd have never guessed. You don't have

any accent, and you write as if English were your mother tongue."

"My father had us educated in English and French. I lost all traces of my accent when I went to live with my uncle in Massachusetts."

"Armenian," Ted repeated. They were sometimes called "Christian Jews"—they too had known hostility, ghettos, even pogroms, though they called them by different names. "I met an old Armenian when I was in Russia. He was propped up against the side of a building, he was wearing rags. I thought he was a beggar. He was an illegal money changer, and after we negotiated for some rubles, he asked if I was Armenian. I told him I was Jewish, and he shook his head and shrugged, saying, 'Same thing, really.' I don't think I'll ever forget that man. He was a survivor of the so-called Turkish deportations."

"So am I," Jo said slowly. Her mind was wandering, and buried images returned with a dismal clarity. "We were taken to a desert camp. They intended to let us die of thirst. My father organized an escape. We made it to the mountains, but then we were set upon by Kurdish soldiers. They killed my father, grandfather, and brothers. Then they . . ." Jo stopped and closed her eyes; she could hardly put into words what she had seen, what she had hidden for so long, what was recreated only in her nightmares. "They raped my sister and mother many times, then stabbed them to death with knives. I saw it all from where I was hiding with my friend Mushgin. He tried to cover my eyes, but I saw it all." Jo stopped and let out her breath. "I often used to dream about it. About the wild horses that trampled my father, about the rape. But they say time heals all wounds, and in recent years I've had such terrible dreams only now and again. When I first came to

Chicago, I wanted to avoid any physical relationship with a man. David was safe—he thought of me as a child. He took me under his wing and he guided me. Then he began drinking again, and everything went wrong."

"You weren't lovers?"

Jo half-smiled. "Oh, we tried once. David couldn't get involved with me that way, and he didn't really satisfy me either. But he was gentle, he enabled me to overcome my fear."

"Oh, Jo, I don't know what to say."

Ted's face was pale, and his hand covered hers, squeezing it gently.

"David came into my life when I needed him. In my heart, he became my father and brothers. He helped me, he gave me hope, and I guess I fell in love with him. Not as a woman should love a man, Ted. But as a woman loves her father and brother."

"I understand," Ted said sincerely. "How did you finally escape? How were you able to witness your parents' murder without being killed yourself?"

"Mushgin," Jo replied. "Mushgin was the baker's son. He was with us. He was my playmate and my friend, though he was a few years older than I. He had taken me up into the rocks to look for small animals or some vegetation we could eat. He said that sometimes near the big rocks, sweet grass grew. We heard the Kurds' horses, and Mushgin said we should hide. We saw everything because the Kurds had torches. Mushgin covered my mouth so I couldn't scream. We stayed in hiding till morning, holding each other and crying. Then Mushgin and I left. We wandered for days, and were found by Greek soldiers, who took us across their lines. Eventually we were put into a camp in Athens. Then we were separated and Mushgin was sent to

relatives in Syria and I was sent to Salonika. I never
saw him again," she added sadly.

Ted finished his wine. "Let's walk," he suggested.
"Let's walk and talk some more."

He paid the bill and they left the little restaurant,
emerging into the misty fog of a London night. Ted
took her arm and held her close to him.

"I know about the Armenians," Ted told her. "You
know, for centuries the Jews and the Armenians have
been treated the same way. Both peoples have been
aliens—they've lived among those with strong prejudices. In the Ukraine the Jews are aliens among ignorant Christians who believe we eat Christian children at
Passover."

"It's strange how similar the folklore of prejudice is,"
Jo observed. "The Armenians were aliens in a Moslem
land. They said we captured Moslem children at Easter
and held them captive, torturing and killing them."

"The Turks were brutal."

"Not all Turks. None of us would have survived had it
not been for the friendship of some Turks. I was born
and brought up in Istanbul, and we summered near
Lake Van and were there when the deportation orders
came. We had many Turkish friends in Istanbul, and
some in the village where we summered. In Istanbul
some Turks risked their own lives to urge an end to the
deportations and massacres, and Turks in our village
brought us food at great risk to their personal safety.
Turkey is the bridge between East and West, is at once
Occidental and Oriental. There's enormous wealth and
severe poverty; it's a culture where only the fit survive.
There are highly educated, humane, and kind Turks.
There are ignorant, fearful, and inhumane Turks. The
Europeanized Turks fought for our rights, but they lost
to a combination of political threat and ignorance. Tur-

key is not like America, there is no great middle class, and there are no newspapers to tell people of injustices. Good people who might have helped us couldn't help because they didn't know, or they were roughly silenced. But even Turkey is changing. It isn't like it was." She smiled. "Do you know the parliament under Ataturk has over ninety women! And of course, now there is freedom of the press."

"I wish you had told me all of this in Chicago."

"I couldn't talk about it then."

"Does our past trap us in our future?" he asked.

"I think it only determines the path we take, but I also think we can force ourselves to change direction. I have no regrets, Ted." She looked up into his face and forced herself to smile. "Tell me about you. Tell me about your wife."

Tell me about your wife? What a simple question, Ted thought. A simple question, but the answer was as emotionally complicated as Jo's relationship with David Driscoll.

He had been in Moscow four months. They were the winter months—long cold, dark, and dismal. He was lonely and bored. And Russian women? The ones he met were broad-shouldered, wide-hipped, short, and bedecked in clothes that gave the impression they were in perpetual mourning. Then he was introduced to Irena, who came to work as a translator at the Soviet press bureau. She was thin, almost frail. She had long blond hair and blue eyes. She was, he learned, half Jewish. Her father came from close to the Finnish border, her mother from Moscow. She was an only child and her one desire in life was to escape the dreariness of Russia. They were, he realized now, a matched set. What had originally brought them together was their mutual dislike of Moscow. He began seeing her, and one thing led to another. Eventually he slept with her, and belatedly he realized it was lust without passion. He left Moscow in the spring, but when he returned, he found Irena was pregnant. Honor won out. He married her and together they planned her escape from Moscow through Finland. By the time Irena arrived in Berlin, she had lost the baby. The German doctor who examined her told them she could have no children. Months passed and Irena changed. She stayed in their Berlin apartment as if she feared going out. She shrank from physical contact with him as if she blamed him for the loss of the child. They lived together, but they lived apart. Should he say to Jo: "She's a strange woman and I'm miserable"? No, it sounded all too common. He wouldn't whine, and he wouldn't complain. His marriage was of his own making, and though he regretted it, Jo was the one person he couldn't tell.

"Irena? She's a lovely girl. I think you'd like her, though you're very different," he said after a moment.

"I'm sure I would like her. Is she Jewish?"

"Half. Her mother was Jewish. But her mother's family didn't practice the faith. Really she knows very little about the religion or customs of the Jews."

Jo watched Ted's expression. It seemed to have changed; he looked tight, almost as if he were holding something back. "Is she happy in Berlin too?"

Ted shrugged. "I think she would be happier in New York. Never having been to America, she refuses to believe that all Americans aren't wealthy."

"I thought that once," Jo told him.

"But you were only fourteen. Irena's twenty-five."

Jo stared ahead. Ted's tone had changed as soon as he began to talk about his wife. No, no, she thought. I'm imagining it.

"There's the hotel," Ted said, pointing through the fog.

"Have we walked so far?"·

"Jo, seeing you has meant a lot to me . . ." He leaned over and drew her into his arms and kissed her suddenly. It was a long, deep, penetrating kiss, and she gave way to it, leaning against him.

Then she pulled away abruptly. "No, Ted. Stop it. Don't do this." She stood looking up into his face. There were tears in his eyes, and his expression was one of longing and pain.

"I'm sorry, Jo. I really am."

She nodded. "I have to go." She turned and ran down the street toward the hotel. Tears formed in her eyes, and she dared not look back. Oh God, I wish I hadn't seen you, she thought. I wish to heaven we hadn't met again.

"Hitler, the German Svengali,"
by Jo Gregory.
September 1930. Dateline: Berlin.
Exclusive to *Profiles*.

Fifteen

To: Jo Gregory, Foreign Correspondent, *Profiles*
From: Sam Rattner, Editor in Chief

It's been decided to relocate you in Berlin as of July.
Please make necessary plans. Wire Konrad Baer, 106
Nollendorfplatz, Berlin, of your time of arrival. Herr
Baer is an excellent photographer we have engaged to
assist you when necessary (he has worked free-lance for
a number of American journals). He will help you to
relocate and provide you with a contact list.
                                        Best of luck,
                                                Sam

Go to Berlin! Jo's first reaction was personal and less
than enthusiastic. The American press corps in Berlin
consisted of no more than nine correspondents. There
was no way she could avoid running into Ted, and, she
confessed to herself, that might mean another emotional upheaval.

On another level, she was ecstatic. This assignment
meant she could devote herself entirely to international
news and analysis. She was the only woman journalist
to have this kind of plum. What's more, she repre-

sented *Profiles*, now one of America's leading magazines and virtually the only one expanding during the
current depression. Her success stemmed from the fact
that two of her stories had won prizes, and from time to
time she herself made news when her name was linked
romantically with some famous personage. Indeed, that
had happened only recently when she had gone to
London to interview Sultan Sir Mohammed Shah, Aga
Khan III, one of the richest men in the world. He was
in England to attend the Round Table Conference on
Indian constitutional reform and he insisted he be interviewed at the sprawling country estate of a friend. Jo
found herself invited to the estate for the weekend. The
interview was held over a two-day period while the Aga
Khan toured the stables and rode the countryside on
some of the finest thoroughbreds in England. Horses
were his passion, and Jo had ridden with him, causing a
certain amount of predictable gossip, which was duly
reported by the British papers with such leads as "Beautiful American Reporter Rides with Aga Kahn" and
"Weekend Rendezvous."

David had written her a letter in which he teasingly
dubbed her "The Princess of International Journalism." He must have said it to others as well, because
now all her press colleagues jokingly called her Princess.

Profiles was not the only publication for which she
wrote, though it was the one she appeared in regularly.
Over the years she had continued with INS, and recently the Hearst papers had bought the occasional
column from her. When she first received her Berlin
assignment from *Profiles*, she had been afraid of losing
her INS job. But David was overjoyed she was going to
Berlin, and Hearst promised her further assignments.

*   *   *

Jo stood expectantly by the information desk in the crowded Friedrichstrasse Bahnhof. She was wearing her new long-waisted rose silk crepe dress and an impish summer straw hat trimmed in the same dusty rose as her dress.

Why did she half-expect to see Ted appear out of the crowd? It was nonsense. She couldn't possibly run into him except at a press conference or reception. Berlin is a big city, she assured herself again and again. When we meet, it will be casual. I can be as remote as I want. Silently, and for the hundredth time, she vowed not to become involved with Ted Kahn again. He's a married man, she frequently reminded herself. And no matter how strong the attraction, I won't allow myself to be alone with him. The past is the past.

"Miss Gregory? Jo Gregory?"

The sound of her name caused her to whirl around nervously toward the speaker. He was a tall, thin young man. Somehow, she had expected someone older. "Herr Baer?"

His pale lips pressed together and he nodded. "You look like your picture," he said in near-perfect English and with an expansive wave of his hand. "And very fashionable. I was afraid you'd turn out to be one of those dowdy women reporters dressed in a mannish suit."

Konrad Baer did not suit his name. His face was long and narrow, his eyes gray, and his skin slightly sallow. He was, she noticed, not only thin but also small-boned, almost delicate in appearance. He seemed nervous and ill-at-ease, and his hands moved constantly when he spoke. Her first reaction to him was one of instant familiarity. It was as if she had met him before. Then with a flash she knew. He not only resembled Antoine physically but also moved his hands in the same way and gave an overwhelming impression of femininity. "I'm glad you had no difficulty recognizing me." She smiled warmly, hoping to put him more at ease.

"No, no. Here, let me take your case. I have a car waiting."

Jo followed him through the station and out into the warm July sunshine.

"Have you been to Berlin before?"

"No. This is my first time in Germany."

"Ah." He nodded his head up and down as he opened the car door for her. "Nollendorfplatz," he instructed the driver. Then he climbed in beside her. "I hope you like the flat." He smiled, leaned back, and seemed to relax slightly. "Of course, if you don't, you can move. I made the arrangement for only one month. It's near my studio, so it's quite convenient."

"What kind of neighborhood is it?" she asked.

"Oh, mixed. I'm not sure how to put it in English. Bohemian, I would say. Though some of Berlin's better citizens would say it's a red-light district. Many artists, photographers, and writers live there. Some American writers too."

Jo almost laughed. Briefly she thought of the house on Erie Street and its inhabitants. "Good. It sounds like the kind of area I'm used to."

"One American told me it was Berlin's Greenwich Village."

"Then I shall be at home there. It's very kind of you to have found a place."

"It's furnished. I decorated it myself. I do hope you like it."

"I'm sure I will." She didn't tell him how little her surroundings meant to her. As long as it had the necessities, she would be happy.

The car turned onto a square. Jo looked out the window and noticed the flower stalls and bookshops.

"Turn down that street," Herr Baer directed. "Stop at the third building."

The three-story stone building was just around the corner, off the square on a tree-lined street. The houses must once have been massive private homes, Jo thought. Clearly now they had been converted into flats and studios. The car glided to a halt and Herr Baer scrambled out with her suitcase. "Have you shipped your other belongings?"

"Yes. They should come tomorrow."

"I'll make arrangements to have them delivered. Here, this way."

Jo followed in his wake, up two flights of stairs. He paused and fumbled with the key, then swung open the door. "Here," he said proudly.

Jo stepped into a cheery little three-room flat with yellow curtains and spotless white furniture. Herr Baer had gone so far as to put flowers on the table. "It's lovely," she said, turning. "You have very good taste. There's nothing I would want to change."

He beamed and blushed slightly. "As we will be working together, please call me Koni."

"If you will call me Jo."

He nodded and walked into the kitchen. "I have hardly stocked the cupboards, but I did buy some tea, milk, and sugar. There are several markets on the square. I didn't want to shop for you because I don't know what you like. But if you wish, I'll come with you the first time, in case you have trouble with German labels."

"I'd really appreciate that," Jo told him as she sank into the cushions of the small sofa and kicked her shoes off casually. "I think I shall eat out tonight. Koni, will you show me Berlin?"

"Of course. You will want to see the Romanische Café—all the writers go there—and of course the Bristol Hotel, the various government buildings . . ." He scratched his clean-shaven chin and went on with his list. Jo watched his fingers as they moved in the air—he had long feminine hands, almost delicate, she decided. He finished his recital: "I shall come for you tomorrow at ten."

"Oh, I was hoping you might show me some of Berlin's nightlife tonight. I've heard so much about it."

He surveyed her carefully with his gray eyes, then lifted his brow questioningly. "You might not like the club I frequent."

"Is there music?"

"Oh yes."

"And good food?"

He nodded.

"Then I'll like it."

"I'll come back for you at nine. Perhaps afterward you will come to my studio and examine my work."

"Sounds good," she agreed. "Now perhaps I should unpack and get used to my surroundings."

"Until nine, then." He smiled. "Oh, here, you may need your door key."

Jo took the key and walked to the door, closing it after him. Then she returned to the sofa. She decided she liked Koni, and she knew it was because he reminded her so of Antoine.

Jo turned her thoughts away from Koni and got up and hoisted her bag to the sofa. It was time to unpack, time to get settled in her new environment.

"Feminia," Jo said, looking at the gaudy flashing light above the door of the nightclub. She felt strangely underdressed as a tall woman in a sleek black sequined gown pressed past them with a slight shove and a swish.

Berlin, or what she had seen of it, came alive at night. The streets were full and the crowds were loud and gay. There was something almost hysterical in the atmosphere, something she couldn't define but which she found exhilarating.

Koni pushed open the purple door of the club and guided her down a hallway that was nearly dark save for weird flashing purple and green lights.

"Ahhh!" A garish orange-haired creature blocked their way, her mouth outlined in fuchsia lipstick, her eyes heavy in green and black mascara and eye shadow. Triangular swatches of bright pink rouge covered her cheeks, and she wore a red gown trimmed with feathers. "Ahhh!" she shrieked throatily in their faces, and Jo froze.

"Feminia, Feminia, Femina! What a lovely face! What lovely hair, darling, is it real?" Long fingers stroked Jo's hair.

Jo nodded dumbly.

Koni took her arm, though not protectively. "Don't mind her, she's an old queen and she's jealous of real women." He pulled Jo into a cavernous room. Music blared from the bandstand, and outlandishly dressed couples swayed together on the dance floor. Koni led her to a small table on a raised balcony. "We can see the floorshow from here," he told her, pulling out the chair.

Fascinated and intrigued, Jo took in the entire scene. What was it about the women in this place? They were all tall, broad-shouldered, and moved with exaggerated female motions. And never had she seen such clothes! Fox stoles and feathers, turbans with jewels. tight dresses with long slits, spike heels, and the most atrocious jewelry imaginable.

The lights over the stage dimmed and the dancers faded away. A tall, shapely woman in stunning white appeared onstage. She had masses of long blond hair, and her translucent dress was augmented by rhinestone-studded veils. She took the microphone and began singing in a deep, husky voice: "*Und der Haifisch, der hat Zahne* . . ." The audience clapped wildly and Jo recognized the music as being a song from *The Three Penny Opera*. She listened appreciatively to the song, "Moritat," moving slightly to its seductive rhythms.

"Ah, you like Weill?" Koni said, hoisting a glass of white wine that had been unobtrusively delivered to their table.

"Oh, very much. The singer is . . . well, stunning."

"And he's all mine." Koni's gray eyes glistened mischievously. "Do you understand, Jo?"

Jo knew her mouth had parted slightly in surprise. "He?" she repeated, suddenly feeling like a fool as she again thought of the name of the club—Feminia. And of course that was why Koni reminded her of Antoine. They were both homosexuals.

Koni laughed. "He, they are all male . . . well, not all. There are some women in the audience. They come for the entertainment. It's good entertainment, yes?"

Jo laughed lightly. "Very good. But you should have told me sooner."

He tilted his head. "My way of letting you know about me. I was thinking of how to handle it, and when you said you wanted to come out tonight, I thought to myself: What better way? Would you have come if you'd known?"

"Yes."

"This is as good an introduction to Berlin as any." He

leaned over. "I suppose you thought me nervous this afternoon. I was, you know. You're my boss, in a way, and the foreign currency I earn from this job means a lot. I was thinking how I would have to hide myself from you, then I decided not to bother. I said to myself: Risk it. Perhaps she will understand. Do you?"

His gray eyes were intense and his long fingers moved on the white tablecloth like a cat's exploring paws. "Yes. You remind me of someone I once knew. Someone I liked very much. Your private life is of no concern to me," she answered quite honestly. Then she smiled, trying to put him completely at ease. "Besides, I like it here. Will he sing another song?"

Koni beamed. "Oh, yes. May I order for us?"

Jo took a sip of wine. "Of course."

In the hours since he had met her at the station, it seemed to Jo as if Koni had gone through a metamorphosis. Shy and withdrawn initially, he emerged during their evening at Feminia as extroverted and flamboyant. Now, standing in his studio surrounded by his work, she saw another side of his multifaceted personality.

On his walls, more than a hundred black-and-white photographs begged her for attention. They were haunting, vibrant portraits. Some were of old bearded men with dark expressive eyes, others were of children huddled together. Their faces were questioning, their bodes gaunt, their mouths set in a kind of resignation more often seen on the faces of the aged.

"I took them in the Warsaw ghetto," Koni told her. "Others were taken in Slovakia."

"They're remarkable," Jo commented in a near-whisper. She shivered inwardly, unable to escape the eyes of a small child who hid in a doorway, her face illuminated, though the rest of her body faded into shadows—ominous shadows, Jo thought. These were

the faces of Jewish children, but their expressions were
the same as the children she had known in the Greek
refugee camps. "They remind me of children I once
knew," she confessed. "Armenian children."

Koni nodded. "Waiting for death," he said solemnly.

She turned to look into Koni's face. The gaiety of the
evening was gone. He was serious and somber. Like an
onion, another layer of him had been peeled away,
revealing a tender inner core. "Are you Jewish?"

"Yes."

He pressed his lips together and his mouth twisted
into a wry smile. "Jewish and homosexual. I am doubly
vulnerable."

"I know there is a lot of anti-Semitism in Europe . . ."

"More every day. It's happening again. I can feel it.
You haven't been here long enough to know, you haven't
seen the signs."

Koni's eyes had taken on a glassy appearance, as if he
were intoxicated with a demonic vision of the future.
The same future that was Jo's past. She felt a sudden
impulse to tell him, so he would know she understood.
"I'm Armenian," she confessed. "I know what it's like
to live in a ghetto, to fear the majority, to wait for the
next time they descend to wreak havoc. My grandfather
saw his family killed when the Turks tried to kill us all
in 1897. I saw mine killed in the deportations and
massacres of 1915."

"I knew there was something different about you. I
sensed it when we first met. I don't show these photographs to everyone. I took a chance showing them to
you."

"Why?"

"They're part of me. They're my homage to my own
people. To a people I think are waiting for death. I
showed them to someone else, and he asked, 'Why do

you waste your talent taking pictures of grubby children when you could be photographing film stars?' I couldn't explain because it is something that must be understood—how would you say it?—'internally.' "

"In the gut," Jo almost said, thinking of David's favorite phrase. "I'm grateful that you trusted me," she told him.

His expression changed once again. A nervous smile appeared, and he walked across the room and took her arm. "I should take you home now," he said laughing. "It could ruin my reputation having a woman in my rooms so late at night."

They walked silently across the square. Even though it was three in the morning, the streets were still filled with people and the Nollendorfplatz had come to life under the stars of the warm July evening. Jo inhaled and wondered why she didn't feel exhausted.

At the far corner of the square an organ grinder played out a merry tune and a monkey danced at the end of a long red rope. Couples sat on the grass kissing, and groups of people huddled together discussing politics and drinking schnapps from an open bottle.

"Do Berliners ever sleep?" Jo asked.

" 'To sleep, perchance to dream,' " Koni replied. "Dreams bring nightmares. We must force ourselves not to sleep. We must make the most of—"

Gunfire crackled and suddenly the square was filled with the sound of beating drums, whistles, and shrieks. People scattered in all directions, and Jo felt Koni pulling her along, forcing her down behind some thorny shrubbery which tore at her stockings and scratched her legs.

"*Deutschland, Erwache!* Germany, Awaken!" A band of youths invaded the square. One waved a gun in the air, firing it at random. Others beat on pots with iron hammers, and the rest spread out like a swarm of evil insects, hitting the people in their path, swearing and cursing. Over and over they screamed their slogans: "*Deutschland, Erwache!*" and "Death to the Jews!"

A man screamed under their relentless blows, pleading from his knees for them to stop hitting him. The organ grinder abandoned his instrument, and wriggling monkey in his arms, fled, only to be intercepted by three of the loathsome youths. He was fist-whipped until he fell to the ground. There he wailed, as before him the tethered, helpless, squealing little monkey was clubbed to death.

Jo watched in utter horror, and was reminded of another night long ago. She could hear Koni breathing, just as she could remember hearing Mushgin breathing in frightened gasps. Then, as suddenly as the youths had come, they were gone. Like the Kurdish horsemen of her childhood nightmares, they ran away, leaving only the echo of their barbaric curses in the still night air.

She heard the glass window of a shop near the square shatter. Then there was absolute silence, save for the hysterical sobs of the organ grinder as he lamented the loss of his simian partner.

Jo looked at Koni questioningly as she pulled herself up from behind the hedge.

"Nazi youth," he muttered.

"Where were the police?"

"Never fear. When it's safe, they'll be along. Come on, they're gone."

"God," she said in a near-whisper. "Does that sort of thing happen often?"

He nodded. "More than it used to, not as much as it

will happen in the future." He smiled at the irony, held
out his hand, and bowed from the waist. "Welcome to
Berlin."

The sweet aroma from bouquets of carnations filled the
room. Along the far wall, long tables with spotless
white linen cloths bore a variety of foods hidden away
in heavy silver serving dishes. In spite of the mingling
crowd, all conversations were muted by the heavy persian
rugs and high ceilings.

Teams of formally dressed roving butlers circulated
with trays of canapés and glasses of pink champagne in
long-stemmed crystal glasses. Jo looked around uneasily. Certainly the entire Berlin press corps would be at
this dazzling reception at the British embassy. Reporters, she well knew, seldom missed an official reception,
especially one which offered free drinks and good food.

"You do look stunning," Koni said, lifting to his mouth
a cracker covered with caviar.

"Thank you. I bought this dress this morning."

"Ah, did you go to one of the shops on the Kurfurstendamm?"

The Kurfurstendamm was Berlin's Fifth Avenue, a
street filled with unimaginable expensive boutiques and
couturiers. But she had not gone there. Her smart gold
dress had been purchased at Ka De We, a quite ordinary department store on the Tauntzenstrasse, though
its highly stylish belt had been bought in a boutique.
"No," she whispered back, "only the belt."

Koni sipped his pink champagne and raised his eyebrow. "Accessories are *so* important. But I really think
it's your fur. I must say it gives you an air of dazzling
elegance."

Jo touched the fox stole. Koni, she decided, would not be impressed to learn that she had bought it in a second-hand store in Paris, where it had been abandoned by a down-and-out member of the former Russian nobility.

"Are you expecting someone? You keep looking around like a thief in search of the security forces." He laughed. "This *is* the British embassy, you know."

"You're psychic," she answered. Koni *was* amazing. In the few weeks since her arrival, they had become good friends. He sensed her moods easily, and he seemed to have the gift of being able to predict the outcome of events. Sometimes, however, she truly felt as if she were with another woman. When they discussed politics, he was male and serious. He was the same when he photographed a subject for her. On those occasions he was completely professional. He carefully read her material so he could take just the right photos. But at other times he was flippant, perferring to discuss clothes and high fashion, furniture and design. He was extraordinarily witty when he wanted to be, and he could be biting, sarcastic, and even catty.

"I have an old friend who lives in Berlin, a correspondent. Perhaps you know him, Ted Kahn? I thought he might be here tonight." It was inevitable that they would meet. Day after day, Jo had followed up stories for INS, and always she expected to meet Ted. But so far their paths hadn't crossed. In a way, she was grateful; in another way, she wanted to face him and have their destined meeting occur. Then, she reasoned, she could relax and put thoughts of him out of her mind.

"Of course I know him," Koni responded quickly. "I did some work for him three months ago." Then, with a slight gush he added, "He's really quite gorgeous, but regrettably as straight as a pin and quite married."

"Do you know his wife?"

"No. But then, neither does anyone else. She never accompanies him anywhere. I've heard she's ill. Well, frankly, I've heard she's mentally ill."

Jo knew her expression must have revealed her surprise as well as her dismay.

"I see you knew each other quite well," Koni said thoughtfully.

Jo didn't bother to contradict his conclusion. She only nodded and turned around to look at the long formal reception line. Ted was there shaking hands with the British ambassador.

"Would you excuse me? I've just seen a friend," Koni said as he discreetly disappeared into the milling crowd.

Jo nodded and watched as he made his way toward a tall distinguished member of the embassy staff. Feeling as if she were in a trance, she walked toward the area just at the end of the reception line, where Ted could not help seeing her. Then, she reasoned, the worst would be over.

"Jo." Ted's eyes fell on her and she thought his face flushed slightly. "I heard you were in Berlin. I wondered when we would meet."

He sounded remote, formal. Jo forced a smile.

"We're having an awkward silence," Ted said, shifting his weight from one foot to the other.

Jo looked up into his face. "I thought we might meet last week," she said softly. "I went to the Nazi-party press conference."

"Jews aren't welcome," he answered. "Even American Jews."

"I haven't gotten used to Berlin yet." Small talk. They were making small talk. She wanted to say a thousand things to him, but nothing came—she couldn't verbalize a single one of the emotions she felt.

"I hear you're using Koni Baer as a photographer. He's very good. I used him once. He's gay, you know. But very likable."

"We get on well. The first night I was here he took me to Feminia," she said.

Ted laughed. "Shock treatment. But Berlin's full of clubs like that. In fact, it's full of transvestites. Where are you living?"

"Just off the Nollendorfplatz."

"Colorful neighborhood. I'd prefer it myself, but Irena doesn't like it."

Jo deliberated whether or not she should ask after Irena. Koni's comment had left her confused. Moreover, the fact that Ted's wife might be mentally ill added a dimension to her dilemma she was not prepared for. She decided not to ask. "Well, it is a strange city. I'm still not sure how to assess it. Ever since I got here I've felt as if I were watching a carousel spinning round and round. On one side of the carousel there's complete madness, and on the other there are club-wielding Nazi thugs."

His dark eyes studied her carefully and he nodded his agreement. "That's an interesting way to put it."

"I feel every inch the observer."

"That's what makes you such a good reporter."

Jo smiled at his compliment. In a very real sense they were professional equals. Ted had a fine journalistic reputation. Oddly, they had won the same number of professional honors and, she thought with amusement, he too had a nickname. He'd been dubbed by his colleagues "The Professor." That, she knew, was because of his thoughtful, well-written analyses.

"How do you feel?" Jo asked. "Are you only an observer?"

"I'm all too involved."

Jo looked away from his penetrating gaze. Here they stood talking about one thing while they were both thinking about something else. His eyes were almost pleading, and he reached for her hand. "Jo, I need to talk with you, be with you. Not here, but tomorrow. Say you'll have lunch with me, please."

Jo's lips parted. Yes. No. The two simplest words in the English language, but either was now laden with conflict. "All right," she said hesitantly.

———

Ted sat at a corner table in the Romanische Café, staring abstractedly at a plant that sat on the nearby windowsill. Its leaves curled in rebellion against the smoke-filled atmosphere of the noisy room. Why had he asked Jo to meet him here? There was no serenity, and no privacy. That was it, of course. It was a public place. He simply didn't trust himself to be alone with her, even though that was what he really wanted.

"You look a million miles away."

Ted looked up and nodded. "Please sit down, Jo."

Jo sat down uneasily, glad she had come but wishing she had not. The waitress came and put down a carafe of red wine and two glasses.

"I took the liberty of ordering wine. Do you want to try the house special for lunch?"

"That's fine."

Ted ordered and the waitress hurried away. Ted poured the wine and lifted his glass. "To your success in Berlin."

Jo sipped the dry wine slowly. "Thank you."

"I wanted to talk to you . . ." He cleared his throat. "Now I don't know what to say."

"I know what must be said," Jo told him as she

leaned over. "Ted, we have to see each other now and again. Our work makes it inevitable. We shouldn't feel awkward or embarrassed together."

"Promise me you won't run away the way you did in London."

His eyes were intense as he leaned even closer. Jo felt the old longing, the desire that had plagued her in London when he had kissed her. She couldn't make him any promise. She was drawn to him, but he was a married man. She wanted to run now, just as she had run in London.

"I know you feel about me the way I feel about you. Jo, I have no right to say it, but I love you. I've always loved you. When I kissed you in London, I knew you felt the same. How can we go on ignoring our feelings?" He vowed not to tell her that his marriage was a terrible mistake. That was a problem he had to solve for himself, though at the moment he hadn't the slightest idea how.

"Ted, I will leave if you persist." Jo struggled to gain full control over herself. She ignored his words and forced herself to deny them. "I didn't feel what you think. I don't now either," she lied. "Ted, I was only shocked."

"All this because I'm married. The Aga Khan is married too. So, I believe, is Mr. Lloyd George." He hated himself as soon as he made the comment.

"You know perfectly well that all those stories are silly gossip," she snapped. "Ted, I want to be your friend. You must try to understand that friendship is all there can ever be."

He looked down at the tablecloth, his face knit in a frown. "I had hoped—"

"Don't say it. Friendship or nothing, Ted. I have my

career and my friends. I have no intention of becoming the mistress of a married man."

"I wouldn't ask you to be my mistress, and I can't ask you to wait."

"No, you can't," Jo said firmly.

"My feelings for you won't change, Jo. I've been a fool, and I know it."

"Please, Ted. Please don't make me leave. I want your friendship, and that's all I want."

"I suppose you think if we practice, we can pretend there's nothing between us."

"It's not what I think—it's a question of what we must do."

He half-smiled. "I wonder if I'd love you more or less if you weren't so morally upright."

The waitress came with their steaming-hot lunch and Jo looked up gratefully. She wasn't as morally upright as he thought. Her legs felt weak, and she knew her heart was pounding wildly. If they'd been alone, if he had taken her in his arms, she wouldn't have had the courage to say no.

"Will you have lunch with me again?"

"Perhaps."

"If I promise to discuss only politics and the rise of the Nazi party?"

She smiled and nodded. "See that you don't break your promise."

The weak September sun broke through the clouds as Jo walked toward the Romanische Café, directly across the square from the Kaiser Wilhelm Memorial Church.

She passed under the graceful old trees. They were alive with birds; indeed, all Berlin was alive with birds—

sparrows, magpies, nightingales, and thrushes. They
sang above the traffic, they filled the parks with discordant sounds. That was one of the startling characteristics of Berlin. The city was filled with gardens; more
than half its land was devoted to parks. She had heard
that wild boars roamed the woods of Berlin, and she
knew that herds of deer and flocks of sheep were not
uncommon sights. Still, in spite of its rural charm,
Berlin was a city of striking and cohesive architecture, a
booming, wild, exciting, stimulating city. Mark Twain
once called it "the German Chicago," and the temptation to make the comparison didn't stop with Mark
Twain. Bertolt Brecht, whom she had recently interviewed, was writing a new allegerical work called, *Saint
Joan of the Stockyards*, in which Berlin's youthful Nazi
thugs were to be portrayed as Chicago criminals, wearing pinstriped suits and broad-brimmed felt hats.

Jo herself saw the comparisons between Chicago and
Berlin. Both were modern, planned cities beset by
poverty. Both had an abundance of prostitutes, bars,
rich restaurants, fine hotels, good theaters, and music.
It was not the same kind of music, though in fact jazz
was also popular in Berlin's nightspots.

But what the two cities shared most was the dynamic
of anger which lay just below the surface of their outward image of carefree hedonism. The rich were very
rich in both cities, and the poor were starving. Berliners, even more than other Germans, resented the Versailles Treaty, which had subjugated them.

Most Berliners demonstrated their resentment by
living fast and hard, as if each day were their last.
Others, the thugs who burst forth shrieking slogans and
often beating people in the streets, screamed their frustrations to the world. They were the youth, young
people without a foreseeable future.

Jo shifted the strap of her purse from one shoulder to the other and continued across the square. She had agreed to meet Ted for lunch, though today, of necessity, their lunch would be shorter than usual.

Again she asked herself if it were right to go on seeing Ted once a week for lunch. I look forward to seeing him too much, she thought, chastising herself for giving in to this difficult and emotionally troubling arrangement.

"I've got a table!" Ted emerged from the crowded restaurant and took her arm, guiding her through the din of noon-hour diners.

"I only have time for a sandwich," Jo told him as she sat down. "Ted, Hitler is in town and he's granted my request for an interview."

Ted half-smiled. "That's a coup."

"I think he agreed because I made the request before the election."

"Well, he's certainly news now."

"I wish he weren't," Jo said, picking up the menu.

"I never thought it would happen. I thought the desecrated synagogues, the hate literature, and the swastika would pass. I never dreamed that the Nazis would get twenty percent of the vote. I still think it will pass."

Jo nodded and murmured, "I hope so." Ted, she well knew, was revolted by the anti-Semitism, but he had a curious fascination with it too. Strangely, Koni was the same. It was as if they had both stepped back into the history of their people and were reliving a racial nightmare. She guessed that fear was never far beneath the surface of any individual Jew.

"How's Koni?" Ted asked after ordering their sandwiches.

"Depressed. He's trying to get out. He's applied for a visa. He wants to go to England."

"He's got a right to be depressed, but I hardly think leaving the country is necessary. There have been waves of severe anti-Semitism before in Germany. Hell, it's part of German history."

"Koni says it's more organized now. He says the timing is perfect."

"He tends to be a trifle melodramatic, you know."

"But insightful," Jo pressed.

The waitress brought their order and Jo began eating immediately. "I really do have to hurry."

"Where's the interview?"

"At Goebbels' offices on Hedinmanstrasse. I'm glad Hitler is in Berlin. I really didn't want to go to Munich."

"It's a beautiful city. I go there all the time."

"I remember, you have family there."

"Cousins."

Jo didn't ask if he took Irena, but she suspected the answer would be no. In any case, the subject of Irena was off limits. They never discussed her. Jo took the last bite of her sandwich and gulped down her coffee. "I'm going now."

"Call me at the office tomorrow and tell me how it went."

"I will," Jo responded with a wave.

Jo sat nervously perched on the edge of a straight-backed chair in Goebbels' outer office.

She thought of Louise Bryant, and wondered if she had been so apprehensive before meeting Mussolini. Certainly the two men shared more than their dedication to fascism. Mussolini had deprived Italian women of the vote, limited their ability to own property, and lectured constantly on their "inferiority" and usefulness only as mothers. Hitler now led the only party in the Reichstag without women members, and in his public speeches he too relegated women to the home, declaring they had no place in the working world. Still, Gerta Schmidt, who ran an exclusive and expensive jewelry store, had told Jo that Hitler appeared to have great appeal to German women. "A great many of my wealthy patrons have sold their jewels to help finance the party," she confided. Gerta Schmidt and Anya Braun, who was a designer and owned a boutique, were both valuable contacts. They knew and dealt with the wealthy and were a good source of both gossip and news. Koni, who had a never-ending list of contacts, had introduced Jo to both Gerta and Anya.

Jo reviewed the notes she had spent weeks compiling while researching Adolf Hitler's background. She had talked to Gerta and Anya and been introduced to several well-off matrons who had met Hitler. She had talked to lesser members of the party, and she had read back issues of papers and magazines. She felt well-prepared, even though up until this very morning her requested interview had not been confirmed.

Hitler's rise to power was remarkable, she allowed. Until the election of 1928, the National Socialists were an obscure political party. They won twelve seats in the Reichstag, or less than three percent. But on September 14, that same party under Hitler's leadership won 107 seats, or twenty percent. But Hitler did not sit in the Reichstag himself, as he was not a German citizen— Goering served in his place.

The National Socialists were now the second-strongest party in Germany, and even they seemed shocked at their success. Shocked or not, there was no question about the cause of that success. The cause was Adolf Hitler, the dispossessed Austrian who had risen to power in Bavaria. The National Socialists, she concluded, prospered because of the climate created by the depression.

But what made people follow this man? Jo asked herself. Those who had met him said he was compelling and hypnotic. Such descriptions caused her to wonder if he were a modern-day Svengali who had cast a spell over a nation of Trilbys.

Jo recalled what Count Hugo Lerchenfeld, the former Bavarian prime minister had written in the New York *World:* "The ancients believed in the existence of demons, powerful spirits between the gods and men. Goethe defines the inexplicable, incomprehensible in nature and humanity as demonic. Hitler is demonic."

"You may go in, Miss Gregory," the secretary informed her. Jo summoned herself and prepared to meet the demon.

He was standing up when she entered the room, and he was shorter than she. Jo smiled and mumbled her thanks that he had granted her an interview and forced herself to recover from her initial surprise at his physical appearance.

He was not only short but also potbellied. He was quite the opposite of impressive. In fact, from her own perspective, he was entirely forgettable. His mustache was like Charlie Chaplin's, and his face was devoid of expression save for the unpleasant impression she had when looking at his flabby jowls. To one side, a fragile, effeminate intrepreter stood nervously by a straight-backed chair, his eyes focused on the carpet. Jo was momentarily fascinated. He reminded her instantly of a performer at Feminia.

Jo nodded to him. In three months she had mastered quite a lot of German, and while she could certainly ask her prepared questions in German, she knew she would not understand all the nuances of Herr Hitler's answers. For that reason she was glad the interpreter was present, as he guaranteed that there would be no misunderstandings.

She was motioned to a chair, and Herr Hitler sat down opposite her, while the interpreter took a straight-backed chair between them.

Hitler asked in German that the interview begin. He checked his watch. "Thirty minutes," he grumbled. "Not a moment more," he added in German.

"You've modeled your National Socialist party after the Fascists in Italy—after Mussolini. Can you tell me what the philosophy of National Socialism entails?"

It was as if she were a puppeteer who had pulled a string, or as if he were one of the wind-up toy dogs they sold on the streets of Berlin. Wonderful little dogs, one minute they were dormant and dead, the next they were going in rapid circles, a sharp mechanical bark emanating from their gaping little mouths. Herr Hitler was like that; he snapped into action as if set down fully wound.

Herr Hitler's eyes suddenly flashed. His eyes, Jo thought, were a key to his power, to his ability to sway his public. They were the eyes of a madman, of a person possessed. They seemed to have no pupils, but were only bottomless blue pools that rippled when he spoke, and that did indeed cast a spell. His eyes, his voice, his gesticulating hands compelled, and even though he didn't answer the question, Jo had to fight feeling satisfied with his reply.

He had answered that fascism was essentially a na-tionalistic movement. That he would expel foreign ele-ments, take over the banks, abolish department stores, and return the entire economy to "small" businessmen and natural German entrepreneurs. "Enough of greasy profiteers!" he shouted. "Expel the dirty foreigners! Eliminate the parasites!"

The interpreter began a long, tedious translation. And Jo inhaled, scribbling on her notepad but knowing that what she would write later would be drawn from her impressions more than his answers.

As soon as the interpreter had finished, she asked, "By foreigners, whom do you mean?" She squelched her desire to point out that he himself was a foreigner, an Austrian in exile.

"The Jews," he responded instantly. "Look at America, where all the banks are controlled by Jews. But there *is* an American—an American who could save you!" He whirled around and pointed proudly to Henry Ford's picture, which hung on his office wall.

Of course, Jo thought. Ted had once shown her Ford's anti-Semitic ravings in the Dearborn Independent.

"You would expel all the Jews in Germany?" she asked.

His hand rose, his fist doubled, and he pounded on the side of his chair. "All!" he shouted, his dark eyes flashing. "I would deport all of them!" His face broke into a wide smile. "You think people would object? You think the German people would care? I suppose you think the world would be shocked? No! No one cares what happens to the Jews. No one cares if I deport them. Look, who remembers the Armenians? Who remembers how the Turks eliminated the Armenian curse within their borders?"

Jo stared at him. She was so stunned she felt frozen.

Hitler stood up while the interpreter droned on.

Jo did not interrupt the little man, even though she had understood Hitler all too well. Her mouth felt dry, and confused thoughts flooded her mind.

She dreaded even having to ask this hate-filled little misfit of a man another question, but she soon discovered she was mercifully saved the chore by Hitler's own colossal ego.

He began answering questions she hadn't asked, took over the entire interview, directing her to make notes on this and that, laughing, and actually trying to flirt with her. He paraded around the room, pausing now and again for interpretation. Then quite suddenly he looked at his watch. "This interview is over," he announced. Then he strode out a side door and the interpreter was left to show her out.

Jo hurried away from Goebbels' office, grateful that Hitler had ended the interview with such military punctuality. Doubtless he had anticipated her begging for a longer period of time, but she hadn't. Indeed, she only wanted to flee this terrible man who was indeed a Svengali with powerful eyes. God help Germany, she thought to herself. She prayed that this mad demon would not find too many Germans he could bend to his will.

Sixteen

Jo pulled her coat around her and hurried down Unter den Linden, Berlin's crowded version of Pennsylvania Avenue. She turned quickly into the famed Bristol Hotel.

She had walked from the Reichstag, a little to the north, choosing to stroll along the banks of Landwehr Canal. It was fall, and the chestnut trees were losing their leaves, the grass had turned brown, and only a few hardy flowers still bloomed. It was the season of transition, not just for the weather, but for the city, and indeed for all of Germany.

Was everything so different? The answer was yes. Not all the changes were visible to the eye; some, to use Koni's words, "had to be felt." Berliners were still sophisticates. The well-dressed women who paraded the Kurfurstendamm still sauntered at a leisurely pace, pausing now and again to look at the displays in shop windows. But it was not unusual to see a well-dressed matron sporting an expensive silver swastika instead of a designer's pendant. It also seemed to Jo as if the numbers of uniformed men had grown almost overnight. Yet the street vendors hawked their wares, the pastry shops and coffeehouses were filled to capacity, and Berlin continued to have an atmosphere of nervous excitement.

Yes, that was it. That was how she would describe it in her article. A nervous excitement, a prelude to breakdown, the frantic hustling, the contrast, the purity and wickedness, the Communists and the Nazis, black and white. All middle ground in Berlin had been erased. If you lived here, if you spoke German, if you partook of the pleasures of Berlin, you were either for or against what was happening. Berlin was a city without grays, and all the issues that had racked national political debate for so long were now reduced to one simple rhetorical question: "Can we live under fascism?"

Jo slipped into a booth in the Hotel Bristol's least elegant restaurant and ordered coffee. She unfolded a copy of *Das Wissen der Nation*, a Nazi paper. In it was an article on the type of woman a good Nazi should marry. It warned against sophisticated society girls, actresses, breakers of sports records, and any young woman who earned her living in a liberal profession. "The Aryan is urged to select a good industrious and pure girl who is known to be an adept housekeeper with an affection for her children—even though she may be stupid," it bluntly stated. The article went on to describe physically this ideal woman—blond, blue eyes, oval face, and white skin.

The absurdity of this Nazi garbage might make an outsider laugh. The outsider was the problem, she thought. Only those who were here and had been here for some time were not outsiders. Outsiders might laugh at Nazi proclamations in papers such as *Das Wissen der Nation*, but they marveled at other aspects of National Socialism and gave it a respectability it did not deserve.

Herr Walter Funk, the new chief of the German

Official Press Bureau, grandly proclaimed that two million Germans had returned to work. He stated that when Hitler had become chancellor in January, the unemployed numbered over six million. Now, a year later, the Germans were engaged in huge public-works projects: new motor roads, new settlements in sparsely populated areas in East Prussia, the cultivation of wasteland, and the encouragement of new branches of production. Funk sang out that there was new hope for the masses, and his song was heard around the world. Unfortunately, the lyrics of the absurd racial doctrines were drowned out by the drumbeat of the economic thrust.

And how things had changed! In Jo's first year in Berlin, she and Koni had listened to the biting songs of the throaty Lotte Lenya as she spit out the words written by Bertolt Brecht to the tunes of Kurt Weill. But now Brecht and Weill were gone, and the cabarets were closed. Berlin had been a city with a population that lived on the streets. The sidewalk cafés were filled every night. Street entertainers flocked to the parks and drew crowds on the sidewalks. Seamy strip shows vied with the symphonies for customers, pornography shops were side by side with fine bookstores. Everything was for sale or could be rented. Berlin had been frantic, invigorating, wild, lustful, insane. And now, in one short year since Adolf Hitler and his Nazi party had swung into power, a kind of puritanical fear had swept over the city, turning it into a Victorian beehive filled with self-righteous drones.

Jo remembered that in May 1932 she had gone to Paris to interview Amelia Earhart, the first woman ever to make a transatlantic solo flight. Paris had seemed tame compared to Berlin. She had gone to London in late thirty-two, and found it was even tamer than Paris.

She remembered returning to Berlin joyfully, because the city inspired her. It kept her working at fever pitch. Of course, she had always hated the Nazis, but until they took total control, one could temporarily forget them and simply give in to the wiles of the city. But now the Nazis could not be put aside. They had come to power, they had subverted the city.

She thought briefly of Ted. During her first year in Berlin, they had run into each other frequently. But then Ted began traveling. For a time, nearly nine months in fact, he had moved himself to Munich, where the Nazi-party headquarters were located. He was back in Berlin now, but they had run into each other only once.

Jo lit a cigarette and watched the smoke curl in the still air. She always felt her heart quicken when she saw Ted, was always aware of the longing in his eyes. But Irena was ever present, a reality that could not be ignored.

Jo finished her coffee and checked her watch. It was nearly three and she had to go to the INS office and pick up some mail. If I hurry, she thought, I can pick it up and still be home by four.

The INS office, located three blocks off the Unter den Linden was anything but imposing. It consisted of two small rooms in an office building, and was staffed only by Mavis Adams, a secretary whose main job was to oversee correspondence and run the teletype machine.

The office's bare furnishings consisted of two filing cabinets, the teletype, and a typewriter. Its sole reason for existence was to clear stories coming in from the Soviet Union and send them on to the United States, and to send Jo's stories out from Germany, Poland, Hungary, and Austria. In point of fact, Jo had never filed a story in Hungary or Poland, but she had traveled twice to Austria. In spite of its size and limited staff correspondents, INS was reasonably efficient. Fast-breaking stories were picked up off the European wires and translated. But the main source of European news was the granddaddy of the wire services, Reuters, which had, since the end of the war, pretty well controlled the news flow out of Europe.

INS did not compare with either the Associated Press, the oldest of the American news-gathering agencies, or United Press Association. They were the two largest of the American wire services and had reporters and stringers all over the world. The other major wire service operating out of Berlin was Universal, which the Hearst papers subscribed to in spite of the fact that they owned INS.

Mavis Adams was a quiet middle-aged woman who went about her work rapidly and efficiently, seemingly unrattled by the constant sound of the teletype and the ever-ringing telephone. Mavis was American, but she was married to a German and had moved to Berlin in 1923. Her German was excellent.

Jo closed the door of the office and looked around. Mavis was on the phone, so she walked to the teletype and watched it print out the stories on the A wire.

"Are you really interested in that?" Mavis asked.

She had put down the phone, and Jo turned. "I just came in to pick up my mail."

Mavis shuffled through the papers on her desk. "Just this one letter," she said, frowning, "but it's from the boss, so I thought I'd better have you come and get it."

Jo took the proffered letter. Jim Wilson was the head man at INS and she had never met him. Perhaps, she contemplated, they weren't happy with her dispatches. Perhaps they were sending in another reporter. She ripped open the envelope.

Dear Miss Gregory:

I know we've never met, so let me begin by saying how pleased we are with your work. You've done a crackerjack job for us in Germany. I sometimes find it hard to believe the dispatches were written by a woman.

Your dispatches are not, however, the reason for this letter. The reason involves David Driscoll, who usually deals with your stories. Henceforth, Willie Collins in New York will be the person you deal with.

Driscoll has taken what I guess we would call a permanent leave of absence, which is to say, he wasn't fired. The poor bugger has been extremely ill and it seems he's been dealt the final hand. The doctors tell him he has only a few months to live, so he decided to spend those months at home in Hannibal. I understand you know him quite well, so I thought you ought to know the truth. Sorry to be the messenger who brings bad news. Keep up the good work.

Sincerely,
Jim

Jo stared at the letter and pressed her lips together. David was dying. . . . She fixed on the last few lines and couldn't seem to make sense of them.

"Bad news?" Mavis asked.

Jo nodded. "Of a personal nature." She almost choked on the words as she folded the letter and stuffed it in her purse. She mumbled a hurried farewell to Mavis and ran out of the office, her large dark eyes filled with tears.

"A few months," she kept repeating under her breath. It didn't seem possible, it didn't seem real. David Driscoll had once been the most important person in her life, and though their relationship had been turbulent, she still felt a strong bond of affection for him. Long ago they had come to terms with their individual needs, but

not before they had shared a knowledge of each other's
darkest secrets. It didn't matter now that they had been
apart for so long. What mattered was that David was
sick and dying and that she was in Germany and he was
thousands of miles away.

Jo hurried down the street. She didn't feel the raindrops or the wind. The crowds of workers hurrying
home pushed past her without concern, the noise and
traffic seemed somewhere in the distance. Tears ran
down Jo's face, and she made no attempt to brush them
aside. Her thoughts were suddenly full of David, and
she saw his face in her mind's eye and remembered
him as he had been in Salonika fourteen years ago.

There was no question about what had to be done. Jo
knew, she knew as surely as she knew anything. She
would have to go to David. She would have to be with
him. David Driscoll was her family; she couldn't let
him die alone.

———

Jo climbed the steps to Koni's studio. He would be
upset to learn she was leaving, but it was only fair to
tell him first. Perhaps her replacement would also employ him, or perhaps Ted could find some assignments
for him. She planned to discuss the various alternatives
with him, and even, she had decided, offer to sponsor
him if he decided to immigrate to the U.S. He wanted
to leave Germany—about that there was no question.
But he was holding out for England, where, he insisted,
he would better fit in.

She stopped to catch her breath on the third-floor
landing, then continued up the last flight of stairs. She
paused again outside the door, then knocked and called
out his name.

She frowned when there was no answer, and checked her watch. Surely he was home. She had phoned him earlier and told him she would drop by on her way back from INS.

She shrugged and put her hand on the doorknob. "Probably gone out for cigarettes," she said to herself, turning the knob.

The door opened and Jo stepped into the studio apartment. "Koni?" she called once again, and then walked down the foyer toward the center room. It was a large airy room with a skylight, the room in which Koni displayed his work. Beyond it were a kitchen, a bathroom, and a bedroom. To one side of the center corridor was Koni's well-equipped darkroom.

Jo opened the door to the living room and her mouth opened in shock. "Koni!" she screamed, and her hands flew to her mouth at the scene of utter wanton destruction that lay before her.

His masterful photographs of ghetto children were knife-slashed to bits, furniture was overturned, and lights were shattered. In one corner, Koni's broken tripod lay in pieces, and next to it his expensive Hasselblad had been torn apart and smashed. On the stark white walls the word *Juden* was scrawled in bright red paint. Instinctively Jo ran to one photo—her favorite, the portrait of a small child taken in Warsaw. The knife slash went right across the child's neck, and Jo let out a sob, as if the child herself had been brutally attacked. She took the dangling photo in her shaking hands and turned around slowly. It had been a Nazi Youth gang, there was no question about that. She had heard of such random attacks, of wanton destruction, of people being taken away in the night. Jo shivered. "Koni!" She called his name again and suddenly was totally filled with terror. It wasn't red paint, it was blood. She ran down

the hall. The bedroom door was ajar. She screamed
again and closed her eyes, nearly sinking to the floor in
agony and shock.

Koni was sprawled across the bed like a rag doll. He
was nude, flat on his stomach. A leg from one of his
tripods had been jammed up his rear, there were pools
of blood on the floor, and on the walls his attackers had
written in German, "Death to the queer Jew!"

Jo gurgled and then vomited violently as wave after
wave of nausea gripped her. She slammed the bedroom
door to cut herself off from the gruesome sight in the
bedroom and forced herself back to the living room,
inching along the wall, holding it for support. She staggered to the sofa and collapsed, momentarily curling
into an embryonic ball, as she was again sick. "God in
heaven," she moaned, and rocked back and forth. Moments passed, perhaps a half-hour. Then, still in a daze,
she picked up the phone, her hands shaking violently,
and dialed Ted's office number.

"Ted Kahn," his voice echoed out of the receiver—
strong, soothing, competent. It was Chicago, not Berlin. He was holding her and she was leaning against
him. She was beginning to admit how much she loved
him, but there was too much in the way, too much to
overcome.

"It's Jo," she managed. "Come to Koni's . . . please,
Ted. Come now." Tears streamed down her face. It was
one of her nightmares . . . it wasn't really happening.
David wasn't dying and Koni hadn't been brutally murdered. She would wake up soon. . . . She let the phone
drop into the cradle and slumped to the floor, clutching
one of the sofa pillows in her arms as if it were a child.
She began to sob violently, burying her face and pounding the pillow with her fist.

                    *   *   *

"Jo!" Ted stood over her.

Jo looked up at him, her eyes large and wide, her whole body still shaking. "I didn't know what to do," she said in a near-whisper.

"I came as fast as I could. Christ! What's happened?"

She dropped the pillow and lifted her arm, pointing toward the bedroom. "In there . . ." She choked out the words and then closed her eyes.

She heard Ted walking down the hall. She heard him open the door, and she heard him swear loudly and close the door again. She sat where she was, unable to move. Then Ted was back at her side, lifting her to her feet, steadying her.

"We have to get out of here," he told her firmly.

"Shouldn't we call the police?" She stared into his eyes, then buried her face in his chest and began crying again.

"No. We can't be implicated. Besides, they won't do anything anyway." He pulled her back and shook her slightly. "Jo, I'm going to take you home. You have to be able to walk out of here."

She nodded dumbly as Ted buttoned her coat and forcefully turned her toward the door. "Come on," he urged.

"The negatives," Jo heard herself say. "Ted, I have to take the negatives." She moved her hand abstractedly around the room at the slashed pictures.

"Wait here." He went into the darkroom and returned with four files of negatives. "Now, come," he said, opening the door. "I have to get you home."

She gripped his sleeve and looked up at him pleadingly. "Don't leave me."

Ted nodded silently and led her down the stairs, out into the cold November air. "I'll get a cab," he offered.

Jo shook her head. "It's only a few blocks across the square. I have to walk."

He took her arm and they walked slowly across the Nollendorfplatz. Jo stared at the barren trees. Her feet felt as if they were barely touching the ground, and all she could think was that there were no birds singing today.

Ted took the key to her apartment from her purse and opened the door. "Your clothes are stained," he said matter-of-factly as he helped her out of her coat. "Jo, I think you had better take a hot bath. Listen, it will make you feel better. I'll go out and get some brandy. You need something to make you sleep."

"I don't want to sleep."

He looked at her tenderly and brushed her hair with his hand. "I'll be right back, then we'll talk. Go take your bath."

She nodded. "I feel numb, I can't stop shaking."

"You're going to be all right. It's shock." He prodded her toward the bathroom. "I'll be back in ten minutes."

"Don't leave me," she pleaded.

"Ten minutes. I won't be gone a moment longer."

Jo nodded and went into the bathroom. She ran the bath, watching as the steam curled up off the water. When it was full, she climbed in and submerged herself nearly to her neck. Ted was right—the hot water was soothing and she felt herself begin to relax slightly.

The door of her apartment opened and closed. "I'm back," Ted called out. "You okay?"

"Yes," Jo answered. She lay in the tub for another ten minutes, then emerged and wrapped herself in her long soft woolly bathrobe. Her dark hair curled into ringlets from the steam, and she shook it out, allowing it to fall loose on her shoulders.

Ted smiled at her as she came back into the living room. "I haven't seen your hair loose in years." He held out a brandy snifter. She looked incredibly beautiful, he thought as he stared at her, more beautiful than she was in his daydreams. Her skin was like ivory, her hair rich and dark, her eyes—her huge eyes—as compelling as ever. She had been beautiful when he first saw her ten years ago. But then she had youthful looks. At twenty-eight she had the voluptuous appeal of a ripe mature woman, and her face had character as well as superb structure.

Jo lifted the brandy snifter to her lips and took a sip. The amber liquid trickled down her throat and filled her with warmth, even though she still felt other-worldly and numbed by the day's horrible events.

Ted patted the couch and she sat down next to him, resting her head on his shoulder and closing her eyes. She shuddered slightly. "How could anyone have done that? Oh God, all I can think of is how much he must have suffered." She started to cry again, wrenching sobs.

Ted held her tighter and stroked her hair. "I don't know" was all he could say.

Ted moved and Jo gripped his jacket. "Please don't leave me. I can't stand to be alone. I can't."

He pulled her full into his arms and let her bury her face in his chest. "I'm not going anywhere," he assured her.

"It's like that night . . . all the blood, as if the whole world was bleeding . . ."

Ted stroked her hair and gently rubbed her back. She was strong, but everyone had a breaking point. Koni's murder had brought back too many memories for Jo. They washed over her like the tide coming in on a deserted beach. "I won't leave you," he said again.

Jo closed her eyes and snuggled closer. She felt as if she were alone walking through a dense fog out of which faces appeared—bloodstained, tortured faces. Her mother, her father, her sister and brothers, then Antoine and Marcella . . .

The fog closed around her and she was aware only of Ted. She was in his arms and he was comforting her as if she were a child. His hands moved slowly on her back, easing away her fears, warm and strong. Her arms were around his neck, and she could feel his hot breath in her ear, and his hands as they loosened her robe and moved across her trembling flesh.

"I love you," he was saying, and she was moving with him in the fog. . . . Where did comfort end and lovemaking begin? She wasn't sure, and she didn't care.

She felt his hands on her breasts and she knew her nipples had hardened. His body was across hers now, naked and strong. She moved beneath him as if in a dream, and he filled her with warmth and passion.

"I love you," he said again.

Jo held onto him tightly, afraid he would disappear, terrified he too would be swallowed up by the violence of the bleeding world.

One night. One stolen night. They would never speak of it again. She would go home to David and he would go home to Irena. But tonight they needed each other. It was the dream that ended the day's nightmare.

It was mid-December when Jo reached Hannibal. The small town on the Mississippi, Mark Twain's town appeared much as David had described it. The river was magnificent, wide, and emphasized by high bluffs But this time of year there was no greenery, save the sparse pine trees that dotted the countryside. The willows and poplars that clung to the bluffs were barren and stark, like scrawny old women, their gnarled arms seeming to reach for something to cling to. Those trees near the water glistened with ice, giving them a fairy-tale quality.

The river cutting its way through the gorge it had carved over the centuries moved sheet ice from somewhere upstream. Small waterfalls caused freezing on the sides of barren cliffs, resulting in natural ice sculptures that hung in weird formations from the rocks. In all, Jo's first impression was of a quiet, underpopulated winter wonderland.

David's farm was two miles out of Hannibal, and she had to wait three hours to get someone to take her. The old man who eventually turned up was known by the nickname "Complaining Ed," and it didn't take long for Jo to discover why.

"Have to hitch up the team and take yah ova by sleigh," he proclaimed in his strange accent. "The road along the river is iced good, and then there's gould-blasted snow on top of it!"

"I'll pay you well," she told him.

"Money's not everything, young lady! It takes time to hitch up the team, and then I gotta think on whether I can get back by nightfall. Mighty treacherous after dark. Lotta work, lotta considerations to think on."

Mercifully, he considered while he worked, and after a long while announced they could leave. "Bad weather," he muttered. "Bad weather, bad farm prices, and now we've had us a dang-blasted Democratic President in the White House for near a year. I don't like it one bit, no ma'am, not one bit. I was born a Republican, and I'm going to die a Republican. Don't trust Democrats, never have."

Jo let old Complaining Ed, complain. She bundled herself under woolen blankets and watched as the sleigh made its way down a long winding road. The farmland covered rolling hills, and the houses were far apart. Complaining Ed told her that wild deer roamed in the woods, but the only evidence of life she heard was a dog howl now and again as the sleigh passed by.

Perhaps I should have told David I was coming, she thought when she finally stood on the doorstep of the old farmhouse.

David opened the door and stood there, his mouth open.

"I've come a long way," she said. "Are you going to invite me in?" She forced herself not to react to his appearance. The David she remembered had been robust, but now he was a walking skeleton with sunken cheeks and dark circles under his eyes. His hair was terribly thin, and his skin sallow.

He smiled weakly. "Child, I never thought I'd see you again." The door opened wider, and Jo waved sending Complaining Ed back to town.

That had been three months ago, three heartwarming and heartbreaking months.

Jo finished drying the dishes and casually hung the cloth over the stove handle. David was lying down, as he usually did after breakfast. It was March now, and the snow beyond the kitchen window had given way to puddles of icy water.

"Wait till May," David told her. "Wait and see how beautiful the spring is. It's peaceful. It's like heaven here in the spring."

Jo blinked back tears. That was what he wanted. He wanted to live till spring so she could push his wheelchair through the woods and he could listen to the bird and watch the new leaves appear on the trees. Let him have that, she prayed. Let him have just one more spring.

David, she acknowledged, had changed with his illness. Even though he had grown much weaker since her arrival in December, he seemed stronger in other ways. He dictated his book to her, showing more discipline than in all the years she had known him. They talked for hours, and she discovered that David had become a philosopher.

She walked into the living room and poked at the fire. He was on the old worn sofa, a quilt covering his sleeping form.

"Stop tidying up," he said, opening his eyes. "Stop playing mother and come and sit down, child."

Jo sat in the chair next to the sofa. His brow was furrowed and she wondered if he was in pain again. Sometimes he tried to describe the pain, but usually he endured it silently. But there were other times when he screamed out and she had to give him the medication the doctor had left. It was morphine. It dulled his mind. It made him sleep. But today David seemed alert and eager to talk.

"I want to write a chapter on what the news ought to be," David told her. "I was tied up in simple reporting. I wanted to say things, draw conclusions, make observations, but I couldn't. I became an ambulance chaser. I was getting the facts—what time did it happen, who was the person, what was he like? I never asked why, because *why* involved conjecture. I was obsessed with the idea that the public wanted only facts, wanted some kind of objectivity. I was afraid to offer opinion, and that fear destroyed me as a writer."

"Even reporting facts can't be objective," Jo offered, "because the facts are always selected, and there's a

form of bias and censorship in the selection process."
The horrible image of Koni sprawled across the bed
drenched in blood flashed into her mind, as it so often
did. She couldn't have reported that objectively—she
couldn't write about the Nazis objectively and she knew
it.

David nodded. "I'm a cynical man. I always looked
for the worst. I rejoiced in tragedy because I knew
tragedy sells."

"We're all cynical," Jo acknowledged. "But even so,
we have to know that we can influence opinion. We're
capable of making news as well as reporting it. David,
the press is the conscience of the people. We have an
obligation to report facts and prod our readers."

He smiled. "You're right to be idealistic. You're right
to want the best. I've had to face myself in the last year.
I've finally admitted that I didn't want journalism to
change." David smiled. "I wanted it to be a job I could
fill. I was afraid that new ideas and trained reporters
were a threat to me. Jo, I've said it before, and I'll say
it again. I was never the man you thought I was. I
couldn't live up to your perceptions of me. I was never
a knight in shining armor."

Jo touched his cheek gently. "I know that, but I care
for you anyway. David, you may have needed me, but
you always overlooked the fact that I needed you. You're
my family."

"Have I told you how glad I am that you came?"
David took her hand and held it. "I'm a coward. I
didn't want to be alone. I can admit my cowardly way
now. I can see myself." He let out his breath. "In my
own way, I do love you. I always have."

Jo fought back tears. "And I love you, David." No
the way I love Ted, she thought silently, but another
kind of love. She turned and looked at David. He was

asleep. Such sleeps came on him suddenly, and she knew that one day he would not awaken. David's life was slowly ebbing away.

The river at floodtide ran bank to bank below the bluffs, and its current carried broken branches, dead trees, planks from decayed docks—winter's debris. The Mississippi at floodtide was an awesome show of power, a mad rush to the sea born of the melting ice in a thousand tributaries.

The trees were overburdened with new fresh green leaves. The ground was soft and smelled of the early-morning rain. It was ready to till. The deer grazed lazily now, and baby squirrels scampered up trees, emulating their mothers. Raccoons, rabbits, and small foxes tended their young, darting now and again out of the bushes near the farmhouse. The wildflowers bloomed, and acres of grassland turned yellow with dandelions and goldenrod. The sun shone warmly, mild winds blew across the fields, and spring's new life was in evidence everywhere.

David was suddenly better. His pain eased, he laughed as Jo pushed his wheelchair down a rough path through the woods adjacent to the farm. " 'What is so rare as a day in June?' " he asked, quoting James Russell Lowell.

Rare. Yes, Jo thought to herself, those days in early June were rare. Rare and precious. David's book was completed, and a wire had come from New York telling her "Berlin Nights," a series she had written, had won a Pulitzer Prize.

David was filled with joy for her. "I'm holding America's finest journalist captive," he joked. They celebrated with wine and a special dinner. David held her

close and kissed her tenderly, saying, "I'm proud o
you. You're a fine writer, and if your father were alive
he'd be proud too."

His declaration brought tears to her eyes, and for the
first time she felt she had truly fulfilled her father'
dream.

Two weeks of respite. Two weeks without cries o
pain, two weeks to enjoy the annual rebirth of spring
Two weeks of hope that his remission would be perma
nent. It was a wicked trick of the cancer that was eating
his lungs. It was too short a time. Death came quietly
and suddenly, like a rainstorm on a summer's day.

"Edit and sell the book for me," he had asked her. ".
haven't got a lot to leave you, but I'll leave you the
book and this farm."

"You leave me with more than that," she told him.
"David, you rescued me. You were someone I could
love, and you came into my life when I was afraid I'd
never be able to trust anyone. You leave me with
memories, good memories."

"Take care of yourself, child."

Jo promised she would, and he closed his eyes for the
last time as his hand slipped from hers.

Fresh earth on a simple wooden casket. Prayers and
incantations, a priest offering the final blessing to a lapsed
Catholic: "Dust thou art, man—to dust thou must return."

Jo looked around at the budding spring—life-death.
David was dead, but she knew her own life had to go on.

———

August 1934. "Ted Kahn and Entire American Press
Corps in Berlin Go to Nuremberg for Annual Nazi
Rally." Ted conjured up the headline and began to

write the story mentally, fantasizing about what might have happened but hadn't.

There had been a strong feeling among the members of the press that the whole Nazi mess might explode into an internal bloodbath. On June 30 Hitler had massacred the leaders of the S.A., including its chief, Ernst Rohm. But of course Hitler didn't stop with the purge of his own S.A. He went on to order the murder of his predecessor as chancellor, General Kurt Von Schleicher, and his wife. It was thought, perhaps even hoped, that disenchanted members of the S.A. would retaliate, thus ending the maniacal leadership of the little Austrian.

Ted shook his head. No such luck. He stared at the crowd below and lit a cigarette, trying to look as if he were actually listening to Hitler's loudly expressed harangue. There were thousands of people below the press box; hundreds and thousands of uniformed members of the S.S., the Schutzstaffel, or elite guard, and the S.A. the Sturmabteilung, or brown-shirted street brawlers. The S.A. was thought to number a million members, and the S.S. a hundred thousand. Clearly they thought of Hitler as their savior, and there wasn't even the slightest hint of rebellion in their ranks.

Nauseated by the mesmerized sea of faces, Ted looked around at his colleagues. William Shirer was covering for Universal Press and the Hearst papers.

United Press Association was represented by a fellow named Fleisher, also a Jew, but one who kept an even lower profile than he himself did.

On the whole, Ted thought, the American press corps was an interesting bunch. They all spoke German well, protected their contacts, and mingled socially, though they worked in competition.

Ted focused his eyes on a single person just below the press box. He was a tall lad, stiff and straight in his uniform. He was the personification of the Aryan myth. A boy with white-blond hair, blue eyes, the build of a young Adonis. But his blue eyes were vacant as he stared at his idol, the lunatic house painter whose arms extended outward as if to embrace all of Germany, perhaps all of Europe.

"The German Svengali," Jo had called him in her article. Svengali, the character from DuMaurier's novel *Trilby*. Svengali, who had bent the innocent girl to his evil will. Jo had been right. Hitler was a hypnotist, but he was a hypnotist with the ability to cast a spell over masses.

Ted's mind wandered and he tried to conjure up a vision of Jo in order to blot out the sound of Hitler's voice. He could see her kneeling, her white coat touching the grass, as she fed the birds in the park. If he tried, he could almost hear her lilting laughter and her soft voice. He remembered with absolute clarity the night they had spent together, and he longed for her in all his thoughts, even though he prayed she wouldn't come back to Germany.

One of his contacts, a Protestant minister, had been killed. He could have rationalized the minister's death because he was, in fact, involved in a resistance group. What revolted him most was the fate of the minister's family. The children had been killed in their sleep, and his young wife had been maimed and permanently blinded when acid was thrown in her face. She was arrested and led away screaming. He heard she had been incarcerated in an insane asylum.

His mind wandered to Irena. She stayed in their apartment all the time now. She had totally lost touch with any reality, and she played with dolls like a child and wandered about talking to herself. Two psychiatrists had examined her at great length and both had proclaimed her harmless but quite insane. But Ted could not send her to an institution in Germany, so instead he hired an elderly woman who looked after her. Soon, he contemplated, he would have to send her to the United States. He had written to two institutions—one in the rolling hills of Vermont, and another in New Hampshire.

Ted returned his gaze to the youth, then glanced again at the fist-waving Hitler.

"Germany has done everything possible to assure world peace. If war comes to Europe, it will come only because of Communist chaos," Hitler proclaimed. Ted began listening again. Hitler was off on the Communists again. That, he thought, would appeal to anti-Reds in America. The crowd was on its feet, cheering wildly and chanting.

Then they quieted, and Hitler's arms raised toward the ceiling. The klieg lights blazed behind the platform, and the audience was awash in flags.

Hitler was starting on the Jews now. "The alien life and form of ideas injected into and forced upon nations by Jewish intellectualism, which is racially without a basis, led to an alien, rootless state and internationally to complete chaos in cultural life."

The crowd roared and Ted stared at the floor beneath his feet. How could so many people swallow this crap? How could Jewish intellectualism be racially without a basis? Did intellectualism need a racial basis? He glanced sideways at Fleisher, who was making notes, a bland expression on his face. Ted admired him; he knew his own face was flushed with his internal anger. Koni's tortured body haunted him, as did the bodies of the minister and countless others.

"We will deport foreigners!" Hitler shouted. Flags

waved; people shouted and stomped their feet. They were an army of robots.

"Deport." Ted mouthed the word. For the Jews, Germany was turning into a fantastic journey through hell. The crowd went mad. Ted silently clenched his fist. There were resistance groups he knew about. You couldn't go through life always being just an observer, he decided.

Seventeen

Jo listened to Ted's voice as it came out of the tapes-
tried speaker of her tabletop RCA radio. For this moment, once a week, he was in the living room with her,
seemingly near, though in fact he was thousands of
miles away broadcasting from Berlin. His voice fluctu-
ated with the transmission. It was sometimes high,
sometimes low. Now and again it disappeared, overcome by static. Radio was an imperfect medium.

Ted's report dealt with the Nuremberg Laws, a dra-
conian bit of fascist legislation that deprived German
Jews of their rights. It was a known fact that church-
men, socialists, and artists of whom Hitler did not
approve had also been persecuted, but it was for the
Jews that Hitler reserved most of his venom. In his first
year of power, which Jo well remembered, he had
removed them from public office and decreed that they
could not in the future hold office. The next year,
seeing that his first decrees met with approval, he went
further. He removed Jews from the stock exchange,
forbade them to own businesses—especially department
stores or publications of any kind. He began eliminating

411

them from law and from medicine; he weeded Jewish students out of the universities and gymnasiums.

Now he had introduced the Nuremburg Laws. These laws deprived Jews of citizenship, making them instead "subjects." The laws forbade Jews marrying non-Jews, they forbade extramarital relations between Jews and non-Jews, they even prohibited Jews from employing Aryan women.

As Ted spoke of the Nuremberg Laws, she could tell he was holding back, trying hard not to concentrate on anti-Semitism, but rather trying to report what was going on in the way that a non-Jew might.

Ted Kahn was in a terribly difficult position. He was one of two American Jewish newsmen in Berlin.

Jo recalled her recent lunch with Arnold Harris of the *Globe.* Arnold was short and stout and had piercing sea-green eyes behind wire rimmed glasses. He was a perceptive writer and had just returned from a two-year stint in Berlin. He explained that while Ted's American passport protected him, many sources were unavailable to him. "Day by day, his personal life is affected by growing restrictions," Arnold had told her. "Jeez, it's a miracle he can even do his job. Frankly, I think he ought to get out. The whole scene is putting a real strain on the guy."

Arnold's comments about Ted had come without prodding. The two of them had been discussing the performance of the Berlin press corps generally. Jo had wanted to ask a hundred questions, but she had restrained herself. Too much interest in Ted Kahn would arouse Arnold's insatiable curiosity.

"A real double bind," Arnold had added as he thoughtfully touched the bridge of his glasses. "Poor old Ted. He's tied in knots in Berlin and can't drum up any interest Stateside in the plight of the Jews."

Jo had silently agreed. The owners, publishers, and editors of the American press continued to insist that the public was not interested in anti-Semitism. Even the *Times* carried nothing on the German legislation.

Ted had just spoken about the Nazi dictum that Jews were disloyal, a "foreign" influence, a scourge to the rebuilding German nation. Jo listened, and she almost felt Ted was speaking to her. No, Hitler had not lied to her that day in 1930. He had been inspired by the Turks' treatment of the Armenians. He had studied their methods. Equally troubling was the attitude of the Jews. Like the Armenians, German Jews remained apparently complacent, choosing to believe that a shift in the country's economic fortunes would cause a change in the attitude of the state toward them. They chose to believe that "things would improve" or that by compliance they could prove their loyalty. But it wouldn't happen. It hadn't happened to the Armenians, and it wouldn't happen to the Jews.

Hitler and his Nazi followers were adhering to a set pattern. They first played on old prejudices and fears; then they limited rights. Soon they would find a way to identify their victims, perhaps by confining them to certain areas, as the Turks had confined the Armenians to the Armenian quarters in Turkish cities. Next the deportations would begin—deportations that would end in camps where Jews would be killed.

Jo covered her eyes with her hand, as if to blot out the returning image of Koni. The Berlin police had written it off as "a homosexual killing." They hadn't even bothered to investigate. But it wasn't a homosexual killing. Koni was a victim of the Sturmabteilung, the brown-shirted street brawlers known as the S.A. Some of them were, as Ted said, "rough trade." They marked their potential victims for both political and sexual reasons. They often raped before they murdered.

Jo's thoughts returned to her recent lunch with Arnold. "The S.A. is said to have a million members," Arnold told her. "Christ, Jo, you can't imagine what it's like now. I was in Nuremberg for the Nazi-party rally. Remember that story you wrote, the one where you called Hitler a Svengali? Well, I thought of it then."

Jo smiled. It was a compliment to have a story that old remembered by someone as hard-nosed as Arnold. "I found him hypnotic," she commented.

"Christ, that's putting it mildly. The son of a bitch went on for hours. Longest damned speech ever heard. God, it was awesome, awesome and sickening." Arnold had shaken his head. Then, changing the subject quickly, "Why don't you go back to Europe? I mean, really, Jo, I think there's going to be another war. Ted may be the most frustrated reporter in Berlin, but the rest aren't exactly contented with the space their coverage gets. You've got clout, you know. There isn't another Pulitzer Prize-winner in Europe. Editors will print you. You've got a following, and that's something most reporters don't have."

"I might go back to Europe, but I won't go back to Berlin," Jo told him.

"Because of what happened to Koni?"

Jo nodded. It was a half-lie. Koni's brutal murder had left her shattered for months; it obliterated her pleasant memories of Berlin and replaced them with memories of sheer revulsion. But the real reason she wouldn't go back was Ted. They had both succumbed to need and temptation once. But Ted was too fine a person to leave his sick wife, and being near each other would only increase their desire and frustration.

David had died in the spring of 1934. Jo had come to

New York and resumed writing for *Profiles*. She was their best-known writer, and she was able to travel all over the United States. She chose her own assignments and had total editorial freedom. Her byline was famous and she earned a salary well above the average journalist's. She could write her own ticket, but she had decided that ticket would not take her to Berlin.

She glanced at David's manuscript on the mantel. She had edited it and written an introduction. The original was now being readied for publication. David had left it to her. "My legacy," he told her. She smiled to herself. The publisher said it was going to be a huge success: "It may even outsell Ben Hecht!" She hoped it would. She regarded *Chicago Years* as a fitting memorial to David. When he had finished it, a short month before his death, he had handed it to her and winked. "Always finish what you start, child. It's taken me years to learn that lesson."

Jo reached over and turned off the radio. The news was over, and the announcer had just introduced Bing Crosby, who was crooning his theme song, "When the Blue of the Night . . ." Jo walked to her desk to pick up her notes. Her editor had insisted she interview William Saroyan, a young, jovial, optimistic Armenian-American writer whose book of short stories *The Man on the Flying Trapeze* had recently set the literary world of New York on its ear. When Saroyan discovered she too was Armenian, he insisted she meet him in a coffeehouse. "He's the world's most optimistic man," her editor had said, Jo sighed and glanced at the radio. "I could use a little optimism," she allowed.

Jo sat in the small Armenian restaurant and drank thick, syrupy coffee, the kind of coffee she had not had for years. She inhaled the aroma of cumin which filled the air, and turned now and again to watch as the dedicated chef turned the spears of lamb over an open flame. Destiny, she thought, played strange tricks.

"You put your past behind you!" Saroyan boomed, fingering his mustache. "Of course, in one way you must—you have to write in the English language and you have to write with an understanding of North American culture. It's imperative that a writer be understood. I have no patience with expatriate writers who go on writing in their mother tongue. But you can't put the past entirely behind you! You have to retain lessons from our experience as a people. You have to carry those lessons on into your life and your writing."

For some reason Jo could not even define, she began to tell him about herself. She told him about Garabed and Nass, and about her desire to escape the confines of an immigrant community she saw as limited and stifling.

"Garabed Gregorian?" He repeated the name she gave him, rolled it off his tongue, and laughed. "A small world. I knew him in Fresno."

"Fresno was his dream. He wanted to live like a king on his own vineyards."

"Ah," Saroyan laughed. "Vineyards do not give forth without hard work. Your uncle Garabed was a no-account. In general, we are a hardworking, literate, good-natured people. But we have our no-accounts. Was it because of the likes of Garabed you cast your heritage aside? Come, come, now."

"Not the memories of my family," she protested. "I haven't lost those."

"But your memories are not all pleasant?"

Jo explained, and he touched her hand warmly. "I too was raised in an orphanage. I too had no formal training in writing. And I too began young. I am, after all, younger than you."

Jo nodded. She was thirty and would be thirty-one in four months, and he was three or four years younger. But he seemed older than his years, and his stories had maturity and universal appeal.

"What do you want to do?" he asked her.

She told him about Hitler, about how she perceived the situation in Germany, even about Ted.

"You want to go back to Europe and write about the Nazis. I can tell that from the way you speak. You see, it is not enough to remember the fate of your immediate family. You must remember the fate of our people. You see a similarity. You see that the Nazis will do to the Jews what the Turks did to us."

"It's not a vision. Hitler told me himself." She had paused then and told Saroyan about her interview with Hitler.

"Then you have a moral obligation to return. You must convince as many people as possible of the danger. You see, if you do not, you are truly casting aside your heritage, perhaps the most important aspect of it."

"Yes," she replied even as David's words rang in her ears: "Finish what you start."

"You must use your experience to show others that history is repeating itself."

He drank his coffee and they talked at length about his stories and the plans for his next book, titled *Inhale and Exhale*. "Humor and courage," he told her, "are the ways to conquer adversity. And optimism, ah, you must have that. They say that everyone must die, but I believe that in my case, an exception will no doubt be made." He laughed and winked. "Perhaps for you too."

"Choose the future, not the past," Saroyan told her. "But use the past, don't discard it. Make of our tragedy— our people's tragedy—a lesson. And for heaven's sake, stop running! You can eat sarma, dance to Armenian tunes, tell our stories, and speak our language without becoming a person like Garabed Gregorian!"

When Saroyan left, Jo chose to stay for a time in the tiny restaurant. She sat at the table and drank coffee and scribbled notes for her story on Saroyan.

She left the Armenian restaurant humming, and she walked all the way to the *Profiles* office.

———

Alvin Hendrix, the new editor of *Profiles*, was forty. He had intense blue eyes, a full head of snow-white hair, and a dazzling smile. In spite of his white hair and conservative manner of dress, he had a boyish enthusiasm and a cynical tongue. "You've really got a bee in your bonnet," he observed, raising one eyebrow. "I'm overjoyed that you want to go back to Europe, but I warn you, it's a mess. A fire sale!"

"I think I'm prepared."

Alvin clapped his hands together joyfully. "Hell, you're the only reporter that can make news as well as write it! Shit, I think we ought to drop you into Ethiopia for a firsthand look at what the fascists are doing. You're going to look sexy as hell in battle fatigues. As the only woman front-line correspondent, you'll make headlines, then *Profiles* will reap the full benefit of your byline."

"I want to go to Berlin," she said tersely.

"Sure, of course. Where else would you end up? But not first. Come on, Jo, be reasonable. Ethiopia for a look-see at David and the fascist Italian Goliath. Then on to Italy to observe what's happened there, then maybe a jaunt around the European capitals to get a feel for the whole fascist movement. Then you can go to Berlin."

Jo nodded her compliance. He was right. A total assessment would give her Berlin stories depth.

"I'm going to get the ball rolling upstairs. You get your passport in order and run over to Bellevue and find out if you need any shots to go to Ethiopia. Then start packing."

"I'll need a photographer," she put in.

"I'll make an arrangement with someone who is already on the ground. Maybe Calvin Haggerty. He works free-lance."

"Fine, but I'm not staying behind Italian lines. I'll want to see the Ethiopian side of things too."

Alvin grinned. "Start in Addis Ababa, then. I'm not worried about the shooting, but listen, don't drink the water." He winked. "I've heard they've got more parasites in Africa than we've got rats in Harlem."

Jo's mind raced. There was a small Armenian community in Ethiopia's capital. It was a good place to start to build contacts for a real inside story.

June 1936. "American Reporter Missing in Ethiopia!" The headline was two inches high, and beneath it was a five-by-seven photo of Jo in army fatigues, interviewing two Italian foot soldiers. The story was typical of the *Sun*, long on sensationalism, short on facts.

It described her as a courageous, diminutive black-haired beauty who dared venture behind enemy lines in "a wild, uncivilized country." "This miss," the writer ventured, "always gets her story."

"Hogwash!" Jo said, putting the paper down on the leather seat next to her. The train slowed to an agonizing crawl as it approached Geneva.

Calvin Haggerty sat opposite, his feet stretched out

on the seat next to her, his arms behind his head. He chomped vigorously on his Chicklets, but somehow managed to laugh at the same time. "I thought you'd get a kick out of it. Hell, when I saw it, I almost split a gut. Picked it up in Paris and saved it for you."

Jo gave him a disparaging glance. Calvin had met her in Paris and agreed to go on to Geneva with her to take some photos. "You saved it because it's your photo," she grumbled.

"Not often I sell a picture as many times as that." He grinned and counted the sales on his fingers. "Worth about two hundred and forty beers, that one." Calvin valued everything in beers. His camera, he grandly proclaimed, was worth four thousand beers.

"I dislike the *Sun*," Jo told him. "It's a rag."

"They sell papers."

"Undeniably. Did they do a follow-up?"

"Oh sure. Everybody knows you're safe and sound. Alvin's in some kind of ecstasy. Says your next story will sell a million copies of *Profiles*. He says I should take you out for dinner in Geneva and blow the old expense account."

Jo glanced again at the week-old copy of the *Sun*. "Enemy lines," she muttered disapprovingly. "They're pro-Italian. What absolute nonsense. The Ethiopians aren't our enemies, they aren't really anyone's enemies. And," she added with a touch of anger in her voice, "they've been civilized for two thousand years."

"I'm sure you'll set the record straight."

"I wish you'd come with me," she said, looking him in the eye. "I've got pictures, but they aren't as good as yours."

"Listen, I'm great, not just good."

She ignored his bragging. Calvin wasn't as much of an egotist as he sounded, and frankly, she was grateful he had agreed to meet her in Paris. They were going on to Geneva to take exclusive pictures of the Emperor of Ethiopia as he addressed the League of Nations. It wasn't Calvin's type of assignment, but she had talked him into it.

"You haven't said a lot about the fall of Addis," he prodded. "In fact, you haven't said much about your whole experience behind Italian lines."

Jo couldn't meet Calvin's eyes. She stared out the window and talked slowly. "I saw a village of unarmed women and children come out with rakes and hoes to defend themselves against an armored division. I saw old men mowed down by submachine guns. In Addis it was brutal. Mussolini allowed his troops to decimate a helpless civilian population."

"And you? How did the Italians treat you?"

"Bowed and scraped," she answered. She tapped the *Sun* with her finger. "I suppose they thought they had accidentally killed me and that would cause an adverse reaction in the U.S. They were overjoyed when they found me."

"The *Sun* seems to have thought the Ethiopians killed you."

"That's absurd. They want someone to tell their side of it—I was virtually the only reporter on their side of the shooting."

"And what is their side?"

"It's the ultimate international sob story," Jo answered, knowing Calvin would at least understand the terminology. "Calvin, tomorrow Haile Selassie will speak to the League. I guarantee there won't be a dry eye in the house. I'm going to write the story. I'm going to let people know what really happened in Ethiopia."

"Nobody's going to do anything about it. Haile Selassie is going to get tea and sympathy. Ethiopia's down the

fascist drain. It's not worth even one beer to the powers
that be."

"It has to be seen for what it is, a prelude to war."

Calvin grunted. "Somebody else's war, sweatheart.
The U.S. is staying out."

Jo turned to look at him. "In the short run, maybe.
In the long run, I think we'll be in."

Calvin snarled good-naturedly. "Warmonger," he said,
winking.

———————

It was a lovely warm June evening on the terrace of
Geneva's Palace Hotel. Jo was dressed in a clinging
green silk print dress with a high neck and bare back.
Four strands of perfectly matched pearls hung around
her neck. They were a gift from the Aga Khan and had
come one day by messenger, accompanied by a note
that simply read "For writing the truth and not yielding
to the exaggerated rumors of our intimacy." The soft
folds of her dress caressed her sheer dark stockings.
She wore impossibly high-heeled black satin shoes. They
were the kind of shoes she seldom had the opportunity
to wear and they emphasized her shapely legs. When
she was working, she was stylish but practical. Here in
Geneva she gladly yielded to fashion and returned to
the softness of silks and satins and elegant accessories.

Calvin was typically sprawled out, his feet resting on
one of the empty wire chairs. A huge stein of German
beer sat in front of him, and he looked at it lovingly.
"Well, you called it," he said with reference to the
emperor's speech. "Not a dry eye in the house. You
send off the story?"

"Yes. Will you have the glossies in New York by the
end of the week for the *Profiles* story?"

"You bet. It cost me five beers, but Ed's flying them in with the weekly pouch."

"That's good of him." Ed Martin, A.P. bureau chief for Europe, wasn't into favors. But of course *Profiles* was a magazine, not a newspaper. They weren't in any kind of competition. In any case, Ed and Calvin were old drinking buddies.

"As I live and breathe! Look who's here! It's America's missing girl reporter!"

Jo blushed and looked up into the face of Tim Huntley. He was the roving European correspondent for the *Evening Herald*. She smiled and held out her hand.

Tim kissed it gallantly and pulled the empty chair out from under Calvin's feet. "Don't mind if I do, old boy," he said, seating himself. "I've been longing for you, Jo Gregory." He leaned over and planted a kiss on her cheek. "Glad you're okay."

"I'm never going to live that story down," she murmured.

"Look, it's not easy for reporters to make headlines. Of course, it helps if they're ravishing and sexy. God, we could use you back in Berlin."

"Don't tell me Berlin is dull?"

"I will tell you. First of all, it's puritansville, and second, the Nazis are damn skillful at news management. Everybody gets the same stuff. They have press briefings galore."

"I hear they have beer parties for the press," Calvin put in.

"Yeah, you get to meet the Nazi celebrity of the week and interview him. It not only takes the joy out of hunting stories, it takes the joy out of drinking beer."

"Impossible," Calvin muttered.

Jo leaned over. "Did you just come from Berlin?"

"Yeah, got off the morning train. I'm headed State-side for a breather."

Jo smiled. Then, trying to sound casual, she asked, "How's Ted Kahn doing?"

"As well as can be expected under the circumstances. Poor bastard lost his wife two months ago, and of course the strain is double for a Jewish correspondent. I don't know why he stays on. Still, he's got an amazing number of contacts. Mostly dissidents."

Tim prattled on and Jo sat, temporarily stunned into silence. "What do you mean he lost his wife?" she blurted out.

Tim shrugged. "She died. You remember, she was always sick. Well, sick in the head. He was sending her to an institution in the States for treatment, and the plane she was on crashed. There weren't any survivors." Jo bit her lip and stared into her drink. She'd been more or less out of contact for seven months during the fighting in Ethiopia. "Poor Ted," she whispered, not wanting to say more.

"Yeah, that's right. You used to be buddies back in Chicago," Tim observed.

"I'll see him when I get to Berlin," Jo said, again trying to sound casual.

"I doubt it. He's become nothing short of reclusive. He actually told me it was a bad idea to be seen with him. I suppose he meant because he's Jewish. But hell, I told him, we're Americans, the dumb German laws don't apply. But I guess he thinks they do. He checks in with the embassy regularly, but he never shows up at any of the press-corps drinking parties. Listen, I've known Ted Kahn for years, and I'm here to tell you he's a changed man."

Jo was only half taking in Tim's comments. "I'm leaving for Berlin on Thursday," she told them.

Tim smiled broadly and leaned over to squeeze her hand. "Well, maybe old Ted will come out of his shell for you. I sure would. Hey, how about I take you out on the town? What's it been? . . . Jeez, it's been four years since I last tried to seduce you."

Jo squeezed his hand back and winked at him. "The answer is the same now as it was then."

Tim mockingly scraped his feet on the floor. "Aw, shucks," he lamented. "Well, you can't blame a guy for trying."

Jo finished off her drink. "I have to go to my room. I've got some writing to finish up."

Calvin pushed his chair back and started to stand. "I think I'll stay down here and finish off a few more pints."

"Don't get up." Jo gently touched his shoulder.

Tim looked her up and down boldly, then shook his head. "If I'd been Mussolini, I wouldn't have let you out of Italy."

Jo turned and waved back at them as she disappeared into the crowded lobby. Why hadn't Ted tried to write to her or get in touch? She mulled over Tim's comments. The word "reclusive" stuck in her mind. That didn't sound like Ted. It didn't sound like him at all.

She crossed the lobby and entered the elevator.

"Miss Gregory!" The short desk clerk ran toward the elevator, an envelope in his hand.

Jo pressed the button to hold the elevator door open.

"This came this evening, forwarded from Paris," the clerk said breathlessly, handing her a somewhat tattered envelope.

For a single second she had thought it was from Ted, but as soon as she saw the rough envelope, she knew it wasn't. She felt puzzled as she turned it over in her fingers. It bore French stamps overmarked with black block letters that read "Syria."

The elevator reached her floor and Jo walked briskly to her room, unlocked the door, went in, and switched on the light. Only then did she carefully tear open the letter.

It was written in a neat Armenian hand, and as she read it, tears filled her eyes.

Dear Josephina,

I know you will be surprised to receive this letter. I saw your picture in the newspaper and recognized your face. You have not changed so much that I would not know you. I see from the story that you now call yourself "Jo Gregory," which sounds very American.

You, I see, have achieved your dreams. Your papa would be proud, Josephina. I am proud. I am sending you my address, and I hope you will write to me.

I finished school at the American University in Beirut and am an engineer currently working for the French. Some months ago I met a French engineer from Canada and he persuaded me to apply to emigrate to that country, where, I am told, a good many people speak French. Only a week before I saw your picture, my wife, Mira, and I received permission to emigrate. We leave in a month's time.

I hope, dear Josephina, that you are as well as you look. Mira is expecting a child, and I want to name it after you if it is a girl.

Write to me. It is a miracle I saw your picture, and I do not want to lose track of you again.

Love,
Mushgin

Jo brushed the tears from her cheek. Her joy for Mushgin mixed with her feelings of apprehension for

Ted. She leaned back and closed her eyes. Today had been a day of messages. They were mixed, good and bad.

Jo looked around the Friedrichstrasse Bahnhof uneasily. There were S.S. standing near the newstand and by the washrooms. There were police by the doors, and brown-shirted S.A. who wandered about swinging their clubs threateningly at their sides. From the moment she had stepped off the train, she had felt a strong sense of paranoia. Still, she had breezed through customs and simply been told to report within a week to the Ministry of Propaganda for her approved press credentials and identity card.

Nervously Jo smoothed out her snow-white linen skirt. She was dressed casually in a straight-cut suit, a round-necked gold silk blouse, and low-heeled white-and-black pumps with a matching bag. She wore her white cloche with the black band tilted slightly to one side, allowing her wavy dark hair to caress her forehead.

"Jo!" she heard Ted shout before she saw him. "Over here!"

She looked around and spotted his waving arm. He was wearing a raincoat and a dark hat. She pushed toward him, then found herself standing awkwardly in front of him. He didn't extend his arms or move to kiss her. He looked stiff and formal, and she was sure he was silently commanding her to act as if they were casual acquaintances rather than close friends and one-time lovers.

"Good to see you again," he said, touching the corner of his hat. "Got your wire. Have a good trip?"

Jo nodded, and he leaned over and took her suitcase.

"I guess we better get you settled in a hotel."

Jo tried to smile. She wanted to throw herself into his arms. "I have to register at the embassy first," she replied.

"Let's get out of here," he said quietly, politely taking her arm and guiding her through the crowds, out into the rainy afternoon.

They took a taxi and he sat in the front seat while she sat in the back alone. "American embassy," he requested in flawless German.

His manner, his voice, and the way he was treating her confirmed the fears she had first begun to feel when Tim was talking about Ted. Ted was definitely involved in something that went well beyond a big story. He was afraid for his friends, and now for her. He was acting like a stranger.

Jo went through the formality of registering at the embassy; then Ted led her down the hall to the press attache's office.

"Alex?" Ted opened the door and peered in.

Alex Austin looked up. "What have you said or written now?" he asked in an annoyed tone. "I know you. You never turn up here unless it's to prepare me to handle another complaint."

"Not this time. I want to use your office."

Alex pulled himself from behind the desk and for the first time saw Jo. He grinned. "Didn't know you were back. God, how long have you been gone?"

She smiled. "Too long."

"Can we use your office?" Ted persisted.

Alex stretched. "Sure, I guess so. Time to go get some coffee anyway." He waved casually and ambled off.

Ted pulled her inside and closed the door. For a long

moment they stood looking at each other. Then he took
her in his arms and kissed her deeply and passionately.
"I wanted to do this when I first saw you," he said,
whispering into her ear.

Jo pressed herself to him. She could sense his desire
and feel her own. "Why didn't you write to me about
Irena? Oh, Ted, I'm so sorry."

"She's at peace now," he said. "Someday I'll talk to
you about it. But not now. Jo, I love you, but I'm not
glad you came back to Berlin. I want you to leave."

She pulled away slightly and looked into his face.
"You're involved in something, aren't you? I saw Tim in
Geneva. He said you were . . . 'reclusive.' Ted, what's
going on?"

His facial muscles tightened. "Christ! I didn't know
you were coming back. Jo, when Irena died, I thought:
That's it—I don't have to be responsible to anyone. I'm
free to take chances."

"What are you involved in?"

"I brought you in here because I didn't even want to
talk out front. There are Germans working in the outer
office. I have to be very careful."

"Ted, you must tell me."

He shook his head. "The more you know, the more
dangerous it is for you. Jo, please leave Berlin."

"No, Ted. I'm staying."

"Jo, you don't understand. When I saw you, I knew
you had guessed something, but you really don't know
how serious it is. I don't want anyone to know how
close we are, and I won't tell you anything."

Jo arched her eyebrow slightly and looked him in the
eye. "Ted, you're being selfish. Just because you're
Jewish, you think this is your personal fight. Well, it
isn't. It's my fight too. You think this is about Nazis and
Jews. It isn't. This is about people. This could happen

anywhere, to any people. It happened to mine. I'm going to stay here as long as possible and let the world know that. I have to do this. I have to do it whether you want me to or not and whether or not you let me in on your own private little war. I came back here to do a job. I was on my way back before Tim told me about Irena. If I can't be with you, I'll do the job anyway."

His face flushed slightly and he pulled her back into his arms and held her tightly. "I think I'm more like Driscoll than I thought," he said slowly. Then, after a moment: "I wanted to go it alone too. I underestimated you. I think I always have."

Jo reached up and felt the side of his cheek with her hand. "Ted, I love you. Tell me, please."

He inhaled. "I'm little more than a courier. But one of my contacts was killed three weeks ago. And before that there was another murder, one that involved the wife and children of the person I was working with. Jo, we can't live together. It's too dangerous for you. I just won't put you in that situation. Anyway, the law prevents us living together—hell, it even prevents us from making love."

"That law doesn't apply to American citizens."

"It hasn't been tested with American citizens."

"We'll be discreet. We'll live separately." She smiled and then added, "But we *will* break the law."

"It's still dangerous."

She looked at him steadily. "Ted, stop trying to protect me. I just came back from a war zone. I'm not child."

"You scared me to death."

She smiled. "I scared myself. It wasn't pleasant."

Ted smiled his sexy crooked smile and put his hand on her neck, drawing her close once again. "I'm nc sure I'm going to know what to do with such a strong-willed woman."

She looked into his eyes. "Take me to the hotel and I'll tell you."

Eighteen

How well the dismal weather suited her mood, Jo
thought as she walked across the Nollendorfplatz. Masses
of rain-laden gray clouds moved across the sky, and a
chill wind blew out of the northeast. The yellow cro-
cuses that had bloomed only yesterday in anticipation of
warm spring sunshine wavered on their stalks as i
shivering in the unseemly damp and cold.

Jo pulled her rain cape more tightly around her and
tried to shake the mental image of young Helmut Hirsch
a youth of twenty, being beheaded. She shivered un
controllably as she suppressed the desire to scream a
the passersby. How could this be happening? How
could the populace be so unconcerned? Their arm
were full of packages, their faces smiling as they greete
one another. *Don't you know what's happened?* Sh
wanted to shout that question from the center of th
square. She wanted the German citizenry to drop thei
fat sausages and loaves of bread and cry out in ange
with her. One cry of protest! One objection! Even
murmur of fear, or of regret. But there was none.

"Oppression is so gradual," Ted had said just tw

nights ago. "You know it's total, but if you try to pin-
point the moment it happened, you can't. It slips away
slowly, like the life ebbing out of a dying man. We're
all prisoners here." His fist had automatically doubled
in frustration. "I was walking in the park yesterday and
I wanted to sit down and feed the birds. Then I remembered Jews can't sit on the park benches, so I kept
walking. Why the hell did I do that? Look what's happening. I'm obeying their damn laws, and so is everyone else! Why don't the Jews rebel? Why don't they
fight back?" He had almost cried, and she knew it was
tension combined with fear.

Jo had knelt in front of him and taken his hands in
hers. "You know better than I do that there *is* resistance."

"It's too little, too late," he said, shaking his head.
"It's disorganized, and the S.S. is highly organized. You
can't trust anyone, not anyone. Look at Hirsch, a mere
courier like myself. They'll kill him, you know. They'll
behead him like they did those two women last month."

"He is an American citizen. Ambassador Dodd is—"

"Is wasting his time," Ted interrupted. "He's a good
man, but they'll chop off Helmut's head and the good
German people won't raise a whisper of protest, not
even a whimper."

Ted had been so right, Jo thought as she again surveyed the faces of the shoppers. Hirsch had been tried
by the infamous "People's Court" and the trial was held
in camera.

Ambassador Dodd was Jo's personal friend. She had
taken a history course from him years ago in Chicago,
and when he came to Berlin, they had renewed their
friendship. William Dodd was a concerned man. He'd
tried everything, even a personal appeal to Hitler.

It wasn't only the boy's youth, nor the fact that he
was Jewish, that caused Jo to be frightened and upset

by the execution. It was the fact that Hirsch, like Ted, had been born in Germany and held dual citizenship. Worse yet, as Ted himself had pointed out, they were both couriers, albeit for different organizations. Still, the similarity of their profiles sent a shiver of fear through her. It had happened to Hirsch, and it could happen to Ted. She silently cursed the cold raindrops, and wished Ted had not gone to Munich. She thought again of Hirsch, reviewing the case in her mind.

Helmut Hirsch and his parents were naturalized American citizens who had returned to Germany when Hirsch was quite young. After the Nuremberg Laws, Hirsch had moved with his parents to Poland, where he was finishing his education, having been thrown out of a German university because he was Jewish. He had come back into Germany, and was arrested on the train as it crossed from Czechoslovakia. His luggage, said to contain incriminating evidence that linked him to an anti-Nazi organization in Prague, was seized. Ted, she thought miserably, had taken that same train more than once, and certainly his luggage had contained the same kind of incriminating evidence.

Jo shook her head. Poor Amabassador Dodd. He was so conscientious. He had been almost in tears when his last plea to Hitler was rejected. Dodd had hoped against hope that the Germans would not behead Hirsch because he was an American citizen.

"I've been here too long," the ambassador had told her only this morning. "I've asked to be relieved of my posting. I want to go home to Chicago. I can't stand Germany any longer. There's no justice here. None at all."

Jo had silently agreed. She had been in contact with Hirsch's lawyer and sister. She intended to do her June profile on the young poet whose life had ended before it began. A memorial, she thought, to one of the few who had the courage to take action.

How long before she would have to write that kind of memorial for Ted? He was taking chances all the time. He was taking one now. He had gone to Munich for the wedding of his cousin and to personally deliver American visas to his family. He had also carried a message to be delivered to one of the leaders of the dissidents. I can't think about it, I mustn't, Jo told herself.

She paused on the opposite side of the square and realized she was standing in front of Gerta Schmidt's jewelry shop. She peered through the rain-stained window, and seeing Gerta at the counter, went in.

"*Guten tag,*" Jo said, trying to sound cheerful, though in fact she felt nothing but sheer anxiety.

Gerta looked up and brushed a wisp of blond hair off her forehead. "May I help you?"

Jo forced a smile. "I've come in to gossip. How have you been?"

Gerta's facial expression was momentarily stricken; then it turned hard and set. Her blue eyes flashed. "Madam, I do not know you, and I cannot chat during business hours."

For a split second Jo stared uncomprehendingly at her. She had known Gerta for six years. Gerta was one of her best "ears," and though she had been a little more careful in the last year not to be seen publicly with a foreigner, she had always been willing to talk. Not that they discussed anything monumental. Gerta only told her how her customers felt about various laws and regulations. In general, they talked about the so-called "New Germany." Jo stood for a moment and knew she looked dumbfounded. Then she glanced round. Did Gerta think someone was watching the

shop? Was there someone in the back room? "I see I
have mistaken you for someone else," Jo said quickly.

"Quite all right, madam," Gerta said, turning away.

Jo left the shop, certain she had seen a look of gratitude on Gerta's face. The tinkle of the bell on the door
rang in her ears, and Jo knew this little incident had
increased her anxiety. I'm being paranoid, she told
herself as she rounded the corner and walked the several blocks to the residential street where her small
house was located. Gerta has simply decided she
shouldn't talk with foreigners anymore. Yet as she walked
along, she couldn't shake the impression that Gerta had
not been alone.

If Ted were here, I wouldn't be so afraid, she thought.
The S.S. was chillingly efficient, and she worried about
Ted constantly. More so today than yesterday.

She let herself into the house and locked the door
behind her. It had been a coach house once, but when
the main house had been converted into apartments
the coach house, which sat to one side, facing the
street, had also been rented out. It was the perfec
place because it afforded a privacy which she could no
have had in an ordinary flat. Jo remembered how
delighted she had been when she found it. Beyond the
back door was a tree-filled yard fenced off from a lane
that intersected with another street. Three of the plank
in the fence were loose, and Ted usually came through
the back. He spent most nights here with her, but he
kept his own room as his official address.

Jo looked around the empty house and wished he
were here. She sank into the sofa and leaned back
putting her feet up. The events of the morning ha
made her sick—not physically, but spiritually.

After a time, Jo pulled herself up off the sofa an
went to the kitchen to make tea. She decided to sta

writing Hirsch's story now, while her emotions were all on the surface. She shook her head in dismay. Ted had been so right! You couldn't trust anyone. Hirsch had been betrayed; so had others, who had been arrested and subsequently beheaded. The Nazis had a network of informers; they often planted such informers as press contacts, hoping to incriminate correspondents who were "unfriendly." But most of the press corps was unfriendly now.

And then, with a chill, Jo thought of Gerta. Informers . . . contacts . . . arrests. Feeling as if she were acting out a role in a bad film, she went to the window and looked out.

Through the leafy branches of the trees in the front yard, she could see the street. On the other side, a long black car was parked. It was the kind of car so often driven by the S.S. Had she been right? Was there someone in Gerta's back room? Was she herself now being watched?

"Name?"

"Ted Kahn."

"I see you were born in Berlin, Herr Kahn."

"I'm an American citizen."

"You're a German subject, Juden!"

Ted stared back into the face of the S.S. officer. "I'm an American citizen. I'm a journalist. I want to contact my embassy. You have an obligation to let them know of my arrest."

Ted was standing in front of the officer's massive desk. The office was unbelievably hot, Ted thought. Then he wondered why, under the circumstances, anything so trivial bothered him. He looked around, thinking that he ought to commit every detail to memory.

The room was plain, the walls a kind of sick mustard color. The furniture looked as if it had been requisitioned from a schoolhouse. Except for Hitler's portrait behind the desk, he might have been a naughty child in the principal's office. In spite of his rapid heartbeat, he couldn't shake the image. The S.S. officer looked stern, like a school principal.

"Who is notified, and when, will be determined at a later time. You travel a great deal, Kahn. Tell me about your trips."

"I travel to gather news. Berlin isn't the only city in Germany." What did they have on him? Why had his family been arrested too? He had delivered his parcel on arrival, and at the time of his arrest he had nothing incriminating on his person. The police had come just before the wedding. They had stormed the apartment like Treasury agents raiding a speakeasy. Then, after keeping Ted and his relatives an hour in the police station, they had transferred all of them to Gestapo headquarters. Ted's aunt Sophie had been hysterical, and the last he had seen of his relatives was when they were led away roughly.

"You seem to have interesting friends. I'm interested in your friends."

"I have very few friends outside the press corps."

The officer smiled. "Yes, the press corps. There's a Miss Gregory. Let's talk about her."

Ted felt his heart stop. "I hardly know her." He was certain it sounded like a lie. He was sure the sound of her name had caused him to react. And he'd said it too fast. The S.S. interrogator would notice.

"Now, now, Mr. Kahn. You can't expect me to be

lieve you hardly know Miss Gregory. She's such a beautiful woman. Aren't you interested in beautiful women?"

"Sure," Ted said. "But I still don't know her very
well."

"Do you sleep with Miss Gregory?"

The son of a bitch was fairly leering. Ted wanted to
lean across the desk and wipe the smile off the bastard's
face. "I don't discuss my sex life with strangers," he
said coldly.

"I think you will feel more like talking to us in the
morning."

"I want to call my embassy."

The officer picked up a small bell on his desk and
rang it. The door opened and four burly S.S. men
surrounded him.

"Show Mr. Kahn our best accommodation," the officer said sarcastically.

Ted walked between them down a long dimly lit
corridor. They opened the door to a small cell and
roughly pushed him in.

"Jewish dog!" one of them said.

Two of them grabbed his arms. He struggled, but in
vain. He was a big man, but they were four and they
were armed. Ted went slightly limp, trying to relax his
body to receive the blows he knew were coming. Don't
give them any excuses, he cautioned himself as the
headline "American Reporter Accidentally Shot in Escape Attempt" mingled with other incoherent thoughts.
One of them punched him in the stomach, and when he
doubled over, the biggest one hit him repeatedly in the
ribs. After a few seconds, one slugged him in the face,
and Ted could feel a slight trickle of blood run down his
chin. Roughly they threw him to the stone floor, and he
only barely managed to cushion the fall with one hand.
Two of them kicked him again. Once in the stomach,

causing him to vomit, two or three more times in his ribs. Then, mysteriously, they left him sprawled on the floor. They tramped out of the cell laughing, and he heard the key turn in the lock on the door.

Ted lay on the concrete floor. He felt certain he had a few cracked ribs and he could feel his face swelling slightly. But it wasn't the worst beating he'd ever had, and he couldn't help wondering why they had stopped.

———————

Jo wondered how it was possible for time to pass so slowly. Every now and again she went to the window and looked out. The car was still there, and she was sure there was someone sitting in it.

If they wanted to arrest her, surely they would come in. Doubtless they only had her under surveillance, but when had it started? Jo slumped into the living-room chair once again. They were waiting for someone, and she was certain that someone was Ted. She walked to the phone and picked up the receiver and started to dial the residence of Ambassador Dodd. Then, just as the phone started to ring, she slammed it down. She had heard there were ways to listen in on phone conversations. If they were watching her house, they might well be listening to her phone. That meant she couldn't call Ted in Munich either.

She came back to the chair. It was getting dark outside. She had to think. After a time, she got up and turned on the lights and the radio. It filled the room with tinny music.

Jo fingered the velvet material of the chair nervously. Ted wasn't due to come home till tomorrow, but when he came, they'd be waiting. She got up and went to the desk. She took out her contact book and Ted's. His was

written in a jumbled code that used the baseball stand-
ings as a key. Still, it wasn't at all sophisticated, and the
Germans knew how to break codes. She took them both
to the sink in the kitchen, and lighting them with a
candle, watched them burn in the sink. She inhaled. If
this were all a product of her imagination, she had just
destroyed something valuable. If not, she had saved
lives.

Jo peered into the backyard. It was an unkempt jungle of shrubbery. She wondered if there was someone
watching the lane. Perhaps they thought Ted was coming back tonight. Perhaps that was an idea she should
foster.

Jo hurried to the closet and put on her light sweater.
Then she picked up her little basket and purse and
went out the door of the house. She jauntily walked
past the parked car, pretending not to notice it. When
she was halfway down the street, it slowly pulled away
from the curb. They were following her! It wasn't all a
product of anxiety and an overactive imagination.

She rounded the corner and came to the place where
the lane exited. She glanced down it and could clearly
see that there was no one there. Then she entered the
wine shop, bought a bottle, put it in her basket, and
walked briskly toward home. The car was not immediately visible, but by the time she closed the front door,
it was once again parked across the street.

She again turned on the lights and put on the phonograph. She didn't bother closing the curtains, instead,
she busied herself setting the table for two, complete
with candles.

When she finished, she went upstairs. She put on
her suit and her good walking shoes, and she loaded all
her cash into her purse together with her passport and
press credentials. She then slipped on her long flowing

robe over her suit and returned to the living room, where she stood for a bit in front of the window. Anyone with binoculars could plainly see she was wearing a robe and that the table was set for two.

Jo walked casually into the kitchen and dropped her robe down the laundry chute. She slipped out the back door and hurried across the yard. The house blazed with lights and the radio was still on. They would believe she was still there waiting for Ted. But for how long? A half-hour at the most, she decided. By then she could be at one of the main-line railway stations.

The night train sped into Munich, Germany's third-largest city. Jo stared out the window, able to see the city's skyline against the pink-gray sky of dawn. It was a beautiful city, located only thirty miles from the base of the Alps. Its architecture was baroque, rococo, and neoclassical, the beauty of which was ruined only by Hitler's new art museum, a horrible eyesore in shining white marble. The Hall of German Art, it was to be called when completed. The citizens of Munich had already dubbed it the Weisswurstpalast, the White Sausage Palace.

Jo hurried through the empty station. She took a cab directly to the American consulate. She didn't have Ted's relatives' address, but she knew it was registered at the consulate. Ted always registered with the consulate. He told them where he was going, and when he was expected back. She checked her watch. It was a few minutes past six in the morning. She would have to wait for the consulate to open.

"How can I help you?" the thin, officious consular official asked. He was obviously annoyed to have someone waiting for him at so early an hour.

"I'm looking for Ted Kahn. He's an American journalist."

"I know quite well who he is," the official replied curtly. The man's tone was one of utter disdain and he looked past her instead of at her.

"I must find him."

"Have you tried his relatives? I think I do have that address. He's quite paranoid, you know. He registered all his addresses. He insists the Germans are following him. Really! Americans are quite safe. I keep telling him that."

"Helmut Hirsch wasn't safe," she responded sarcastically.

"He was a spy."

"He was probably framed. Who knows what he was? The trial was held in secret," she retorted. "Will you please hurry and give me the address."

"I'm not sure I should. It's confidential information."

"Do I have to call Ambassador Dodd?" Jo said angrily. She hadn't slept one wink on the train. She had sat in her compartment and was totally rigid and suffering from constant chills caused by anxiety and fear.

He muttered and disappeared, returning with a file. "Here are all the addresses he's left."

Jo leaned over the half-open file and copied the address, 34 Augenstrasse.

Jo hurried away from the consulate. She hailed a cab and took it to the address.

"Kahn," she told the woman in the first-floor apartment. "Is there a family named Kahn?"

The old woman shook her head.

"A former merchant, there was a family wedding, and a visitor, an American visitor."

The woman's eyes flickered, but she still shook her
head.

"I know they live here," Jo persisted.

The woman muttered at her in German, "This building is not for Jews." Then, without further comment,
she slammed the door.

Jo tried seven other apartments. At each door it was
the same. Eyes cast down, the occupants refused even
to acknowledge that the family lived or had lived at this
address.

Jo wandered up and down the halls, then climbed
the last flight of stairs to the fifth floor. There she found
painters working in an empty apartment.

"Who lived here?" she demanded.

One shrugged. "It's for rent. Do you want an
apartment?"

"Who used to live here?" she said again.

"*Juden!*" one of the painters answered. "But now
they're gone. This building is not for Jews anymore!"
They laughed; then one advanced toward her ominously.
"Are you Jewish, *fräulein*?"

"*Nein,*" she answered, hurrying away. Ted's words
rang in her ear: "The victims just disappear, the neighbors don't talk."

Jo bypassed the miserable consular official she had dealt
with earlier. She demanded to see the consul general
personally.

Mr. Henshaw was middle-aged and as plump as his
officious assistant had been thin. He sat, protected by a
vast expanse of oak desk, stuffed into his chair, a pencil
in his mouth, while he listened to her story.

"And he's disappeared and so has his family," Jo said
with finality. "I know he's been arrested. He must be
released immediately."

"When Americans are arrested, we are notified. Naturally, if they've committed a crime, they are subject to the laws of this country."

"He hasn't committed a crime. He's a respected reporter. I told you, he's Jewish and his family is Jewish. He's an American, but he was born in Berlin."

The man grunted. "A naturalized American."

"He came to the United States when he was a child. This has nothing to do with anything! You must get him released!"

"But I don't know if he's been arrested."

"I know it!" She heard her own voice rise and could feel her anger starting to grow. "Mr. Henshaw, you must do something immediately!"

"But how do you know he was arrested?"

"I told you, I went there. Men were repainting the apartment."

"I'm sure a great many apartments get repainted every year in Munich. Did the neighbors tell you the family had been arrested?"

"No. They wouldn't talk."

"Of course not, because there was nothing to talk about. Listen, I hear these stories all the time." He shook his head in disgust. "You have a very vivid imagination, my dear. These things really do not happen, and they certainly don't happen to Americans. Even Jews who are American citizens are quite, quite safe."

"Such things *do* happen and *this* has happened. I insist you phone the Gestapo and check. I absolutely insist!"

"And who are you to insist I do anything?" He took the pencil out of his mouth and tapped it on the table in irritation. "I tell you, this is all fantasy. Oh, I don't deny the fascists don't like the Jews, but who does? I sit here all day and have to talk to Jews who want to go to

America. And why do they want to go to America? I'll
tell you why. It's because the Germans have caught on
to their little game, so now they want to go to America
to make money and hide behind our liberal constitution."

"That's nonsense!" Jo stormed. "You're as bad as the
Nazis!" She could feel her face growing red, and she
shook in absolute rage at this pompous bastard. "The
Jews of Germany are being persecuted, that's why they
want to leave. And I tell you Ted has been arrested and
if anything happens I will hold you personally responsible. Do you understand?" She leaned over, narrowing
her eyes. "I'm the European correspondent for *Profiles*,
I'm a personal friend of Ambassador Dodd. I can assure
you he doesn't think as you do! I shall phone him and
tell him of your behavior, and if necessary, I will notify
every American correspondent in Germany to bring
pressure on you and this consulate!"

Mr. Henshaw scowled, but he looked nervous now,
and she leaned even closer. "Ted Kahn's network won't
like this either. Having a member of the press disappear is a serious matter, Mr. Henshaw. A very serious
matter. We of the Fourth Estate stick together, and I
want you to do something immediately."

"You're a very insistent woman, but to please you,
I'll call Herr Kurtz at Gestapo headquarters."

"Now," Jo said, collapsing back into her chair.

Mr. Henshaw left the office, and Jo sat there for what
seemed hours before he returned.

"Well, you see, they have no record of arresting your
Mr. Kahn. But they said they'd check."

Jo jumped to her feet. "No, Mr. Henshaw, *you* will
check. You will put on your coat immediately and go to
Gestapo headquarters. You will explain that Mr. Kahn
is a very important person, you will insist that he be

released, and you will insist that you know he was arrested."

"But I don't."

"You *do* know, because I have told you. Mr. Henshaw, if you value your career, you will do as I suggest."

"I don't like being threatened, young lady."

"I am not a young lady. But I am threatening you. I don't usually threaten people, Mr. Henshaw, but I'm tired and I'm desperate. And I promise you, if you don't move heaven and earth to find Ted Kahn, my threat will become your reality."

Mr. Henshaw stood up. He seemed at a loss for words. "Leave your hotel number with my secretary," he muttered. "I'll call you later."

"I haven't checked into a hotel yet. I'll phone in the number."

Jo turned and left. Her anger had enabled her to be self-righteous in protesting Ted's innocence. She prayed to God he hadn't been caught with anything.

Jo checked into the Kemper House and phoned her number in to the embassy. It was a little after noon. She left a call at the desk asking to be awakened at six. Then she went to her room and collapsed onto the feather mattress, sinking into it uncomfortably. She decided she hated German beds. They were too soft, and the covers were giant down-filled puffs that continually slid off the bed unless you remained in one position.

She did not remain in one position. Even with the draperies closed and in spite of not having slept all night, she tossed and turned, beset by nightmares. When she dozed off, she awoke with her heart pounding. False energy seemed to flow through her veins, and it conspired with her thoughts to keep her restless and awake. All the people she had known and loved seemed to parade across her thoughts. All the people who had died. It wouldn't happen to Ted. It couldn't, she kept telling herself. They had waited so long to be together. She loved him so much.

Sometime around 6:00 P.M. she fell into a deeper sleep, only to be awakened by the concierge.

Jo dressed hurriedly and went directly to the post office to make a long-distance call. I've waited long enough, she told herself. She phoned Fleischer in Berlin, she told him Ted had disappeared, and she told him what she suspected. He didn't say much, but she knew he would have the story on the wires within the hour. He was simply a careful man on the telephone.

She walked rapidly back to the hotel and waited for three long hours. No call came from Mr. Henshaw.

Finally she called the Henshaw home, and was told by Henshaw's oblique secretary that "These things take time. Mr. Henshaw will be in touch with you."

She phoned again at ten and was told that Mr. Henshaw could not be reached till morning.

Jo tossed again through the night. Sleep came only in the form of short naps, and her chills continued, leading her to believe she might have a slight fever. At nine, Jo was roused from the edge of sleep by the concierge, who notified her that she was to call the embassy.

She dressed quickly and ran to the phone in the lobby, repeating the number twice for the operator and then cursing when the phone lines cackled with static.

"Ah, Miss Gregory. Yes, I did indeed phone. Yes, I do have news, but I must say, your story to UPI was a bit premature. Your Mr. Kahn is quite all right. It was all a terrible mistake and the Gestapo have apologized for his detainment. His family is being released and sent on their way—they do have their visas."

"And Ted? Where is he? How is he?"

"Quite well, I understand. But I'm afraid he hasn't been writing very complimentary things about the government. He's been declared *persona non grata* and is being deported."

"Deported?"

"Yes. I'm afraid that means you won't be able to see him until he's out of Germany. He'll be leaving under guard in a special car on the midnight train. His destination is Paris. You, I'm afraid, have other problems."

"I don't know what you mean."

"I am instructed to request that you return immediately to Berlin. You are to go directly to the American embassy and remain there. Do you understand?"

Jo nodded dumbly into the receiver. "Why?" she finally asked.

"Because that is the arrangement that has been made. My office is not equipped to handle such complicated matters. Good day, Miss Gregory."

Jo heard him click down the receiver and for a moment she stared at the telephone.

She paid her hotel bill and went to the station. It occurred to her that it might all be a ruse of some sort. Maybe Ted wasn't safe, maybe the consul wasn't telling her the truth. She sat down in an empty compartment and looked vacantly out the window. I'm being absurd, she told herself. Hunger and lack of sleep are causing me to imagine things. And I'm sick too, she decided. But why was she to go back to the American embassy in Berlin?

Jo was ushered directly into Ambassador Dodd's private office.

"Am I glad to see you!" He walked across the room and hugged her.

"Have you heard from Ted? Is he all right? I want you to tell me. I want to hear it from you." She looked into the ambassador's blue eyes.

He pressed his lips together and nodded. "He was roughed up a little, but he's fine. He was turned over to our consular staff at the border. Really, he's quite all right. It's you who are the problem."

Jo was utterly bewildered. "Me?"

"Yes, perhaps you had better sit down." He showed her to a chair and motioned for her to sit down. "You've led the Gestapo a merry chase," he told her.

"I don't understand. I mean, I know they were watching my house waiting for Ted—"

"They weren't waiting for Ted, Jo. They knew perfectly well Ted was in Munich and that he was under arrest."

"What?"

"They were waiting for you."

"But I went out. They followed me, they made no attempt to arrest me."

"Yes, I know. A little walk to the wine store. They didn't move then because they thought you were waiting for someone."

"But I'm not the one who's involved with—"

"For heaven's sake, don't tell me more than I want to know," the ambassador said, holding up his hand to silence her.

Jo closed her mouth and shook her head. "I really don't understand."

"Do you know a person called Gerta Schmidt?"

Jo nodded. "I talk to her a lot. She owns a jewelry store. She tells me what her clients think about this and that, but it's nothing. Why would the Gestapo care about that?"

"I don't honestly know the whole story," the ambassador confessed. "I do know that her boyfriend was in the S.S. and that he apparently tried to assassinate a high-ranking Nazi. He was arrested, and shot in an attempt to escape. The Gestapo decided Gerta must somehow be involved because she's half Jewish. They began watching her shop, and they noted that you came in quite often. Since you are an American reporter, one conclusion seems to have led to another."

"It wasn't Ted they wanted?" Jo said in total disbelief.

"No. And I think they're embarrassed that you slipped away. Of course, they're more upset about the UPI story."

"You don't understand," Jo protested.

"I don't really want to," he replied.

"But why did they arrest Ted?"

"Because the building owner requested his family be moved. A mean little man who thought it would be nice to have them evicted during the wedding. When they got to police headquarters and found they also had Ted, they phoned Berlin for identification verification. He was ordered to be turned over to the S.S. for questioning because he was known to be a friend of yours."

Jo trembled slightly. She felt like a fine crystal wineglass about to shatter. Nervous tension still filled her. "I haven't had much sleep. I don't know whether to laugh or cry."

"I'm going to give you a sleeping tablet and let you get some rest. After that, when you're in control, I'm afraid you're going to have to talk to the Gestapo."

Jo looked at him wide-eyed. She was going to pass out soon, or else wake up and find this was all a horrible dream.

"You could have been arrested in Munich," the ambassador confided. "But they didn't locate you till after the U.P. story was out, and then they couldn't arrest you because it would appear that was why you were arrested. At that point they called me. I persuaded them to let you come back here. I promised you would be available for questions."

"Will they arrest me?"

"Well, they can't as long as you're here. I suspect they've more information now and know you weren't involved in any plot. I don't think they would have agreed to let you come here if they had still intended to arrest you. And fortunately, the story about Ted being arrested puts you in a rather strong position. They don't want to publicize the assassination attempt, and if they arrest you, they'll have no choice." The ambassador shook his head. "Ironic, really. The story you hoped would save Ted has probably saved you. Frankly, at this point I think they'll be glad to get rid of both of you."

Jo's head pounded wildly. "Why was Ted roughed up?"

"Because he's Jewish."

"I really don't know anything about Gerta's boyfriend."

"Good," the ambassador said. "Don't worry, the interview will be held here. I'll be with you. Just answer their questions. My guess is they're only insisting on the interview so they can close the file. You know how the Germans are—everything has to be tidy."

Jo tried to smile.

Ambassador Dodd walked over and put a fatherly arm around her. He held out a bottle of capsules. "Here, take one of these sleeping pills and go upstairs. Lie down and get some rest. I'll set up your appointment with the Gestapo for tomorrow morning."

The ambassador insisted she dress in the primmest outfit he could find. The chic red wool suit she had worn to Munich was too fashionable and far too bright. "You should look like a schoolmistress," he added. In the end, he borrowed a dress from one of the secretaries. It was gray with a huge white collar, and Jo felt not so much like a schoolteacher as like a schoolgirl. She approached the interview with confidence, thinking it ought not to be difficult to sound innocent. She was. She knew absolutely nothing about Gerta's boyfriend.

She was flanked by the ambassador and the embassy legal officer, a nervous young man with a Harvard accent and thick glasses. The Gestapo officer who came was introduced as Commandant Frick.

"Ah, Miss Gregory." He clicked his heels and bowed from the waist. "It's most unusual for us to conduct an interview in the American embassy. I trust you appreciate the fact that you are quite safe and that we have utter and complete respect for international law and the laws of diplomacy."

"Yes. Thank you," she replied.

"I trust when you write about this experience, as I'm *certain* you will, that you will mention how properly you have been treated."

Jo nodded.

"Now, do you know a Miss Gerta Schmidt?"

"Yes, I'm acquainted with her. She runs a jewelry store near the Nollendorfplatz."

"Quite correct. You frequent her shop. You have been seen talking to her on many occasions, and often you take coffee with her in the back room."

"Yes."

"And what do you and Miss Schmidt discuss?"

Jo looked down at the carpet and smiled slyly. "Mostly topics that concern women, Herr Frick. Do you really want to hear about such matters? Who is sleeping with whom, and what fashions are in vogue."

"You're an American journalist. I'm sure your discussions with Miss Schmidt are more than woman talk."

"I'm a writer. She tells me how her customers—some of whom are married to high-ranking Nazi officials—feel about the New Germany. It's vital for me to know how the German people feel. How else can I let Americans know?"

"And what do you let Americans know?"

"I wrote only recently that most Germans seemed satisfied with the government."

"I think the word you used was 'complacent.'"

Jo opened her eyes wide and blinked at him. "Did I? Tell me, what is the difference? If one is complacent, isn't one satisfied?"

Herr Frick cleared his throat. "Why did you run away? We only had you under surveillance."

"I was worried about my boyfriend. He's Jewish. I thought you were waiting for him."

Herr Frick shrugged. "Your boyfriend? Does he help you with your writing?"

Jo smiled as stupidly as she could manage. "A great many men have helped me with my career," she replied.

"I'm sure they have. Are you acquainted with Miss Schmidt's boyfriend?"

"I didn't know she had one. Though I should have guessed. She's very pretty and all her clothes are the latest fashion."

Herr Frick stood up and smoothed out his jacket. "You are either one of the most intelligent women I have ever met, or the stupidest. However, my investigation of this matter leads me to believe that you were not involved with Miss Schmidt in a way that would concern us. Nonetheless, your story to United Press is an embarrassment to my government, and we will no longer tolerate this kind of sensationalism from the foreign press corps. You, Miss Gregory have also been declared *persona non grata*."

Jo stared at Herr Frick. Clearly a great deal more was behind his words. He was grim and struggling to control himself. She shuddered to think what could have happened had not the ambassador stepped in and made an arrangement with the government.

"I have no further interest in this woman," Herr Frick announced, turning toward the ambassador. "We'll sign the safe-conduct agreement and you may see to it she boards the train. We will be most generous. We'll give her five days."

"Thank you." Ambassador Dodd bowed slightly.

Herr Frick was escorted from the ambassador's office, and Dodd sat down.

"I owe you a great deal," Jo said, turning to face him.

"Ted's arrest really was a mistake," Ambassador Dodd told her. He rubbed his chin and shook his head. "I doubt you would have gotten off so easily had it not been for Hirsch's execution. It caused quite a stir, and I suppose the government was willing to make an arrangement with me because two such stories following one on the other would have been very bad indeed."

Jo leaned over and kissed him on the cheek. "Stop in Paris and see us on your way home."

The ambassador smiled. "I will. You know, I'm looking forward to returning to my history books. History in the making is very tiring."

"It's my job," Jo said, managing a smile for the first time in days.

———

The sun streamed through the windows of the room Jo and Ted had taken on the Rue Jacob. It was a wonderful room, sunny and bright. Its walls were yellow with white trim. Sheer white dimity curtains hung at the open window and blew gently in the morning breeze. Jo smiled to herself. Every tabletop in the room was covered with bouquets of fresh flowers. There were pink carnations on the bureau, bright yellow mums on the dressing table, long-stemmed roses in a white basket on the coffee table, and a delicate vase filled with ferns and violets on the bedside table.

The carnations were from Alvin Hendrix at *Profiles* and the card simply read, "Don't let marriage spoil you." The mums were from Calvin and, she thought with amusement, they must have cost him at least four beers. All the rest were from Ted. He stopped at every flower stall they passed and bought flowers.

Leaving Germany was, she realized, like having a yoke lifted from around your neck. Suddenly she and Ted were able to laugh again. They could walk the streets hand in hand, they were free to sit in the park and to do a thousand and one things together that a Jew and a Gentile in Germany were prohibited from doing. Yet the experience in Germany brought with it an increased obligation to go on fighting fascism. They had agreed. After their brief respite in Paris, they would go on to Spain. But for now there was Paris, it was spring, and there were flowers everywhere.

Jo looked into Ted's face. She leaned over him smiling.

He opened his eyes and yawned. "Guess I fell back asleep," he admitted.

"Were you awake earlier?" She touched his hair and kissed his forehead.

"Around eight. I watched you sleeping. I thought you might sleep forever."

She stretched sensuously and put her arms around his neck. For the first time in almost a year they both felt free and unrestricted. Their minds were on each other rather than filled with the apprehension and fear that had become daily life in Germany.

"I feel wonderful," she sighed. "I must have slept for twelve hours."

Ted glanced at his watch. "Twelve hours, thirty-two minutes, and fourteen seconds."

She laughed gently at his teasing. Then, looking mishchievous: "You wore me out."

He looked at her hungrily. Her sheer white nightdress had fallen slightly off her left shoulder, exposing the gentle curve of her breast. Her hair was a dark mass of tangled curls, her eyes, always beautiful, looked back at him longingly, and her naturally sensuous lips seemed to beckon him. Unable to resist, he bent over and kissed the bare curve of her breast, then nuzzled her neck.

"Make love to me," she said softly, touching him intimately.

He lunged at her lovingly, holding her tightly.

She laughed and twisted in his arms, and he held her closer, breathing on her neck, kissing her ears, taunting her with soft caresses.

"You're wicked," she whispered.

"You asked," he replied, lifting his eyebrow. "Of course, it's not proper to make love at ten in the morning, especially when we're married." He touched her smooth stomach and moved his hand down between her thighs, then quickly withdrew it and smilingly asked, "Do you want me to stop? Shall we be proper, prim, and married?"

She closed her eyes and moaned softly. "Don't you dare stop," she said, pressing herself to him as he again ran his hands over her, touching her until she was trembling and ready.

"Oh, I do love you," he whispered as they joined together. She moved beneath him and was part of him as they tumbled together—feeling, inhaling, tasting each other in a growing wild passion that ended with each clinging to the other as one.

They were again on the edge of sleep in each other's arms when a persistent tapping on the door roused them.

"It's the maid with breakfast," Jo said as she struggled out of bed and put on her white satin robe.

Ted pulled up the bedcovers and sat up. He leaned over and took a cigarette from the pack on the bedside table and lit it.

Jo opened the door and took the proffered tray. She was greeted with the fresh aroma of hot dark coffee. The tray held orange juice, hard rolls, jam, two poached eggs, and lean slices of ham and cheese.

"Is the paper there?" Ted asked as he plumped up the pillows.

"Catch." She tossed him the morning paper and put the breakfast tray on the table next to the violets. Then she returned to the bed and leaned over, looking at the headline. The lead story was on the occupation of Bilbao by Spanish Nationalist troops. "It's Tim Huntley's byline," she said offhandedly.

Ted reached over and kissed her on the cheek. "In two days we'll be behind Loyalist lines. Then the byline will be yours."